Set in Stone

Set in Stone

Linda Newbery

LAUREL-LEAF BOOKS

Published by Laurel-Leaf
an imprint of Random House Children's Books
a division of Random House, Inc.
New York

Originally published in hardcover in Great Britain by David Fickling Books, Oxford,
in 2006. This edition published by arrangement with David Fickling Books.

Visit us on the Web! www.randomhouse.com/teens

Educators and librarians, for a variety of teaching tools, visit us at
www.randomhouse.com/teachers

The Library of Congress has cataloged the hardcover edition of this work as follows:
Newbery, Linda.
Set in stone / Linda Newbery.
p.   cm.
Summary: The alternating narratives of art tutor Samuel Godwin and governess
Charlotte Agnew, who work for the wealthy Farrow family in 1898 England,
reveal the secrets that almost everyone in the household is hiding.
ISBN: 978-0-385-75102-5 (trade) — ISBN: 978-0-385-75103-2 (lib. bdg.)
[1. Secrets—Fiction. 2. Incest—Fiction. 3. Identity—Fiction. 4. Family problems—Fiction.
5. Great Britain—History—Victoria, 1837–1901—Fiction.] I. Title.
PZ7.N4715Set 2006
[Fic]—dc22   2005018479

ISBN: 978-0-440-24051-8 (pbk.)

July 2008
Printed in the United States of America
10 9 8 7 6 5 4 3 2 1
First Laurel-Leaf Edition

For Peter Thomas, and long overdue

'To handle stone is to handle the stuff of life and death, of time and change, the mysteries of the Earth itself . . .'

Contents

Prologue

The Wild Girl

1920

Samuel Godwin
Watercolours and Oil Paintings
Private View

The poster is almost obscured by the press of people entering the gallery. Wineglass in hand, I position myself to one side, a spectator at my own exhibition; as the guests file in, I assume a genial smile, and prepare to wear it for the duration of the evening.

Nowadays there are many such occasions, enough to make me droop at the prospect of yet another. How easily we tire of novelties, once their gloss has faded! Twenty years ago, I dreamed of this tedious social duty as the height of my aspiration. If I had thought then, at the start of my career, that people would flock to see my work – and not only to look, but to pay handsomely for it; that I should be fêted, flattered, invited to dine, to comment, to make speeches; that I should be regarded as someone touched by the Muse, not quite in the run of common men – I should have thought it a wishful dream. But this has become the pattern of my life, no longer yearned for. My name, now, seems to stand apart from me. It is a valued signature, two words that command a price; its syllables are spoken by people who consider themselves connoisseurs.

'Ah, Mr Godwin!' The woman bearing down on me, social smile stretching her lipsticked mouth, scarf draped artfully round her neck and secured with a brooch, is of the wearisome type I often meet at such viewings. 'Let me have your attention, before you're quite besieged! I am so curious – do tell me . . .' Manicured fingers touch my sleeve; perfume mingles with cigarette smoke. 'The Wild Girl. She intrigues me so very much. Who is she, I wonder? Do tell.'

I avert my eyes from the archness of her gaze, and block my ears to her gush. Across the gallery, my Wild Girl stares at me from her ebony frame. Although her expression is seared into my mind, although my own hand made every brushstroke that defines her, I cannot look on her without feeling a fresh twist of pain. Her hair, of that rich, extraordinary shade I used to amuse myself by defining – the colour of newly opened chestnuts in their cases, of beech leaves against snow, of polished pennies, of a kestrel's wing – tumbles over her shoulders. Her eyes, not quite green, not quite blue, hold mine in a blend of exultation and pleading. This is my reason for painting her: to hold this moment in suspension, to keep for ever the possibilities it holds.

In the next instant it will be too late. Her plea will remain unanswered, and I will have failed.

My heart clenches.

I do this to her, my Wild Girl. I bring her to these fashionable galleries, I expose her to these scavengers with their ravenous eyes and their predatory cheque-books. Do they really see her? Twenty years ago she would have been as invisible as the rest of my work. Now, because she carries my name (but not her own), she is the object of speculation. Fickle fashion has decreed that my work is collectable. *The Wild Girl* is a desirable commodity.

But not for sale. No, never.

'Come, now, Mr Godwin!' My inquisitor plucks at my sleeve and peers closely into my face. 'Please don't be coy! Is there a story here, I wonder? Such a beauty – she is someone you loved, maybe? She is a real girl – yes, surely.'

I catch the eye of the gallery owner. Knowing how I dislike being cornered, he threads his way towards us, summoning a waiter to refill our glasses. I see my chance to escape.

'She is herself,' I answer, sidling away. 'She is someone I met many years ago.'

Chapter One

Fourwinds

June 1898

It was an impulse stirred by the moon over the Downs that made me decide to complete my journey on foot. Such a night as this, I thought, standing outside the railway station in the moonlight that seemed almost liquid silver, is too great a gift to ignore behind drawn curtains and closed doors. It is to be fully experienced with all senses – lived, inhaled, absorbed.

It had been arranged that my new employer, Mr Farrow, would send a pony-chaise to meet me, but a series of misfortunes had delayed my arrival. My London train had departed late, and I had missed my connection; he must have given up expecting me until the morrow. At this hour there was no conveyance of any kind to be seen. At first wondering whether to spend the night in a local tavern and continue next morning, I then had the idea of walking. I asked the stationmaster to put my trunk aside until morning, explained that my destination was Fourwinds, and showed him the address.

'Mile or so up the lane there, all uphill, then turn left down a rough old track by a copse. Stick on that track and it'll bring you to the gates.' He seemed to feel unduly put upon by my request to store the trunk, and began, with a grudging air, to haul it towards the ticket office.

'I shall send for it in the morning,' I told him.

He accepted without comment the coin I gave him for his trouble. I shouldered the small pack in which I had my necessaries, and set off at once, past a coaching inn – with no coaches to be seen – and out of Staverton in the direction he had indicated.

As the sounds from the inn and the lights from the stationmaster's house receded, I found myself alone, and very tiny, beneath the vast, starred expanse of sky. Coming from the London suburb of Sydenham, where I had lived all my life, I had rarely experienced such isolation as this, such silence. And yet, as my ears attuned to my new surroundings, it was not silence I heard: my feet trod steadily on the stony road; I heard the hooting of an owl, the screech of some unseen creature in the verge, the faintest rustle of grasses sighing against each other. I was on a high, open road, curving over the swell of hillside that I saw as the flanks of some prehistoric animal, deep in slumber. The moonlight was so strong as to throw my shadow beside me on the road as a mute companion; and so I found myself not quite alone after all, taking a childish pleasure in my shadow-self as it matched me stride for stride. I could see quite clearly my road curving ahead, and the clump of trees, inky black, that marked my turning point.

From here, my track took me sharply left. Chalky and bare, it formed rough undulations over the ground, leading me to the brow of a low hill; chalk stones grated underfoot. Fourwinds, the house at which I was to take up employment, apparently lay in a very isolated spot, for I could see no sign of habitation, no friendly lamp in a farmhouse window, no plume of smoke from a shepherd's humble croft. I felt very conscious of travelling from one stage of my life to the next: every step away from the road carried me farther from London, my mother and sister, the art school and my friends there; each tread brought me nearer to the house and its inhabitants, of which, and of whom, I knew very little.

Reaching the highest point of the track, I glanced about me; and saw now that my track descended into woodland, dense and dark. The stationmaster had mentioned no wood; but perhaps the omission could be ascribed to his hurry to finish work for the night. I hesitated; then, as sure as I could be that I had made no mistake, continued on my path down into the valley and the shadows of the trees.

Darkness swallowed me; the branches arched high overhead; I saw only glimpses of the paler sky through their tracery. My feet crunched beech mast. I smelled the coolness of mossy earth, and heard the trickle of water close by. As my eyes accustomed themselves to dimmer light, I saw that here, on the lower ground, a faint mist hung in the air, trapped perhaps beneath the trees. I must be careful not to stray from the path, which I could only dimly discern; but before many minutes had passed, wrought-iron gates reared ahead of me, set in a wall of flint. Though I had reached the edge of the wood, my way was barred. The gate must, however, be unlocked, as my arrival was expected.

I peered through the scrollwork of the gates. The track, pale and broad, wound between specimen trees and smooth lawns; I had some distance still to walk, it seemed. The mist clung to the ground, and the trees seemed rooted in a vaporous swamp. I tried the fastening; the left-hand gate swung open with a loud, grating squeal that echoed into the night.

At the same moment another sound arose, competing for shrillness with the gate's protest: a sound to make my heart pound and my nerves stretch taut. It was a wailing shriek that filled my head and thrummed in my ears; close enough to make me shrink against the gate, which I pushed open to its fullest extent against the shadows of the wall. Whether the cry was animal or human, I could not tell. If human, it was a sound of terrible distress, of unbearable grief. I felt the hairs prickle on the back of my neck, my eyes trying to stare in all directions at once. Instinct told me to hunch low till the danger passed. Dropped into such strangeness, I had acquired, it seemed, the impulse of a wild creature to hide myself and survive whatever perils were near. The metal bit into my hands as I clung to the gate. Attempting to retain a clear head, I reminded myself that I was unfamiliar with the sounds of the countryside at night. It must be a fox, a badger, some creature yowling in hunger or pain.

The next instant, all my senses quickened again as I discerned a movement in the shadow: a movement that resolved itself into a cloaked figure – slender, female – rushing towards me. As I had not seen her approach, she must have been lurking by the wall. In the confusion of the moment, the thought flitted across my mind that this might be a ghostly presence – the setting, the eerie light, the ground-veiling mist that made her seem to advance without feet, all contributed to this fancy. Since she appeared intent on collision, I reached out both hands to ward her off; but, unswerving, she grabbed me by one arm. I saw that she was not woman but girl – an adolescent girl, with hair wild and loose under her hooded cloak – and no ghost, but a living person, breathing, panting, alarmed. For it must have been she who had shrieked.

'Help – please help me!' she begged, tightening her grip on my arm, and peering close into my face.

At once a different instinct was aroused – for now I must be protector, not prey. 'Madam, I am at your service,' I assured her, looking around, steeling myself to confront possible attackers.

'Where is it?' she implored me, her eyes searching mine. 'Where?'

'Madam – miss! Please explain what is distressing you, and I shall gladly give what help I can.'

Thinking that I might take her with me to Fourwinds, where assistance could be summoned, I tried to free myself from her grasp in order to close the gate behind me, but she seemed equally determined that it should stay open. For a few moments we struggled; I was surprised by her strength and tenacity. I tried to shake her off; I almost flung her from me; but she was like a terrier set on a fox, and would not be detached.

'Have you seen him?' she pleaded.

'If you might stand back and allow me to—' I began, but she burst out with, 'No! No! I cannot stop searching, while he is roaming free—'

'Who?' I enquired, looking about me again.

'The West Wind!' she replied, in a tone of impatience; and she tilted her head and gazed about in anguish, as if expecting a gusting presence to manifest itself above our heads.

'I beg your pardon?'

'The West Wind!' she repeated. 'He must be found – captured, and secured!'

The poor young lady must be deranged, I realized, suffering from fits or delusions – had escaped, maybe, from some institution. For why else should a young woman of her tender years be out alone at night, so far from habitation, and on such an extraordinary mission?

With the gate closed at last, I thought it best to humour her. 'I'm afraid I have no idea where to look,' I answered.

She turned her head rapidly this way and that; she gazed at me again. 'Who are you?' she demanded, almost rudely.

'My name is Samuel Godwin, and I am on my way to Fourwinds. A Mr Ernest Farrow lives there.'

'Oh! To Fourwinds!' she repeated, as one struck

by an amazing coincidence – although we were, presumably, in the grounds of that very house. For a few moments she stared at me; then, abruptly, her manner changed. She stepped back, making an effort to breathe more calmly; she straightened herself and seemed to grow taller; she became, in effect, a different person. 'Then – you are my new tutor.' She extended a hand to shake mine, as formally as if we were being introduced in a drawing room. 'I am very pleased indeed to meet you – I am Marianne Farrow, one of your two pupils. Let me lead you to the house, and introduce you to my father and sister.'

Chapter Two

A Disturbance

Devoted to Mr Farrow though I was, I could not deny that he had some rather exasperating habits. Chief among these was his failure to communicate matters of pressing interest to others in the house. It was typical of him that he did not think to mention that an art tutor from London would be joining us at Fourwinds until two days before the young man's arrival.

My employer summoned me to his office, then, as was his wont, carried on writing, bent over his desk, without so much as glancing up at me. Used to his manner, I waited patiently. The delay allowed me to study the details of his appearance: his meticulous attire, his close-curling dark hair, his frown of concentration, and the strong fingers that gripped the pen. The bold, angular script that issued from the pen-nib was a part of his character.

After a few moments he looked up. 'Ah, yes,' he said, bestowing on me the briefest of glances; at once his attention was back with the papers on his desk, which he began to tidy into folders and drawers.

'There is to be an addition to our household, Charlotte! A bedroom must be prepared, and all made ready. A Mr Samuel Godwin will be taking up residence here, to instruct Juliana in drawing and painting, and to carry out some commissions I have in mind. He is a young artist, trained at the Slade School of Art – I have the highest expectations of him. He will be with us on Monday afternoon. Please tell Mrs Reynolds to make arrangements.'

Clearly, no further information was forthcoming; he expected me to have no opinion on the matter. Giving me a nod and a smile, he picked up a letter, tutted with impatience at what he read there, then, when I gave a modest cough to attract his attention, seemed surprised to find that I was still in the room; his eyebrows rose quizzically.

'For how long,' I enquired, 'will this Mr Godwin be staying?'

'Oh, I have engaged him for an indefinite period,' he replied. 'The art lessons will take place daily. Juliana needs taking out of herself, and we will all appreciate a change of company.'

'Marianne loves to draw and paint,' I reminded him.

'Yes, of course,' he replied. 'Well, she can take part in the lessons too.'

'Are the young ladies aware that Mr Godwin is expected?'

'No, I haven't yet mentioned it,' said he, taking an envelope out of the bureau drawer, and writing an address with rapid slashes of his pen. 'I shall tell them at dinner. If you prefer to tell them sooner, please do.'

Dismissed, I closed the door behind me, and stood for a moment on the half-landing before going down to the morning room. If I confess that my first reaction was of displeasure, this may seem surprising; our life at Fourwinds was uneventful, with Mr Farrow often away from home, and few visitors to break our seclusion. The arrival of a young man from London might be expected to provoke interest and expectation. Certainly, when I conveyed the news to my two charges, Marianne was greatly excited. 'An artist!' she exclaimed, several times, as though our new arrival were closer akin to deity than to mortal man. 'Is he famous? Is he handsome, do you suppose? How do you picture him, Charlotte? I think he must have luxuriant dark hair, and a bold twinkling eye. What will he think of us? And he comes from London! – I fear he may find us rather dull. Are you not afraid he will, Juley?'

Juliana said little, and I even less. Mr Farrow's purpose in this arrangement was, I found, perplexing. He could without much difficulty have engaged a tutor to come to the house in the afternoons, as often as he thought beneficial; it hardly seemed necessary for the artist to come and live with us. Yet it was characteristically generous of Mr Farrow, once having thought of a scheme, to spare no expense in carrying it out. His daughters were everything to him; and, as usual, this thought provoked in me a flash of warmth, sharpened with envy. Such is my lot; these jealous pangs are the cost of my happiness here – or, if it is not complete happiness, it is the nearest to it I have ever known.

My hard-won equilibrium was likely to be upset by the intrusion of a stranger. The circumstances of my life have taught me to keep my own secrets, and to respect those of others. With few acquaintances, I value those I can trust; these number very few, and are to be found within the confines of Fourwinds. I did not look forward to admitting a newcomer to our circle.

After a period of reflection, however, it occurred to me that I might find companionship in the new arrangement. Someone in my position can be rather isolated in a household; neither a member of the family, nor one of the domestic servants, she occupies a somewhat in-between role. Mr Godwin would find himself similarly placed. I allowed myself to conjecture that he and I might walk in the gardens together, or enjoy quiet conversations in the drawing room after the girls had retired to bed.

This foolishness was most unlike me, and experience has taught me that high expectations are frequently thwarted; therefore, I prepared myself for our Mr Godwin to be disagreeable, arrogant, or weak-featured, to have an irritating laugh, or odious breath, or a pompous, self-regarding air. Thus, I was pleasantly surprised when he entered the vestibule of Fourwinds. It was late at night, so late that I had assumed he would not after all appear until the morrow. Mr Farrow had retired to his room, and I was roving the house in search of Marianne, who had slipped away while I was reading. No hooves had been heard approaching, nor the rumble of wheels, so I was startled when the front door opened to admit both Marianne and a somewhat bemused-looking young man. Marianne was flushed and excitable, and I knew at once that she had had one of her wandering fits. It was my fault; yet how could I prevent such escapes without either dogging the poor girl's heels like a shepherd's collie, or keeping her under lock and key?

'Charlotte!' she said, coming towards me eagerly. 'Here is Mr Godwin – I found him outside. Such a long walk he's had – all the way from Staverton!'

The newcomer stood, hat in hand, just inside the door. Like most visitors to Fourwinds, though there are not many, he was gazing about him in some surprise at the height and space of the entrance hall, having expected, I suppose, a traditional country mansion, which this most assuredly is not.

'Good evening, Mr Godwin,' I said, extending my hand. 'Welcome to Fourwinds. My name is Charlotte Agnew – I am companion to the Misses Farrow, and Marianne's governess. What regrettable inconvenience you have suffered by having to walk! You must be very tired.'

We shook hands while I made this speech. His hand was warm, his grip firm. He was a tall young man, well-built but not stocky, with springy hair, rich brown in colour, brushed back from a shapely forehead. His eyes were grey, his nose straight and his mouth determined; when he answered, his voice was deep and well modulated.

'I am very glad to meet you, Miss Agnew,' said he. 'No, I am not tired in the least. I preferred to walk on such a beautiful night. But I am sorry to disturb your household so late.'

Though certainly not the flamboyant figure Marianne had imagined, Samuel Godwin was pleasing in person and manner. Although Juliana had yet to set eyes on him, I saw that he had already made a good impression on her younger sister. While I made enquiries about his baggage, summoned Mrs Reynolds to serve his supper and asked her to call Juliana from her room, Marianne watched attentively, her eyes resting with fascination on his face, then turning to mine. Yes, I thought, she is quite engrossed with him, impulsive creature that she is, after an acquaintance of some five or ten minutes.

Mr Godwin gave a detailed explanation of the circumstances that had delayed his arrival, and apologized again; I assured him that it did not matter in the least, and that we were pleased he had arrived safely. With Marianne following, I showed him to his room, which was on the second floor, on the east side of the house, with a view over the gardens and the lake. Afterwards we returned to the dining room, where Mrs Reynolds had set out a meal of cold meat, cheese and pickles. After pouring him a glass of wine, and another for myself, I sat with him at table.

'Marianne,' I said, as she seemed inclined to linger, 'your sister has not come down. Will you go and tell her Mr Godwin has arrived?'

She nodded, and left us.

'I have never seen a more beautiful house!' Mr Godwin remarked. He looked around him at the clean stone arch of the fireplace, at the bay window with its cushioned seats, and the heavy curtains that fell to the floor; he stroked a hand over the smooth-grained wood of the chair adjacent to his. 'Everything chosen with such care! Mr Farrow is a man of very decided tastes. That was evident when I met him in London.'

'Most assuredly he is,' I agreed.

'He is not at home this evening?'

'He is; but he has already retired. I'm afraid we had quite given you up until tomorrow. Please, begin,' I told him, indicating his plate.

Mr Godwin picked up his knife and fork, but stopped there.

'Miss Agnew,' he began tentatively, 'I think I ought to tell you that when I first came across Marianne – I beg your pardon, I mean the younger Miss Farrow – she seemed in great distress. I met her at some distance from the house – wandering, quite alone, and crying out in anguish. I thought at first she was being attacked, or threatened in some way—' He broke off. 'But I see that you are not surprised by this information?'

'Thank you for your kind concern, Mr Godwin,' I replied. 'It is good of you to share it with me. As you are aware, Mr Farrow has engaged you principally to teach his elder daughter, Juliana. Juliana is very different in character from her sister; you will find her quiet and amenable. Marianne, on the other hand, is somewhat excitable, as you have seen.'

'Excitable, indeed!'

'It is merely a phase – it will pass. But you need not concern yourself unduly. She has not always been thus afflicted; it seems to be a malaise of adolescence. She has an over-active imagination – that is all.'

'*All*, Miss Agnew? What is to be more feared than the excesses of imagination? Where can anyone be less easily helped than when lost in fear? For the mind can produce terrors to eclipse anything found in the material world. Can nothing be done to help her?'

'A doctor is in regular attendance,' I told him, rather crisply. 'She has the best possible care. Her welfare is my responsibility; yours is for her drawing and painting. Here at Fourwinds, where everyone knows her ways, she is in little danger of harming herself.'

'And yet she suffers such torment. Poor girl!' I saw sympathy flare in his grey eyes.

'It was unfortunate,' I continued, 'that you first met her in this over-stimulated state. She is otherwise an agreeable and most charming girl.'

Still he had not taken one mouthful. 'I cannot help thinking that Mr Farrow might have warned me of this, when he interviewed me in London,' he remarked, 'since Miss Farrow is to be my pupil. He gave no hint of it.'

'I suppose he did not wish to give unnecessary alarm. In the present circumstances, Marianne has become a little over-excited. It is probable that from now on she will be quite herself, and you will see only the pleasant, attentive young woman who left us just now. Come, please begin your meal.'

He began to eat; at first with polite reserve, apparently conscious of himself as the only diner; then with appreciative eagerness.

'What did you mean, Miss Agnew,' he asked me after a few mouthfuls, 'when you referred just now to the present circumstances?'

'I meant, of course, your arrival,' I told him. 'We are an isolated household here, Mr Godwin. We see few visitors. The sisters spend most of their time in each other's company, and in mine. They rarely meet men; especially, I may say, young men. Juliana, you will find, is a mature and sensible young woman, but Marianne is very different. She is an impressionable girl; her imagination is fed by stories and romances; she likes to indulge in daydreams. It would not be surprising if, thrown into the company of a personable young man, she were to behave, let us say, inappropriately. You see, I know her well. We must trust you, Mr Godwin, to keep within the bounds of propriety.'

He understood me at once. A deep blush crept over his face; he looked at me in consternation, seemed about to speak, but said nothing. Why, I thought, he is hardly more than a boy. Then something even more startling occurred; my own face, as though in sympathy with his discomfiture, began to flush hotly. Averting my gaze from his, I busied myself with wiping an imaginary smear from my wineglass. I am not given to blushing; it is my pride to be always discreet, detached, the perfect employee, almost invisible when I choose to be. At this moment I was far from invisible, with my face flaming like a beacon.

'Miss Agnew, you have my word that—' he began, but was interrupted by the opening of the door. Marianne burst in, followed by Juliana.

'Here he is, Juley!' said Marianne, almost pushing her sister towards us.

Composing myself, I carried out the introductions. Juliana, very self-conscious, very pale, looked wan and lifeless next to her sister's vivacity. She gave only the most fleeting smile as she shook Mr Godwin's hand, and enquired whether he found his room satisfactory. He, I saw, was intrigued by the contrast between the two. Juliana, as told to me by Mrs Reynolds, and confirmed by the photograph in Mr Farrow's study, resembled her mother; Marianne, with her vivid colouring and stronger features, took after her father.

Watching, I was alert to the glances criss-crossing in all directions. Marianne was looking at Mr Godwin with a complacent, almost proprietorial air; he, repeating his compliments about the house, was turning from one sister to the other; Juliana, venturing to give him only the shyest of glances, now lifted her eyes and looked at me directly, in what looked like a plea for help.

'Come, now,' I said briskly. 'It is late, and you have had a long and tiring journey, Mr Godwin. Let us retire – if you have finished your meal. We shall make each other's acquaintance more fully in the morning.'

Chapter Three

Samuel Godwin to Mrs Winifred Godwin

Fourwinds,
Near Staverton,
Sussex

15th June, 1898

Mrs W. G. Godwin,
3 Parkside Avenue,
Sydenham,
London

Dearest Mother,

Although my journey took rather longer than expected, I have arrived safely at Fourwinds, and have been made welcome.

This is a most unusual house, not at all what I imagined. It was apparent when I met him in London that Mr Farrow is immensely proud of his home, and I see now that this pride is more than justified. It has been built to his own specifications, and is intriguing in every detail.

Samuel Godwin

It stands in a very isolated spot, far from any other habitation; clearly Mr Farrow is a man who enjoys seclusion, although of course he could not have imagined that he would live here as a widower, Mrs Farrow having passed away quite recently. My approach — though in semi-darkness — was through woodland and then a small park. You would like the outside of the house. It is grandly simple, half tiled in the local style, with an entrance porch, in the shape of a Gothic arch, leading to heavy double doors; there are gabled windows on the second floor (where my room is located), and tall brick chimneys. Such, at least, was my impression tonight; a fuller exploration of the house, garden and grounds must wait till morning.

Inside is where my surprise began, for here Mr Farrow has exhibited very modern tastes. Instead of furnishing his house in the usual dark wood and rich fabrics, he has chosen everything light and plain. A double oak staircase curves up to a gallery above, hung with paintings which I have not yet had time to examine. Most surprisingly, there is a skylight, so that standing in the entrance hall one has an unencumbered view of the stars — for tonight is moonlit and starry, as you may have observed. The whole building seems full of space, as if a larger house has been concealed within an outer shell so traditional as to fit easily into its surroundings. There is electric lighting in all the rooms — so you see it is very up to date indeed. When I expressed surprise — and appreciation of the convenience, for one simply has to flick a switch to have a whole room illuminated at once — Miss Agnew, of whom more in a moment, told me that Mr Farrow is proud to own the first house in the vicinity to be powered by electricity.

Fourwinds is a testimony to its owner's interest in architecture and the arts. Even my room — in which I sit writing this — is not some cramped attic cell but is generously proportioned, furnished in white and cream, with a bureau, tiled washstand, fireplace, and plenty of space for my belongings. Someone has thoughtfully put a vase of evergreens on my bureau, which is maybe an odd choice for summer, but I have yet to see whether there is a flower garden.

As for the inhabitants of Fourwinds: I must wait till tomorrow to meet Mr Farrow again, as he had already retired for the night, but I was greeted by Miss Charlotte Agnew, an agreeable person who is employed here as governess-companion, and his two daughters, both of them charming young ladies and very well mannered. We are all looking forward to commencing our studies tomorrow. I must confess that I am a little anxious, but will do my best to fulfil Mr Farrow's requirements.

I hope you will enjoy your few days with the Gardiners; I shall write my next letter to you there, with of course a fuller account once I have properly acquainted myself with the household here. Please give my love to Isobel — and, to Monty, a big pat and an extra brushing from me. I miss him most sorely, as of course I do you and Isobel, dearest Mother.

Your loving son,

Samuel

Chapter Four

By Moonlight

Completing and sealing my letter, I retired for the night, but sleep would not come. As I lay in bed, increasingly wakeful, I found myself assailed by childish homesickness, longing for my family, my dog Monty, and the friends I had left behind at the Slade. Inevitably, my thoughts soon turned to my father. The shock of loss came new and raw each time I thought of him. Death always surprises us, even when it is anticipated; and my father's death had been brutally sudden. A strong man in his late forties, scarcely affected by even the most trifling illness, he had been working as usual in his office when he had suffered an abrupt dyspepsia, and had died almost in an instant.

With a sense of bewilderment, I tried to understand that I would never again hear his gruff *Good morning*, or smell the pervading aroma that hung around him, a comforting masculine blend of pipe-smoke, tweed, and carbolic soap. I could not comprehend that he was gone for ever.

Yet relations with my father had not been harmonious. This sense of lingering regret, even of guilt, of unfinished conversations and unresolved disputes, haunted me with unease. I grieved, not because he was dead, but because I could not sincerely mourn his loss.

If it were not for my father's death, I would not now be lying wakeful in an unfamiliar room. I should have stayed on at the Slade College of Art, where I had enrolled, against my father's wishes, with the rather unworldly aim of earning my living as a painter when my studies were completed. His death left us – my mother, my fourteen-year-old sister Isobel, and myself – adequately but not amply provided for. Although our home, in a quiet part of Sydenham, was left to my mother, we were compelled to live more economically than we were accustomed to, and I found myself, at the age of one-and-twenty, contemplating the role of provider. This was not at all at my mother's insistence – she, on the contrary, bravely urged me to continue at the Slade, even though our finances could barely support it – but at my own. It was a duty I felt towards my father, who had worked all his life to achieve prosperity for his family. My artistic aspirations were forced into second place, behind the need to support the household.

As a student of fine art, I knew that any qualification I might gain would be singularly useless when it came to earning a living in the realms of business or commerce. I could, I suppose, have exploited my father's connections to find myself a position in the City, but my heart was not in it. It was with a feeling of hopelessness that I was turning the pages of the newspaper when a small advertisement caught my attention.

> Art tutor required for two young ladies at a quiet country residence in Sussex. Generous salary and comfortable accommodation offered to a suitably qualified person. Impeccable references essential.

The address which followed was not in Sussex, but of a hotel in Kensington. I wrote a letter of application and was invited to present myself. To be brief: I did so, and was interviewed at the hotel by Mr Farrow himself. I took an instant liking to him – to his openness and directness, to his decided expression of his tastes and opinions – and I do not think it unreasonably arrogant to suggest that he liked me in return. He examined very closely the portfolio of drawings, sketches and watercolours I had brought with me, and asked a great many questions about my background, education and upbringing.

My answers, and my references from the Slade, evidently passed muster; two days later, I received a letter offering me the position at Fourwinds, at one hundred pounds per annum, in addition to board and residence. I realized from fellow students, and from my examination of the Persons Wanted columns, that this was rather more than I could reasonably have hoped for.

Gratifying though this was, I wondered that more suitably experienced candidates had not presented themselves; for, although I could provide evidence of

my skill with pencil and paintbrush, I was completely
untried as a tutor. However, the thought of the money
I should be able to send home to Mama and Isobel,
the assurance of a regular income, and the thought of
the free hours I should have in the Sussex countryside
for my own artistic endeavours, swept away my doubts,
and convinced me that I was extremely fortunate.

At the interview, Mr Farrow had told me only the
briefest details of his daughters: that their ages were
nineteen and sixteen, that their mother had died only
recently, and that a governess-companion was in residence. Now, though, the three young women had
entered my consciousness in their own right, and were
no longer the faceless abstractions of my imagination.
Already I found myself intrigued by three very
different personalities. Miss Agnew, whose role in the
household was similar to my own, I saw as a possible
ally. At first – from the severity of her dress, her straight
brown hair parted in the centre and pulled back into
a bun, and the plainness of her features – I had
assumed she was a good few years older than I. When
she sat and talked with me in the dining room,
however, and I observed her at close quarters, I
lowered my estimate to perhaps two- or three-and-
twenty. Her skin was fresh and young, her eyes bright
and keen as a wren's. I saw that here was a young
woman who, conscious of her status, wished to draw
no attention to herself through feminine adornment.
And what of that startling moment when, observing

the treacherous flushing that heated my face, she had blushed scarlet in response, and for a moment seemed as bashful as a schoolgirl? I could not think what had provoked such embarrassment, other than an awareness that she had embarrassed *me*.

As for Mr Farrow's two daughters – they could hardly be more different in appearance, or, apparently, in temperament. Marianne! I am hardly exaggerating if I say that she captivated me at first glance, and that her troubled personality served only to heighten my fascination. Juliana was pretty, but Marianne was a beauty – such hair, such eyes, and those fleeting expressions. Lying wakeful in my bed, I could see her as clearly as if she stood before me now. That hair! – rich and luxuriant, tumbling loose over her shoulders; her eyes, dark and fearful when we had met by the gates, had revealed themselves when we entered the house to be deep in colour, between blue and sea-green. My fingers itched for a paintbrush; I longed for paper or a canvas on which to attempt her image. Indeed, if my art materials had not been in my trunk at the railway station, I should have abandoned sleep to set myself the task of capturing Marianne's likeness, her spirit, her restless energy. And of course I was fully aware that such warmth of feeling from a tutor towards his young pupil was far from appropriate, and that I must conquer or conceal it.

Juliana was so different that the two would hardly be taken for sisters. Smaller in build than Marianne, she gave the appearance of delicacy, even of fragility, and I was not surprised when – after she had bid us goodnight – Miss Agnew told me that she had been convalescing from illness, hence her father's wish to revive her spirits through the drawing lessons I was to provide. Her features were fine, her skin pale and flawless; her thin hair – unlike her sister's springing mane – was dressed close to her head and in coils at the nape of her neck, and shone the colour of ripe barley. She was demure in appearance, even docile. She was, I knew, nineteen years old, but seemed, like her younger sister, to look for guidance to Miss Agnew.

What was I doing here? What should I make of it? My thoughts swung extravagantly one way and then the other. One moment, I could hardly believe my good fortune at securing employment in such a place; the next, I was sure that Mr Farrow would be disappointed in me, that I would prove unworthy of his regard, a dull companion and an ineffectual tutor.

It was impossible; sleep would not come. I flung back my bedclothes and sat upright; then crossed to the window and opened it wide to the night air.

The moonlight was intoxicating. My room faced south; I could see the swell of the Downs against a paler sky; the moon, unbelievably huge, gazed down with cool indifference. I heard a sharp bark, maybe of a fox; the night had a life and an energy of its own. Used to London streets, I revelled in the sense of the unpeopled landscape stretching before me, of meadows and copses and thickets breathing their scents into the night. If I had not been a new arrival, conscious of the impression I must make, I should have found my way out into the grounds, to stand under the sky again, and stretch my arms to its immensity.

Instead I peered more closely at the gardens before me, trying to discern their outline. I saw shrubberies, clipped hedges, walks; a little farther, beyond an expanse of lawn, I saw the cold glimmer of moonlight on water.

When I awoke in the morning it was from a dream of extraordinary vividness, so that I had to shake my head free of it, and gaze around my room several times to convince myself of where I was, and that the dream was not real but imagined. In it, I had been drawn by the liquid notes of a bird to the water's edge, pushing my way through branches. I wondered now if the nightingale – for surely it could only be a nightingale? – had been pouring forth its song outside my window while I slept, for I could not have imagined such tunefulness. Of an intensity and sweetness that shivered over my skin, its song struck in me some chord of desperate yearning – for what, I did not know. In the dream I tried to draw closer, not expecting to see the bird itself, for I knew that it was brown and insignificant, and would not show itself in the summer night, but only to drink in more and more of that throbbing, silvery song, ever varying: now a mellifluous fluting, now low, drawn out and melancholy. Cool leaves brushed my face; I parted them with my hands and, as I found myself close to the lake shore, was arrested by the sight of a female form, dark and cloaked, silhouetted against the water's pale glimmer. As I paused, hardly breathing, she turned her face to me, and spoke. 'I knew you would come,' said Marianne – for she it was. 'But you should know that such beauty will always give you pain, for you can never catch and hold it.'

'What do you mean?' I asked her; but she had turned away and was lost in the trees' shadows, and although I strained for the bird's note, I heard only silence.

Chapter Five

North, South, East

At breakfast, Mr Godwin was visibly disappointed to find me as his only companion; Marianne had already been and gone, and Juliana had not yet appeared downstairs.

'Will Mr Farrow be joining us?' he queried, with a touch of petulance.

'It is his custom to take breakfast alone in his room,' I told him, 'and to spend the morning in his study, attending to business matters. We do not generally see him before luncheon. Today, though, he has asked that you present yourself at his study at ten o'clock. If you have questions relating to your employment here, he will answer them then.'

He seemed appeased. 'I must send for my trunk,' he said. 'It is still at the station – I had almost forgotten.'

'There is no need to trouble yourself,' I assured him. 'I have already sent Reynolds with the pony-chaise.'

'That is most thoughtful of you, Miss Agnew.'

Acknowledging this with a nod, I added, 'Do please help yourself,' and indicated the range of dishes on the sideboard.

When we had breakfasted, I conducted him on a tour of the house. He was full of admiration for its beauties; and I must say that, observing his reactions, his exclamations of delight as we turned a corner or opened a door, I contemplated the house with fresh eyes, remembering my own amazement when first I entered. It is a house that invites the visitor to roam through its rooms, to sit and to linger. Constantly it offers small details to delight the eye: a plaster frieze of berries and leaves, a curving door handle that makes the hand want to clasp it, or a pair of wall lamps shaped like snowdrops. Indeed, it is hard to imagine a house in which beauty and comfort combine more harmoniously.

Mr Godwin was full of praise. 'It seems so solid – so rooted in the earth,' he remarked, as we surveyed the long, low drawing room, with its fireplace of curving simplicity, its cushioned recesses and Juliana's rosewood piano. 'Yet so light and spacious within! Mr Farrow, you say, had a hand in its design, at every stage? Does he have any practical experience of architecture?'

'He interests himself in such matters,' I replied. 'When he inherited his father's London house, and a considerable fortune from property investments, he saw an opportunity to build a house to his own requirements. An older house formerly stood on this site, but was demolished to make way for the new – only a few of the outbuildings remain. Mr Farrow engaged a leading architect, one whose work he admired, and worked very closely with him throughout. Every detail, interior and exterior, is a part of the whole. Mr Farrow suggested some of the more striking features: the high central vestibule, the double staircase and the upper gallery. He wanted to make his own mark.'

'So, Miss Agnew' – we had paused to look out of the glass doors that opened to the terrace, and to the lawn sloping down to an alder-fringed stream, with the rise of the Downs beyond – 'evidently, then, you have been in Mr Farrow's employment for some while? You were with him at his previous residence?'

'No,' I corrected him. 'I have been here for just over a year – some fifteen months. Since March of last year, to be precise.'

'And did you know the late Mrs Farrow?'

'I did not,' I replied. 'The poor lady died at the beginning of that year.'

'How terribly distressing for the two girls to lose their mother,' he remarked, with a sad shake of his head.

'Yes, a most tragic loss indeed. Now, let me show you the gardens— Ah, here is Marianne!'

Knowing my younger charge as I did, I could assess her mental state at a glance. This morning, coming up the lawn towards us, she looked fresh and appealing in a dress of sprigged muslin, her hair looped back; no one seeing her like this, smiling and at ease, could have guessed at the mental disturbance I knew equally well. As I opened the doors to let her in, I saw that she had threaded three daisies into her hair.

'Good morning, Charlotte; good morning, Mr Godwin!' she greeted us. Oh, how I envied her sometimes, her grace, her youthful radiance, and her captivating smile! However, I pushed such thoughts aside, as unworthy of me. To admire is one thing; to envy, quite another.

'Good morning, Miss Farrow,' Mr Godwin returned.

She gave a pretty frown. 'We cannot stick to this absurd formality, if you're to teach me drawing every day. I should prefer you to call me Marianne – it is so much friendlier.'

'Thank you,' said Mr Godwin, with a small bow. 'In which case, I hope you will address me as Samuel.'

He did not glance in my direction, not thinking fit to include me in this. As he should have deferred to me for guidance, I felt nettled, and quickly intervened.

'Your father would wish us to observe the proprieties, Marianne,' I pointed out. 'We shall address Mr Godwin by his proper name.'

He gave me a sidelong look, but went on, 'Miss Agnew is about to take me on a tour of the grounds.'

'Then I shall join you!' Marianne announced. 'We must start at the front – with the North Wind. We won't be disturbed – Papa is safely shut up in his study.'

'The north wind?' said Mr Godwin, holding out both hands, as though to attest that barely a breeze was blowing today.

'Marianne,' I said, to forestall her, 'would you go to your sister's room and ask whether she wishes to join us?'

She would not, however, be so easily diverted. 'Juliana is so slow in the mornings! I cannot think how she takes such an age to get up and dressed. And I want to see what Sa— what Mr Godwin thinks of our

Winds. He is an artist – his opinion will be worth having.'

So rational did she sound that I gave way.

'The Winds are quite a feature of the house,' I told Mr Godwin, leading the way back through the vestibule, out of the front door, and down the porch steps. 'Mr Farrow, having decided on the name Fourwinds, so appropriate for this open situation, commissioned the carvings, one for each façade of the house. Here is the first.'

We stood looking up at the stone figure above the entrance. Having lived here long enough for familiarity to dull my responses, I had almost ceased to notice the carved panels that adorned three of its four sides, hardly sparing them an upward glance as I went about my business. Now, standing beside Samuel Godwin as he contemplated the North Wind for the first time, I was reminded how very striking it is. The elderly male figure, with the proportions of a living person, hoary bearded and with eyebrows that jut above piercing eyes, seems to fly through a blizzard beneath louring clouds; but these meagre words cannot do justice to the sculptor's skill. Mr Godwin drew in his breath sharply and stood for a moment before speaking.

'What do you think?' Marianne prompted.

'Remarkable!' His voice was low and reverent. 'Such a powerful combination of styles, classical and – pagan, one might call it. I am impatient, Miss Agnew, to see the other three.'

Marianne glanced at me but said nothing.

'Who is the sculptor?' Mr Godwin asked, as we walked round to the east side of the house. 'Someone very gifted, that much is evident.'

'His name was Gideon Waring,' I answered. This was not a subject upon which I was keen to embark; yet I saw no way of circumventing it, with Mr Godwin's interest keenly aroused, and Marianne so eager to gauge his responses.

'And is he well known in his field? I confess I am not familiar with his name.'

'Oh, Gideon Waring is a real artist,' Marianne said, over her shoulder. 'An artist in stone. Are *you* a real artist, Mr Godwin?'

'Well, I . . .' the young man faltered.

'Marianne!' I reproved. 'Please remember your manners. Of course Mr Godwin is a real artist, or your father would not have engaged him.'

Mr Godwin, looking embarrassed, repeated his question: 'Is Gideon Waring well known as a sculptor?'

'Moderately, I believe,' I began; but Marianne saved me from further elucidation. She came to a halt, and gazed up.

'Look!' she directed Mr Godwin. 'Here is our East Wind.'

From this side of the house, the windows of dining room and morning room overlook a gentle downward slope towards paddocks and, beyond, the lake fringed with reed-beds; but we were all facing the shivering boy-man on the wall above us, naked and huddled: the East Wind, blown in, it seems, from distant mountain peaks that pierce a storm-ravaged sky. Although the morning was warm and still, with the promise of heat later, the East Wind carving almost made me want to snuggle into an imaginary shawl, and seek the nearest fireplace.

Again Samuel Godwin stood rapt and entranced, much to Marianne's delight.

'I see you have fallen under his spell!' she exclaimed. 'I am so glad – for I could not take to you as my drawing teacher, if you looked on him with cold indifference. Come – let us see what you think of the South Wind. She has a very different character.'

As we moved on, a flicker of movement caught my attention. The unusual design of Fourwinds incorporates a room between ground and first floor on each side, at the turn of the stair; Mr Farrow's study, with its oriel window, occupied this position on one side of the house; on the other side, a linen store. At this elevation he was able to look out at us without being observed from below. His eye, so expert at assessing the qualities of hunter or brood mare, rested on the figure of Samuel Godwin. Unintentionally catching my eye in mid-inspection, he gave a curt nod and the merest twitch of a smile. I nodded in return, and he moved away from the window.

Keeping this little exchange to myself, I followed Marianne and Mr Godwin to the rear of the house. Again we all turned our backs on the vista and looked at the carved figure above window-height: a female figure, full and voluptuous, clad in light drapery. Her eyes half closed, she floats on warm currents, accompanied by flights of swallows.

'Ah yes, very different, but beautiful again!' murmured Mr Godwin.

'Marianne,' I said, while we could still feel ourselves bathed in the balmy atmosphere this South Wind brought with her (for I knew that this was the way Marianne's thoughts transported her), 'it is rather late, even for Juliana. Would you go indoors and tell her we are all out here?'

Marianne appeared not to have heard; her eyes were fixed on Samuel Godwin as he stood in contemplation. After a few moments, he made to move off. 'And now the last!' he said, with a look of eager anticipation. 'How has your ingenious sculptor personified the West Wind, I wonder?'

'Marianne – your sister,' I reminded her gently.

Too late. Her expression was set in the blank stare I knew too well; she stared at me as though trying to wring sense out of my simple words, then swivelled her head towards Mr Godwin, and fixed him with the same unnerving glare.

'Don't you know?' she accused him. 'Has no one told you?'

'I beg your pardon?' he answered, quite taken aback.

Her eyes wavered over his face; she did not speak. When I attempted to take her arm, she shook me off with a gesture of impatience.

'Miss Farrow! Are you feeling unwell?' said Mr Godwin, moving towards her. 'May I assist you?'

'Yes, maybe we had better go indoors,' I added. 'Come, Marianne!'

She backed away, and I saw that she was trembling. 'He is roaming free – always, roaming free!' she said with difficulty, as though the words were wrenched from her.

Mr Godwin glanced at me, then made another attempt. 'Miss Farrow! You cannot be well. Do take my arm, please – maybe a quiet walk on the lawn will restore you.'

Marianne's shoulders began to heave; a large, single tear coursed down her cheek. 'Where is he?' she sobbed. 'Where is the West Wind? Will he never be found?'

'Marianne, please,' I began, but she threw me an agonized glance and turned, ignoring Mr Godwin's proffered arm, to run back the way we had come, her long hair flying out behind her. About to excuse myself and go in pursuit, I saw her veer down the slope towards the paddocks, then jink back again as she caught sight of Juliana, who was sauntering across the lawn. Marianne gave a loud sob, and rushed towards her sister.

Naturally, Mr Godwin was most perturbed. 'She was speaking of the West Wind when I met her last night, by the gate!' he told me quietly. 'What is it that upsets her so? Could we perhaps look at the carving in question – might that offer a clue?'

He was about to move off to the west side of the house. I held up a hand to forestall him. 'Mr Godwin,' I said, 'the West Wind carving might well provide us with useful information, if we knew where to find it. What Marianne said is true. There *is* no West Wind –

or, if there is, it is not to be found on these premises. I see that I must furnish you with a fuller explanation. However,' I added, pulling out my pocket watch, 'that had better wait until later in the day. It is almost time for you to meet Mr Farrow.'

The glass doors to the drawing room were unlocked; I guided him through them, to avoid passing Marianne, who was now weeping in her sister's arms. Samuel Godwin threw her a doubtful glance as we entered. He considered me, no doubt, rather matter-of-fact in my dealings with her. As for myself, I felt only irritation that Marianne had twice since his arrival shown herself at her most hysterical. Knowing her as I did, I suspected that she was quite deliberately making herself the centre of attention.

Chapter Six

A Solitary Man

At one minute to ten precisely, I was standing outside Mr Farrow's study door. Anxious to make as good an impression as I had evidently made on our first meeting, I had washed my hands, brushed my hair and smoothed it down with water; I was determined that Mr Farrow should have no reason to fault my turnout or manners. Yet, fiddling with my necktie, and checking that my fingernails were perfectly clean, I could not help feeling like a schoolboy summoned to his headmaster.

I rapped on the door, hoping to convey a confidence I did not feel.

'Enter,' called a deep voice from within.

I did so. Mr Farrow, seated at a desk by the window, rose to his feet as I approached. He was a large man, almost burly; I remembered my surprise, on that first meeting in London, for I had expected him to be considerably older. My mental picture, derived only from the wording of the advertisement he had placed, the implication of country seclusion, and the hotel address in a discreetly expensive part of Kensington, was of someone grey-haired and retiring – slightly built, and cautious of his health, formidable in terms of intellect and status. This picture had proved wrong in almost every respect. Mr Farrow, vigorous, without a trace of grey in his thick dark hair, could not have been much above forty. He was a handsome, sensual-looking man: strong featured, with full lips, and eyes of the darkest brown.

'Good morning, Mr Godwin,' he greeted me now. 'I am very glad to welcome you to Fourwinds.' Offering his hand, he shook mine in a painfully wringing grip. 'I trust you are settling in comfortably? Everything is to your liking?'

'Very much so, sir. It is a most beautiful house you have here.'

'Have a seat, do.' He gestured towards an uphol-stered carver chair by the fireplace, and turned his own – for he had been seated facing the window – towards it. Then he tugged at a bell pull. 'I shall send for coffee. You will take coffee?'

'Thank you, sir,' I replied, though breakfast was so recent.

'You were late arriving last night,' he went on, with a quizzical lift of one eyebrow that turned statement into question.

I explained about the delayed train, the missed connection and my urge to walk; then a maidservant arrived and took the order for coffee. This gave me a few moments to assess my surroundings.

Every room I had so far seen contained small surprises; this, though intended as an office and with

44

one wall lined with bookshelves, was entirely panelled in light wood, and featured several small alcoves and cupboards, as well as a most beautifully carved oak surround. A narrow oriel window allowed daylight to enter, and the occupant to glance outside, without offering the distraction of a larger window.

I was rather surprised that such a robust-looking individual as Mr Farrow should choose to spend his mornings shut away indoors; I should not have been surprised if his pleasure instead had been to ride early on the Downs, or to venture out with dogs and rifle. A case on the wall held guns – a rifle and two pistols – though all three looked unused and highly polished. I had seen no dog at Fourwinds, and felt a sudden pang of loss for Monty, our fox terrier at home. How he would have enjoyed exploring the countryside here, and chasing rabbits on the Downs! – but at this point I called myself sternly to attention.

A framed photograph of my employer's two daughters stood upon his desk; another, of a lady in a broad-brimmed hat, holding an armful of lilies, I assumed to portray his deceased wife. When he saw me looking at it, I felt that some remark would be appropriate.

'I am very sorry, sir,' I ventured, 'to learn of your sad loss – I mean of the late Mrs Farrow.'

'Thank you. Yes, a sad loss indeed,' he replied. He spread the fingers of one hand and examined them, his features pensive and downcast. After a moment, he added: 'You have met my daughters, of course?'

'Indeed I have. Such very charming young

ladies—' I began, but he went on, 'It is mainly for Juliana's benefit that I have engaged you, Mr Godwin. She has some modest artistic talent, I believe. She needs taking out of herself. She's been ill, you know – she is physically well now, but has not recovered her spirits. She spends far too long brooding around the house. Your company, and a purposeful occupation, will restore her well-being.'

'I assure you that I shall do all I can to engage her interest and encourage her talents,' I replied. 'And the younger Miss Farrow?'

My dream came back to me then, in all its intensity and strangeness. I wondered if Mr Farrow might offer some information about his other daughter's peculiar changes of mood – for, surely, it was Marianne whose spirits most obviously needed reviving – but his reply was offhand.

'Yes, of course. Marianne may as well join in the lessons, if it amuses her to do so. She has no aptitude, as far as I can see. But she likes to chatter on about nothing in particular – don't let her make a nuisance of herself. Now, what d'you think of my house? You're an artist. You must have an eye for details that would be missed by the casual visitor. A sense of aesthetics, of the guiding principles of a building. What do you say?'

I had already told him that I considered Fourwinds to be beautiful; evidently he required a fuller appreciation. 'I have only just now had a brief tour, with Miss Agnew,' I told him, 'but I am very impressed. It is not at all what I expected. I very much admire the lightness and spaciousness inside, yet it stands so well in the landscape that one would hardly suspect it was newly built.'

I began to feel lost for words; architecture was not my discipline. Yet he seemed pleased. 'Ah! You understand! Solidity and strength without; light and modernity within. I like to surround myself with beauty. Nothing mass-produced or factory-made here, Mr Godwin. I employ honest, skilled craftsmen. Attention to detail makes a harmonious whole. To combine the best of the new architectural thinking with traditional craftsmanship and materials, that was my aim. I flatter myself that I have not done too badly.'

'Then you have fulfilled it most admirably – you and your architect,' I assured him. 'Truly, it is a beautiful building, but also a comfortable family home.'

As soon as I had uttered these words, I felt how tactless they were, how ill judged. The poor man's hopes must have been dashed – to plan such a beautiful dwelling for his family, to imagine them living here happily, their voices in its rooms, their footfall on its stairs – only to have his wife snatched away to an early death! Mrs Farrow's absence must be felt as a huge blank, a great emptiness at the heart of Fourwinds. Having experienced for myself the unfathomable loss, almost the mystery, of an untimely death in the family, I could guess at his feelings.

'Well, I hope you'll be happy here,' he said, with no sign of reproach. 'To be honest with you, I shall welcome male company. I lead rather a solitary life here in this houseful of women. I hope we may enjoy a congenial conversation from time to time, over a bottle of good wine and a few cigars. Yes?'

He sat back in his chair, looking at me with evident approval while the maid brought in the coffee. I could not help feeling flattered by the attention of this powerful, forthright man. His ease and assurance, and the sense of mutual liking, encouraged me to think that I should do well here.

After the coffee was poured, Mr Farrow became businesslike again. 'Now. I have another reason for bringing you here. I liked what I saw of your work, Mr Godwin, when we met in London. You've brought more samples to show me, from your portfolio?'

'Yes, sir, I have – but they are in my trunk, which is being brought from the station as we speak.'

'I want to see them. You have already shown me that you have the right kind of feeling for my house. Your painting style pleases me as much as your sensibility. Spirit of place, that's what I see in your work. I want to commission a series of paintings from you. Fourwinds, exterior and interior. Yes, you see' – he gave a self-mocking laugh – 'I like to see myself in the style of an eighteenth-century landowner. Proud of my surroundings, and the mark I've made on the landscape. My picture gallery stands in readiness. The paintings hung there are drab things that have been in the family for years. They're only filling the space; they don't suit this house. I aim to replace them with fresh new works.' He looked at me keenly. 'Will you do it? Take on the commission?'

'Indeed I shall!' I said, with an eagerness which

seemed to amuse him. It was a step towards earning my living as painter, rather than as humble teacher. Mr Farrow was an influential man, I had no doubt. If I could please him with my work – and I vowed to make every conceivable effort to do so! – other commissions might follow.

'Good, good,' he said, nodding. 'You'll have plenty of free time here, time for painting. Very well. You may take up your tutoring duties immediately. We'll meet again this time tomorrow, when I shall explain more fully what I have in mind. Bring your portfolio.'

My spirits were high as I wished him good morning, and descended the stairs. The fates that had chosen me as protégé of such a man as Ernest Farrow had been generous indeed.

Chapter Seven

Juliana

As soon as Samuel Godwin went to keep his appointment with Mr Farrow, I sought out Juliana, who was sitting in the morning room with her embroidery. She was particularly fond of this room, it having been her mother's. Although I had felt anxious for Marianne, I found her reclining on the chaise longue, reading a book, and showing no remnant of her recent distress. This rather confirmed my opinion that her outburst owed more to melodrama than to genuine anguish.

'Well, Charlotte.' Juliana greeted me with her quick, demure smile. 'What opinion have you formed of Mr Godwin? Will he be a good tutor, do you think?'

'He seems a most agreeable young man.' No treacherous blush threatened my composure this morning; I could not think what had come over me while I sat with the newcomer at his supper the night before. 'But I shall reserve further judgement until I have seen him at work. Your lessons will, I suppose, commence this afternoon?'

'Tuh!' went Marianne, from her chaise longue; I had not believed her to be listening, so engrossed had she seemed in her book. 'The art lessons are merely Papa's excuse – don't you see, Charlotte?'

'What can you mean?' I challenged her.

'Surely you must have guessed Papa's real reason for bringing Samuel Godwin here?' she replied. Her cheeks were flushed, her eyes bright.

'I have not,' I returned.

'Why, he is to marry Juley!' Marianne said, in triumph. 'Is that not obvious?'

'To marry . . . ?' I echoed. Perplexed, I gazed first at Marianne, then at her sister: who, I observed, showed little surprise on hearing this startling piece of news; rather, a concern that it had been spoken aloud. 'But that would be preposterous, if it were true! Juliana is only nineteen, and we know next to nothing of Mr Godwin. Why should your father wish to arrange a marriage to someone with neither wealth nor connections?'

A silence answered my question: Marianne looked at her sister, her lips parted; Juliana continued sewing, only the faint blush of her cheeks betraying emotion. She was always mild mannered, yet even she would surely have countered Marianne's remark with a strong denial, unless – unless there were some truth in it.

It was not in Juliana's nature to keep secrets; or so I had thought.

'Surely your father can have mentioned no such plan!' I exclaimed, looking from one sister to the other. 'I would be more than astonished if he had.'

'Of course not!' Marianne replied. 'But it's obvious to anyone with eyes to see.'

'Marianne!' her sister reproved, snipping a thread.

'Manners, Marianne,' I said crisply. 'I am certain that Mr Godwin himself has no such idea – so he must be as blind as I am to what you consider so obvious.'

Marianne turned a page of her book. Seating myself next to Juliana on the sofa, I felt nettled by this exchange. I thought I had the confidence of both sisters; particularly Juliana, who was sometimes, I thought, over-dependent on my company, seeing me almost as a substitute for her mother, though I was close to her own age. Now, it seemed, the introduction of a personable young man to our company had inspired them to collude in silly fantasies. With Marianne, I was used to wild imaginings, but her sister I credited with more practical sense.

'You don't believe me,' Marianne observed.

'I most certainly do not,' I returned. 'Marry Mr Godwin? I don't understand how such a notion has entered your head. Nothing in Mr Godwin's person or manner makes the idea objectionable; but why would your father make such an arbitrary choice? He cannot suppose Juliana to be incapable of attracting admirers without his interference. There must be plenty of eligible young men among his acquaintances.'

'Yes! But when do we ever meet them?' Marianne retorted, giving me a knowing glance, in which I read her absolute assurance that she was right. Juliana only bent more attentively over her needlework. It was true that I had already asked myself why the girls' father had chosen to install Mr Godwin at Fourwinds; but this theory was too outrageous to be seriously considered. If anyone were likely to contemplate marriage, it would more likely be Mr Farrow himself, still vigorous, handsome and in his prime, than his daughters. At this point I curbed my thoughts swiftly: he was only recently out of mourning for his late wife. How I felt for him! The merest sight of his girls, each in her own way so charming, must give him pain; every hour spent with them must remind him most sharply of his loss. It is a hard burden for any man to bear. The most doting of fathers, he would do anything likely to contribute to his daughters' happiness; but, surely, he would not attempt to procure a husband for Juliana in this way, as if she were a plain spinster of thirty with no other hope of marriage?

No, no! I shook my head, endeavouring to clear it of such nonsense. Ernest Farrow liked to see himself as a patron of the arts. He was encouraging a promising young painter, just as he had encouraged his architect; and, later, the stone-carver Gideon Waring, ill fated though that project had turned out to be.

'Juliana, I thought you would consider this idea of Marianne's as unlikely as I do,' I remarked. 'What have you to say?'

She did not look up from her sewing. 'To marry, and to have a home of one's own, is the ambition of most young women.'

'Is it yours, Charlotte?' Marianne asked me, with a mischievous little smile.

'You know it is not. Whom should I marry?'

'Papa won't trouble himself to send for a husband

for *me*,' she said, a little fretfully. 'Juley is his favourite; anyone can see that. I'm sure I don't know why.'

'Oh, no,' Juliana murmured, with a quick shake of her head.

'Marianne, that is quite absurd!' I replied. 'You know your father is utterly devoted to both of you. Besides, you are far too young to be thinking of marrying.'

'But Juliana is not,' said Marianne.

I turned to her sister. 'So you would not object to leaving Fourwinds, to marry and set up a home of your own?'

Honesty compels me to own that I was thinking principally of myself. My tenure here, of course, could not last indefinitely; I should be foolish to think so. Inevitably, Juliana would marry; if not soon, then within a few years; so would Marianne; and what need would there be for Charlotte Agnew? I did not like to think of it. I had made my life here; I had no other.

'If I should be so blessed,' said Juliana. She paused, and gave me a sidelong glance, a look of sweet tenderness. 'If that should happen, Charlotte, if I should leave Fourwinds – I hope you would come with me. I could not bear to be parted from you.'

Such a dear, kind-hearted girl as she was, she had sensed my disquiet. I smiled my gratitude.

'Nor I,' said Marianne promptly. 'I should insist on coming too. So, Juley, you and your husband will need quite a large house, to accommodate us all.'

'There will be plenty of time to consider such matters,' I told them, '*when* the occasion arises. That is not likely to be for some while.'

'It's a great pity that Mr Waring had to leave,' Marianne remarked.

I gave her a stern glance. 'Why, what has *he* to do with anything?'

'We were talking of Juliana's future husband.' Marianne was in mischievous mood. 'He would have suited her better than anyone, even though he had no money.'

'I should hardly think so!' I reproved.

She gave me a look of playfulness mixed with defiance, but did not defend herself.

Juliana blushed hotly. 'Mr Waring was a good friend to me,' she said, casting her eyes down. 'I wish he were here still.'

'While we are on the subject,' I told them, lowering my voice, 'I should warn you against speaking of Gideon Waring in Mr Godwin's hearing. He – I mean Mr Godwin – is already curious, having seen the three Winds. We need only say that Mr Waring was working on the sculptures when your father found reason to dismiss him. That must suffice. I know how the servants gossip. We cannot prevent that, but it is a subject best avoided amongst ourselves.'

'Miss Hardacre too,' said Marianne. 'Papa is very good at finding reasons to dismiss people, when it suits him to do so.'

'Please, Marianne!' Juliana, glanced up, still flushed. 'You will make Charlotte anxious for her own position, and there is no need for her to feel doubt on that score. No one could suit us more perfectly than you do, Charlotte. You are almost a member of the family.'

At this comparison with my predecessor, I have to admit that I felt a glow of satisfaction, almost of self-righteousness; but Miss Hardacre, like Mr Waring, was not someone I wished to hear mentioned.

'Your father would never dismiss anyone without good reason,' I added, 'and I sincerely hope I shall never give him cause for displeasure. Marianne, it is time for your French lesson. Where are your books?'

'I shall fetch them. But you needn't worry about Samuel,' she assured me. 'I am quite sure he isn't a gossip.' She uncurled her legs, knocking her book carelessly to the floor; then she stood, stretching both arms above her head. 'Oh, I feel so restless today! Charlotte, you will find me an inattentive pupil, I am afraid.'

She was quite right: I did; though her distraction was matched by my own.

Chapter Eight

Mrs Matthew Dearly, née Hardacre, to Miss Juliana Farrow

Orchard Cottage,
Rampions,
Near Staverton,
Sussex

22nd June, 1898

My dearest Juliana,

I must apologize for the delay in replying to your last, since you have told me how you look forward to my letters. You would be forgiven for thinking me very neglectful. However, you will see that we have been very much occupied of late, and you will see why, for you must be surprised by the address I have given. Yes, we have come to live at Rampions, not five miles from Fourwinds! We have been so very lucky! We had thought ourselves quite settled in Petersfield, but then the head gardener at Rampions became ill and was forced to retire, and so Mr Vernon-Dale was looking for a replacement. The groom there, with whom Matthew was friendly, wrote with the news, and Matthew applied immediately. It is a wonderful advancement for him, with four under-gardeners to supervise, and the splendid grounds of Rampions, and most importantly we have for our home the gardener's cottage, which is as comfortable and well appointed a dwelling as I could hope for, and quite sizeable — indeed I prefer to call it a villa, with its own vegetable plot behind and flower garden in front. Rampions is so very grand that I think everyone who comes here must be quite astonished by its splendour. I must say that I am very glad to find myself once again in Sussex, not because I was in the least unhappy in Hampshire — how could I be with Matthew for a husband, and darling little Thomas? — but because it brings me back to the place I know and love best. And, dearest Juley, it returns me to the vicinity of Fourwinds, and to you and dear Marianne. I know that your father has appointed a new companion for you in my place, but I hope that you have not entirely transferred your affections and that there is still room in your heart for your Eliza. I flatter myself that there is. Mrs Matthew Dearly has a very different ring to it than Miss Eliza Hardacre, does it not? I am still the very same person, however, and quite unchanged in my devotion to you and your sister, even though I am now a married woman with husband and home of my own.

Now, Juley, how shall I come to visit you? For your father would be averse to my visiting Fourwinds. Indeed, as he was so instrumental in helping us to remove to Hampshire, it will displease him to learn that we have now made altogether different arrangements for ourselves — though maybe he need not learn _immediately_, if you understand my meaning! It would give me the greatest pleasure to welcome you to my new home; but I am quite sure your father would not permit that either. If he still travels to London, as used to be his wont, to deal with his business affairs, and stays there for a few nights, maybe you would let me know, so that I could arrange for one of the grooms here to drive me to Fourwinds? I can hardly wait to see you again, and I am sure that you must be longing to see Thomas — Tommy, as we call him. He is such a delightful child, pretty, playful and sunny-tempered. Thank you so much for the toy bear you sent for his first birthday. He plays with it devotedly.

I wonder whether you have any news of Mr Waring? I have not heard a word of him since our paths separated so abruptly — but this and other news can wait until we have the chance to spend a few hours in each other's company.

With affectionate best wishes, dearest Juley, to you and to Marianne,

Your devoted friend,

Eliza

Chapter Nine

Sleepless

At Fourwinds, spending so much time alone, I had ample time to examine my motives. What did I think I was doing, in my efforts with pencil and paintbrush, with oils and washes?

I could only discover a strong desire to make my mark on the future, to achieve something memorable that would outlast my life. But how could this be done? Why, among the countless millions of humans that thronged the Earth, should I believe myself to be set apart by some special gift? Did I seriously believe that I had the talent to outshine the countless unremarkable painters who squinted and stared, who mixed their colours, who dabbed and brushed and smeared their marks on canvas in the naive belief that it would grant them immortality? Was it only conceit on my part, a childish desire for fame and admiration?

I knew only that without the compulsion to draw and paint, to render on paper or canvas what I saw about me, I should consider my life to be quite without purpose.

* * *

The Farrows went to church in Staverton on Sunday, and I with them. Before and after the service, I was introduced to several people; my arrival at Fourwinds had caused, it seemed, a flurry of interest. I supposed that life in this quiet country place was so uneventful that change of any kind provoked comment and speculation. At these encounters, Mr Farrow introduced me as 'an artist of great promise', 'an immensely talented young painter', and other such heady descriptions. I did not choose to question his judgement; rather, I began to believe it myself, to think that there must be some latent spark of genius in my work which was apparent to him, if not to me.

Strangely, however, he seemed completely wrong in his assessment of his daughters' abilities. Whenever we spoke of the drawing lessons, his concern was all for Juliana, for her need to regain health and spirits. Yet, from the start, it was evident to me that Marianne was the one with artistic promise. Juliana had a fussy, hesitant approach, over-concerned with correctness: I should have to work hard, I saw, to make the best of a very modest talent. Marianne, on the other hand, had boldness, a feeling for place, and a style that could be termed slapdash but which needed only a little discipline to smooth its roughness.

On my second Sunday at Fourwinds, after attending church and doing justice to Mrs Reynolds's good roast beef and apple pie, I excused myself and went outside to look at the Wind carvings. I studied them in detail, and made a careful drawing of each, trying to emulate the clean precision of blanched, smooth-grained stone.

Then, turning to a blank page, I walked round to the west side of the house and stood looking up at the space which should have been occupied by the missing piece, the West Wind. I saw it, I fancied, in my mind's eye.

I was no connoisseur of sculpture, but there was something about these carvings that strongly appealed to me. Each stone figure seemed to have its own living presence, its own personality; and none revealed all its secrets at once. The North Wind seemed wearied of his duties, as if he would fain have changed places with his opposite on the south wall. The East Wind – the beautiful youth, bared to the elements without so much as a conventional fig leaf or wisp of loincloth to conceal his nakedness – looked fearful, hounded by Furies. The South Wind, smug by comparison in the balmy breath of wind that disturbed her tresses, gave a knowing, sidelong glance that was almost sly. Their maker seemed to have taken his inspiration from Roman or Greek figures, infusing them with a pagan mischief that spoke of medievalism. By now I had found other evidence, too, of his presence – of his humour. Beneath one roof quoin, a gargoyle head looked down at passers-by with a jeering expression. On a window ledge, a stone lizard stood poised; on another, a tiny monkey crouched. It was almost as if the sculptor had placed small jokes around the building, to reward the attention of the close observer.

Keenly interested in this Gideon Waring, I had committed his name to memory the instant Charlotte had uttered it. Here, I felt strongly, was a man whose work spoke of authority and sureness; whose identity was stamped on everything he touched. I had not heard the name before, but wondered if Waring lived locally and if I might see more of his stonework. I envied him his assurance, for in my painting I had yet to find a style I could call my own; I allowed myself to be swayed by one influence after another, as the whim took me. In comparison with the gifted Mr Waring, I felt myself to be a skilled copier, at best.

Looking around me, I saw a wrought-iron seat against the hedge that screened the vegetable garden. I sat, and drew. The afternoon was warm and still; the merest of breezes carried the scent of a rambling rose that sprawled against the house wall; I was content.

Here at Fourwinds, I resolved, I should find myself as an artist. While all my needs were provided for and I had limitless time to devote to my work, I should define and strengthen my style; I should find a painterly expression that was unmistakably my own. Yet, completely at odds with this ambition, I drew now in imitation of Gideon Waring. I was sketching the West Wind as I thought he might have executed it.

'No, no.' I imagined his voice in my ear; imagined he had crept up on me and looked over my shoulder, amused and sceptical. 'No,' he would say. 'That is not it at all.' Disturbingly, when I tried to give a face to the person I had summoned, the features appearing in my mind were those of my father. 'Painting's all very well as a leisure interest,' he admonished me, 'but you'll never make a living at it. How d'you think you'll ever support a wife and family? Keep it as a hobby, boy, that's my advice to you.'

What would he think of me now, my father? He would disapprove; he would find me a disappointment. When I announced my intention of studying at the Slade, he had all but washed his hands of me, only grudgingly persuaded by my mother to give me a meagre living allowance. My solitude here was allowing thoughts to surface, uncomfortable memories which I preferred to suppress. I had let down my father; but, equally, he had let me down. I found myself recalling an episode in which I had set up my easel in the park, and was absorbed in trying to capture the autumnal light through trees, when my father had approached, walking briskly, with Monty on his lead. Father threw a disparaging glance at my canvas, which I tried to turn away from his view; then he told me, 'You're squandering your time, Sam. What can you hope to do that's not been done a thousand times before? Photography's the thing now – your paints and canvases will soon belong in museums.' And he had stumped on across the grass, calling irritably to the dog, who showed me the whites of his eyes in a regretful look before trotting after his master. Monty, I consoled myself, would have preferred to keep me company, lying close by my easel while I painted.

This memory infected my idyll, wrenching me like the pain of colic. I groaned, and tore the page from my sketchbook, crumpling it in my hand.

As I rose to my feet, Marianne walked towards me from the southern side of the house, carrying a tapestry bag. She did not notice me at first; when she did, she quickened her steps and approached me, her face alert.

'You were drawing him!' she cried. 'I know you were, and now I have spoiled it.'

Him? The figure I had drawn was female.

'No, you have spoiled nothing,' I assured her, revealing the torn page clenched in my hand.

'Let me see!'

She attempted to wrest it from me, but I resisted. 'It is not worthy of your attention, believe me.'

'You are trying to put things right!' She looked at me keenly. 'You know how important it is – and I am grateful. But you cannot know the West Wind, Samuel. Be glad that you cannot.'

I was newly struck by her strange zealousness. 'Why do *you* not attempt its likeness?' I suggested, on an impulse. 'I should be most interested.'

'Maybe.' She spoke off-handedly, her interest quenched as suddenly as it had been aroused. Giving me a vague smile, she moved across the grass to sit on the bench I had just been occupying. I stood and watched, but she paid me no further attention; she sat quite still, gazing up at the empty space on the house wall. After a few moments I walked on, wondering where I might find Charlotte, and left Marianne to her meditation. When I turned to look, I saw that she too had brought sketchbook and pencil, and was drawing almost feverishly, with quick upward glances at the blank space, as if drawing something that was not there. She had only been waiting for me to be gone.

*　　*　　*

My days had settled into an agreeable pattern. After breakfast with Charlotte, and sometimes with one or both of the girls, I worked alone for most of the morning. I wanted to produce a set of detailed preparatory drawings, which I would show Mr Farrow before beginning to paint. Inexpressibly proud, and more than a little anxious, at being entrusted with this commission, I was determined to fulfil it in a manner which exceeded all expectations. I roamed around the house, inside and out, with a speculative eye, considering the angles and approaches I might choose.

The early part of each afternoon was devoted to my drawing lessons with Juliana and Marianne. Charlotte accompanied us, taking, I supposed, the role of chaperone; she sewed, or prepared Marianne's French lessons. I could scarcely describe my routine as arduous; when my pupils tired, I had free time for walks on the Downs, from whence I could look down on Fourwinds amidst its trees and lawns, or in a southerly direction to the distant sea. Often, Juliana went out on horseback; she had a white mare, called Queen Bess. Marianne, it seemed, was not fond of riding, had no horse of her own, and preferred to spend her afternoons reading, or sketching by the lake shore.

Although there were only five of us at Fourwinds, dinner was served each evening in formal style. Mr Farrow sat at the head of the table, Marianne to his left, Juliana to his right, with me beside her. Charlotte's place was at the far end, facing Mr Farrow, in the position his wife would have occupied; indeed, he looked to her to preside over meals, to give instructions to the cook and housekeeper, and in fact to take on several of the tasks a wife would have performed. Did she, I began to suspect, have designs on becoming the next Mrs Farrow? Many a young woman in her position, employed by a wealthy and presentable widower, would have nurtured such a hope. I looked at her keenly for evidence of scheming, but what I saw instead was single-minded devotion – to her employer as much as to her two charges. Whenever Mr Farrow spoke, her eyes rested on him with a fond, attentive expression; yes, I thought, she wishes to become a part of this family, and must surely wish without hope of fulfilment, for I cannot see Mr Farrow choosing to pair himself with Miss Charlotte Agnew. She was less plain than I had thought her at first glance – her quick eyes gave her an appealing liveliness – but was always simply dressed, even for dinner, without adornment. In our conversations so far, she had revealed little of herself – she plied me with questions about my family, my upbringing, my ambitions, but gave only vague answers to those I asked her in return. Although our routines brought us into contact several times each day, I scarcely knew more about her than I had at first meeting.

Always, there were four courses, and wine; the food was excellent, and the company congenial. Afterwards, in the drawing room, Juliana played the piano, with Marianne – who declined to play, on the grounds that she never practised adequately – turning the pages for her. As I sat at ease, or strolled on the lawn in the rose-scented dusk, or contemplated what the morrow might bring, I considered myself to be luckier than I deserved.

I had only one cause for regret. I missed my Slade friends, Chas, John and others; missed the laughter, the uproariousness, the high spirits of student life. I missed the classes, the silent hum of concentration, the smell of turpentine and pencil shavings; the noisy meals in the refectory; the squares of clipped grass where we sprawled to talk and argue, and, outside, the London streets, and the public house where we spent many an evening, each of us making a pint of beer last as long as possible, teasing Johnny for his hopeless adoration of the girl who worked in the furniture shop. Twice, I began to write to Chas and John; twice I put my letter aside, unable to employ the jocular tone we used among ourselves, and unwilling to give a serious account of my new surroundings and acquaintances. London, home and the Slade seemed fixed in the past, like moths on a collector's board, already withered and fading to dust.

Late on the evening of my encounter with Marianne in the garden, I sat by the open window of my room, my sketchbook before me. Over the last few evenings I had been amusing myself by drawing portraits. I had decided that I would reward Mr Farrow's patronage by surprising him with a portrait of his daughters. Experimenting with this first sketch, and finding that I did have some ability to capture the likeness of my subjects, I had added –

on a whim – Charlotte, standing behind the two sisters.

Looking afresh at the three images that gazed back at me, I was struck by what each face revealed of the personality behind it. In Juliana's – mild, composed, tranquil – I read sadness. Marianne's expression, though I could not do justice to her extraordinary, vibrant beauty, held boldness, a spirit of defiance. And Charlotte? Charlotte had been the hardest of all three to capture, her features unremarkable, her expression hard to define; but what I saw, now that she was committed to paper, was her sharp mind, her cleverness. She was, I realized, someone I should not underestimate.

I was more tired than I had thought. Abandoning paper and pencil, I moved to the open window, gazing out at the midsummer dusk. A dog barked somewhere, far off; I heard the lowing of cattle; the trees were lush with leaf. The quietness of the evening soothed me; I made ready for bed.

At first I must have slept heavily. Much later, something woke me – the screech of a bird from outside, maybe – and I lay for a few seconds in the silvery darkness, unable to remember where I was. When I realized that I was not, after all, in my bedroom in Sydenham, with Mama and Isobel in adjoining rooms, everything downstairs just as I knew it, and Monty snoring gently on the front doormat, which was his preferred sleeping place, I felt a renewed longing for home. I should have given much at that moment to walk down our own familiar stairs and to find everything just as I knew it.

No hint of dawn light yet penetrated the curtains. I turned, pushed back my sheets – for the night was warm – and composed myself for sleep. But in vain. From time to time, at troubled periods in my life, I have experienced the impossibility of falling asleep; my brain seems intent on resistance, and every determined effort, every shift of position or deliberate banishing of troublesome thoughts, results only in more emphatic wakefulness. My mind was racing with accumulated impressions, at such speed that I was almost dizzied by my mental workings.

Marianne! As so often, my circling thoughts settled on her. A small sigh escaped my lips as I conjured her – her glances, her long-limbed movement, the swirl of her hair. My bedding seemed unbearably hot and restricting; I flung back the covers altogether, and lay on my back, gazing at the ceiling. I struggled between a yearning for sensuous fantasies, and the knowledge that such thoughts must be curbed in their infancy. Marianne, I admonished myself, was barely a year older than my sister Isobel; she was my pupil, and I her teacher. My role, I began to feel, would be far easier if she had turned out to be plain of feature and dull of brain. I must control myself, must stop indulging my wanton desires; yet the heat of my blood and the prickling of my skin allowed no restraint.

Impatiently, I rolled over, rammed my face into the pillow and closed my eyes tightly; but sleep would not come.

At last I sat up, thinking that I may as well acknowledge defeat and spend the time profitably; turn on my lamp, sit at my bureau and continue working at my sketch. On the point of rising from my bed, I was arrested by a sound in the gallery beyond my door.

A slow footfall came near; then seemed to pause. The hairs rose on the back of my neck, just as Monty's hackles rose when, from his doormat observation post, he heard the tread of a possible intruder on our front path. I waited for a rap on my door, but none came. Silently, I stood; crept close; applied my ear to the keyhole. I heard a woeful sigh; then the footsteps moved on, more quickly. I heard the creak of a floorboard as the nocturnal wanderer passed towards the stairs.

The fear that had gripped me by the gateway, on my first approach, returned now with full force. In those taut-stretched seconds I could easily believe the place to be haunted by a restless or vengeful ghost. I had read stories in which newcomers to country houses find themselves witness to apparitions; in those moments I imagined myself as the central figure in such a drama. My hand on the doorknob, I paused to make certain the footsteps had passed away; rapidly, I removed it on hearing the return of the slow tread, which now quickened and seemed to approach my door almost at a run. Then, on a rising wail, a voice spoke:

'Never sleep! Oh, I shall never sleep!'

I might have reflected that the phantom was expressing my own thoughts precisely, had I not been stirred into action by a realization that this was no supernatural manifestation, but Marianne, on another of her strange roamings. At once I opened the door, and called her name softly. It must have been the beginning of dawn after all, for the dimmest of light revealed her to me, standing by the gallery railings. Clad in a white nightgown, with her abundant hair loose about her shoulders and tumbling down her back, she could, after all, have been taken for an apparition of the kind beloved by writers of sensation novels. But my next thought was of the physical danger she was in. She stood gazing up at the skylight; then, gripping the balustrade with both hands, she leaned over and gazed down at the vestibule two floors below. I caught my breath. If she leaned too far – if she lost her balance!

'Marianne!' I called again, more sharply. I moved carefully towards her, anxious not to startle her, for I feared precipitating disaster rather than averting it.

I trod so carefully that the floorboards gave scarcely a creak; she showed no sign of noticing my advance. Indeed, in spite of her complaint of not sleeping, I wondered if she were, in fact, asleep and dreaming; I had heard of such things. As soon as I drew close enough to be sure of securing her, I reached out, caught her wrist, and put my other arm around her shoulders, turning her away from the balustrade and the dangerous drop below. She spun round to face me.

'Oh – oh!' In shock, she was hardly able to breathe normally. For a moment she seemed about to faint; I held her, keenly conscious of the scent of her hair, its tickle against my face, and the firm smoothness of flesh beneath the nightgown. Next instant I heard the opening of another door behind me; heard the words, 'Is that you, Marianne?' spoken by Charlotte; and she was with us.

'I found her here,' I offered; 'she was walking in her sleep, I believe.'

Charlotte nodded. 'Marianne?' she said softly, with a touch on the other's sleeve. 'You are awake now? You know where you are?'

Marianne looked from Charlotte's face to mine and back again; blinked several times, and swallowed with an effort. 'I am sorry. I thought— Oh, but I am too late!' She began softly to cry.

'Come,' said Charlotte. She looked at me over Marianne's head. 'We must take her back to her room. There is a couch there – I shall fetch my blankets and sleep there for the rest of the night, in case she should try to wander again.'

Together we shuffled along the gallery and down the stairs, supporting the weeping girl between us. On the first floor, the bedrooms were larger and spaced farther apart. We passed the room I knew to be Mr Farrow's, with his dressing room next to it, hearing regular breathing from within; then Juliana's room; and now Marianne's, where the door stood open. We guided her to the bed, where, seated, she seemed gripped by a new distress.

'You must not tell Father! Promise me you will not?'

'Hush, dear.' Charlotte stroked her hand. 'Don't upset yourself.'

'No, no – you must promise – both of you!' Marianne's eyes searched my face in anguish.

'I promise,' I told her. Truly, I think I would have promised her anything she asked of me.

'Charlotte, you must promise, too! He will want to send me away, like Mama—'

Charlotte's eyes flicked to mine. Then she busied herself with details: switching on the lamp, smoothing the pillows and coverlet. 'Hush! Hush! You must get into bed – we shall talk in a moment. Mr Godwin, you had better leave us now. Thank you for your assistance.'

Self-conscious in the flare of lamplight, bare-legged and in my nightshirt in front of the two young women, I did as Charlotte asked; but waited outside the room for her to reappear. After their voices had murmured for some minutes, she did so, and prepared to climb the stairs to fetch her blankets; but I intercepted her.

'Charlotte! What did she mean by—?'

Raising a hand, she silenced me. 'We cannot talk now. Come down early to breakfast. I shall tell you then.'

The night was long in passing, for sleep eluded me completely.

Chapter Ten

Of Unsound Mind

After her escapade, Marianne slept soundly for the remainder of the night. It is needless to relate that I did not, though I made myself as comfortable as possible on the couch at the foot of her bed, and must have dozed intermittently. From now on, I decided, this must be my regular sleeping place. The risk of Marianne wandering around the house, or even outside it, as I suspected she had done on at least one occasion, was too alarming to contemplate. A bed must be made up for me here; I should tell Mrs Reynolds at the first opportunity.

At my usual hour of rising, I returned to my own room to wash and dress, leaving Marianne to sleep on. I had not forgotten my obligation to Samuel; on the contrary, I had lain awake through the dawn hours preparing exactly what I should say to him. We met in the dining room, as arranged, before the rest of the house was astir. The table was set in readiness, but Alice had not yet brought in the hot dishes.

'Mr Godwin,' I began, as soon as we had

exchanged Good Mornings. 'There are several things I need to explain to you.'

'I should be grateful,' said he. 'I have a good many questions to ask.'

'I am quite sure you have,' I returned. 'Let me begin by telling you that, as you must have guessed, Marianne has wandered in her sleep before. Most often, it is of short duration: she comes to her senses before leaving her own room, and I know of it only because she has confided in me. On occasion, though, she has left her room; even, I am afraid, ventured outside the house.'

'She could easily come to harm!' Samuel said, in great concern. 'Last night – she could have fallen from the upper gallery. If she should wander outside, the risk is even greater – there is the lake, or she might stray so far as to lose herself in the darkness—'

'Yes, yes,' I replied, a little piqued by his assumption that I had not thought of these hazards for myself. 'The disturbance has become more frequent of late, and that is why I have decided to supervise her more closely. From now on I shall sleep in her room, keeping the door locked from inside. I am a light enough sleeper to depend on waking if she rises from her bed.'

He nodded approval. 'And the cause? Do you attribute it to the poor girl's distress at the loss of her mother – is that when it began?'

'I believe so. As you know, I was not here at the time, but from what I know of the circumstances, it must have been a terrible ordeal for such an impressionable girl.

Besides her mother's death, there was her sister's ill-health and lengthy convalescence.'

'Are the two events related?' Mr Godwin asked. 'The mother's death and the daughter's illness? Is there, I mean, some hereditary disease in the family?'

'Possibly,' I replied, after a momentary hesitation. 'Mr Farrow has hinted at it, though naturally the subject is a painful one. Shall we sit?' – for we had stood till now at the window, looking out at the smooth-ness of lawn, the trees beyond, and the horses grazing in the paddock.

Although I had planned my subsequent speeches, I did not find it easy to continue.

'The nature of the illness . . . ?' Samuel prompted.

It was with reluctance that I went on. 'Mrs Farrow, the girls' mother, died in a tragic accident. It is not impossible that she took her own life, while – "while of unsound mind" is the phrase customarily used.'

'What kind of accident?'

'A fall.' Again, I found the words hard to utter. 'She fell from the upper gallery. Her neck was broken and she died instantly.'

Samuel's mouth opened in a soundless O.

'It was Marianne who found her,' I continued. 'It was in the early hours of the morning – while the rest of the household slept. Marianne, hearing some sound, emerged from her bedroom to see her mother standing by the railing. She called out in alarm, upon which Mrs Farrow leaned farther, and lost her balance; either that, or she deliberately threw herself into the stairwell.'

'How dreadful!' Samuel said, in a shocked, small

voice. 'And how do you know this, since it was before your employment here? From Marianne herself?'

'No. I have heard it from Mrs Reynolds. It seems to have been decided in the family that the matter should not be spoken of, and delicacy forbids me to seek details from Mr Farrow or the girls. But you can conjecture, I am sure, as to the effect on sensitive young minds. And, of course, there is no way of stopping the servants from talking.'

'Marianne, I imagine, must blame herself – she believes that she caused the accident, by startling her mother?'

'That must compound her distress, I am quite certain. It is almost eighteen months since the tragedy occurred, but such a dreadful memory must be vivid and raw in Marianne's mind, especially in dreams.'

'And Mrs Farrow? Was she also prone to sleep-walking?'

'Not that I have heard,' I replied. 'Neither Marianne nor Juliana has ever mentioned it. From Mrs Reynolds, I understand that Mrs Farrow was rather delicate – much confined to the house. I have seen her photograph, of course; she was a very handsome lady. Of the two girls, Juliana resembles her the more; Marianne takes after her father.'

'So young to die! Such a terrible loss to the family!' Samuel said, more to himself than to me; then he added, 'What can Marianne have meant, last night – this morning, rather – when she spoke of her mother being sent away? Did Mrs Farrow go to a sanatorium, maybe, or a nursing home?'

'I suppose that is possible,' I replied. 'But really, I cannot tell you. I am not aware that she ever did go away.'

Samuel gazed out of the window for some moments, absorbed in thought. My ears strained towards the servants' wing for sounds of our breakfast arriving; strong coffee would revive us both, after the restless night.

'In what particular way,' he asked, turning to me abruptly, 'was Mrs Farrow of unsound mind? Did Mrs Reynolds speak of it?'

'Very little. She has given me the impression that Mrs Farrow was always rather reserved.'

Samuel frowned. 'But now it is feared that *both* daughters may be following the same way? I am thinking of Juliana's recent illness and convalescence. The nature of her illness – was it a mental disturbance of some kind?'

'That is what I have been led to believe,' I answered. 'All I can say is that I know Juliana well, and that both girls are very dear to me. I have never seen any sign of instability in Juliana, nor of the over-wrought excitement we have both seen in Marianne. As you are aware, Juliana is far more placid in tempera-ment than her sister. Maybe the period of rest, away from home, allowed her to adjust to her loss, and to face it in a way that still eludes Marianne.'

'It strikes me as very odd,' said Samuel, with a frown, 'to send only one sister away, leaving the younger one in the house where the tragedy occurred! Where, every day, she must come across reminders not

only of the mother she has lost, but – each time she
mounts the stairs or crosses the hallway – of the very
place where the fatal fall took place! I don't understand it.'

'Yes, I cannot help but agree. No doubt Mr Farrow
had his reasons. He would always act in the best interests of his daughters, of that I am quite certain.'

Samuel gave me a quizzical glance. 'Your loyalty
does you great credit! You have lived in Mr Farrow's
house for more than a year – you must know him
well?'

'It is not difficult to feel loyalty to such an
employer,' I answered promptly. 'I know Mr Farrow
as the most admirable of men and the kindest of
fathers.'

At this point, Alice entered the room, pushing a
trolley loaded with coffee pot and serving dishes.
Seeing us seated and ready, she must have thought us
impatient, or herself late, for she apologized profusely.
'No matter,' I assured her, glad of the interruption.
However, there was to be no easy avoidance of
Samuel's further questioning, for Juliana was never
down early, and Marianne likely to sleep peacefully
for some while more.

At first he seemed preoccupied with examining
everything on the table. He picked up a knife and
smoothed two fingers over its handle; next he examined the salt cellar, and admired the lustre of a plate.
'Everything so well chosen,' he remarked; 'so harmonious! Mr Farrow's good taste, and attention to detail,
is evident in everything I see – every door handle,

every plate and glass, every item of furniture – to say nothing of his willingness to pay for the best.'

'You are right, of course,' I said, though I could not see where this train of thought was leading.

He looked at me. 'And yet there is one thing about the house that is incomplete, unfinished – and this, it seems, gives considerable distress to Marianne. I must know more about the stone-carver, Gideon Waring. Why was his work abandoned – such an important final touch, the carvings that give the house its name?'

'Come, Mr Godwin,' I said, rising from my seat. 'This good food must not go to waste.'

He followed me to the sideboard. 'I have noticed before,' he remarked, 'how you avoid the subject – but that only arouses my curiosity all the more.'

Lifting the lid of a chafing dish, I served myself with poached eggs. 'On the contrary. I am quite willing to tell you what little I know. You must remember that I have never encountered Mr Waring, for he left Fourwinds before I arrived.' I returned to my place. 'There was evidently a dispute between him and Mr Farrow. Mr Waring had been living here while he carried out the work, in Yew Tree Cottage, one of the outbuildings. He was at work on the fourth carving, the West Wind, when a fierce altercation resulted in Mr Farrow dismissing him. It is not known whether he destroyed the final carving, or took it away with him. Coffee, Mr Godwin?'

'Thank you. And the cause of the dispute?'

'That I do not know.'

Samuel assimilated this, and ate his bacon in silence.

'And yet,' he went on, after this pause, 'Mr Farrow was not offended enough to abandon the whole project? He could, if he wished, have discarded or sold off the first three Winds, and engaged another sculptor – but he did not. The North, East and South Winds are in their positions, and the fourth wall remains blank. Surely he intends to complete the sequence?'

'I believe so. The girls, you see, have become fond of the first three Winds, and insisted on their being placed in position. Mr Farrow once mentioned his wish to find another sculptor, to make the West Wind in imitation of Gideon Waring's style. However, such a man is not easy to find.'

'I should think not!' he exclaimed. 'It would be a pity if the West Wind were a poor imitation of the other three. But I am most curious about the nature of the quarrel. It cannot have concerned the quality of the work; that much is evident. About money, then? Mr Waring did not think he was being paid enough?'

'I have told you, I don't know,' I said. 'As it is not my concern, I have wasted no time in speculation.'

He was silenced by this rebuff. At that moment Alice interrupted us, bringing hot water and fresh toast. 'Excuse me, Miss Agnew, but Mr Farrow has finished his breakfast and wishes to see you in his study at nine o'clock.'

This was unusual, but I was not sorry to terminate the conversation with Samuel. Quickly completing my meal, I excused myself and tidied my hair and dress before going to Mr Farrow's study.

He called, 'Come in,' in answer to my knock; not looking up from his papers, he gestured that I should sit. Waiting, I found myself gazing at the photographs on his desk. There were two: one showed poor Constance, Mrs Farrow, smiling over an armful of flowers; in the other, Juliana sat on a garden bench while Marianne stood behind, an arm draped across her sister's shoulder. It was a foolish fantasy of mine to picture myself as a part of this family grouping; to think of Mr Farrow's glance falling on my image, his face softening into a smile of affection, in moments of distraction from his work. Since I was all but invisible to him, this was a ridiculous indulgence, but one which I permitted myself from time to time.

After a few moments he put down his pen and shuffled his papers together. He was brief.

'Charlotte, I have pressing business matters to attend to in London; I am leaving today, and will return on Friday,' he informed me. 'I shall stay at my club. Tell Reynolds to have the gig ready; I shall take the midday train.'

With a nod, I assured him that I should see to it. He continued: 'On Saturday, the Vernon-Dales and the Greenlaws are invited to dinner; I intend to introduce them to Mr Godwin. I should like you to act as hostess, since Juliana is not up to it; you may draw up the menu with Mrs Reynolds, and she will take care of everything else. Maybe you could see to the flowers.'

'Yes, Mr Farrow, it will be my pleasure,' I assured him, in some surprise.

I waited to see if he had any more to say; but as he did not, I turned to go. Then he added, 'I have arranged to see Mr Godwin; perhaps you would remind him to be prompt, for I am in a hurry to leave.'

Outside his door, I stood for a few moments considering what I had just heard, before making my way to Marianne's room to see if she were awake. No dinner party of any sort had been held at Fourwinds during my time there; as far as I knew, Ernest Farrow had not entertained guests since the death of his wife. What could have prompted this unwonted hospitality? Was it really all in honour of Samuel Godwin? If so, I wondered, slowly climbing the stairs, what role was he expected to play? Resident artist, protégé . . . or potential suitor for Juliana?

No! It was a ridiculous notion. Marianne might entertain the fancy if she chose, but I was not so foolish. I walked briskly along the corridor and rapped on Marianne's door, to see if she were awake.

Chapter Eleven

Sketching

Occupied as my mind had been during the wakeful hours of the night, I now found even more to puzzle and absorb me.

I recalled my mother's words, at home in Sydenham, when I told her of my good fortune. 'Four-winds does sound a delightful place!' she had remarked. 'My only worry, Sam, is that you may find it too dull there, too quiet. You are accustomed to London, and to the company of your friends at the Slade – you will be lonely.' Though I had dismissed her anxiety, my concern had been that my situation with the Farrows might lack the challenge – and the need to compete with my art-school fellows – necessary to develop my skills.

By now, however, I had formed a rather different picture. Fourwinds was delightful indeed, constantly surprising me with new discoveries: the face of a Green Man, almost hidden by carved leaves, in the arch of the door to the servants' wing; the beauty and craftsmanship of a simple wooden bench in a corner of the garden; a window-catch shaped like a dragon.

Yet the harmonious setting, in which no detail had been overlooked, in which nothing was ugly or out of place, was at odds with the lives lived within its walls. I could no longer cross the vestibule, or climb the staircase, without seeing the broken, spread-eagled form of Mrs Farrow there, so vivid that I had to avert my eyes; without hearing Marianne's cry as she witnessed her mother's fatal plunge. I could no longer sit at Mr Farrow's dinner-table without contemplating the dreadful loss he had suffered, and which he must face anew every day of his life. I could no longer look at Marianne – and of course I frequently *did* look at her, for my eyes tracked her every movement – without wondering what torment lay behind her beautiful eyes, or at Juliana, without speculating that the calmness of her manner hid mental disturbance of a less obvious kind. Having myself only recently sustained the shock of bereavement, I could appreciate that the spectacular manner of Mrs Farrow's death could hardly have caused more distress to her husband and daughters.

The announcement of Saturday's dinner party, at least, seemed to herald an end to formal grieving. 'Well, you are in favour,' Charlotte remarked, after Mr Farrow had given me the news.

Unsure of her tone, I looked at her askance. 'You will be present?'

'Of course,' Charlotte replied. 'It is my duty.'

I stifled a smile. How typical of Charlotte, to represent the promise of pleasure as merely an extension of her duties! For myself, I was looking forward to the occasion, for it showed that my role here was not merely as art teacher and employee, but as valued member of the household. Mr Farrow had hinted that the Saturday dinner guests were wealthy and influential people: that, in other words, if they liked the work I did for *him*, further commissions or recommendations would be likely to follow.

Anyone observing me that afternoon as I conducted the daily drawing lesson would have considered that Samuel Godwin was a fortunate fellow indeed. Juliana, Marianne and I had arranged our stools in the shade of a holm oak; the weather was fair, my companions charming. Beyond the paddock, the grazing horses, and the trees in full summer beauty, the sweep of the Downs was hazed in blue. The gentlest of breezes cooled our faces; the burbling of skylarks and the scream of swifts filled the sky with those most exuberant of summer sounds.

Juliana had expressed a wish to draw the horses in the paddock, and in particular her white mare, Queen Bess. Charlotte, evidently considering by now that the girls were safe with me unchaperoned, had gone indoors to make arrangements for Saturday with Mrs Reynolds. Marianne had tired of our company, and had wandered down towards the lake, to draw the bulrushes by the little boathouse; and thus, for the first time, I found myself alone with Juliana.

As a pupil, she was inept. Horses are not the easiest subject, especially for someone with as little knowledge of their anatomy, and such poor powers of observation, as Juliana. I suggested that she execute

a series of rapid sketches, to free her style a little; but
the bulbous joints, ungainly postures and stiff necks
she produced on paper did no justice to the graceful
animals before us. She was nothing, though, if not
diligent. Where Marianne would have tossed her
pencil aside and given up in disgust, Juliana toiled on,
painstakingly trying to put my advice into practice.
Our concentration – for I, too, was attempting to draw
her favourite, although I know little of horses – was
broken only by the occasional remark, or request for
help from my pupil. I noticed that something seemed
changed in her manner today, as if she were nour-
ishing a secret excitement. Juliana – in complete
contrast to her sister – was not given to outward
displays of feeling; so when I say that her manner
suggested excitement, I mean that she revealed it in
small, private smiles, and occasional fidgets and
murmurings as she surveyed her work.

Meanwhile, I had become interested in the
outbuildings on the opposite side of the paddock,
behind the stables. Usually, from the house and
garden, these buildings were concealed behind the
stable block, but our present vantage point brought
them into view. The stables, new and with every
modern convenience, had been built at the same time
as the house; but the ivy-covered cottage I was looking
at, together with some tumbledown structures nearby,
obviously pre-dated the recently built Fourwinds.
These outbuildings, I assumed, had belonged to the
earlier dwelling, the old house of which Charlotte had
told me.

'That,' I remarked, noticing the inky dark of the yew tree that partly obscured the roof, 'is Yew Tree Cottage, I presume?'

The effect on Juliana was instantaneous. A deep flush reddened her cheeks; she turned her head so that the brim of her hat shielded her face from me; but too late. I had seen.

'Yes, it is.'

I could not think why the mere pronouncing of its name should cause such consternation, but here was my chance – away from Charlotte's controlling presence – to ask some pertinent questions.

'Mr Waring, the sculptor, used to live there, did he not? Is it inhabited now?' I put to her – though the place wore such a neglected, shut-up look that this did not seem likely.

'It has stood empty since Gideon – I mean, Mr Waring – left us,' Juliana answered.

'And he went away quite suddenly, I understand? Before the Four Winds project was completed?'

'Did Charlotte tell you that?'

'Yes. But she gave no reason for his sudden departure.'

To my surprise, Juliana said, without prompting: 'It was my father's doing. He took against Mr Waring for nothing at all! He would not be satisfied until he had driven him from the premises.'

'He must have had some good reason, surely?'

Juliana merely shook her head, not seeming to trust herself to speak.

'You were aware of this at the time?' I enquired.

'Yes, I—' Again her cheeks flushed deeper. 'I liked Gideon Waring, you see. I thought of him as my friend. Father did not know – he would have forbidden it – but Miss Hardacre and I used to come across to his workshop, to watch him and to talk with him. And sometimes I came alone.'

'Miss Hardacre?'

'Our governess, before Charlotte came. She went away, too – to be married.'

'So,' I said, 'your father must have had some particular objection to your acquaintance with Mr Waring?'

'I do not know what it was. When he found out, Father was angry. And then Gideon left very suddenly – I did not even have the chance to wish him farewell. I was so sorry – I—' She looked at me sidelong, with evident consternation at saying so much, but plunged on: 'I felt his loss very keenly. He was such an . . . interesting man. And kind, too— Oh, if only he were here now! I miss him so.'

'I see.' I sketched on for a few moments, thinking over this revelation. Clearly my own company did not make up for the loss of Gideon Waring's; but Juliana had spoken with such uncharacteristic impetuousness that I did not think she intended to slight me.

'You say that your governess went away to be married,' I ventured. 'You don't mean that she became Mrs Waring?'

'Oh, no! No! That was only—' Visibly, she checked herself. 'Eliza – Miss Hardacre, as she was – is very happily married to Matthew Dearly, a gardener. They lived for a while in Petersfield, but have lately come back to Sussex – Matthew Dearly has taken up employment with Mr Vernon-Dale.'

'Vernon-Dale?' I repeated. I had been introduced, briefly, to the Vernon-Dales at church; they were among the guests Mr Farrow had invited to dinner on Saturday.

'Yes, the Vernon-Dales, at Rampions. It is a grand house and estate not far from here – you will no doubt see it. Might I . . . ?' Juliana glanced at me, then away.

'Yes?' I prompted.

She took a deep breath. 'Mr Godwin – might I ask a favour of you?'

'Of course you may. What is it?'

'I should like you to keep a secret from Papa. You see' – she gave me a look of beguiling openness – 'I plan to invite Eliza to visit me, while he is away.'

It could not escape my notice that heightened colour and animation gave Juliana a glow her features lacked in their customary repose. The delicacy of her skin, the pale-gold gleam of the tendrils of hair escaping from her brimmed hat, the direct gaze of her blue eyes, made a pretty picture indeed. Marianne's looks were so striking that she easily eclipsed her sister when they were together; but, alone, Juliana had charms enough to command male attention.

However, I was puzzled by her request. 'Why should a visit from your former governess require secrecy?'

'Because, you see,' Juliana said, 'Papa would not like Eliza to come here. He dismissed her, and sent her away.'

'He dismissed *her*, as well as Mr Waring?'

'Yes,' said Juliana, casting her eyes down at her

sketchpad; absently, she resumed drawing.

'Was there any connection between the two dismissals?'

'I am quite sure there was not,' Juliana replied, not looking at me.

I began to feel a stirring of alarm for my own security; but quickly told myself that Mr Farrow was too fair and reasonable to discharge two of his employees without good reason. A solution came easily to mind.

'Is it presumptuous of me to suspect that there was a – a romantic attachment between Mr Waring and your governess?' I conjectured. 'And that your father took exception to it?'

'I cannot say what Father may have thought,' Juliana answered; but a renewed crimsoning of her cheeks spoke otherwise.

'As for keeping your secret,' I continued, 'I shall follow Charlotte's lead; if she agrees, then so shall I. In return, can you tell me something?'

'What is it?'

'I should very much like to meet Gideon Waring. Do you know where I might find him?'

'I would tell you, if only I knew,' Juliana said, with a small sigh. 'But unfortunately I have no idea where he went.'

Our conversation was put to an end by the arrival of Marianne, who had wearied of drawing, and wanted her sister to accompany her on a walk around the lake. 'Do join us, Samuel!'

'Perhaps – in a moment,' I told her. 'I must work here for a few more minutes.'

Samuel Godwin

Completing my drawing of Queen Bess, which I thought good enough to please her mistress, I pieced together the new information I had received, and found that it added up to some rather interesting totals. After only a short while, I packed away my drawing materials and, instead of joining the two young ladies, made my way across the paddock to Yew Tree Cottage.

Chapter Twelve

Visitor

On Thursday at luncheon, Juliana waited until Alice had cleared away the dishes before mentioning, with studied casualness, that she expected a visitor that afternoon.

'Oh? Who is it?' Marianne asked eagerly.

There was a pause; then Juliana answered, with a touch of defiance, 'Mrs Dearly.'

'Dearly?' repeated Marianne. 'Oh, you mean our Eliza! How odd *Mrs Dearly* sounds – I shall always think of her as Eliza, or Miss Hardacre. But I thought she was in Hampshire?'

'She lives nearby, now,' Juliana told her. 'She is at Rampions – almost our neighbour.'

'At Rampions?' I repeated. 'Employed by the Vernon-Dales? I am most surprised to hear that.'

'Why, Charlotte?' asked Juliana.

What I *meant* was that Miss Hardacre had left Fourwinds under a cloud, so presumably without the good character reference which a family as eminent as the Vernon-Dales would require. Instead of broaching this topic, however, I said: 'Because the Vernon-Dales have no need of a governess. Their children are quite grown up, are they not?'

'Yes – but Eliza is married now, and no longer a governess,' Juliana replied. 'Her husband, Matthew Dearly, who used to be at Oak Lodge, is head gardener at Rampions. It is an excellent advancement for him – the gardens there are very splendid.'

'Is your father aware of her new situation?'

'I don't know – I suppose so,' Juliana said, off-handedly.

Very rarely did I find cause for annoyance with Juliana; but now I *was* displeased with her, for delaying this announcement until such a late stage.

'I am surprised you did not think to mention this sooner,' I remarked, trying to conceal my pique.

'You sly thing, Juley!' Marianne said, her eyes shining. 'Inviting Eliza here while Papa's out of the way!'

'You may think it very clever,' I reproved, 'but I should not need to remind you both that I am in charge of the household while your father is in London. What am I to say to him? Juliana, I am surprised at you for compromising me like this.'

'Father need not know,' Juliana said, uneasily meeting my gaze. 'You won't tell him, will you? And Mr Godwin has already promised not to.'

'I see. So you have confided in Mr Godwin before you thought of telling me?' This time I could not help sounding offended. Samuel was peeling an apple and affecting disinterest; but, glancing at him, I saw the flicker of his eye, and knew he was attending closely.

'Oh, Charlotte! Please don't be cross.' Marianne got up and put an arm round me, like the impetuous little girl she sometimes still was. 'We love you just as much as we ever did Eliza, don't we, Juley? You know we do. You needn't feel envious.'

'I am not envious,' I replied, though in truth I was a little irked that she had not said *more than.* 'The point is that you know full well that your father would not welcome Miss Hardacre here – I mean Mrs Dearly,' I amended. 'If I allow it, he will hold me to blame.'

'Then, if he finds out, we'll tell him it was Juley's idea,' Marianne returned, 'and that you knew nothing of it – which is quite true.'

If I am honest, my curiosity about my predecessor soon got the better of my peevishness, though I continued to make a show of disapproval. At half past three, Eliza Dearly arrived in a pony-chaise, driven by a young man in shirtsleeves and a peaked cap. My charges hastened to greet her; I, however, waited in the vestibule, from whence I watched with utter incredulity as she lifted a small boy down from the chaise seat. While she gave her driver instructions as to what time he should return, Marianne took the infant from her, all but smothering it with exclamations and cooings, while Juliana gazed at it fondly.

My heart was beating fast as I shrank back behind the curtains. Of course, she had the child now; even the lowliest servant at Fourwinds knew this, although Juliana had made no reference to it. Not for a moment had I imagined that she would have the temerity to bring it here! It was improper enough for her to visit during Mr Farrow's absence; bringing that child with her was nothing short of outrageous. Juliana, surely, could not have intended that?

While I loitered there, uncertain how to react, Marianne took the toddling boy by the hand, in the manner of a doting aunt, and led him towards the lawn. What a happy party they looked, the four of them!

Decisive intervention was called for, I knew; duty told me to step forward and inform the visitor that, in Mr Farrow's stead, I must ask her to leave the premises. In my hesitation, however, I was lost. Nothing in Mrs Dearly's demeanour showed any hint of her former disgrace; on the contrary, an observer might think her an established friend of the family, with every right to come visiting whenever she chose. Her confidence stripped me of mine.

In these first few moments, I formed the opinion that my predecessor gave herself airs. She was, I estimated, two or three years older than I, and tolerably handsome. She wore a high-necked blouse of striped fabric, a narrow, belted skirt and a broad-brimmed hat; crossing the few yards to the lawn, she twirled a parasol, talking all the while. 'Well, my dears, you're both looking the picture of health! How good it is to see you after so long – and to find myself back at Fourwinds! Who would have thought that your governess would return in such style? I declare, the place has not changed one bit – I could almost fancy that we are about to resume our lessons! What happy times we had, did we not? Tommy, Tommy, what do you think of this splendid house?' she addressed the child, who, unsurprisingly, offered no opinion.

Stepping forward, I asserted my presence. Mrs Dearly surveyed me boldly.

'Oh!' Juliana was ruffled for a moment; then she turned to her guest. 'Eliza – this is Charlotte, Miss Agnew, who now fills your place. Charlotte, may I introduce you to Mrs Dearly?'

'Welcome to Fourwinds,' I said, formally, and without cordiality. 'As I expect you are aware, Mr Farrow is away from home, and unable to greet you himself.' It would have taken a keener sensibility than Mrs Dearly's to hear the implied reproof; and subsequent conversation confirmed that this first impression was not mistaken.

We shook hands. Mrs Dearly gave me a condescending smile, while her gaze swept over my unremarkable features, and my plain grey dress. Look what you are, her smile seemed to say, and look how comfortable *I* am. Steadfastly I held her gaze. How could she, with her past, presume to intimidate *me*?

'Oh, and here is Mr Godwin,' cried Juliana, attempting to cover any awkwardness in the situation with uncharacteristic vivacity. 'Mr Godwin, come and be introduced.'

There was far more warmth in the smile and the handshake Eliza Dearly offered our young artist; her eyes lingered on his face and form. 'Well, Mr Godwin, I suppose you know you are quite the talk of the neighbourhood?' she simpered. When Samuel expressed surprise, she went on: 'Oh yes! Everyone is agog to see your paintings. Mr Farrow is a generous patron, is he not? I can only hope that this project turns out more successfully than his last.' She raised her eyes to the North Wind, who glowered above us as if displeased with the warmth of the midsummer day. 'Has the missing statue ever been found, or is the west wall still blank? Ah, the artistic temperament must be treated with caution. Do you not agree? Mr Godwin, are *you* temperamental? Do you fly into rages, or brood darkly for days on end?'

'I am sorry to disappoint you,' said Samuel. 'I have never felt that I should be tolerated if I did. From what I have seen of Gideon Waring's work, I have the greatest admiration for it and for him; but I don't understand why artists should expect to behave any differently from other people.'

'Ah, then I wonder if you are genuinely an artist!' Mrs Dearly admonished him. 'Everyone knows that true artists have volatile temperaments. I shall be very disappointed if you never rage, sulk or fly into a jealous passion.'

Her tone was teasing, but Juliana answered with all seriousness: 'Mr Waring never raged or sulked. He was the most even-tempered man I have ever known.'

'And *he* was a genuine artist,' said Marianne. 'No one could doubt that.'

'Indeed, he was even-tempered; but who knows what depths of passion lurked beneath?' answered Mrs Dearly, with a look of intolerable knowingness.

This was not to be endured. 'I think, Juliana,' I said, though really my point was directed at Mrs Dearly, who seemed to have no inhibitions at all, 'we had better find another topic of conversation. You know that we do not talk of Mr Waring.'

Mrs Dearly gave me a haughty look, as though the lowliest kitchen maid had dared to advise her betters. My gaze fell on the little boy on all fours on the grass, who was staring, eyes and mouth round with astonishment, at a bee that buzzed in prospecting spirals close to his head. Marianne swished the insect away, and the child sat up, waving a plump hand in imitation. He was, I have to concede, a pretty and engaging boy, with straight dark hair and alert eyes; but conversation about *him* was not to be encouraged, either.

'Tea will be served in the garden, under the cedar tree,' said Juliana, breaking the awkward pause.

'How delightful!' Mrs Dearly adjusted her hat. 'I am so longing to hear all your news!'

Chairs and a table had already been set out on the south lawn, beneath the cedar's spreading branches. Alice brought tea, bread-and-butter and cake, crockery and hot water; Juliana had made arrangements with the domestic staff without consulting me, and I wondered whether she had also ensured their silence. My demure miss was revealing depths of deviousness I had never suspected.

We settled ourselves in the shade. Samuel proved to have an unexpected affinity with little Thomas, taking on the task of amusing the boy. Soon he got down on all fours behind his chair, hiding all of himself but his hands, which he shaped to represent various kinds of animal: elephant, donkey and chicken, each accompanied by the appropriate sound. The little boy stared, frowned, broke into disarming chuckles, and crawled behind the seat in evident expectation of finding a whole menagerie concealed there. Against my better judgement, I found myself smiling indulgently. It was unfair, of course, to blame this innocent child for the wantonness of his conception.

While Juliana gave her attention to this game, Mrs Dearly chatted on, eagerly questioned by Marianne, and I had no need to do anything but listen. Here was a young lady so pleased with herself that she felt everyone else must share her absorption; she talked endlessly about Rampions, the number of staff employed there, the gardener's cottage (which she referred to as a villa), her vegetable garden, and how admirable a wife her husband found her. Before twenty minutes had passed, I had heard quite enough. Excusing myself, I said that I had matters to attend to indoors, and wished her a stiff farewell.

It was pleasantly cool in the house. Seating myself at the bureau in the morning room, I began to read Marianne's French composition. Although the errors sprinkled liberally throughout her work made me tut, I was soon absorbed; so much so that I gave a start of surprise when a voice spoke close behind me.

'What, back at your work already?' It was Samuel, looking over my shoulder. 'Surely you needn't shut yourself inside on such a glorious afternoon?'

Recovering, I turned to face him. 'Thank you, Mr Godwin, I am quite purposefully occupied. I tire of too much leisure. You seemed very taken with Mrs Dearly's boy,' I remarked. 'Are you fond of small children?'

'I am, rather,' he replied, looking for a moment quite wistful. 'A cousin of mine has a little boy of Tommy's age – he reminded me of family days at home.' He sat on the chaise longue, and reclined there for a moment without speaking; I steered my thoughts back to the composition, until Samuel asked me, quite without prelude, 'Are you happy here, Charlotte?'

Startled, I replied, 'I beg your pardon?'

'Miss Agnew, I should say,' he amended. 'You appear – as Miss Agnew – to be the perfect employee: discreet, quietly mannered, considerate. Pardon my impertinence, but it is Charlotte I am enquiring about – not Miss Agnew the employee. What of her? Is she happy here?'

'I hardly know,' I replied, with an embarrassed little laugh. 'It is not something I spend time contemplating.'

'I sense that your own happiness takes second place to that of the two young ladies.'

'What else is expected from a paid companion?' I returned. 'I am very fond of Marianne and Juliana, of course. Maybe excessively so.' Immediately regretting this, I turned back to the page I was scrutinizing.

'Please excuse me if I'm curious about you,' Samuel persisted. 'What keeps you here? What of your life before? You have told me so little. Do you have a family? In answer to your questions, I have told you all about mine – introduced you, in effect, to my mother, my sister – even to the dog. Do, please, return the confidence.'

It is in my nature to be secretive. This has never

presented a difficulty, since most people, I have found, are interested principally in themselves; it is easy enough to be considered a good friend, even a confidante, by the simple means of listening, and sympathizing. Someone in my position is rarely called upon to analyse her feelings, or give her views on the life she finds herself leading.

'I have no family,' I replied. 'I am alone in the world. That is all you need know.'

'I am sorry,' he said.

'Then you may spare your pity,' I told him. 'I am quite accustomed to my role in life.'

He looked likely to press for further details; then thought better of it, and sat gazing out of the window. Following his glance, I saw Juliana and Mrs Dearly strolling together along the lower lawn, Juliana carrying the boy in her arms.

'Please,' I told him, 'don't linger inside on my account. There is more congenial company to be found outdoors.'

To my amazement, I saw a smile twitch at the corners of his mouth.

'Do I amuse you, Mr Godwin?' I asked him sharply.

'Only in that your disapproval of Mrs Dearly is so transparent,' he replied, in what I considered an impertinent manner. 'Your feelings are clearly read in your face.'

'My conduct towards her has been entirely appropriate. I only wish she would show the same sense of decorum; yet I suppose that is hardly to be expected.'

He nodded. 'You dislike her intensely – do you

not? You were firm on that point within moments of meeting her.'

'I am mortified that you think my feelings so easily read,' I returned.

Undeterred, he went on: 'I would go so far as to say, you had made up your mind *before* meeting her. Am I right?'

'Since you were present at luncheon, when the visit was discussed, that is hardly a remarkable deduction,' I pointed out.

'And nothing you see in the lady induces you to change your opinion?' he persevered.

Rustling the pages of Marianne's essay, I replied, 'Neither her station in life, nor her conduct, entitles her to be considered a *lady*. Do you have some particular reason for this interrogation?'

'Only this. Let me hazard a guess,' said he. 'You have reason to suspect that Mrs Dearly's little boy, there, is not – as one would naturally assume – the product of her recent marriage. No – you believe that his sire is none other than our elusive sculptor, Gideon Waring. Am I right? Hence, your stern disapproval of his mother? And of Tommy himself, endearing though he is?'

'You have a fertile imagination, Mr Godwin.'

'I like to think so – but here, it is not imagination at work, but a simple piecing together of information,' said Samuel. 'Mr Waring left Fourwinds suddenly, after an altercation.' He enumerated his points on his fingers. 'Miss Hardacre, as she then was, also left in disgrace. Miss Hardacre had been in the habit of visiting Mr Waring's cottage. A little more than a year later, she returns with an infant son. What other conclusion can possibly be drawn?'

'If you choose to spend your time gossiping with the servants,' I said, with my eyes still on the page before me, 'you will no doubt hear all manner of things.'

'Oh, come – must you be so prim and frosty?' he admonished me. 'Is this not what you believe about the boy's parentage – did Mr Farrow hint as much, when he engaged you in Miss Hardacre's place?'

With a huff of impatience, I put down my pen. 'Very well – yes, you are quite right, though I cannot see why it concerns you. It may be as well for you to know, now that Mrs Dearly has returned to the neighbourhood, that she is not welcome here – whether or not Mr Farrow is at home. This visit has been most unfortunate. He will, I know, be displeased when he finds out she is living nearby.'

Samuel made a steeple of his fingers and pursed his lips, looking ludicrously pompous. 'But what if a misjudgement has taken place?' he pursued. 'What if Thomas's father is not, after all, Gideon Waring – but Mr Dearly, the gardener?'

'You have just now pointed out strong reasons to the contrary. You need only consider the dates involved. Thomas Dearly is a little over a year old – which means he was born in May last year. Eliza Hardacre left here just before Christmas – her marriage, in Hampshire, must have taken place between then and the birth. In other words, although her child was certainly conceived out of wedlock, her marriage took place in time to avoid further disgrace.'

'And is it impossible,' he said, smiling, 'that she had been courting her husband while she was employed here? Would that not be a more likely explanation?'

'Only if her behaviour were even more reprehensible than I believe it to be,' I replied crisply. 'Even *she* would surely not keep company, as one might put it, with two men at once!'

Samuel smiled at this. 'So,' he went on, 'you are quite certain of her liaison with Mr Waring?'

'Mr Farrow left me in little doubt of it,' I told him. 'Besides, Marianne—'

His attention sharpened. 'Yes?'

'Suffice it to say that Marianne – who, you must remember, was only fourteen at this time, a mere child – has a – how shall I put this? – a precocious awareness of things that no child ought to be exposed to.'

'She has told you this?' said he.

'In so many words. No wonder the poor girl is distressed.'

He looked puzzled. 'But Marianne showed no reluctance to entertain Eliza this afternoon. She seemed delighted, especially with the little boy.'

A glance silenced him. 'I know Marianne far better than you do, Mr Godwin,' I assured him. 'You must take my word for it that Miss Hardacre proved herself completely unsuited to the teaching and supervision of young girls. That is why I am so anxious that her visit here must not be repeated. Mr Farrow does not wish his daughters to come under the influence of such a disreputable person. Her past cannot be forgotten, merely because she now presents herself as a respectable married woman – for which she ought to consider herself very fortunate. Mr Matthew Dearly must be a forgiving man indeed.'

Infuriatingly, Samuel laughed. 'You would prefer her to be a penniless outcast, it appears – to suffer for her sin? You would like her to grovel at the workhouse door, or beg for scraps by the roadside?'

'On the contrary. I should never wish such misfortune on anyone, and certainly not on her blameless little boy,' I told him. 'But I do wish she did not give herself such airs – it is her assumption of superiority I find intolerable.'

He looked at me with a knowing smile.

'You think yourself very clever, I see,' I retaliated. 'What is the meaning of that complacent look?'

He only smiled the more; and I may as well acknowledge that he would have won over a woman of less resolve. His face was flushed with the beginnings of sunburn, for he had unguardedly been walking without a hat; he looked the picture of ease and contentment.

'I was merely thinking,' he said, 'that your pride in your charges does you credit. A sister could not show more devotion than you do towards Marianne and Juliana. And therefore you are bound to dislike Miss Hardacre, for your jealousy of her is transparent.'

'*Jealous?*' I retorted. '*I?* You are gravely mistaken if you think I could possibly feel any envy of – of that—'

'You bear her a grudge,' he insisted, 'because of the affection shown to her by both girls. You do not like to think that she once occupied your place, and still occupies their thoughts.'

This was provoking beyond measure. Deciding to remove myself to my room, I stood, and collected up my papers. 'Well, Mr Godwin,' I told him, 'if you have quite finished entertaining yourself in this fashion, by analysing my character, you must excuse me. I have work to do, even if you do not.'

It gave me great satisfaction to sweep out of the room, leaving him staring after me.

Chapter Thirteen

Watched

I had left my curtains open while I slept. The exuberance of birdsong woke me; it was already full daylight, although a glance at the mantel clock told me that the hour was barely past five. Slipping out of bed, I went barefooted to the open window, and looked out.

My spirits lifted in response to the glory of the midsummer morning. The lawn, and the lake beyond, were hazed in gold; the smooth line of the Downs beyond was misty pale. A fox trod stealthily across the grass – pausing to look this way and that, to sniff the air, before walking on unhurried, as if the world were spread out for his pleasure. I saw the narrow muzzle, the delicate tread of his paws, the rich copper of fox-fur against grass; almost, I fancied, I smelled the sharp, feral tang of him.

Suddenly impatient at being indoors, I dressed quickly, crept down the stairs, unlocked the front door and let myself out. I stopped in the porch to put on my shoes, which I had left off till now to avoid waking sleepers in the bedrooms I passed.

The air was as cool and refreshing as spring water.

As soon as my lungs filled with it, and my feet trod the dewy grass, I felt elated; coming out so long before the house was awake, I was claiming these early hours for my own, a delicious secret I shared with the creatures who inhabited them. I made my way down to the lake, and stood on its nearest shore, looking out at the water's surface, where the faintest of mists lingered. The shore was fringed, for the most part, with rushes; at the farthest end, sheltered by willows, a small landing-stage had been constructed, with a boathouse and wooden jetty. A moorhen with her brood of chicks bobbed across the water, quickly vanishing into the safety of rushes; I heard the *cra-a-ark* of some other unseen bird.

I stooped to dabble my fingers. Here the sand sloped invitingly into the water, which was clear of weed, and would, I estimated, be deep enough for swimming. At once the idea was irresistible. I glanced around, rather as the fox had done, to ensure that no one was near; quickly I threw off my clothes, laid them on a log-seat, and waded in. Sandy mud oozed between my toes; the shock of cold water against skin now repelled, rather than invited me; but it would be weak-willed to change my mind. Gasping with the unexpected chill, I plunged my head under the surface and pushed away in the first strong strokes. Yes! At once I was exhilarated, filled with pleasure in the cool caress of the water, the powerful thrust of my arms and legs, the complete absorption of mind and body.

I swam the length of the lake, towards the boathouse and jetty, some fifty yards; then turned again. Here I paused to tread water, aware of the commotion I had made, of my rough intrusion into this tranquil place. As the ripples in my wake subsided, and I made only the small movements necessary to keep myself afloat, I listened intently to the lake's own sounds: barely discernible movements in the rushes, stirrings of willow leaves in the faintest sigh of the breeze, the melodious phrases of a thrush close at hand; and behind it all, the swelling, joyous cacophony of birds from the trees and woods farther off.

I find that I cannot understand what happened then – how, so suddenly, the atmosphere of the place seemed to change. I felt a soft touch against my ankle, a feathery, brushing sensation; there was water-weed here, which I had not seen. As I moved away, I found my legs threshing more of the stuff, which seemed intent on tangling itself about me. Fibrous and strong, it did not yield easily to my kicking, and for a second – I am sure it was no more than that – I was gripped by a fear that I should find myself held firm and pulled underwater. What can I have been thinking? – of marine legends, I suppose, tales of sirens, of deathly music and of drowned sailors – but in another moment I had freed myself, and was swimming again. Although I should have been able to laugh at my discomfiture, to resume my pleasure in being alone in such surroundings, I found that I could not. Above me was golden sunlight and birdsong, but my mind was occupied with what might lurk unseen in the depths beneath my flailing legs. I could almost feel the blubbery touch of fish mouths against my limbs, the slime of eely creatures that might rise from the mud at the lake's bottom, the bloated touch of drowned flesh – all I can say is that, overcome with an unease that amounted almost to horror, I struck out for shore as fast as I could swim.

As soon as my feet met the sandy bottom I pushed myself upright, wading, splashing out of the shallows; then I looked around me, thinking that I had truly taken leave of my senses for those bewildering moments. The sun struck warm on my skin; a turtle-dove crooned in the willows; what danger could I possibly have feared? My best course, I decided, would be to re-enter the water and swim for a few more minutes, until I felt calm. But at that point, looking down, I noticed a scarlet trickle of blood from my right foot, issuing from a small gash near the ankle. In my haste, I must have struck against some rock or obstruction underwater, though I had been quite unaware of any painful collision. I sat on the log-seat, pushing aside my heaped clothes, to examine the wound; it bled profusely, though it did not appear deep, and now I felt the stab of pain, which made me wonder that I had not noticed it before.

A pocket handkerchief would soon staunch the flow, if I had one about me. I reached for my jacket – and realized, in the same instant, that I was not alone.

Across the lake, a man stood watching me. He was half concealed by the thick reed-bed on that side of the lake, so that I could see him only from the waist up – clad in a white shirt, with sleeves rolled up, and a tan-coloured waistcoat. He was so still and silent that I wondered for how long he had been standing there – whether he had seen my wild dash from the lake.

From his posture, and the fact that he made no move either to hide himself or to speak, I assumed that he must have some right to be in the grounds. An employee of the house, perhaps? A stable lad I had not yet encountered? Recovering from the shock of seeing him, I registered that he was a young man of perhaps my own age, taller than I, with hair that shone corn-coloured in the sunlight. An intruder, possibly – a poacher? Who else was likely to be abroad so early in the day but someone illicitly snaring rabbit or hare, or fishing in the lake?

Conscious of my nakedness, I grabbed at my shirt and, standing, held it to me. I felt obliged to challenge him; his curious silence inhibited me, but there was such arrogance in his stare that I felt his presence must be explained. 'Hello, there?' I ventured – feeling that this was scarcely adequate. He responded with a curt, unsmiling nod.

I began to struggle into my clothes, clumsy with haste. The stranger stepped back from the reeds – in order, I assumed, to reach a firmer path and to make his way towards me, by which time at least I should be semi-clad and more ready to conduct a conversation.

But I was wrong. While I was occupied in dressing, he had ducked out of sight.

'What the—?'

Now thoroughly annoyed, I looked this way and that to see which direction he had taken; for the lake, in its tree-fringed hollow, was surrounded by lawn on one side and rough grass on the other, and I did not see how he could get away unobserved. There he was – having cut back behind the willows, he was now walking with a long stride towards the stables. Reaching the fence, he vaulted it easily, and disappeared behind the buildings. I considered giving chase, then rejected it, as he looked both fitter and taller than I; and I was still barefoot. If he were determined to get away, he had outpaced me already.

I wondered what the time was, for I had left my pocket watch in my room. An age seemed to have passed since I left there, but my adventure must in reality have taken less than an hour; it was still too early for Reynolds, or his stableboy, to be about his work. Still, though, I put on my socks and shoes (forgetting the gash to my foot, which I rediscovered later, aware of a congealing stickiness in my shoe), and followed the interloper towards the stables.

All was quiet here. It being midsummer, the horses – some five or six – were turned out to pasture, only being brought in when needed. The stables were unoccupied, an open-sided barn sheltering the pony-chaise and the gig. White doves, a dozen or so, were pecking about in the yard; they fluttered up to their cote below the weathervane, with a whirring of wings, as I approached. The stranger, then, could not have come this way, or he would have disturbed these birds before I reached them. He must have gone behind the buildings, on the side farthest from the house – in the direction of Yew Tree Cottage.

The day before yesterday, I had found its door locked. Today, I intended to take the simple measure of asking Reynolds for the key: doubtless he would be its keeper, and would assume that I had some legitimate business there, such as setting up my painting studio in a private place away from the house. If anyone else – Charlotte, or Mr Farrow – were to find out, and challenge me, I could simply say that I had been assessing the possibilities.

For the first time it occurred to me that the person I was following might be none other than Gideon Waring himself: the man who so strongly aroused my curiosity. With this realization jangling in my brain, for I had expected Mr Waring to be considerably older, I walked up the flagged stone path towards the cottage.

Clad in flint and tile like so many buildings locally, it must once have been an attractive little dwelling. Now, with the windows blank, and the wood of the doorframe beginning to rot, it looked sadly neglected. A picket fence marked out its garden, which had recently been used for the growing of vegetables, but had now gone wild and weedy. Bees were already busy in the honeysuckle which, trained over a rudimentary porch, almost obscured the door; the sweet honey fragrance filled my senses as I approached.

Grasping the handle, I felt it turn in my grip. The door swung open, revealing a single room inside, with a brick fireplace, and stairs rising ahead – I had seen this much before, looking in through the dusty glass. As then, the room was completely bare. Floorboards creaked as I stepped inside.

'Hello?' I called out, my voice echoing. 'Is anyone here?'

Silence answered me. Stealthily I moved through the empty cottage – a simple kitchen at the rear, and the two small rooms of the upper floor, one with a fireplace. All were empty, and swept clean. From upstairs I looked out at the garden behind, shadowed in the immensity of the yew tree, and at a tiny outbuilding by the boundary fence which was, presumably, an earth-closet, with logs stacked neatly under a lean-to roof beside it.

I turned again. 'Mr Waring?' I called to the echoing rooms, though it was obvious that there was no one to answer. I felt thwarted: so close, yet he had escaped me! He must be living nearer at hand, though, than either Charlotte or Juliana had led me to believe; maybe he had taken lodgings nearby. A few enquiries would surely give me the information I sought.

Outside, I pulled the door closed behind me, wondering whether I should find it locked again if I returned, and made my way across paddock and lawn to the still-sleeping house – rather amused that my day had already contained so much, before the other inhabitants of Fourwinds had so much as left their beds. Instead of entering immediately, I paused to look again at each of the Wind carvings in turn, seeing them in a fresh light now that I thought I had glimpsed their creator. I was beginning to feel well acquainted with their faces and expressions: the weary resignation of the North Wind, tired of plying his icy gusts and cold showers; the concupiscence of the South;

the resentful, hunted look of the East – who, handsome fellow that he was, now struck me as bearing a passing likeness to the man I took to be his maker.

I frowned, looking away from the compelling sidelong glance of that stone face and trying to replace it with the flesh-and-blood features I had seen so briefly. I had already credited Mr Waring with remarkable gifts, with dedication to his art, and with a sensual awareness that enabled him to breathe life into cold stone. To these attributes, I must now add the less appealing one of vanity – since a man who could use himself as model for this beauteous youth must be vain indeed.

And, if Charlotte were right, he had compromised Miss Eliza Hardacre. Little Thomas Dearly, as I recalled, bore no obvious similarity to the man I had met, but Charlotte had been quite adamant that Waring was indeed his father. Could it be, perhaps, the proximity of Thomas that kept Gideon Waring in the neighbourhood? In which case he must also be aware that the Dearlys had returned from Petersfield . . .

I was getting myself quite lost in a maze of speculations. Huffing a sigh, I turned away, and came face to face with Charlotte Agnew, dressed as usual in plain grey, but looking neat and fresh.

'Good morning, Mr Godwin,' she greeted me. 'You are up early – but you sound as though you have the weight of the world on your shoulders!'

'Not at all,' I assured her, and added, suddenly reckless: 'I believe I have seen Gideon Waring – here, this morning, in the grounds.'

Charlotte's face was a picture to behold. Her eyes became quite round; her mouth opened soundlessly; it was the first time I had seen her lost for words. Instantly I regretted having spoken – not because of the shock I had given her, but because I now doubted the sense of what I had said. On what did I base the supposition that the person I had seen was Gideon Waring? On nothing at all, beyond the bare fact that I had seen a strange person by the lake – and a vague resemblance, probably only imagined, to the East Wind. He was more likely to be a stable lad, a poacher, or an intruder from the village, up to no good, who had run away on seeing me.

'You have seen Gideon Waring?' Charlotte repeated, incredulous. 'You had better explain.'

Chapter Fourteen

Mr Arthur Deakins, Solicitor, to Miss Charlotte Agnew, on Behalf of Mrs Henrietta Newbold

Deakins and Murdoch, Solicitors,
8 Connaught Chambers,
Eastbourne,
Sussex

22nd June, 1898

Miss Charlotte Agnew,
c/o Mr Ernest Farrow,
Fourwinds,
Staverton,
Sussex

Dear Miss Agnew,

It is my unwelcome duty to write to you with grievous tidings. I believe you may be unaware that your grandmother, Mrs Henrietta Newbold, is gravely ill at her home in Eastbourne. She is attended there by a nurse, and has asked me to contact you as a matter of urgency. I must stress that, if

119

you wish to see her, you should make your way to 3 Sussex Esplanade without delay.

Please accept my apologies for writing with such distressing news. I shall be available at my offices, where I will be pleased to offer such assistance as you may require.

With sincerest good wishes,

Arthur J. Deakins

Chapter Fifteen

Summoned

'You have seen Gideon Waring?' I repeated, incredulous. Almost, for a moment, I thought I had another sleepwalker on my hands, especially as Samuel looked somewhat dishevelled, as though he had thrown on his clothes in haste. 'You had better explain.'

He did so; telling me that he had been taking an early walk beside the lake, when he noticed the man he took to be Waring watching him from across the water.

'But you have never seen Mr Waring,' I pointed out. 'Whatever makes you conclude that he was the man you saw?'

'Let me describe him,' said Samuel. 'A younger man than I expected. Tall – taller than I. Light hair and a tanned face – rather handsome, from my brief impression – virile, I should say.'

It was impossible not to make an expression of distaste. Mr Waring's virility had manifested itself all too obviously.

'That is all I had time to see,' Samuel went on, not noticing. 'But he made off towards Yew Tree Cottage – that is what made me suspicious.'

'Well,' I said, troubled, 'never having met him myself, I cannot tell from your description whether or not it was Waring you saw. It is possible. The simplest way to find out would be to ask the girls, but I should not like them to hear that he has returned – if he it was. What can he be doing here? I thought he had long gone! What might bring him back? Might he have left something behind in the cottage, and returned to collect it?'

'I followed him in that direction,' said Samuel, 'but he did not stop there. I went inside, but found the place empty.'

'Surely not. The cottage is kept locked.'

'Maybe,' said Samuel, 'but it was not locked this morning.'

'I must ask Reynolds whether he knows anything of this,' I said. 'It makes me uneasy to think of that man being around, especially with Mr Farrow not at home.'

'You don't think,' Samuel queried, 'he intends some harm?'

'I have no reason to think him vengeful. But only consider the circumstances. He was sent away after a bitter quarrel with Mr Farrow; he left the same day, taking all his belongings with him; and now he seems to have returned, not openly by calling at the house, but by sneaking into the grounds in the early hours of the morning. And apparently he has a key to the cottage. I cannot choose but find it a matter for concern. We must be on our guard, and I will tell Reynolds and the gardeners to keep a sharp lookout.

One of them may know where he is lodging. Mr Godwin, your hair is wet, and here' – I permitted myself the liberty of plucking a thin green frond from behind his ear – 'is what appears to be water-weed. Have you been swimming in the lake?'

He reddened. 'I have. It was so tempting.'

'And so you plunged in. Well, well. If you will excuse me,' I said, turning away, 'I shall go and see if Marianne is awake. You will be glad to know that she spent a peaceful night, without disturbance.'

Re-entering the house, I mounted the stairs. If I am honest, I must confess that at that moment I was struggling to contain feelings of envy. How glorious it must be to be strong and male! To be able, on a whim, to cast off one's clothes and dive into cool water, to swim freely as otter or water rat! Contemplating it, I was irritated by the swish of skirt around my ankles, the tug of petticoat beneath it, the clasp of my stays; moreover, I was impatient with myself, with the neat, constrained person I presented to the world. The role I filled so efficiently had *become* me, so completely that I felt myself defined by it. Charlotte Agnew, governess, companion. What was I, besides?

Shaking off this futile discontent, I knocked gently on Marianne's door and entered. Mr Farrow was expected home today; there was much to do. After breakfast I should see Mrs Reynolds to ensure that everything was in order for his return; but, first, I intended to speak to her husband. After talking for a few moments to Marianne, who was brushing her hair and almost ready to come down, I went into

the servants' wing and sought Reynolds in the
kitchen. As usual at this hour, he was seated at the
table with a plate of bread, ham and eggs, while his
wife busied herself at the range. Without preamble,
I enquired whether he had seen anything of the
errant sculptor.

He looked surprised at my question. 'No, miss! I
ent seen him, not since he went away.'

'Has anyone been sleeping in the cottage?'

'No, miss,' he replied. 'Kept locked up, it is.'

'Mr Godwin found it unlocked this morning, and
went inside,' I countered.

'Well, I can't understand that,' he said, with a
frown. 'Key's over in harness room, but that's kept
locked an' all, and the key to *that* door I keep with
me.' He patted the bunch of keys he kept attached to
his trouser belt.

'And there's only one key to the cottage?' I asked.

'There is now,' said he, 'but there used to be two.
Mr Waring had his own, and left in such a hurry he
never give it back, not as I know of.'

'Tell me,' I said, 'was Mr Waring a tall, handsome
man, with a tanned face and light hair?'

Reynolds grinned. 'Not sure as I'd call him handsome, miss – though there's one at least would think
so.'

His wife gave him a warning glance.

'Hair, face – yes, that could be him,' he finished.

'Then he *has* been here! You haven't heard
anything, have you, in the village?' I included Mrs
Reynolds in my question, as well as Alice, who was filling

a jug of hot water from the urn, and the kitchen maid, preparing vegetables.

'Not a word,' Mrs Reynolds replied. 'And folks would talk, if he showed his face. Specially now the other one's come back,' she added with a sniff.

This I took to indicate Mrs Dearly, for whom I knew she had little regard. 'I'm sure you're right,' I said, and turned to the two maids.

'Nothing, miss,' they assured me.

'If you should see him – any of you – will you be sure to tell him to leave the premises or, if he will not, to come to the house?' I looked for assent at each in turn. 'Of course, you should inform me or Mr Farrow at once. And please, Mrs Reynolds, be so good as to warn all the servants, both in and outside the house.'

All of them nodded gravely. Proceeding to the dining room, I was joined there by Samuel and, shortly, by Marianne. With a meaningful look at Samuel, I reminded him not to mention his encounter in Marianne's presence; he gave a nod of understanding, and we talked instead about Mr Farrow's return, and our plans for the day.

While we were serving ourselves, Alice re-entered. 'The post's just arrived, miss, and there's this letter for you.'

With some surprise, I took the envelope she handed me. I assumed the letter to be from Mr Farrow, with some forgotten instruction, perhaps, but the envelope was addressed in copperplate handwriting I did not recognize. Who could be writing to me? As far as I was aware, no one knew of my whereabouts, other than the inhabitants of Fourwinds. Perplexed, I sat at my place, opened the envelope, and read its contents; then, immediately, I read them again. With a quick glance at each of my companions, I refolded the letter and slid it back into its envelope, which I laid beside my plate.

'What is it, Charlotte?' asked Marianne. 'Aren't you going to tell us?'

'Not bad news, I hope?' Samuel half rose to his feet.

'Nothing of importance,' I answered, regaining my composure. I gestured to Samuel to sit. 'But I'm afraid I must leave Fourwinds for a day or two.'

'Leave?' cried Marianne, as though it were quite out of the question. 'But where to, and why?'

My hesitation must have been clear. 'I am called upon to go to – to Eastbourne. This matter need not detain me there for long. I shall return as soon as I can. It's fortunate that your father will be home later today,' I added to Marianne. 'I shall write him a letter of explanation, then pack my bag.'

'So, this is all you're going to tell us?' Marianne exclaimed. 'That you're going to Eastbourne? What is it that takes you there?'

'A business matter,' I told her. 'Would you please pass the salt?'

Marianne would not be put off. 'A business matter that makes you turn quite pale? Come, Charlotte, this won't do! What business have you got in Eastbourne?'

Samuel held up a hand to restrain her. 'Please! Let Miss Agnew collect herself.'

'I have told you all that it is necessary for you to know,' I answered. 'It is a distant family matter, that is all.'

Both of them looked at me quizzically; Samuel was first to speak. 'I understood that you *had* no family, Charlotte.'

'That's what you've always told us!' Marianne reproached.

'Immediate family I have none,' I answered. 'I have only one or two very distant relations I have not seen for many a year.'

She looked sceptical. 'Yet they are able to summon you at a moment's notice?'

'Marianne, that is enough,' I told her. 'I shall write a letter to your father giving all necessary explanation. Please allow me to finish my breakfast in peace.'

As soon as the meal was completed, I went to Juliana's room, and found her sitting in her window seat, still in her peignoir. The face she turned to me, reluctantly, and only after I had addressed her three times, was puffy and tear-stained.

'Juliana, what is amiss?' I implored, hurrying to her side. 'What has upset you?'

She let me hug her, but turned again to gaze out of the window. 'Forgive me, Charlotte. I am very low in spirits today.'

'Why? Are you unwell?' I placed a hand on her forehead. 'Maybe you're a little feverish. Should I summon Dr Fletcher? Return to bed, and I shall ask Alice to bring you something on a tray.'

'Thank you, Charlotte,' she said softly, 'but I am

not unwell, and have no need of a doctor. Allow me a little time to recover myself – that is all I need.'

'Is it—?' I paused. 'Have you got your monthly visitor?'

She hesitated, then replied: 'Yes. Yes, it is no more than that. I shall feel better soon.'

'I wish I could spend longer with you, dear,' I said, 'but I must go and pack my bag. I am called away.'

'Called away?' She looked at me in alarm. 'By whom?'

For explanation I gave the same account as I had provided downstairs, receiving in response the same bafflement.

'*Must* you go?' she implored me, searching my face. 'How shall I manage without you?'

'I must – but it will not be for long,' I assured her. 'Please don't fret, dearest. I shall be back as soon as I can. Mr Godwin is here, and your father will be home today. Why not rest on your bed until you feel quite well?'

'Charlotte' – she took my hand, and gazed at me earnestly – 'dear Charlotte, you are my only ally – you know how I depend on you! I want you to promise me something. Will you?'

'If I can, dear – what is it?'

She looked down. 'I want you to speak privately to Samuel. He must not marry me. For his own sake, he must not. Will you make sure he never entertains the idea?'

In amazement I stared at her: at her parted lips, and her eyes, wet and shiny with tears. I smoothed back a strand of hair from her hot face.

'But, Juliana, this is quite absurd! Whatever has got into your head?' I tried in vain to read her expression. 'You cannot mean that Mr Godwin has made advances to you? Surely not, on so slight an acquaintance!'

'No – no!' She almost smiled. 'No, Samuel is quite innocent. This is Papa's idea. Do you not see?'

Puzzled, I shook my head. 'I confess, I do not! I was astonished when Marianne first mentioned it. As for broaching the subject with Mr Godwin himself, what would be my purpose, when I am quite sure that no notion of marriage has ever occurred to him? I might seem to be urging him to consider it, rather than dissuading him. I don't mean that he is unaware of you as an eligible young woman; he has eyes in his head. But he is your father's employee, newly arrived here, and he has no means of supporting a wife, even if he wished to.'

Besides, I could have added, it is your sister who draws his gaze with her wild beauty; Marianne is the one who fascinates and intrigues him. This I had observed, the very first time the three had sat together at their drawing lesson; and I had seen it, since, every time Samuel was in the same room with Marianne. His eyes followed her, almost guiltily; whenever he was not looking at her, it seemed only with a conscious effort to direct his attention elsewhere. Yes, he was Mr Farrow's employee, and Marianne still a child; but how could an artist's eye not be attracted to such exceptional beauty?

It might have given Juliana some comfort to be informed of this; or it might not.

'Please, Charlotte!' Juliana persisted. 'You do not believe me, but you will come to see I am right.'

'Very well,' I conceded. 'But not yet. You must tell me as soon as you see yourself in imminent danger of being married against your will, and I shall confront Mr Godwin then. Meanwhile, I shall be alert to any signs.'

If I were ever required to act on these words, I should have been truly amazed; but Juliana was pathetically grateful, and thanked me over and over again.

'The last time we discussed this subject,' I reminded her, 'you seemed certain that marriage, and a comfortable home of her own, is every woman's desire. Have you changed your mind on that point? Is it Mr Godwin himself you object to? Do you have a different husband in mind? Or is it simply that you resent being pushed into a marriage not of your own choosing? – though I have yet to be convinced that your father has any such plan. Or do you have other reasons besides?'

Juliana reddened; detaching herself from me, she rose from the window seat to look at herself in the mirror. Seeming dissatisfied with what she saw, she turned away, picked up a brooch, put it down again, and fiddled with the other items on her dressing table.

'No, it is not Samuel Godwin I object to,' she said quietly. 'He is kind, attentive, gentle – and quite handsome enough. Indeed, I think I might come to love him – if – if there were no other considerations. And certainly I have no other husband in view. I really think, Charlotte, I had better not marry at all.'

Quite unable to understand her, I comforted her as best I could, promising to return for a final goodbye when I had packed my bag. The timing of the solicitor's summons could hardly have been more unfortunate.

Chapter Sixteen

At the Cross Keys

By mid-morning Charlotte had gone, driven to the station by Reynolds. Her departure, with Mr Farrow also absent, left me mindful of my responsibility for the girls, and thankful that Mrs Reynolds was on hand, lest any crisis should occur which required female superintendence. I had meant to begin the first of my paintings of the house, positioning my easel on the lower lawn; but now I changed my plan, feeling that I ought to keep the girls within my sight. There was really no cause for unease, but my early-morning encounter with the man I took to be Waring, and my awareness that Juliana was very much out of sorts today, urged me towards caution.

I did not feel it appropriate to take my pupils down to the lake today – for no more rational reason than that my undignified scramble out of the water was still fresh in my mind. Using the fierce heat as an excuse, I set up a still-life arrangement in the morning room: a bowl of fruit, a jug and a crumpled napkin. We all set to work with our watercolours; the subject, however, failed to engross any of us. 'Oh, this is so dull!'

Marianne burst out; and though I pointed out that many a Dutch master had been amply stimulated by compositions such as this, I privately shared her impatience. Helping Juliana, whose efforts with watercolour were even less adept than her pencil drawings, I left her sister to work alone, which she preferred.

As Juliana's tutor, I could feel satisfied that I was making some progress; but as Marianne's, I could not. She showed an obstinate reluctance to be guided, wanting to find her own way; only unwillingly did she let me see her work. She had no patience at all, and resisted all my attempts to make her slow down, to look and to see. It was evident that she did not respect my judgement as she had respected Gideon Waring's. Her question as to whether I was a 'real artist' had gone unanswered, but she perturbed me with her implication that I was not. Soon, her huddled absorption – seated in the corner of the bay window, so that I could not glance over her shoulder – told me that she had turned her attention to something other than my arrangement on the table.

'Oh, I do hope Charlotte won't be away for long!' Juliana kept saying. 'It feels so strange, not to have her here with us – I don't like it.'

I probed a little, asking whether they had any idea of the mysterious relative whose demands on Charlotte seemed so urgent, and whether she had been called away like this before, but both sisters seemed as puzzled as I. Time weighed heavily on our hands. Juliana's mind was clearly not on her work; in fact, she seemed to have been weeping, and looked likely to sob again at any small provocation. I was a little surprised that Charlotte's absence should affect her so piteously – for, after all, she had left us only for a night or two. I made myself particularly attentive to Juliana, guiding her hesitant efforts with wash and brush, praising any small success. Before long, Marianne announced that she was tired of drawing, and intended to continue with a French translation she had begun with Charlotte. She left to fetch her books, but did not return.

Soon Juliana, too, excused herself. 'Would you mind if we finished the lesson a little early, Mr Godwin? I confess that my heart is not in it – which is no reflection on your teaching, but rather on my own distraction. I am feeling a little low and lethargic today.'

I offered my sympathy and asked if I should fetch Mrs Reynolds, but Juliana assured me that a short walk outside would refresh her, and declined my offer of company. I put away the painting materials, and went outside, where I could at least keep her in view. Slowly, pensively, she made her way along the east side of the house, pausing to pluck off the withered head of a rose, and to scatter its petals on the grass. Reaching the south terrace, she moved down to the garden seat beneath the cedar. I hesitated, not wanting to intrude; turned, and almost bumped into Marianne, not having realized she was close behind me. Good: she could offer her sister comfort, where I could not. There was no sign of her French reader; she still had her sketch-book in her hand. She dodged aside; as she passed, she gave me a strange little smile, evidently thinking she had caught me at something furtive.

At that moment I saw Reynolds walking in his stiff-legged manner up from the stables, and remembered my intention of asking for the key to the cottage. Having now examined the building, and ascertained that it was quite empty, I had no real need to return; but I used the excuse to intercept him. He seemed surprised by my request, but assured me that the cottage key was available from the harness room, and that I could have access at any time I wished.

I thanked him, and asked: 'When Mr Waring left here, did you have any idea where he went?'

Having expected him to say that he did not, I was surprised when he answered promptly: 'He put up at the Cross Keys a few nights, that much I do know. Where he went after, I couldn't say.'

'The Cross Keys?'

'Big coaching inn, by Waverley Cross.' Seeing my unrecognizing expression, he added: 'Staverton road, then left on the Portsmouth turnpike.'

'But he's not there now?'

'Shouldn't 'a thought so. Good while back, this was.'

'And how far is it to the Cross Keys?'

'Five mile or thereabouts.'

I thanked him, immediately wondering how soon I could make my way to the Cross Keys; for that must surely be Mr Waring's current lodging place, whatever Reynolds thought. My opportunity came sooner than expected, when I joined the two young ladies for luncheon.

'Will you ride this afternoon, Juley?' Marianne

asked her sister, who was still pale and untalkative, and eating little.

'I don't think so,' Juliana answered.

'Poor Queen Bess!' Marianne continued. 'She will consider herself quite neglected!'

'*You* could take her out for an hour or so, Marianne, if you wish,' said her sister.

'Oh no – you know I am not fond of riding, and it is far too hot. I should melt quite away.'

'I think I shall rest in my room this afternoon,' Juliana said, after Alice had come in for the plates. 'I did not sleep well last night, and am fatigued.'

'I shall sit with you,' said Marianne. 'I can complete my translation while you sleep.'

And thus they effectively dismissed me from their company. On an impulse, I said: 'Juliana, would you allow me to borrow Queen Bess this afternoon?'

'I did not know you were a horseman, Samuel.' Marianne leaned towards me with her customary eagerness. 'Why not take Guardsman, Father's horse? He is standing idle in the paddock, and is far more suitable for a gentleman to ride.'

'I make no claim to horsemanship!' I said hastily. 'I have no more than rudimentary skill – and would not presume to ride your father's horse without his permission. I have a mind to explore the surrounding area – it will help me with the paintings your father has commissioned,' I prevaricated, 'and it would be very pleasant to do it on horseback. Queen Bess would suit me admirably – I am not heavy, and she would carry me easily. Is she quiet and well mannered?'

'Yes, indeed! She is perfectly amenable, and you are most welcome to borrow her.' Juliana seemed pleased to oblige. 'She will be glad of the outing. I have rather neglected her these last few days. I am only sorry that we have not thought of offering you a horse before now. It is very remiss of us.'

I found Reynolds and bade him saddle the mare for me – finding out, meanwhile, that his only assistant in the stable yard was a heavy, slow-witted fellow who bore no resemblance to the golden-haired man I had seen by the lake that morning, thus eliminating the possibility that it was a groom I had encountered. Soon I was riding out through the gates, past the place where I had first met Marianne. In comparison with the anxiety I had felt then, I now seemed so established at Fourwinds, that home, Sydenham, the Slade and my friends there had all but faded from my consciousness.

As I had told the girls, I was no horseman, but I felt comfortable enough on Queen Bess's back. She was willing and obedient, as befitted a lady's horse; a stronger-mettled steed would have taxed my abilities and left me no time to contemplate the simple pleasure I felt in the sun on my face, the regular clop of hooves, and the woods and hedgerows heavy with midsummer growth on either side of the track. The air was heady with new-mown hay; the meadow next to the track was shorn and pale, with haycocks stacked in rows; thistledown drifted on the merest breath of air beneath the trees, and a thrush sang from a tall elm. I could easily have felt myself drowsed and lulled by the quiet of the afternoon, had not my errand pressed me forward.

The Cross Keys was soon reached. It was a low, sprawling building of flint and tile, spanning an archway which led through to a stable yard behind. A collie dog basked in the sunshine; there were, at this hour of the afternoon, few people about. I dismounted, tied the mare's reins to a wall-ring, and entered a low-ceilinged tap room. Two gentleman farmers, as I took them to be, sat over a late dinner of pies and potatoes; the innkeeper, aproned and drying his hands on a towel, came to see what I wanted. Wishing him good afternoon, I ordered a pint of ale and sat with it at the serving bar before asking my question.

'I believe that Mr Gideon Waring, a sculptor, stayed here for a while, a year or more ago?'

'Waring . . . Waring,' the man mused, counting out my change. 'Aye, I believe he did. Longer ago than a year, though. If it's the man I'm thinking of, it were closer to two years. Tall feller, quiet, well set up?'

'That sounds like him!'

'Aye, he put up here for ten days or so. Harvest time, I remember that.'

'Has he returned since?'

He pursed his lips, considering, then slowly shook his head. 'Not to stay here, he ent. No, I've not seen him.'

'Do you know where he went after leaving here?' I began to feel that my mission was futile; why should this innkeeper, with any number of guests passing through, have more than economic interest in a man who had visited briefly so many months ago?

'That I don't know.' He was already diverted by one of the farmers, a corpulent man with a bulbous nose on which each vein was drawn in purple, who had come to the bar counter and was jingling the money in his pocket.

'I'll trouble you for two more pints, Frank, if you please,' said this burly fellow; then, turning to me, 'Now, young sir, pardon me for interrupting, but I can point you at a man who'll tell you about the sculptor you're enquiring after. You're the new artist living at Fourwinds, is that right?'

'I am. Samuel Godwin is my name.' I wondered how he knew, then recalled Eliza Dearly's remark that I was the talk of the neighbourhood, to which I had given little credence.

'Jack Nelson,' said the farmer, shaking my proffered hand.

'You'll know Charlotte Agnew, then,' said the landlord, looking at me. 'Miss Agnew, I should say. Used to wait at table here. Give her my regards if you'll be so kind.'

I nodded; this I could scarcely believe, but, more interested in wresting information from the farmer, I let it pass. 'Can you really help me, sir?' I tried to gaze not at his nose, but at the kindly pale eyes behind it. 'I should be most grateful.'

'Indeed I can – you'll find the man not two furlongs from this spot. Take yourself down to St

Stephen's, in the village there, and speak to Ned Simmons.'

'Ned Simmons? And I'll find him at St Stephen's Church?' I repeated, thinking the man referred to might be vicar or verger.

'Aye. He'll be there now, up the tower, most like. Stonemason, see. He and your sculptor used to drink here of an evening, both being in the same line of trade.'

A stonemason! With a quickening sense of excitement, I paid for the farmer's two pints, for which he thanked me profusely. Then I downed my ale as fast as I could, thanked both farmer and innkeeper in turn, and took my leave.

I remounted the patient mare, and guided her in the direction the farmer had indicated, towards the nearby village.

This settlement proved to be no more than a small gathering of cottages with one or two larger dwellings. The church tower – of the squat, square Norman variety – showed above a cluster of trees, behind a lych gate. Here, once more, I tethered Queen Bess, my hands clumsy with haste and excitement. I could scarcely bear the thought that the stonemason might have downed tools for the day, or even finished his work and left the area. My fears, though, were quickly allayed: I saw rough scaffolding erected around the tower, a canvas bag of tools lying open on the ground, and heard, from above, the regular *tink, tink* of metal on stone. A ladder led up the flint tower, but the person wielding the chisel was not in sight.

I made my way through lichen-encrusted gravestones to the base of the tower. Cupping both hands around my mouth, I hollered: 'Mr Simmons? Mr Simmons, are you there?'

The tinking ceased; a few moments later a peaked cap appeared over the edge of the balustrade, and a face beneath it.

'Who's that?'

'My name is Samuel Godwin. May I speak with you?'

Cap and face bobbed out of sight. I waited; thought I should have to yell again; then a booted foot planted itself on the ladder, followed by another, and then by the whole form of the stonemason as he backed nimbly down the rungs. In a moment he was standing beside me. He was a small man of perhaps forty, shorter than I, and wiry as a jockey. Impatient at the interruption, he rubbed dust off his hands.

'Yes, what is it?'

'I beg your pardon for calling you away from your work, Mr Simmons. But I wonder if you can help me? I'm in search of a sculptor named Gideon Waring, and I understand you knew him.'

'Oh?' He jutted his chin at me. 'And who might you be?'

'My name is Samuel Godwin. I'm employed by Mr Ernest Farrow, at Fourwinds.' I held out my hand; after a moment's pause, he returned the gesture and we exchanged a perfunctory shake.

He scrutinized me with astute brown eyes. 'Are you on Mr Farrow's business? Has he sent you after Waring?'

'No – no.' I felt it best to be frank. 'He knows

nothing of this enquiry. Since seeing Mr Waring's stone-carvings at Fourwinds, I've become very curious about him. I want to meet him if I can, and learn more about his work.'

'And what might you be – land agent? Accountant?' He looked at me narrowly.

'I am neither. I am drawing tutor to Mr Farrow's two daughters, and he has also commissioned me to produce a series of paintings of his house.'

Simmons gave me a wry look. 'You want to watch your back.'

'What do you mean by that?'

'What I say.' Ned Simmons crouched by his canvas bag, taking advantage of the unexpected grounding to select a small chisel.

'Mr Simmons,' I tried, feeling that I was getting nowhere, 'if I assure you that I am not acting for Mr Farrow, that in fact he knows nothing of my attempts to track down Gideon Waring, and that my interest is simply that of an aspiring artist who feels the greatest admiration for another's skill – would you consider telling me what you know? Chiefly, whether you know of Mr Waring's current whereabouts?'

Straightening with the tool he had chosen, Simmons looked at me sternly. 'Mr Farrow won't know of this? Nor even that you've spoken to me here?'

'He shall not,' I assured him.

'Then – I shall tell you this.' He still seemed anxious to overcome severe doubt before proceeding; he looked me up and down, rubbed his chin, peered into my face. 'Promise, mind?'

'I promise!'

'Then – if I have your word – I can tell you that Gideon Waring went from here to Chichester, to take up work at the cathedral there. Whether he's still there or not, I've no way of knowing.' He moved back towards the ladder; about to ascend, he turned to add: 'That's all I can tell you. Anything else, you'll have to get from him. Good day.'

Chapter Seventeen

On the Promenade

In Eastbourne, I had little to do but wait.

As I wished to forestall any suggestion that I might stay at my grandmother's home, I took the precaution, before reporting there, of finding alternative lodging. Securing a room in a boarding house near the railway station, I paid in advance for two nights, hoping that would suffice. In any case, I had no intention of staying longer.

Three Sussex Esplanade proved to be part of a prosperous terrace facing the sea: a three-storey house, with steps up to the front door, which had a polished brass knocker in the shape of a lion's head. A maid answered the door; on introducing myself, I was shown into a sitting room. Here I was joined by the resident nurse, a capable-looking person with quiet, assured movements, who impressed on me that I had arrived not a moment too soon.

'You must prepare yourself for the worst,' she told me gravely. 'Your great-aunt cannot last for more than a day or so.'

No one here, other than the solicitor, knew that

Mrs Newbold was in fact my grandmother; I offered no correction. It had suited her, and now it suited me, to pretend that our relationship was farther removed.

With hushed footsteps, this kindly nurse led me into the sick room; the invalid lay there in semi-darkness, the curtains being closed.

'It is Charlotte,' I told her. 'Charlotte Agnew.'

Her eyelids fluttered half open. I had no way of knowing if she recognized me. It was many years since I had seen her face, and I could not now assume an affection I did not feel.

'I am sure she is aware of your presence,' said the nurse, 'and is comforted by it, even if she cannot speak.'

As soon as was decently possible, I excused myself. Telling the nurse that I would return later, I escaped to the seafront and the gaiety of the holiday-makers who thronged there.

Outside in the air, I found that I was hungry after my train journey, and ordered a meal in a small eating-house on the promenade. Unaccustomed to eating alone in public, I did not linger. Leaving, I bought a copy of *The Times* from a news vendor, thinking that I might find a seat in one of the esplanade shelters, or even hire a deckchair, and sit reading for a while. I spent an hour or so in this fashion, enjoying the novelty of having both time and money to spend. Mr Farrow paid me eighty pounds a year, and as all my needs were met at Fourwinds, and I rarely left the place, I had no real demands on my income; indeed, I was in the fortunate position of not having to concern myself with money. It occurred to me now that I might look in the shops for presents to take back for Juliana and Marianne; even, if I wished, I could buy something for myself.

Finding a bench that had only one other occupant, I sat reading my newspaper until I felt my senses muzzed by sleep. This was most unlike me; the break with routine seemed to be affecting me strangely. Collecting bag and newspaper, I walked slowly along the promenade, occasionally diverted by the antics of swimmers or by children and dogs playing on the beach. Soon I found that the rhythmic plash and sigh of the waves, and the high scream of gulls, had lulled me into a peculiarly ruminative state of mind.

Removed from Fourwinds, I was not quite my accustomed self. The encounter with my grandmother had shaken my equilibrium, reminding me sorely of my childhood. The sympathy I felt was not for the dying woman but for myself, for I owed her little enough. She had disposed of me. Yes, she had provided for me: had paid for my board and lodging, and had sent me to a mediocre boarding school; that, however, was chiefly for the sake of her conscience. She did not love me, did not want to acknowledge me as her relative; I had seen her only rarely. The life I had made for myself at Fourwinds owed nothing to her. There, in my known habitat, I was Miss Agnew, Charlotte: admirably filling my role, which required that I efface myself and think always of my two charges. So absorbed was I in their lives, that my own seemed of little importance. I permitted myself the somewhat complacent thought that Juliana and Marianne would be missing me, for we had never before been parted. This dependence was mutual. I did not like being away from them, and was uneasy at the thought of conversation between them and Samuel Godwin without my presence. My disquiet, however, was more than that. Without Marianne and Juliana, away from the pattern of meal times, lessons and conversation, away from Mr Farrow, whose habits and foibles I knew so perfectly, I felt bereft: not only of them, but also of myself. Uprooted from my familiar surroundings, transplanted abruptly from open downland to this Englandedge where the sea constantly fretted and eroded the land – who was I? If anyone had put such a simple question to me, I almost felt that I should be at a loss for an answer. The syllables of my name had become empty puffs of air, meaningless.

Slightly giddied, I continued to walk along the seafront. To outward appearances I must have presented exactly the same figure as usual: a slight, unremarkable young woman, plain of feature, and dressed in grey, quite without jewellery or other adornment. Within, however, I was gripped by a sense of bewilderment, almost of panic. What was I? – I was nothing. Here, I cared for no one, and nobody cared for me. What if, by some unthinkable circumstance, I should remain here, and never return to Fourwinds? I should be utterly alone. No friendly or respectful glances would come my way as I walked through the town; no one would notice me as I passed. Anonymous in the crowd, I should be lost.

Gripping the railing of a flight of steps that led

down to the beach, I felt overcome by faintness, and closed my eyes against the glare. After a few moments, I felt a grip on my arm, and warm breath close to my cheek.

'You all right, miss? Been taken poorly?' The face that looked into mine was round, rosy-cheeked, with tendrils of hair escaping from beneath a cap: it was the face of a mature woman with girlish looks. She carried a jug of milk. 'Why not come and have a nice sit-down? Cup of tea'll soon put you to rights. On the 'ouse, mind.' She gestured towards a kind of caravan down on the beach, to which she had evidently been making her way; it had a striped awning, and deckchairs on the sand nearby. 'Come on, duck, give me your arm.'

'Thank you. I will.' Suddenly I felt overwhelmed by affection towards this kindly soul. Someone had seen me after all; responded with fellow-feeling, and offered me help. She clucked her tongue in concern as she guided me down to the sand: 'Steady, now – watch your step – that's the way.'

By now feeling somewhat foolish, I sat in a deckchair until I had recovered. After drinking a second cup of tea, I insisted on paying for both, then bade farewell to my Samaritan, and walked along the very fringe of the waves, even though my shoes soon filled with grit and pebbles.

Here, I took myself firmly in hand. Far from becoming invisible, I had made an exhibition of myself, attracting the attention of strangers. Charlotte Agnew reasserted herself; she straightened her back and lifted her chin, and looked the world levelly in the face. What had I been thinking of, to allow myself such foolish indulgence? Walking on, I took deep breaths, filling my lungs with salt-laden sea air, feeling strength and confidence returning.

My progress along the beach brought me close to a family group who sat on rugs, enjoying a picnic, sheltered by the edge of the promenade and by a canvas screen. They, of course, did not notice my glances. The group comprised a young mother dressed in white, a uniformed nursemaid, a tiny baby, swaddled, and placed in the shade of a screen, and a sailor-suited boy of maybe two years. This boy's attention was intently fixed on a pair of donkeys giving rides to children farther along the beach; as I watched, he made a dash for freedom, toddling with arms outstretched, struggling for balance on shingles that shifted beneath his feet. 'No, Teddie!' called the mother in alarm; the nursemaid darted after him and led him firmly back, with a wry grimace, while he wriggled and wailed. Putting down the pastry she had been about to eat, the mother gathered the resisting boy into her arms and rocked him. 'Be patient, Teddie! We'll go and see the donkeys in a little while.' In her place I should have put him aside with a harsh reminder to behave himself, but her face was soft with tenderness. Unaccountably perturbed, I turned away to the water's edge.

As I stood gazing out at the calm aquamarine surface that was barely ruffled, the merest frills of waves hardly disturbing the pebbles, for the tide was full in, I found myself puzzling again over the conversation I had had yesterday with Juliana, and her strange insistence that she ought not to marry. The cause of her tearfulness could only be the visit from Eliza Dearly and the infant Tommy. Why, though, should she be so upset by the new proximity of the governess she had been fond of, possibly even as fond as she now was of me? And why should Eliza Dearly's happily married state provoke so firm a resolution in Juliana to remain a spinster? Try as I might, I was at a loss to understand. Could it be a delicate revulsion against what she had witnessed of the liaison between Eliza and Gideon Waring? Yet if that were the case, why invite Eliza to Fourwinds at all? And she had shown no aloofness of manner towards the former governess. On the contrary, she had been in a fluster of delight, and hardly able to take her eyes off little Tommy—

Tommy! Barely could I prevent myself from smiling as I pictured the charming little boy, and recalled Juliana's tender face as she carried him. It seemed she was deeply attached to the child; I thought of her furtive excitement before the visit, her low spirits after—

The answer slipped into my mind as cleanly as a penny into a slot machine. Although I always prided myself on missing nothing, I had missed everything. A cold frisson of shock trembled through me, although the sun was still hot. I startled myself by exclaiming aloud; stumbled, and almost overbalanced.

It was impossible – unthinkable – unendurable –

and yet, and yet, though every fibre of feeling rebelled—

– it made clear sense – supplied all answers, filled all gaps—

Juliana, not Eliza Dearly, was the boy's mother.

No, no! How could my mind even admit such a grotesque possibility? It was preposterous – intolerable! My mind reeled; every instinct in me struggled to repel the notion. I turned and walked along the shore, the pebbles and the waves blurring hotly before my eyes. How could I entertain such a thought, about my beloved Juliana?

Every instinct recoiled; yet each moment supplied an answer to a puzzling question. Each new thought convinced me that I must be right.

I walked and walked, until I was hot and almost feverish. If this were so, how thoroughly I had been taken in! By Mr Farrow, and most of all, by Juliana herself! I thought I had Juliana's trust; believed I was her confidante – but how much she had hidden from me!

Now, dizzied and shocked, yet forcing myself methodically to re-examine the situation, I realized that Juliana's illness and convalescence away from Fourwinds, attributed to a nervous disorder, had coincided with Tommy's birth.

What, then, of Eliza Dearly, and her role in this? I found that I had even more to condemn than before. If my surmising were correct (and it *must* be correct), she had most grievously abused her position of trust at Fourwinds by allowing Juliana to be corrupted by that most wicked of men, Gideon Waring. Indeed, when I realized that Juliana must have been barely seventeen at the time of the child's conception, scarcely more than a child herself, I was filled with such disgust that I must have protested aloud, for a passer-by turned to look at me before moving on hastily, as though I were a madwoman. How vile, how reprehensible their conniving must have been! For how else could a well-brought-up young girl find herself so irredeemably compromised, without being manipulated by two older people she ought to have been able to trust?

'Juliana!' I murmured. 'What is to be done?'

No answer presented itself. Instead, I found myself marvelling at how much Juliana had concealed. What troubling thoughts must possess her daily, yet she had managed to keep me in ignorance! Any feelings of reproach I felt towards the poor girl were quickly suppressed as I realized what a burden of guilt and shame must be her lot. Clearly, I must return; most urgently I must find a way of letting her know that I had guessed her secret. Most assuredly she would find comfort in that.

What of Samuel Godwin? How did this affect his position?

Could Marianne have guessed rightly? Had Mr Farrow brought the unsuspecting young man to live at Fourwinds, not for his artistic ability, but in order for him to confer respectability on Juliana, by marrying her? I turned this idea over and over in my mind, considering it from all angles. Was it possible? No doubt Samuel, if he complied, could benefit from such an arrangement: I knew Ernest Farrow well enough to appreciate that once he had decided on a course of action, he planned everything. If Samuel Godwin were his choice, he had chosen well; Samuel could be as good, as kind, as considerate a husband for Juliana as she might have chosen for herself.

What, now, should I do with this knowledge? Keep it to myself, for Juliana's sake? Encourage Samuel, connive to throw them into company together, extol her virtues to him, and his to her? At this point, however, a new question arose in my mind: was Samuel as innocent as I supposed, and quite unaware of the scheme? Surely, yes; I had spent enough time in his company to form a reliable judgement of his character, and could not believe him capable of deviousness or cunning.

While my thoughts raced, I continued to walk in one direction along the tide's edge, then to retrace my steps in the other, so that my feet almost wore a groove in the pebbles. It was not possible for me to leave Eastbourne yet; now that I was here, I was obliged to wait until the business with my grandmother was concluded.

It would not be long. The nurse had assured me of that.

Leaving the beach at last, my head still teeming with possibilities, I walked back to Sussex Esplanade, stopping on the way to purchase a large bunch of carnations from a flower seller on the street corner. Reluctance slowed my pace. It was not my intention to stay long; my duty fulfilled, I should not return until the morning. Yet it was with a feeling of surrender that I knocked on the door for the second time, and was conducted again to the sick room.

It was alarming to see a person so close to death. My grandmother's features retained their hawkishness. Her mouth was slightly open; her lids fluttered and her eyes rested on me for a second. In her look I read reproach, as though she were affronted at being brought to such an undignified extremity. Quietly her attendant moved around the room: filling a water glass, adjusting the turn of the sheet, arranging my carnations in a vase and placing them on a chest of drawers opposite the bed, not so close that their perfume would overwhelm the sleeper. Her tasks completed for the moment, she sat by the bed and folded her hands, apparently prepared to keep vigil for as long as necessary. I, on the contrary, was already impatient to leave, although I felt that form required me to sit a little longer.

'You have not seen your great-aunt for some while?' the nurse asked me gently.

'Not for several years,' I replied, not adding that I barely recognized her.

'There is no one else you can summon to keep you company? You are Mrs Newbold's only relative?'

'No. She has a son, though I do not know of his whereabouts.' Why had my grandmother's staff not told her this? 'I expected him to be in attendance.'

She looked at me in surprise. 'You do not know? You were not aware that her son was a soldier in Africa

– that he was killed last year, in the Transvaal?'

No, I did not know. Concealing my ignorance as best I could, pretending that the heat, and the shock of this sudden illness, had made me confused and forgetful, I soon excused myself, and left my grandmother in the care of her nurse and servants. She led a comfortable life here. My feet trod thick, well-brushed carpet; there were paintings on the walls in heavy gilt frames; glass-fronted cabinets displayed collections of silverware and china, and a chandelier twinkled in the hallway.

The death of the uncle I had never seen (half-uncle, to be accurate) explained the solicitor's letter, and why I had been summoned. As far as I could tell, I was now my grandmother's only relative in this country. Some spirit of contrition, or maybe some whim, must have urged her to instruct the solicitor to trace and contact me, after all the years of estrangement. It was too late: she could summon me to her bedside, but was powerless to command any feeling of sorrow or loss.

In the morning the blinds were down. The maid looked tearful as she opened the door to me. 'Oh, miss – you're too late!'

Quickly the nurse came to meet me, extending a sympathetic hand. 'I am so sorry, Miss Agnew. Your great-aunt has passed away, not half an hour ago. Please accept my condolences.'

Chapter Eighteen

Mr Charles Latimer to Samuel Godwin

Slade,
London

Friday, 1st

Dear Godwit,

    What's become of you, you scoundrel? Are you so busy that you can't spare a minute to write? I've given up expecting to hear from you. Can only assume that your new life there, buried in the South Downs in your rustic retreat, is so fascinating that you've completely forgotten your friends at the Slade, who bade you a fond and tearful farewell such a short while ago. Johnny says you must be completely engrossed with the young ladies there, and that's your reason for neglecting us — we can think of no other explanation. What a job you have fallen into! Hard work it must be indeed, spending every day in feminine company, guiding their delicate hands, nourishing them with morsels of praise. We are agog to hear full descriptions of your pupils, and how you get on with them. Every morning we bound towards the letter-rack in the happy expectation of finding a letter, even a postcard, from you — and every time we slink away downcast and quite flat-footed with disappointment.

Well, you may have forgotten us, but we haven't forgotten you. Life goes on here much as usual — but soon we will be disbanding for the summer, and we are making plans. I shall be heading for the Aegean, for a few weeks of sustained hard work beneath the sun's hot rays, while acquainting myself with the local wine. Johnny will be travelling up to Scotland to don a kilt and stalk the heathery hills while he awaits the start of the grouse season and permission to blast poor defenceless birds out of the sky, barbarian that he is. But first -

We are reluctant to set off on our travels without reacquainting ourselves with our dear, lost, lamented Godwit. Johnny, you may remember, has an aunt and uncle in Brighton, and we are planning to spend next weekend there before parting for the next few weeks. Brighton is not far from you — does your employer let you out, now and again? Can you plead with him that you need a rest from your strenuous labours, your back-breaking toil, the relentless pressure of your duties? That you would benefit from the refreshment of sea air, a dip in the briny, convivial company and an evening in an alehouse?

Come, Sam, do say Yes. If your answer is No, Johnny and I will be forced to conclude that you have forsworn our company for ever, and that you regard our devoted friendship as the merest trifle to be cast aside on a whim.

Your friend — neglected, dejected, but I hope not rejected -

Chas

Chapter Nineteen

Partnered

I should not have picked up Marianne's sketchbook when I found it lying on the oak settle in the vestibule – but on an impulse I did, and was shocked by what I saw as I flicked back its cover.

This was what had occupied her during our unsuccessful still-life lesson that morning; *this* accounted for her huddled position in the bay window, and her mischievous expression. In watercolours, she had painted a double portrait, of Juliana and me – not skilled, but recognizable enough. We were seated together at the table, our heads close, and Marianne's brush – agile, if not subtle – had caught a moment in which I appeared to be explaining something to my pupil, turned towards her, pencil in hand and lips parted in speech, while she in turn gazed back at me with a fawning expression which I can only say I had never noticed in reality. The picture did not disturb me, though, as much as its caption. Underneath the drawing, Marianne had written in a flowing hand, *Betrothed*, and had added a border of hearts entwined with flowers.

It was only Marianne's jest, I felt sure of that; yet the mere suggestion was enough to perturb me. Her vantage point – observing me and her sister so closely engaged in discussion, from across the room – had put the foolish notion into her head. I knew from my sister Isobel and her friends that young girls will amuse themselves with such nonsense. Yes, I hoped that was all – fervently hoped that Juliana did not share the notion that my attention to her was anything other than that of drawing master to pupil. Replacing the sketchbook precisely where I had found it, I consoled myself with this thought: that if Marianne imagined me to be romantically interested in her sister, she must be quite unaware that she herself figured so largely in my daydreams.

The household being busily occupied in preparation for the evening's dinner party, I was able to put the matter out of my mind; but it returned in force later.

Charlotte's absence was keenly felt by everyone. By Mr Farrow, who had needed her to welcome the guests and ensure that all ran smoothly; by Marianne, who wanted advice on dress and hairstyling; by Juliana, who, simply, never wanted to be without her; and lastly, by myself, for I should have appreciated her quiet guidance in this unfamiliar social situation. As it was, Charlotte had evidently done all she could beforehand: arranging the menu and the seating plan with Mrs Reynolds, and hiring two extra maidservants, one to help in the kitchen and another to wait at table with Alice.

The guests, some of whom had been strolling around the garden, assembled in the drawing room, where the large doors stood open to the evening air. There were six of them: the Vernon-Dales and the Greenlaws, all of whom I had met briefly at church; a stylish lady introduced as Annette Duchêne, who was the Greenlaws' house guest; and a Mr Eaton, Mrs Greenlaw's brother, a horse-breeder. I felt myself under scrutiny as I joined them, and was introduced to the two I had not already met. More, I seemed to be the subject of interested speculation; indeed, I suspected that the evening's main purpose was to bring me into the society of these people. Mr Farrow had, evidently, boasted of my ability – and, even, of my reputation as a painter sure to make my mark in the coming years. He had every faith in the soundness of his investment; pride and ambition made me content to trust his judgement, and eager to accept his valuation of my worth.

'Mr Godwin – we are so pleased of this chance to become better acquainted!' said Mrs Vernon-Dale, a formidable woman of fifty, steelily masculine of feature, and clad in a stiffly beaded dress which gave the appearance of armour. 'I'm so looking forward to seeing your work. Have you exhibited much?'

'Very pleased to see you again.' Her husband was gruff, moustached, slightly stooping, and I guessed that he would feel more at home with rifle or golf club in his hand, rather than a crystal glass. 'I hope we'll be able to have a proper chat later.'

'*Enchantée!*' Miss Annette Duchêne was, as I have already said, a very striking woman – fashionably dressed, with dark hair twined up into a clasp-and-flower arrangement on top of her head, and a dress of rose silk that bared a great deal of her shoulders and bosom. She took my hand and gave me a fleeting glance which I can only describe as flirtatious.

'I do hope you've settled here happily, Mr Godwin?' Her hostess, Mrs Greenlaw, was far more matronly, encased in tight burgundy satin. 'Do you have family of your own? Shall you be at church tomorrow? Maybe you'd care to join us for sherry afterwards?'

Mr Greenlaw wrung my hand in a strong grip. 'Good evening – good evening. You must come and dine with us some time. Your work here keeps you busy, I suppose? Do you do portraits? I've been thinking of commissioning one for some while – you know the sort of thing – my wife and I and the dogs, house in the background?'

And finally Mr Eaton the horse-breeder, a tall man with black, bristling eyebrows that seemed to compensate for thinning hair: 'Pleased to meet you. From London, are you? A Slade man? Finding it a bit quiet here in the Downs, I suppose?'

Our number was completed, of course, by the three Farrows. Juliana was dressed in dove-grey, a shade that was all wrong for her, emphasizing the pallidity of her complexion; her hair was dressed simply, even demurely, and she wore only small pearl earrings for adornment. Over her dress she wore a light beaded shawl, which she kept tugging more closely about her neck and bosom. Marianne, by contrast, had chosen a dress that perfectly suited her colouring: a silk gown of dark fir-green. Her hair was arranged in an artfully casual style that twisted up some of its abundance into jewelled combs, while a few long tresses – gloriously chestnut against the green – tumbled about her shoulders. She looked quite enchanting; my eyes were irresistibly drawn to her. Impertinent young madam that she was, she boldly looked me up and down as she entered the room, assessing my turnout, and gave me a private nod and smile that said: *Yes, I see you have made an effort. Well done – you will do nicely!* I returned the look, expressing approval of her dress and coiffure in what I hoped was a brotherly or even an avuncular manner, although I feared that my fascination with her must be written on my face for all to see. Juliana, beside her, remained unaware of this unspoken communication. Her fingers fumbled at the edge of her thin shawl. She was ill at ease in this social situation; indeed, one might have thought that Marianne was the elder sister, Juliana the debutante.

Finally, Mr Farrow himself. Presiding, he cut an impressive figure – the black and white of dinner jacket and dress shirt giving him a dramatic, almost flamboyant appearance, with his florid colouring, strong features and thick hair. It struck me anew that he was a handsome man, still in his prime, and with status and wealth besides. While I was thinking this, I noticed Annette Duchêne's eyes resting on him appreciatively.

He might remarry; indeed, it was more than likely. This had crossed my mind before, in connection with Charlotte; but here was an altogether different prospect. I would have wagered, too, that the possibility was not far from Mademoiselle Duchêne's thoughts. Aha, I thought: if Charlotte were here, she would find a formidable rival in this stylish mademoiselle, with her coquettish glances and teasing smiles! I would have been much diverted by seeing them seated at the same table, so strikingly contrasted in dress and demeanour.

As we moved through to the dining room, I found myself partnered with Juliana. She looked up at me shyly as I pulled back her chair, then cast her eyes down, as was customary with her. She had not revived in spirits since Charlotte's departure. Although I should have preferred to sit next to Marianne, it was perhaps as well for my composure that I did not; and I determined that if Juliana did not enjoy the evening, it would not be through want of effort on my part. I made myself attentive, engaging her in conversation. There was little competition from her neighbour to the right, Mr Eaton, who was delivering a monologue to Mrs Greenlaw about breeding stock and bloodlines. Following this thread, I made a remark to Juliana about the comfortable paces and excellent manners of her mare, Queen Bess, and asked where she went on her rides. While she answered me, my gaze returned to Marianne, who seemed bored by the comfortable Mr Greenlaw; she looked boldly back at me, noted my solicitousness towards Juliana, and smiled approval. Only then did I remember what I had seen in her sketchbook; I felt my face flush with heat. The sharp-eyed miss noticed that too, of course; made her own interpretation, and was highly pleased.

On my left I had Mrs Vernon-Dale, whose

conversation with Mr Farrow, throughout the soup and the fish course, was all about her plans to extend and landscape the garden at Rampions. A new greenhouse was to be added, and a conservatory to the house, and the kitchen garden extended. Mr Farrow took only polite interest in this, until Mr Vernon-Dale, seated opposite, interrupted. 'Has Marguerite told you about the head gardener I've taken on? Capital fellow. Dearly, his name is. Matthew Dearly. Used to work for the Radcliffes at Oak Lodge.'

'No – surely not!' my employer said brusquely. 'Their gardener moved away to – er, Hampshire, wasn't it? I believe Francis Radcliffe mentioned that.'

'That's true – he did, but he's back again,' said Mr Vernon-Dale. 'I can tell you he's transforming the place. Already licked those lazybones under-gardeners into shape.'

I watched Mr Farrow closely. He picked up the decanter, refilled Annette Duchêne's glass, then called to Alice for more wine. 'Conservatory, you say?' he continued to Mrs Vernon-Dale. 'Have you found a good architect?'

'Matthew Dearly? Hasn't he married that young woman who used to be governess here?' Mrs Greenlaw asked the table at large.

'Yes, yes – they've moved into our Orchard Cottage. Did you know that your old governess is married now, with a child of her own – a fine little boy?' Mr Vernon-Dale said genially to Marianne.

Juliana made an abrupt, almost involuntary movement, dropped her napkin to the floor and began to fumble; I went to her assistance, retrieving it. Alice returned with the wine and moved from place to place, collecting the fish plates.

'We have heard something about it,' Marianne said, with perfect composure. 'I am very happy for her.'

Mrs Vernon-Dale narrowed her mannish features into a frown. 'Didn't she leave here rather suddenly though, Ernest?' she asked Mr Farrow. 'Weren't you displeased with her for some reason?'

'Aha!' cried Annette Duchêne, leaning forward. 'I detect a mystery! Come, let us hear more!'

'It was only a trifling matter,' Mr Farrow said lightly. 'Nothing I propose to bore you all with.'

'Governesses,' Marianne cried, 'should expect to be governess all their lives, do you not think? They must not expect to find themselves husbands or bear children, like other women.'

No one knew how to receive this bold remark until Annette Duchêne burst into a peal of mirth: 'You are very droll, Miss Farrow!' Others laughed politely, the meat course was brought in, and the awkward moment passed. Mrs Vernon-Dale continued talking to Mr Farrow about the design of her conservatory and the plants she planned to cultivate in it; but as soon as the vegetables had been served, everyone's glasses filled, and the sirloin of beef pronounced excellent, her husband introduced another dangerous topic.

'What news of that sculptor fellow, Ernest? I see that your west wall is still blank. Did the scoundrel really make off with the last of your carvings? I hope you had not paid him.'

'What is this?' demanded the alert Mademoiselle Duchêne. 'Another mystery? A vanishing sculptor, a stolen carving?'

Mr Farrow explained briefly; while he did so, I glanced at Juliana, who drank half a glass of wine very quickly, then looked embarrassed when the maid hastened to refill her glass.

'But what will you do?' burst out the impetuous French lady. 'You cannot have only three of four Winds! Another sculptor must be found!'

'That,' said my employer, 'would not be easy. Another sculptor, yes. One who could complete the series without giving the effect of dissonance – I do not know where he is to be found.'

His eye fell on me as he spoke – maybe he was thinking that, with my Slade background, I should number armies of stone-carvers among my friends. Knowing as I did that Waring himself was to be found in Chichester, not twenty miles away, I felt that this intelligence must be written on my face; but I shook my head sadly, and sipped at my wine. Of course, there were sculptors among my Slade acquaintances, my friend John Hickford for one. I thought of the letter I had received this morning from Chas, with its invitation to Brighton. I could easily put Mr Farrow in touch with a dozen or more sculptors, or at any rate student sculptors, but I was not yet ready to give up the search for Gideon Waring.

'They seem to me rather curious, your three Winds,' stated Mrs Vernon-Dale. 'Almost clumsy, to my eye. I could have recommended you a sculptor every bit as accomplished. Come, Mr Godwin, you are an artist, even if stone is not your medium – what is your opinion of them?'

'I think they are quite extraordinary,' I replied. 'Pagan and classical both at once – and with such lively characterization that I feel I know each one personally.'

Mademoiselle Duchêne – who did seem rather easily amused – laughed at this fancy. 'This is your artistic sensibility at work, Mr Godwin,' she told me – and my name had never sounded more charming than when given French pronunciation. 'I see only slabs of stone, attractively carved into human forms.'

'I agree with Samuel,' said Juliana – almost the first time she had spoken to the whole company. Everyone waited for her to say more, but she fell into an embarrassed silence.

'You see,' said Marianne, 'we are extremely fond of our three Winds. Are we not, Juliana? We pay homage to them each day – even speak to them. You will think me very childish, but sometimes I have asked the North Wind to stop blowing, and to yield to the kindlier South!'

'And so you have no West Wind to converse with?' Annette Duchêne looked most entertained by the idea. 'I hope you do not stand talking to a blank wall?'

'No – but it is my deepest wish that the West Wind should be found.' Marianne spoke so intently that all eyes turned to her. 'Where is he, if not here? Roaming, gusting and blowing at will? The house cannot be at peace until the West Wind is safely in his place – until the blank is filled.'

'Marianne, you have been reading too many novels – filling your head with nonsense,' said her father, with an attempt at a laugh.

'It is not nonsense,' replied Marianne, quietly resolute.

'So, Miss Farrow, you require this vagrant Wind of yours to be properly affixed to his wall, his wings clipped, his flight ended?' proposed Annette Duchêne, entering into the conceit.

'Yes!' Marianne replied seriously. 'I do.'

'Well, Ernest,' put in Mr Greenlaw, in a jovial tone, 'I was about to say, that I am surprised you have kept the three pieces this dishonest fellow did complete – that you have given them such prominence. I think I should sooner have abandoned the whole project, or started again with a new sculptor—'

'I agree,' said stern Mrs Vernon-Dale; 'a man like that is not to be encouraged. He has abused your patronage, Ernest. He should not be given the satisfaction of considering his work highly prized.'

'– but I see now,' continued Mr Greenlaw, 'that Marianne and Juliana are so attached to these Wind figures that it would be a great pity to take them down, or destroy them.'

'Destroy them?' cried Marianne. 'No!'

She looked wildly at me; I was reminded of her sleepwalking. I hoped fervently that this unfortunate discussion would not provoke another wandering fit tonight, while Charlotte was absent; but then I imagined her footsteps outside my door, myself rushing to her aid, my arm around her, her hair tumbling down her back, thick and fragrant, the thinness of her nightgown – I felt myself almost giddied by these thoughts, and quickly called myself to attention.

'Smash them to pieces?' Marianne was saying. 'No one could do them such violence – it is unthinkable!'

'Of course it is, dear,' Mrs Greenlaw soothed. 'But don't worry your pretty head. I'm sure no one would think of it.'

'Did you never see the missing West Wind?' asked Miss Duchêne. 'Either the figure itself, or any sketch?'

This, I did not know – I looked from Marianne, who sat forward with lips parted, to her father, whose expression was quite the opposite, closed-in and tight.

'No,' he replied. 'If there ever was a carving, or a sketch, I never saw it.'

'Well, well.' Mr Vernon-Dale had evidently tired of the subject. 'I am quite sure that a competent sculptor can be found, if you are determined to continue. I can put you in touch with several, Ernest.'

The plates were cleared again; through dessert, cheese and fruit, the conversation moved to safer topics. It took three hints from Mr Farrow before Juliana led the ladies into the drawing room; Annette Duchêne's skirt swished against my chair as she passed, and I caught a drift of her musky perfume. When the door was closed behind them, cigars were dispensed and port passed round. My employer asked Mr Eaton about a new stallion he was having shipped over from Ireland; the man needed little encouragement, and the conversation was all about horses and racing until we rejoined the ladies.

If Charlotte had been present, I do not doubt that she would have poured and served the coffee, but in her absence the task fell to Juliana. Looking at her pale face and the worried expression she tried to conceal with frequent smiles, I realized how taxing she had found this evening. Determined to say something to cheer her, I remarked, as she handed me my cup and saucer, 'I am glad to escape from the horse talk; I could not think of two sensible words to say.' I had spoken in an undertone; Juliana rewarded me with a grateful smile. As I moved away towards the sofa, I heard Mrs Greenlaw whisper to Mr Farrow, more audibly than she could have intended, 'Just look at the dear girl – she is quite head over heels! What a handsome couple they make! When may we expect an announcement?'

This remark startled me into consternation; and I confess that I distanced myself at once from Juliana, and sat beside Mrs Vernon-Dale. When, a little later, Mr Farrow indicated that Juliana should play the piano for us, it was Marianne who turned the pages of her score. Now, I could allow myself to sit and gaze without fear of drawing attention to myself. A pretty picture they made: Juliana, devoting her mind, eyes and fingers to Chopin, was more assured than she had been all evening; Marianne stood, poised and attentive by her side, her hair glinting copper in the pool of light from the lamp; in my mind I stored details of her pose, its litheness and unselfconscious grace, to draw later. At one point I glanced across at Mr Farrow, and saw him regarding his daughters with a look of justifiable complacency and pride. Catching my eye, he looked quickly back at me with an odd expression – chin high, a taut smile that was almost a scowl – that I found hard to read: Defiance? Warning? An acknowledgement that no man of flesh and blood could be immune to Marianne's beauty, and that he had read my thoughts? Discomposed again, I attempted to hide it by joining in the clapping from the guests – for at that moment the last chord resounded around the room, and Juliana looked up, then down again, with a quick, tight smile.

'Enchanting!' proclaimed Mrs Greenlaw. 'What delightfully accomplished daughters you have, Ernest! Marianne, will you not take your turn, and sing for us? I know you sing beautifully.'

Marianne declined, and soon the guests departed – Mr Greenlaw wringing my hand, and repeating his suggestion that I should go and dine with him and his wife – and, almost immediately after, the two girls wished me goodnight. No doubt they wanted to talk privately about the evening. About to retire to bed also, I found myself pressed to stay a while with Mr Farrow, and to drink brandy.

We returned to the drawing room. The night was warm, and the double doors still thrown open to the indigo night. I heard an owl call; its low, thrilling *whoo-woo* stirred something within me, and I felt that I should rather walk outside alone, down to the lake, to look at the moon reflected there. I did not want to desert my employer, however, if he wanted to talk.

At first he said little; he poured generous measures of brandy into balloon glasses, offered me a cigar, then reclined on the sofa, smoking, and looking at the ceiling. I wondered why he wanted my company, for in this contemplative mood he might have been content with his own. However, I was gratified that he felt no need to keep up a flow of talk. We smoked, and sipped our brandy, in quiet companionship.

'Well, I think that went off very well,' he remarked, after a while.

'Indeed – the fare was excellent, and I am quite sure everyone enjoyed themselves.'

He looked at me through blue smoke-haze. 'Not too dull for you? Mrs Greenlaw's a terrible bore, of course, but her husband's a sound fellow. If he wants you to paint their portrait, I'd strongly advise you to accept.'

'Portrait painting is not my speciality,' I pointed out.

'He's no connoisseur; he'd be easily pleased. But it's up to you. Damn pity Charlotte couldn't have been here this evening. She knows how to handle people, in her unobtrusive way. It put a strain on Juliana, I know. Still, she conducted herself well. You helped her a great deal, for which I'm grateful. And so, I'm sure, is she.'

I was beginning to feel wary of any mention of Juliana. 'Are you afraid of a recurrence of her illness?'

He looked at me steadily. 'Oh no. That's quite in the past – she's made a complete recovery. It was a – a malady of adolescence, that was all.'

'A nervous complaint?' I ventured, remembering what Charlotte had told me.

'Of a very minor kind. You know what young girls are like. You've a sister, haven't you?'

I nodded, though Isobel was of robust constitution.

'Now, about tomorrow,' my employer continued. 'I have business to attend to, which will keep me at home. Would you accompany the girls to church? Juliana would be sorry to miss it. With Charlotte away, it will be just the three of you. I should be grateful.'

I hesitated, guessing how my appearance with Juliana on my arm would be interpreted by others besides Mrs Greenlaw. But I would also be Marianne's legitimate escort . . . and besides, I saw that if I agreed to this, it would give me an advantage when I wanted to absent myself from Fourwinds for a day or two. 'Yes, of course,' I said. 'It will be my pleasure.'

'Thank you – I'm obliged.' Mr Farrow swirled the amber liquid in his glass. 'You'll know a few people now, of course. That friend of the Greenlaws, Mademoiselle Duchêne – she's a handsome woman. Stylish, but rather overdressed for my taste. Spends a lot of time in Paris, I hear. Of course, it's hard for Juliana to put her in the same room as a woman of fashion like that.'

I nodded, wondering what he was leading to; but he fell silent, and continued smoking for some minutes, occasionally giving a sigh, whether of contentment or tiredness I could not tell. I sipped my brandy, and he sipped his; the clock ticked, and a moth blundered against the mantel.

'There's something I shall always regret, you

know,' he said, after an interval. 'I always wanted a son. Girls are fine in their way, but – well' – he waved his cigar as if in explanation – 'it's not the same. They'll marry, of course. A son, though – he'd inherit this place, have sons of his own. What's the use of it all, without a son to leave it to?'

I watched him, thinking: Yes, I see where your thoughts are leading. If you marry Annette Duchêne – or any other eligible and attractive woman, young enough to bear children – you still have the chance of producing the heir you so badly want. I gave a murmur of assent, which was encouragement enough for him to continue.

'Constance, you see,' he went on, 'lost a baby boy. My son. Stillborn. Four years after Marianne. After that, there was one miscarriage after another. Wretched business. A terrible drain on her strength. Eventually the doctors said there must be no more. Oh, I paid for all sorts of physicians, second, third and fourth opinions. The best doctors money could buy. But they were all agreed. Connie's health wouldn't stand it.'

'I am sincerely sorry,' I said in a low voice, 'for your loss – and that Mrs Farrow suffered so greatly.'

He closed his eyes, lying back. 'I am a fortunate man in many ways, Samuel. You can see that from everything I have around me. But that . . .' He gave out a slow exhalation of smoke, then opened his eyes and looked at me. 'It is the tragedy of my life.'

Unsure what to say to this, I began to stutter a reply, but he went on: 'You're a young man, fit, in your prime, with talent and a purpose in life – at your age, everything seems yours for the taking. But it can turn sour, more quickly than you imagine. Things start to go wrong, there are obstacles you never dreamed of, you lose your direction and blunder off, and there's no finding your way back. Don't let it happen to you, Samuel. Marry, that's my advice to you – marry, and have a son to carry on your name, a son you can be proud of.'

While he spoke, he turned away from me and lay back with his eyes half closed. I gazed at him through a veil of smoke, with the pleasantly warm, floating sense of having consumed more alcohol than I was used to – quantities of wine, port and now brandy. Urgently I wanted to say something profound, to contribute to the intimacy he seemed to be offering.

'If I can be of any help, please say the word,' I offered. My words slurred themselves together – and whatever did I mean? – but at the same time I felt a curious, heady freedom.

'There's only one thing you need do.' His voice seemed to float towards me. 'Stay with us. Stay with us here. I promise you, you will never regret it.'

Why should I want to leave? I caught myself up in confusion, unsure whether I had only thought this, or spoken it aloud; but abruptly, Mr Farrow seemed embarrassed by what he had just said.

'Well, I won't keep you from your bed,' he told me, pushing himself upright. 'It's been a long day. Thank you for all you did this evening.' He stoppered the decanter, stubbed out his cigar, and replaced the lid of the Havana box. 'Goodnight, Samuel.'

I bade him farewell, but instead of ascending the stairs to my room, I went through the open door and walked out to the lawn, relishing my elevated mood, the touch of the night air on my face. Looking up at the dizzy spread of stars, I felt that I could release the hold of gravity and tumble into their depths. That sweep of sky ought to have made me feel minuscule, insignificant, but instead I was filled with a sense of my own importance. The grass seemed to bear me up springily; my head swam as though I were afloat on swelling waves; I felt peculiarly exultant, as if my well-being were assured from this point on, and I need do nothing but allow fate to sweep me, like a bobbing cork on a tide, from one piece of good fortune to the next. My father must have been a fool, to disparage me so; for here in contrast was a man who valued my qualities, and was generous with the praise and encouragement my own father had denied me.

I had severely misjudged Ernest Farrow. Even tonight, I had suspected him of calculating the benefits of a union with Annette Duchêne. Instead, he was seeking in me the son he lacked; he had almost pleaded with me to accept what he offered. Whether he wanted me for substitute son, or son-in-law, I was unclear. But as I stood on the lawn, giddied by stars, anything seemed possible; anything I chose.

Chapter Twenty

Scarlet

I had no choice but to extend my stay. I paid for another night at the boarding house, and informed Mr Farrow by telegram that I should have to remain in Eastbourne until Monday; there were funeral arrangements to be made, and no one but myself to make them. Moreover, I should have to see Mr Deakins, the solicitor.

Impatient with all of this, I longed to return to Fourwinds, the quiet of the downland surroundings, and my dear girls, especially Juliana. No sooner had the door closed behind me, and the nurse been left to perform her final services for my grandmother, than I was seized by a mood of recklessness. As I wandered, my feet took me to a parade of the smartest shops. Going into a ladies' outfitters, I was quite bedazzled by the array of dresses, hats, undergarments, shoes, adornments and fripperies of all kinds. Of course, I should have to appear in mourning until I left Eastbourne; a special department offered very luxurious mourning clothes in velvets and silks, though I saw no reason to waste money on them. Since my wardrobe was predominantly grey and black, I should have no difficulty in presenting myself suitably. While I was choosing a pair of gloves for Juliana and a hair comb for Marianne, my eye was caught by more brightly hued items.

Half an hour later I left the shop, with my packages wrapped in tissue. One of the wrappings concealed a blouse of vivid scarlet, high-necked, with a ruffled front. When I should ever wear it, I had no idea; it was a foolish extravagance. Yet, as I made my way towards the premises of Deakins and Murdoch, Solicitors, I felt a secret, furtive pride in owning such a boldly colourful garment.

In a sombre office lined with shelf upon shelf of heavy books and files, Mr Arthur Deakins received me, and offered his condolences. He was a man of perhaps fifty, with a shiny forehead and a bristling, tobacco-stained moustache.

'I may as well be frank,' I told him, since I was neither tearful nor downcast, 'and tell you that I have not seen Mrs Newbold for more than eight years; when we did meet, her treatment of me was coldly formal. Therefore I cannot claim to be much saddened by her death. I am greatly surprised, in fact, that she thought of sending for me. I am afraid that I must leave all arrangements for her burial in the hands of a funeral director, since I must urgently return to my place of employment, and cannot stay here beyond Monday.'

'I see.' He raised an eyebrow at this. 'Well, Miss Agnew, your grandmother has done all she could to ease your burden. Her Will is very particular in its instructions concerning the funeral.'

'Mrs Newbold must have had some reason for telling you that she is my grandmother,' I told him, 'but she has always disguised this relationship by calling herself my great-aunt. That is what is believed in her household, and I see no reason to change that perception. She could not let it be known that I was her daughter's daughter, so the fiction was created that she was my great-aunt, and that I was the offspring of her nephew, who was widowed and incapable of caring for me.'

Mr Deakins nodded. 'Thank you, Miss Agnew. I am acquainted with some of the details, but you may be able to furnish me with more. Your mother, Mrs Violet Morris, is also estranged? There has been no contact between you since she departed for Kenya?'

'That is correct. Although I cannot speak with any certainty, I doubt that there was much contact between my mother and grandmother. My grandfather died while I was still a baby, and my grandmother remarried soon after. On this second marriage, she moved up in the world, and seemed desirous of casting off all reminders of her first. I was an embarrassment to her.'

Hearing the note of bitterness in my voice, I knew that I had said too much, and fell silent.

'You have had to make your own way in the world, Miss Agnew?' Mr Deakins said, in a kindly tone.

I did not want his sympathy. Looking down at my hands, I saw that I had picked at the skin around one thumbnail until it bled. I could have told him more: of the drabness of my South London boarding school, of the uninspired teaching, the dull food and the sparse dormitories, of the weeks I spent alone there while the other girls went home for their holidays. Yet I had learned one valuable lesson there. Since my own wits were all I had to rely on, I had better sharpen them.

'Yes,' I replied. 'I stayed on at school as pupil-teacher, before finding my present position as governess. But, Mr Deakins, I have not come here to talk about myself. Please continue.'

He shuffled his papers. 'Presumably, you're aware that your grandmother's second marriage, to Geoffrey Newbold, resulted in a son, Edward? He would of course have been her heir, but he was killed in the Transvaal, only last year.'

'Yes, I have heard that.'

'Edward Newbold was barely twenty – it was a grievous loss to his mother, and, needless to say, he was unmarried and died without issue. Soon after his death, Mrs Newbold summoned me to make amendments to her Will. Of course, it would be more usual for relatives to hear of the contents of the Will at a later stage than this, but since you are here only for a short time, and your mother, the only other interested party, is not in the country, I see no harm in mentioning it to you now. Until recently, your grandmother had left everything to her son – the house, her investments, and her late husband's substantial shares in the London, Brighton and South Coast Railway. After Edward Newbold's sad demise, she asked me to change her Will, leaving all her assets, excepting the house, to your mother.'

'I see. They are considerable, I suppose.' How I longed to finish with this tedious business and leave the dusty, dimly-lit office! Oppressed by the dinginess of the furnishings and shelves, I wanted to walk on the beach and gaze out at the sea. What could this matter to me? As soon as my grandmother was in her coffin, I could dismiss her from my thoughts; as I had done these eight years or more.

'Yes, indeed,' Mr Deakins replied. 'Mr Newbold was a shrewd businessman; by the time of his death he was a moderately wealthy man. But, my dear young lady, you surprise me by showing no curiosity about your grandmother's house!' His mouth twitched into a smile beneath his moustache. 'Miss Agnew, Three Sussex Esplanade is left to you.'

Next day I could accomplish nothing, for it was Sunday. In the morning I went to church, where I offered the most perfunctory prayers for my grandmother, though I felt it was insincere to do even this. My church-going was, in any case, a matter of form rather than compunction; I went chiefly because Juliana insisted, with much fervour, on attending each Sunday. If she were here, warm-hearted creature that she was, she would undoubtedly shed more tears for my grandmother, a complete stranger, than were likely to escape from my own dry eyes.

Juliana! The realization that had come to me by the tide's edge seemed newly outrageous each time I considered it. Demure Juliana, the mother of an illegitimate child! Impossible – yet, each time, fresh consideration convinced me that it must be so; it could not be otherwise. At St Nicholas's, our parish church, she did not simply go through the motions, as Marianne and I did, of kneeling, singing, and making the required responses. She seemed genuinely moved by the hymns, the prayers and the sermon, and was usually quiet and withdrawn in the gig on the way home, while Marianne and I talked together. Poor girl! What mental torments she must have concealed – and my anger rose more strongly against Hardacre and Waring every time I thought of them. How they had taken advantage of her compliance, of her unsuspecting good nature!

As Mr Deakins had told me, my grandmother's stipulations regarding the funeral were very precise; she had even arranged for the payment to be made from her estate. Thus, there was little for me to do but set things in motion with the undertakers, and send out cards announcing the death, giving the time and place of the burial. It was to be a costly business; she had ordained enough pomp and ceremony to satisfy an entire dynasty of mourners. There was to be a hearse and two mourning coaches, each drawn by four horses; there would be plumes of ostrich feathers, brass handles to the coffin, and a velvet pall over it; there would be pages and coachmen. Her acquaintances, I trusted, would suffice to fill these carriages, though I should have no means of knowing. Mr Deakins would attend, as her representative.

On Monday, I made arrangements with the undertaker, then returned to Sussex Esplanade to inform my grandmother's staff that her funeral would take place on Friday. Summoning the cook, maid and boy, I gave them their instructions: they must receive the mourners after the burial, and provide refreshment; after that, they should place dustsheets over the furniture and shut up the house, for their employment would be at an end forthwith. Mr Deakins would arrange payment, and provide each of them with a written character reference, which would help them to find new positions. The maid, a good, earnest girl, became red-eyed and sniffy at this, while the cook only looked cross, and the boy bewildered. Thanking them for all they had done in my grandmother's service, I suspected that they had had an easier time of it than they would find elsewhere. When they left the house at the end of the week, the keys would remain with the solicitors until such time as I required access.

When would that be? What should I do?

'Of course,' Mr Deakins had said in his office, surrounded by files and deeds and legal reference books, 'you will wish to resign from your post as governess? In your position I should sell the house, buy a smaller one and invest the proceeds to give myself an income. You could make a good deal more from the sale of the furniture and paintings, if you wished. I can recommend a reliable valuer.'

I told him that I would do nothing until I had given the matter further thought. Now, however, I looked around the house, roaming from room to room. *My* house, as I should soon be able to call it, when all the formalities were completed. It seemed so improbable that I laughed aloud, startling myself with my irreverence, and in a house of mourning! Shocked at my behaviour, I was in such a flippant mood that I could not make myself care. Maybe I was suffering from shock, for I certainly felt as light-headed as if I had consumed a quantity of wine or spirits.

Everything the house contained would be mine too, to keep or dispose of as I wished: Mr Deakins had explained that. Looking around, I adopted a haughty air, ready to find fault with everything. Used as I was to the spaciousness of Fourwinds, and to the simple lines, sturdy materials and good craftsmanship favoured by Mr Farrow, I saw my grandmother's house as intolerably cluttered: the walls were hung with gloomy portraits and landscapes, the reception rooms were crammed with any number of little tables, plant stands, chiffoniers, upholstered chairs, screens and footstools, and every available surface was covered with a tasselled or embroidered cloth and loaded with ornaments. What should be done with it all? The challenge was enough to make me quail.

Well, I need not trouble myself with it now. I left the house, and stepped out again to the breezy promenade. Still in a peculiarly frivolous mood which I hardly recognized, I reflected that I had more freedom now than ever before in my life. Soon, with money and property, I would be a woman of means. If I chose, I could send a telegram to Fourwinds to say that I would not be returning; I could ask for my belongings to be forwarded to me. I had enough money about me for a train ticket and a hotel; I could go wherever I chose. What was to stop me? Now, today, I could go to the train station and buy a ticket for London, or Edinburgh; I could cross the Channel to Deauville, Calais or even Paris, and live there independently; when I ran short of money, I could ask Mr Deakins to sell some of my grandmother's valuables.

This flight of fancy was short-lived, however, and by the time I was seated on the train back to Staverton, I had scolded myself into a more sober mood. Whatever had I been thinking? How could I have contemplated abandoning Marianne and Juliana and Mr Farrow – my only family? Reynolds met me with the pony-chaise, and, jolted and jaunced over the rough ground for the few miles back to Fourwinds, I had time to regain my composure, and for Charlotte Agnew, governess and companion, to become herself again.

What use to me were money, investments, or a house in Eastbourne? All my material needs were met at Fourwinds; and what I lacked, no amount of money could buy.

Chapter Twenty-one

Marianne

On Monday evening after dinner, I set up my stool and easel on the north side of the house, with paints and brushes arranged on the grass at my feet. Mr Farrow was in his study, the girls in the drawing room; the front door was open, and occasionally Marianne came to look out at me. She did not speak, but tiptoed back indoors, with pantomimed gestures of *Artist at work – do not disturb*. Charlotte was expected back on the late train, and Reynolds had gone with the chaise to meet her.

I mixed my colours and looked at the patterns of light and shade, of brick and tile and stone. In this picture – which was not one of Mr Farrow's suggestions – I wanted to capture the cool of evening, the shadows stealing across the grass, together with the simple Gothic arch of the porch, and the steps leading up; through the open door, glimpses of lit lamps, flower vases and wood panelling within, and the sweep of stairway. The North Wind sculpture would be in shade – merely hinted at, in cold blue-grey tones. More detailed renditions of the three Winds would be painted separately. Rather, I mean, of all four – for I could not resist giving my interpretation of the West. Mr Farrow could discard it if he chose.

I made marks on my canvas, I sat back and considered, I looked and I looked. Turtledoves nearby were crooning from a treetop; I smelled crushed grass and leaf mould, the fertile scents of the earth; swifts hurled themselves in arrow-clusters high above, screaming their summer cry of freedom and joyousness. To my right, the sun was setting in a glorious striation of golds and purples, so that the west façade, out of my view, must be ablaze in light. I felt that I would not exchange my situation for all the riches in the world. Truly, I had fallen in love; I had fallen under the spell of Fourwinds. I wanted to think of the place as my own; so utterly had it claimed me.

Listening, I tried to hear whether Juliana was at the piano indoors; its sound on the air would have completed the perfection of the evening. She had been playing earlier in the afternoon. I had not recognized the tune, but it was probably Chopin, her favourite – something minor key, part playful, part regretful. Its mood of longing had pulled me to the doorway of the drawing room, where I stood very still, watching her. She was alone; her face was still and serious, drawn into a pretty frown of concentration, her head bent; her lack of awareness of being observed added charm to the tableau. I could paint her like this, I thought; for today I felt my fingers itching with more pictures than I could hold in my head, my mind tingling with light and colour and atmosphere. If I did so, I should want to paint the music, to have the air of the room filled with its tones, so that the observer could hear as clearly as see, could be saddened and gladdened and teased by it. Although I did not want to break the spell by letting Juliana see me, I loitered there, knowing that if I stepped forward into the room, she would reward me with a look of welcoming radiance.

Now, catching myself smiling all over again, I allowed myself to entertain the fancy that this, if I chose, could be my future. I saw myself as Juliana's husband; imagined myself approaching my pretty wife at the piano, stooping to kiss her, inhaling the scent of her perfume, her hair; I would ask her to play my favourite piece, and she would gladly oblige.

Why not?

The idea was not of my own devising, but once planted in my mind it was proving difficult to dislodge. With it came the knowledge that, in this little scene, Fourwinds would be mine, or destined to be mine – for Juliana would inherit, and I with her. If we had a son, he would be heir to Fourwinds, and Mr Farrow's purpose would be achieved, at one remove – for this conjectural son would be a Godwin, not a Farrow.

Why not? What is to stop you? goaded my insistent inner voice.

I do not love her, I answered at once.

No, you do not, but that can easily be overcome.

But what of Marianne?

You must forget Marianne. She is not for you.

But . . . but . . . I do not like this scheming way of thinking. It sits uneasily with thoughts of marriage.

Do nothing. Be compliant. Accept what is offered you.

This train of thought was disturbing, for I feared that persuasive inner traitor.

Leave me alone. Don't tempt me like this.

Briskly, matter-of-factly, I marshalled my arguments. I was only one-and-twenty, still young to be thinking of marriage; I had no means of supporting a wife; when I did consider it, I should marry for love, and for nothing less. Juliana was a pleasant, amiable girl; she would be a loving and devoted wife to – to whoever was lucky enough to win her . . .

Finding that I did not like this thought either, I called myself to attention, and set myself the task of mixing the precise shade of purplish-grey I needed for cold shadow on stone. I managed to concentrate for some while on the rendering of shade around the figure of the North Wind.

When I heard the clop of hooves and the rumble of wheels, I realized that the light had faded too much to continue. I began to put away my tubes of paint, leaving my brushes to soak in turpentine. The chaise bowled up to the door, and Charlotte alighted, thanking Reynolds for coming out so late to meet her. Hector, the pony, had seen me in the shadows; his ears pricked alertly towards me, like those of a gun dog.

'Good evening, Charlotte! Let me take your bag.' As I stepped forward, Reynolds touched his cap and drove on towards the stables. The tread of hooves quickened to a neat trot, fading beneath the trees; the warm smell of horsehide and sweat lingered behind. Charlotte and I stood smiling at each other.

'I am happy to see you back,' I told her. 'I hope you're not too tired after your journey?'

'I am very glad to return. No, not tired at all.'

I felt then that I should very much like to speak to Charlotte alone – to tell her of all that had happened during her absence – but, of course, both girls clamoured for her company. My enquiries about the nature of her visit to Eastbourne were met with the same reticence as before; all she would say was that it was some business matter concerning a distant relative, something tedious, and not quite concluded. 'I may be called upon to return there, at some time in the future,' she added, 'but it's of no great importance, and need not concern us now.'

We had moved into the vestibule. I saw Charlotte's eyes lift to the study door on the half-landing; and as if prompted by her glance, the door opened and Mr Farrow came down the stairs towards us.

'So! You have come back. I hope you had a tolerable journey.'

She turned towards him, smiling. 'Good evening, sir. Yes, I—'

'Well, we have managed perfectly well by ourselves.' He stood between Juliana and Marianne, his arms resting lightly on their shoulders. 'We hardly noticed you were gone. Our dinner party went splendidly without you.'

My eyes were on Charlotte's face; I saw her glad expression change to one of hurt rebuff, which she immediately concealed. 'I am pleased to hear it,' she replied.

'*I* missed you!' said Marianne, ducking away from her father, and taking Charlotte's arm. 'So did Juley! Let me tell you all about the guests, and the ladies' dresses, and—' She would have moved into the morning room, but her father said, 'Don't bore Miss Agnew with your chatter, Marianne.'

'I am not bored,' Charlotte replied.

Mr Farrow nodded. 'Well, it's good to see you back,' he said.

'Charlotte, you must be tired, and hungry besides,' said Juliana. 'I have asked Mrs Reynolds to have something ready.'

I wished I had thought of that myself – for Charlotte had looked after me better, when I had been the weary traveller. Fifteen minutes later she was seated in the dining room with a light meal of soup, bread and fruit.

Shortly after, at my urging, the two girls retired to bed, content that she was back under their roof. I stayed on, taking my chance for the private conversation I had wanted; but of course, the two subjects most occupying me could not easily be broached with Charlotte. Namely: the contrivances that seemed intent on pairing me with Juliana; and the determination I had formed, of travelling to Chichester at the first opportunity, to seek out Gideon Waring. Instead, I attempted to make up for Mr Farrow's brusqueness.

'Don't take to heart what he said just now – for I could see you felt slighted. We all missed you sorely, especially at the dinner party. He felt your absence as much as we did, I am sure. This is just his way.'

Charlotte looked bleak for a moment. I understood how highly she prized Mr Farrow's approval, and how keenly she felt any slight. Quickly she changed the subject, asking me about my impressions of the dinner guests, and how the drawing lessons were progressing, and whether there had been any more instances of sleepwalking on Marianne's part.

'No, I think not,' I answered. 'Juliana, at her own suggestion, has been sleeping in Marianne's room, and neither has mentioned any disturbance. I'm sure, though,' I added, 'that all of us will sleep more soundly, now that you're back with us.'

'Thank you, Samuel, for all you have done during my absence. Knowing that you were here made me a good deal easier in my mind than I should have been otherwise.'

It struck me at once – this was the very first time she had dropped her reserve sufficiently to address me as Samuel. Secretly pleased, I protested that I had done nothing at all; and on that cordial note of mutual appreciation, we wished each other goodnight.

Upstairs in my room, I sat as usual with my windows thrown open to the air, for I loved to hear the night sounds: the owl that haunted the grounds, the baaing of sheep from the hillside, the little nameless squeaks and cries of small animals or birds about their nocturnal business. After a while, at the risk of attracting moths and other flying insects, I turned on the lamp, and fetched my sketchbook.

It had become my custom, for the half-hour or so before getting into bed, to work on a set of drawings

I did not intend anyone to see. Some were of Juliana, for I had become intrigued by the sadness that belied her habitual air of mild content. Most, though, were of Marianne, and from memory, for I would not risk discovery by putting pencil to paper in her presence.

Whilst in London, and a frequent visitor to galleries and exhibitions, I had become much interested in the work of Dante Gabriel Rossetti. My tutor at the Slade had been scathing on the one occasion when I mentioned this, condemning Rossetti for lack of technique and for sensationalism. He directed my attention instead towards Ingres, Stubbs, Reynolds and Gainsborough, but Rossetti's paintings continued to attract me. More accurately, I should say that his women fascinated me, with their bold glances, their sensually curved lips, and their rippling manes of hair. Since I had come to Fourwinds, Rossetti's Mary Nazarene, his Beata Beatrix, and his Damsel of the Holy Grail, had been replaced in my thoughts by Marianne. Marianne as I dreamed of her, Marianne as I tortured myself my imagining her: her flesh-tones, her wondrous hair, her peculiar intensity that seemed to impress her personality on mine. Maybe Marianne matched the ideal that these paintings had formed in my mind, and that was why I had immediately been attracted to her; or perhaps her beauty and personality had supplanted all other images, making me almost believe that Rossetti had her in mind while he gazed at his model.

I worked at my drawing, concentrating on the glint of eye-white, the lips softly parted, the texture of hair. I could possess her in this way, if in no other.

Footsteps in the corridor outside barely disturbed my concentration; I assumed it to be Charlotte, on her way to her room. When the steps paused at my threshold, I listened more keenly. After a pause came a light rapping at my door – yes, Charlotte it could only be, come with some query, or some important reminder.

And so my smile was for Charlotte as I opened the door.

It was Marianne who stood there – in a long white nightgown, a fringed shawl of peacock blues and greens thrown over it, her hair loose about her shoulders, and her eyes – the eyes I had just been trying to capture with line and shade – looking brightly into mine. Had it not been for the intentness of those eyes, I should have suspected her of sleepwalking again. I found myself thinking of Ophelia, in the Millais painting – beautiful drowned Ophelia, clutching her posy of wild flowers, her hair floating on the water.

'Samuel, let me come in.' She was almost past me – quickly I stretched out an arm to the doorframe, barring entry.

'You cannot!' My heart was beating so powerfully that I felt sure Marianne must hear it.

'I want to show you something.' She held, not a posy, but her sketchbook. 'Please, Samuel, don't be stuffy. It's important.'

The gallery was in darkness; the household was asleep; the only light came from the lamp on my bureau. 'What is it?'

'Let me in – I'll show you.'

I hesitated; no one need know. 'Very well – but only for a moment. It is not seemly, Marianne, for you to visit me here, and at this hour – you know that.' I dropped my arm, and as she entered, quickly crossed the room to close my own drawing pad, which lay open on the bureau.

She made a small sound of derision at my warning. 'I saw your light – I knew you were still up. What are you doing, so late?'

'Reading,' I lied. I saw her eyes flickering round my room with interest, resting on each of my possessions in turn. 'Now, what is it that cannot wait till morning?'

She flicked open her sketchbook, and held it out to me. 'I wanted to show you this. The West Wind. I know you are just as intrigued as I am. I meant what I said at dinner, Samuel – the West Wind must be found! Everything will go amiss, until he is in his place.'

She gazed at me earnestly – almost passionately. Not for the first time, I found myself wondering if she could really be in her right mind; this seemed such an obsession with her.

'He?' I queried. 'You are sure of that?'

'Oh yes.'

Taking her drawing, I carried it over to the lamp to study it. She waited in silence. I looked up at her; looked back at the page.

'You see,' she offered, 'when I picked up your sketch the other day, I saw that you had been trying to guess – but you had made him female, and quite different in character.'

'You looked at my sketch?' For a dizzying instant I thought myself discovered; then gratefully remembered that the drawings of her were in a separate book, which never left my room.

'Yes.' She coloured slightly. 'You left it lying on the bench while you went to fetch something. I did not think you would mind.'

I did mind; but could hardly reprimand her, in the knowledge that I had been identically tempted by *her* sketchings. 'My attempt was all wrong, you say – how can you know that?'

'Because . . .' She came nearer, and gestured towards the book in my hand.

I turned the page and looked. 'When did you draw this?'

'Some while ago – when Mr Waring was with us.'

'And you copied this? From a sketch of his? Or – from the carving itself?'

She darted me a look in which fear and daring were mingled. 'Yes. I have seen it.'

'So a carving exists? You have seen it here? Marianne, you have never told me that – though I am certain I've asked you. Where was it?'

'I did see! Why won't you believe me? No one else did. Gideon was . . . secretive, about his carvings. He would never let Papa see the pieces until they were finished. But he let me watch him in his workshop. He never minded.'

'Why was that?' I asked sharply.

'Because I was interested. I loved to watch him at work. His hands – how skilled they were, how clever.

The same way I love to watch you paint, now,' she said simply, 'when you don't object.'

She was standing a little too close. My senses were so full of her that I could hardly breathe. If I moved my hand towards her, I could entwine it in her hair, trace with my finger the smooth line of her neck – I swallowed, making an involuntary gulping sound – surely she could not be unaware? With one movement I could draw her to me, let my arms enfold her strong, supple body, I could inhale the perfume of her skin, her hair, I could—

'Marianne,' I said, and making a stern effort to master myself, I took a step back, colliding awkwardly with the chest of drawers, 'you must go now. Goodnight.' I stepped round her, moving towards the door. 'I hope you will sleep well. Thank you for showing me this,' I added, realizing that I still held her book. 'Maybe I shall borrow it another day, if you agree. I should like to make a copy.'

'Keep it now!' Following me, she paused in the doorway. 'I want you to look at the other drawings there. Samuel, please?'

'Of course, if that is what you wish.'

She left without wishing me goodnight, as if suddenly anxious to be gone. I waited while she ran lightly down the stairs towards her own room; then closed my door, went to the window and inhaled deeply. Marianne! Breathing out, I pronounced her name soundlessly. Blood was pulsing fast through my veins; I was tingling and hot; to tell the simple truth, I was on fire with longing. This, as I have said, can be

an almost comical state when observed in others –
how mercilessly Chas and I had teased Johnny for his
lusting after the furniture-shop girl! But, experienced
like this, urgent and insistent, it called upon some
deep, powerful instinct – an instinct that seemed to
make me one with the night outside, with the stars in
their courses, with the unseen creatures that lived and
spawned and fought and died. What compelled their
actions was the same irresistible force that stirred every
part of me now. It was almost a torture to stand here,
attempting to calm myself by will alone, when my
blood and my heart and all my senses yearned for
fulfilment.

I went to the washstand and splashed cold water
over my face, hands and neck, soaking my shirt in the
process. Roughly towelling myself, I paced the floor a
few times; then remembered that Marianne's room
was directly underneath, and that she might hear. She
could already be in bed: I pictured her abundant hair
spread on a pillow, her eyes closed, her body warm in
sleep – then let out a groan as I tried, against hope,
to banish such thoughts from my mind.

Her drawings. I would look at her drawings, and
apply my mind sternly to composition and execution.
Sitting at my window, I took up the book she had
handed me, and opened it at its first page.

She had been right to say that my imagined version
of the West Wind was very little like hers. Allowing for
the roughness of her technique, she had caught something of Waring's style – the clean line, the simplicity,
the animation. My West Wind had been a benign

female zephyr, rather anodyne, lacking the character of her brothers and sister. The figure Marianne had drawn certainly did not lack personality. He was male – I had supposed that balance and symmetry required a female, but he was emphatically male – less ethereal than his brother the East, more solidly muscled, more human. It was the face that demanded attention. Possibly, what I saw was attributable more to Marianne's heavy-handedness than to the sculptor's intent: a face that could have belonged to a medieval gargoyle, a face contorted with malice and scheming. Even the posture suggested creeping, spying, and furtiveness. I looked and looked, and saw that with his opposing pairs of Winds – if Marianne's rendering was at all accurate – Waring had created various contrasts: not only the obvious warmth and coldness, but also youth against age, fear against aggression, innocence against cynicism. More than ever I longed to see the original of this, the living – for I could not avoid thinking of it as living – stone. Had Mr Farrow, I wondered, seen it and disapproved? Rejected it, even – asked Waring to start again? Could that be the cause of the rift – rather than, as Charlotte supposed, Waring's liaison with Eliza Hardacre?

I turned the page, turned again, and again. Marianne must have drawn the sketches that followed in the grip of feverish obsession, even hallucination. She had drawn the stone figure not once, but many times; the pages seemed to tell a story. In her clumsy drawing, the gargoyle figure rose from his stone back-ground and became a living, breathing man; he stole up on the benign female figure of the South Wind, he gripped and overcame her, he twisted her to face him, he clasped a hand over her mouth – I caught my breath, unable to believe what I saw in the final drawing. I saw male and female body locked together; I saw grasping hands, spread legs, a humped back; I saw the act of coupling, grossly delineated—

In revulsion I turned away; then looked back, trying to make sense of what Marianne had drawn.

How could she have imagined such a thing?

Immediately the answer supplied itself: *She had not imagined.* Charlotte's words floated into my mind: 'Marianne has seen things that no child ought to be exposed to.' And I knew that I was looking at Gideon Waring and Eliza Hardacre, as Marianne must have seen them – must, surely, have stumbled across them, caught unawares in careless fornication.

If *I* were shocked by what I saw here, what impression must it have made on her tender young mind?

I slapped the book shut, feeling that I was in possession of something incriminating, something filthy. What could be Marianne's motive in bringing it to me? Why did she wish me to know what she had seen? Was there, perhaps, a kind of bravado in it, a wish to show me that she was not a child? I recalled her fear that the West Wind was gusting free; that it must be recaptured and fixed in place on its wall. Did she feel *herself* at risk, while it roamed?

I let out an appalled exclamation; I stood, sat on my bed, stood again; I was quite beside myself with the shock of realization.

It was Waring she feared; it must be. In her torment she had confused him with the Wind of his creation. Had he – had he dared to force his attentions on *her*, taking advantage of her innocent interest? Good God – the thought was not to be tolerated! And was *this*, then, the reason for his dismissal?

I paced my room; I sweated; I was nauseous with loathing and impotent with anger; my fists clenched in futile aggression.

And part of my anger was turned against myself. Had I not – only now – been indulging, even enjoying, my own aching desire? For an instant I felt the same revulsion for myself as I did for Gideon Waring; I felt tainted with his lasciviousness. Yet I could not quite call it lasciviousness; there was such pure, instinctive, single-mindedness in my yearning that I could not believe it harmful, either to myself or to the unwitting Marianne.

But *this* . . .

Eventually, slowly, I undressed for bed. I was certain I should not sleep, but was woken by early bird-song, my head teeming with images of faces and bodies, twining, grappling and writhing. That grinning gargoyle visage leered at me, mocking and triumphant.

Chapter Twenty-two

Proposal

My feelings on returning to Fourwinds were very much mixed.

Having looked forward to everything being exactly as I left it, of course I was disappointed. Juliana, though evidently much happier than when I had left her, was so irrevocably changed in my view that I hardly knew how to look at her. Samuel I planned to manipulate for my own ends, or rather for Juliana's. Mr Farrow seemed intent on demonstrating that I had not been missed at all; it was his way, I suppose, of showing disapproval. As for myself: I was not quite the person who had departed only a few days ago, though I had determined to say and do nothing with regard to my changed circumstances. Only Marianne, full of chatter and excitement at my return, was quite as I expected.

Naturally, they were curious, all of them (Marianne overtly, the others with more discretion), about how my time had been spent in Eastbourne, and who I had seen there. Fobbing them off with vague replies, I diverted the conversation to what had happened at home during my absence, and was gratified to learn that the dinner party had given enjoyment to all concerned. Juliana, indeed, looked as though she had more to tell me, when we were alone. However, after I had given them their presents, the two girls retired to bed, leaving me with Samuel.

Having spent so much time alone in Eastbourne, I was glad indeed to see him again. Looking at his kind grey eyes, his nose a little reddened by the sun, and a dab of green paint on one cheek (for he had been painting by the north front when I arrived in the pony-chaise), I felt a rush of affection that almost made me forget my own deviousness. Dear boy: he was such an innocent, so open in his nature, so good-hearted! Although only a year his senior, I felt decades older in worldly wisdom and scepticism.

He told me a little more of the dinner guests, and of his attendance at church with the two girls. 'But how I ramble on!' he concluded. 'I am tiring you – I am sorry.'

'Not in the least,' I assured him; and, almost involuntarily, reached out a hand to smudge away the paint-mark from his cheek. He seemed to stop himself from flinching; then regarded me with surprise, as well he might. 'Pardon me,' I said, flustered; 'I could not help it – there is paint on your cheek which I have been longing to wipe away. But I am afraid the mark is still there.'

'It is oil paint,' he said, with a little laugh. 'Thank you, Charlotte – you treat me, I see, like one of your charges – like a little boy who bears the remains of

203

his meals on his face. I have some turpentine in my room; that will remove it.'

'Well, it is late.' I rose to my feet. 'Has Marianne been sleeping soundly? You have made no mention of any disturbance.'

He assured me that she had, that Juliana's bed was made up in her room and that I could retire to my own; and we parted for the night. As soon as I had unpacked my few things, looking with some bemusement at the scarlet blouse, which I consigned to a hanger at the very back of my wardrobe, I felt overcome with tiredness, almost too weary to prepare for bed.

Although I slept heavily, I was awake at my usual early hour, my mind very much occupied. Full of purpose, I washed and dressed. With my new resolution strong in my mind, I must lose no time.

Since my revelation on the beach at Eastbourne, in all the hours I had spent worrying and brooding, I had concluded that Samuel must, after all, marry Juliana. It was abundantly clear now that Mr Farrow had brought him to Fourwinds with precisely that end in view. No doubt there would be considerable enticements: Mr Farrow would provide Juliana with a generous dowry, and would build Samuel's reputation as a painter. Juliana's objections to such a marriage could, I felt, be overcome, if she believed Samuel to be genuinely attached to her. Samuel, for his part, would not marry Juliana unless he came to love her;

but this, I felt, could be brought about, with a little unobtrusive guidance from myself.

Unless I broached the subject at the first opportunity, I should be assailed by doubt. After breakfast, having arranged with Marianne that her studies would recommence at ten o'clock in the morning room, I went to find Juliana where I could speak to her alone. Having slept in the bed made up for her next to Marianne's, she had returned to her own room to dress her hair.

'So, my dear, how are you?' I began. 'I was so pleased last night to see you in better spirits than when I left.'

She was seated at the dressing table, hairbrush in hand. 'Maybe a little,' she replied, with the smallest of smiles.

'Please, let me.'

She turned to face the mirror; I stood behind her, and with gentle strokes took over the brushing. Such straight, silky hair she had, the colour of ripened wheat; so delicate in its fineness, each strand so easily broken. I must take great care.

'Mama used to do that for me, when I was a little girl,' Juliana said, half drowsily, soothed by the sweep of the brush. 'Do you remember your mother, Charlotte?'

'Hardly at all.'

'You tell us so little about yourself!' Her eyes in the mirror met mine. 'What do you remember? Surely you must have happy memories of her?'

'None that I can recall. I was so young when she passed away.'

'Poor Charlotte!' Her gaze in the mirror was warm with feeling. 'To have lacked a mother's love! And yet you are so kind, almost motherly yourself. You ought to marry, and have children of your own.'

'I see no possibility of that,' I said brusquely; this was not what I wanted to discuss.

'Do you not, Charlotte?' Her reflected glance flicked up at me, almost mischievous. 'Do you not have tender thoughts of someone very near? Do you never let yourself dream?'

She was referring to her father, of course; I was disturbed by her supposition, but she could hardly be more wrong. 'I don't know who you can mean,' I prevaricated, 'but, I assure you, I am far too sensible to do anything of the sort.' Picking up a hairpin, I held it between my teeth, while I twisted and coiled a lock of hair. 'Before I left for Eastbourne, you remember that we talked about Samuel.'

'Yes?' She looked at me alertly.

'You spoke of your concern,' I reminded her, 'that he might wish to marry you.'

'Marry me?' As though the subject had never been mentioned between us, she gave me another quick upward glance, then cast her eyes down. 'Yes. Of course I remember,' she replied; I saw the faint colour that rose to her cheeks, and knew that I had material to work on. She continued, 'Samuel is a good man, Charlotte – too good for me. At the dinner party, he could hardly have been kinder or more attentive. He saw my unease, and did all he could to smooth my path. I cannot express the gratitude I felt.'

'I hope you have told him?' Securing the strand of hair, I began brushing out the next.

'Yes, I have thanked him,' she said, still flushing; 'inadequately, I am sure.'

'He is, as you say, so good-hearted, so considerate, so affectionate – I should think any young lady would think herself lucky to be escorted by him,' I told her.

Juliana was sharp enough to see my purpose. 'Charlotte! What I have just said – I meant only to commend his qualities, nothing more. Surely you cannot be taking Papa's side – conniving against me? You cannot!' She turned her head away, so that the mirror showed me only her profile. 'Not when you have promised me your help!'

Kneeling by her chair, I looked into her face. 'Juliana – please believe me, when I tell you that your interests are dearer to me than anyone's. I am thinking of your happiness when I say this – that if you could only give Samuel some encouragement—'

She closed her eyes and shook her head rapidly. 'No! Don't ask it of me, Charlotte, please – don't speak of this again! If, truly, you care for me, you will not.'

It was impossible to dissemble any longer; I must speak more directly. 'Dearest,' I said softly, still on my knees, 'I believe I have guessed your secret – I think I know why you said, just now, that Samuel is too good for you, though you are wrong – quite wrong! If you tell me that – that what I believe to be true, *is* true, I think you will find your mind eased – we can talk together, you can unburden yourself. It has drained you, nurturing this secret for so long – I am only sorry it took me so long to divine the truth.'

So still was she, that for a moment I thought she had stopped breathing.

'I am right, am I not,' I said gently, 'that little Thomas Dearly is – is your own child?'

Still she seemed arrested in shock, and I doubted that she could have heard me. Although I did not want to, I was about to repeat what I had said, when she turned away from me with a flinging motion, and covered her face with both hands. As I embraced her, a sob broke from her, shaking her frame.

'Juliana, my love! It is not your fault, what has occurred – most emphatically not your fault!' I murmured. 'Gideon Waring – that wicked man – ought to be taken out and shot, for abusing you so! And Eliza Dearly – I know she calls herself your friend, and she has the care of the boy – but she too has most appallingly misused your trust. My poor girl – what terrible torment you have suffered!'

For long moments she was unable to speak at all. Deep, soundless sobs racked her; she seemed to struggle for breath. Alarmed lest she should collapse, I was almost relieved when she began to weep openly, inconsolably. After fetching first a fresh handkerchief, and then a glass of water, I soothed her while she sobbed. At last, when she had quite exhausted herself, I urged her to lie down on the bed, and rang for a pot of tea, which I intercepted at the door so that Alice should not see her distress and wonder at the cause of it.

'Charlotte,' Juliana said at last in a broken voice, huddling into herself like a small child, 'you are very kind, and I am half glad that you know. But it is impossible for you or anyone else to help me, so please don't attempt it.'

'I won't believe that!' I cried. 'You must not blame yourself! You were hardly more than a child yourself. Blame him – blame *them* – never yourself. It was seeing that woman last week – seeing the child – that has brought it all freshly back to you. Oh, Juliana, if only I had been your companion then, instead of *her* – how different things would have been! But you must think of your own happiness now – your own future . . .'

'I have no future,' Juliana said, in a low, flat voice. 'Only to spend the rest of my life in contemplation of what cannot be changed or put right. Only to carry on as I am. Yes, you are right, I have suffered – I suffer every day and every night in the knowledge of what has happened; and I can see no end to it, for the past cannot be undone.'

'But, my dear, here is a chance of happiness – you must seize it with both hands!' I exclaimed. 'Here is Samuel, who will surely come to love you, if he does not already—'

'No!' Fretfully, Juliana turned her head away and put a hand over her eyes as though finding the daylight too much to bear. 'Can't you see – his presence here only adds to my anguish? Yes, if things had been different – yes, I could love him – maybe I *do* love him. But I am not worthy of him – never, never! Don't you see, Charlotte, what you are suggesting? That I should deceive a good man into marrying me, concealing the fact that I have borne a child? Are you truly proposing that he should be kept in ignorance? That lies and deceit should be the basis on which my marriage is to be built?'

'No, I did not think that,' I ventured, though this part of the plan was hazy in my own mind.

'Then you have hardly thought at all. How can you have, Charlotte?' Juliana remonstrated. 'If you think such a – a hindrance – can be easily put behind me, you have no comprehension of my torments, for all you claim to understand me. How can you begin to know? I have hidden my feelings so very cleverly, have I not? Well enough to keep you in ignorance, you who thought you knew me? But how can I live, otherwise – without keeping my feelings in suppression? When I must spend every day in the knowledge that I have a darling little boy I can only be allowed to glimpse, and whom I hate as well as love – and when I know, know beyond all doubt, that I killed my own mother—'

'Killed?' I echoed. 'How, killed? Juliana, what are you saying?'

She had sat upright to say this; her red-rimmed eyes almost glittered as she gazed at me. Almost in fear, I shrank back, and she gave a humourless laugh.

'Oh – I don't mean that I pushed her to her death. I am not a murderer. But I killed her all the same – she died because of me. The shame and disgrace were too much to bear. I told her! I told her – and she took her own life in the shock of that knowledge. I often think that the only course left open to me – if only I were brave enough – is to follow her by taking my own.' Her face contorted as though for a fresh bout of weeping.

'Juliana, my love!' I implored her. 'You must not think so, not for a moment – it is a – a dreadful distortion!' I moved towards her; but swiftly she regained her self-control, rose from the bed and surveyed her face in the mirror. Fiercely she began to work at her half-complete hairstyle, tugging at the brush, wincing.

Aghast, I watched. Her reddened eyes caught mine in the mirror; at first her gaze flickered away, then returned to meet mine, unafraid. 'Leave me now, Charlotte,' she commanded. 'I must be left alone.'

Outside, I stood by the door in indecision and dismay. My plan, designed to bring her comfort and hope, could scarcely have gone more badly awry. What mischief had I wrought, all unintending?

Chapter Twenty-three

Mr Ernest Farrow to Mrs Matthew Dearly

Fourwinds

3rd July, 1898

Dear Mrs Dearly,

To my consternation, I have recently discovered that your husband has taken employment with Mr Vernon-Dale, and that this has brought you back from Petersfield, where I had thought you were settled. I am surprised that you have not had the consideration to inform me of this move.

I am most concerned that my daughter should not come into contact, whether accidentally or by intention, with yourself or with the child. She is, as you know, of a nervous disposition, and such a meeting would cause her unnecessary distress. I must therefore ask you never to come near Fourwinds or to enter its grounds, and if you should chance to see my daughter in Staverton or its environs, to take every means of avoiding an encounter.

The payments will continue, under the terms of our

agreement, on the assumption that these conditions will be met. As you probably know, I am a close acquaintance of Mr Vernon-Dale, and could if necessary take measures which would render your husband's employment insecure. I am confident that you will take heed of my request and avoid any such unpleasant eventuality.

I trust that you, your husband and the boy are in good health.

Yours sincerely,

Ernest Farrow

Chapter Twenty-four

The Hand of the Sculptor

Artists, as I was discovering at every social encounter, cannot quite be taken seriously unless they exhibit signs of a volatile temperament. Plenty of my fellows at the Slade did their best to live up to this model; as for myself, I could not change my nature, and saw no reason for adapting my behaviour. If anyone mistook my quiet nature for dullness, why, let them – my inner thoughts were my own, and I did not find myself dull company.

Now, though, I found myself consumed by a passion large enough to match anyone's expectations of artistic instability. I could not rest – could scarcely trust myself to speak to anyone in the household – until I had been to Chichester and sought out that villain, Waring.

I informed Mr Farrow that I wished to spend a night away from Fourwinds. Although puzzled, he did not question me further; and when I explained to Charlotte, I avoided telling an outright lie by saying, 'I have had a letter from my friend Chas, from the Slade. He has asked me to join him and another mutual friend in Brighton.'

'I see,' she said. 'I suppose you are tired of our company here.'

'Not at all,' I told her. I had come to find her in the garden, where, in a rather becoming straw boater, she was snipping rose-stems for the dining table. Their sun-warmed scent was around us as we spoke, and a turtledove crooned from the cedar's shade. I could not resist adding, 'You have only just returned from the seaside yourself! You cannot begrudge me the same pleasure.'

She straightened. 'My trip was not for *pleasure*, Mr Godwin.' I noticed the return to formality. 'Do you imagine I have been cavorting in the waves, or playing with bucket and spade?'

'Well! Since you have told us almost nothing, you must pardon the mistake,' I told her.

'It's possible that I might have confided in you.' She flicked an earwig from its rose-petal nest. 'But your sudden haste to leave makes private conversation impossible.'

'I am at your service,' I said, pantomiming listening, hand cupped to ear.

'No, no.' She bent again to select a tightly furled bud. 'Don't let me detain you from your friends.'

'Charlotte,' I said, urged by some rash impulse, 'let me be honest with you. I misled you just now. I'm sorry. It's true that my friends have invited me to Brighton. But I'm not going there.'

'Oh? You have some secret assignation?' She still sounded disapproving.

'Not an assignation – but a quest.' I looked around

to check that no one was within earshot. 'I am going in search of Gideon Waring.'

'Gideon Waring?' Charlotte seemed to receive the name as a blow; her eyes, round and startled, gazed at me from beneath her hat brim. 'You cannot mean that!'

'I can, and I do. I have been making enquiries, and believe I know where to find him. It appears he is in Chichester, and must have travelled from there that day I saw him by the lake.'

'In Chichester! So close!' Charlotte said, though Chichester was half a day's journey away. 'I must urge you to abandon your plan – go to Brighton, if you will, meet your friends, but don't waste your thoughts, or your time, on Gideon Waring! That man is a brute – believe me, for I know more than you do. What can you hope to gain by meeting him?'

Here I faltered, for I could not tell her my true purpose – if, indeed, I knew what that was. The truth was that the sculptor both intrigued and repelled me; but delicacy forbade me to mention Marianne's drawings, or what I suspected. At the very least, I wanted to extract a promise that he would never again come near Fourwinds, or Marianne; but I knew too that when I confronted Waring, I should scarcely resist laying violent hands on him.

'I have my reasons,' I told her. 'However regrettable his conduct has been, his work is fascinating. I want to meet the man who shaped our three Winds – to talk to him. I want to discover what has happened to the fourth. You know how much it would put

Marianne's mind at rest, if the West Wind could be found, and put in position.'

'Yes,' said Charlotte, 'but you are taking too much upon yourself – interfering in Mr Farrow's concerns, and without his permission. Mr Waring's departure from here was acrimonious, and whatever brought him here that morning cannot have been above board. To be perfectly frank, it is no business of yours. Mr Farrow will find another sculptor in good time.'

'Maybe he will,' I said obstinately, 'but I am intent on going, and nothing you say is likely to sway me.'

'I urge you, do not go!' Charlotte repeated. 'Don't go near the man! He has proved himself untrustworthy – he will lie to you – he will turn you against Mr Farrow, against all of us!'

'I repeat – you may protest all you like, but my mind is quite made up that I shall go. And, as you told me, you have never met Mr Waring, so how can you be so sure?'

'I have my reasons,' said Charlotte quietly.

'And I have mine. You must permit me, I think, to do as I please with my spare time? You are governess to Marianne – not, though, to me.'

I had ventured too far. Charlotte faced me with an audible *humph*, her eyes blazing. In her efforts to cut the best blooms, she had ventured off the lawn and into the flowerbed, treading carefully on the dry, crumbled soil; she now began to extricate herself, lifting her skirts, and would, I suspected, have marched off and left me. However, the fabric of her dress had snagged itself on a rose thorn; turning to examine the impediment, she only succeeded in entrapping herself more thoroughly. Pulling herself free would badly rip her clothing.

'Here, let me,' I said, with a touch of amusement, for I knew how it would enrage her to accept my assistance. I bent, and carefully released her skirt, and the petticoat beneath, from the sharp grip of the thorn. In her effort to twist away from me, she almost over-balanced; one arm wavered, while the other hand clasped the bunch of roses. I took the bouquet from her – snagging my thumb as I did so on a thorny stem – gripped her free hand and steadied her as she stepped onto the lawn. Glaring balefully, she almost snatched the roses back from me, and smoothed the folds of her dress.

'If you persist, I shall tell Mr Farrow,' she said – not giving me a word of thanks.

'Very well,' I told her. 'You must do as you think best.'

As I strode across the lawn to the house, I looked down at my thumb, and saw a dark drop of blood oozing from the skin.

Without speaking to anyone else, I asked Reynolds to drive me to the station. I preferred to avoid either giving explanations or telling lies. Since Charlotte's return from Eastbourne, I could not but notice that Juliana was newly saddened, though I had no idea why. As for Marianne: since giving me her sketches, she had seemed embarrassed, barely meeting my eye.

Unsure what, if anything, to say, I returned her book to her room while she was out of doors.

Alone in the dusty railway carriage, watching as the scenery changed from the sweep of downland and hill-pasture to the wide loops of river through water meadow nearer the coast, I was assailed by doubt. Why had I insisted on making this journey? What did I expect to find? I soon convinced myself that the entire errand was in vain. Waring would not be here; he would have completed his work and moved on; I would find the cathedral frequented only by clerics and worshippers, with no mason in sight. I should have to spend an afternoon exploring the city, make a few sketches perhaps, then find myself a night's lodging and catch the train back on the morrow. By now, I was in fact wishing that I had taken up Chas's invitation instead of setting off on this pointless quest.

However, the train soon deposited me in Chichester, where a short walk brought me to a busy thoroughfare lined with prosperous-looking houses and shops. The cathedral spire soared above roofs of slate and tiles, showing me my direction. There was an elaborate market cross at what seemed to be a central point, and stalls set out beneath and around it, selling bread, flowers, cheeses and pies. Hungry from my journey, I ate a pie containing some unidentifiable meat, and paused to get my bearings.

I walked along West Street and was soon looking up at the magnificence of the cathedral from a vantage point close to a bell tower, which stood a little apart. For a few moments I gazed, dwarfed by the cathedral's immensity, thinking of the medieval stonemasons whose vision and skill enabled them to create an edifice of such splendour. Hundreds of years after its conception and building, its domination of the city was unchallenged.

But this was putting off my main purpose. I approached the massive west doors, which stood open to visitors, and stepped inside.

I felt the coolness of stone and air; I felt light and space; I saw the jewel colours of stained glass. Rounded arches, tier on tier, reached at last the final, soaring parabola of ribbed vaulting overhead. Each stone rib leaped towards the centre, to meet three others in a carved stone boss that seemed like a clasp, an affirmation, the keeping of a promise. My nervous cough echoed to the heights; my tread sounded too loud, a clumsy intrusion. How could Waring be here? A man of unrestrained lustfulness, in this sanctuary of peace and prayer?

Walking farther in, I paused, my attention caught by two stone effigies: a lord and his lady, lying side by side as if in bed, he in full armour, their feet resting on absurd little dogs; and the most surprising touch, one of his hands withdrawn from its gauntlet, holding hers. I stopped to look again, unaccountably touched; then pulled out my sketchbook and drew them, in swift lines. For some reason I felt overcome by loneliness – no, of longing, though I could not have explained for what I longed, or for whom. I knew only that I should have liked to have a dear companion with me, someone whose hand I could hold as tenderly as this stone knight held his lady's, someone with whom I could exclaim over the sights and sounds of the cathedral and the city beyond.

There was a lurking unease at the back of my mind, quite apart from the matter in hand. I examined it, and found that it concerned Charlotte, and the animosity between us last time we had spoken. I thought regretfully of my harsh words, and of my departure from Fourwinds without so much as bidding her farewell. I thought of how pleased I had been when she addressed me as Samuel, and how our argument had made her retreat to a frosty *Mr Godwin*, and how dearly I should like her to call me Samuel again.

But I could not concern myself with Charlotte now. I was already letting myself put off what I must do here.

There were two or three people at prayer – I saw hunched backs in the pews, clasped hands, heard words unintelligibly murmured – but no one at work. I retraced my steps to the west door, walked outside, blinking in the sunshine, and there he was, not more than ten yards away! – the man I had seen at the lake, pushing a wheelbarrow laden with tools and chunks of masonry. None other than the villain Waring himself. Ha! The pursuit had been easier than I thought.

I paused, marshalling my resources. I was surprised again at how young he was – still in his twenties, I estimated, though I always imagined him as a more mature man – and, at close quarters, strikingly handsome. Well, looks could mislead. He glanced my way, apparently not noticing the open truculence of my glare; nodded, and pushed his barrow past, in the direction of what appeared to be cloisters on the southern side of the cathedral precinct.

I am not usually in the least aggressive, and it shook my equilibrium to find myself so tensed, so hot with rage, fired up for conflict. My voice stuck in my throat. I coughed, and tried again: 'Mr Waring!'

He stopped, turning to look at me. He was, as I had thought when I saw him at the lake, taller than I; a little older, perhaps; lean and athletic in build. He wore workman's boots and trousers, a striped shirt with sleeves rolled up, and the same tan waistcoat as before; his face was bronzed by the sun. He looked at me curiously; if he recognized me, he showed no sign of it. Since he did not reply, I called again: 'Mr Waring, I must speak to you!'

I was barely able to control my voice, but he answered unhurriedly, and with the roll of a West Country accent. 'I thought you said Waring. If it's him you want, he's up the scaffold there.' He set down his barrow, and nodded towards some planks and ladders rigged up against the southern wall of the cathedral. 'Gideon!' he hollered, cupping both hands around his mouth. 'Gentleman to see you!'

Completely taken aback, I saw the bag of tools at the foot of the ladder. My eyes followed the steps upwards until they encountered the figure of a man. I saw a slim, tall figure; I saw the glint of white hair; a face turned down to look at us. 'What is it?' he called.

I hesitated, unable to shout my business, unsure

even what to say. 'What is it?' repeated the other, with a touch of impatience.

'I must speak with him,' I said.

'Gentleman wants to speak to you,' he yelled strongly.

Gideon Waring paused for just long enough to let me know that it was a great inconvenience to be called away from his work; then placed his tools on the planks near his feet, and lowered himself to the ladder. His slow and careful descent gave me time to calm my jangled thoughts, and to readjust my expectations. This, then, was Gideon Waring – not the younger man who stood by my side. This was the creator of the Winds I had come to love, of the mischievous touches around the house, the Green Man, the little gargoyle faces; this, too, was the seducer of Eliza Hardacre, the careless fornicator, the father of little Thomas Dearly, the would-be corrupter of Marianne. Only with difficulty could I hold all this in my mind as he reached the ground, approached me, and extended his hand, giving me a quizzical glance.

'Gideon Waring,' he said. 'Yes, what is it?'

We shook hands; his grip was strong and firm, his hand dry with stone-dust. The white hair was misleading, startlingly offset by eyebrows of pure black. He was, I judged, around forty; his face was thin and tanned; he had a neatly trimmed beard of white threaded with grey. A high forehead, with hair swept back, gave him a dignified air, rather austere; his eyes, beneath the arched black brows, were blue-grey, and penetrating. I was taken aback again. A sensualist, I had judged him from his work, and his reputation. The man who stood before me, though, had something of the monk about him; an impression heightened by the canvas smock he wore.

'Yes? What do you want of me?' he prompted, since I was quite at a loss for words.

'Pardon me,' I faltered, 'for interrupting you in your work.' My anger was quite dissipated by shock; the accusations I had intended to fling at him dried up in my throat. Thus wrong-footed, I should have to tread carefully. 'My name is Samuel Godwin,' I continued. 'I am employed as painter and tutor by Mr Ernest Farrow, at Fourwinds.'

The mention of those names caused an instant change in his expression, from enquiry to guardedness. I saw a quick glance pass between him and the younger man.

'Mr Farrow?' he repeated. 'And he, I assume, has sent you to find me, for some reason?'

'No,' I assured him. 'I have come of my own accord. I am a great admirer of your work, Mr Waring – indeed, I am fascinated by it.'

He nodded, seeming to accept this as his due.

'I have been curious to meet you,' I continued, 'from the first time I set eyes on your Wind carvings.'

'Have you, indeed?' He looked at me warily. 'So you're living at Fourwinds, are you? Take care to look about you. And how do you find Mr Farrow?' He was quietly but precisely spoken; a man who knew his own mind.

'I have been at Fourwinds only a short time,' I

answered, choosing my words with care, 'and I have formed a good opinion of him, although I cannot claim to know him well. He has been generous to me in commissioning a series of paintings. But I am rather anxious about the outcome. I imagine he is not an easy man to please.'

He answered this only with a curt nod. 'Tutor, you say? So his daughters are still at home?'

'Yes, of course.' I found this an odd question. 'Juliana, as maybe you know, has been ill – she is still frail, but well cared for by Miss Agnew – that is, Miss Charlotte Agnew, who replaced – er – the former governess.'

'Miss Hardacre, Miss Eliza Hardacre,' he supplied, without a flicker of embarrassment. 'Yes – yes. I knew her, of course.'

I looked at him, uncertain what he meant by that *knew*. Surely he could not be boasting of his conquest?

'Juliana ill, you say, and still frail?' he went on. 'I am deeply sorry to hear it – sorry indeed. But, Mr Godwin, you cannot expect me to believe that you have travelled here for the sole purpose of telling me you admire my work? Please credit me with some sense. Mr Farrow must have sent you.'

'No!' His defensiveness revived my suspicions. 'As I have said, your style intrigues me – everything you have carved, from the three Winds to the Green Man in the door arch, and the little gargoyle in the eaves.' At this, he allowed a smile to flit across his features, and I knew that I had pleased him by noticing such details. 'I have been curious,' I continued, 'to see the hand that created them.'

'Well, here it is,' he said, taking me at my word. He pushed back the sleeve of his smock and held out his right hand – work-worn and dusty, with dry skin and chipped nails – for my examination. 'A hand like any other.'

'And to encounter the mind that shaped them.'

My gaze rose from his hand to his eyes; for a second we regarded each other steadily, then he laughed and looked away. 'That I cannot show you – and would not, if I could. The human mind is a mystery, is it not, Mr Godwin? Who knows what it is capable of imagining – and what it is not? Who knows what it can produce, and what it can conceal? I know only the most superficial surface of my own mind. You are an artist, a painter – so I accept your tribute as artist to craftsman. But if you are any kind of artist, you will know that your true self is to be found in your work, rather than in the personage you present to the world.'

'I hardly know where my true self is to be found,' I answered him. 'Or that I should recognize it.' The conversation was taking a confessional turn; I had not come for this.

'Well, you are young. Your work will learn how to speak for itself, as I hope mine does. Now, I have a job to do here, and I cannot stand idle. You must excuse me.' He made to return to his tools.

'Mr Waring!' I called. 'Please – I must speak with you further. Might I return at the end of the day?'

He frowned. 'If you must. Come to my lodgings

at seven o'clock. We are at North Walls, a short step from here.'

He gave me directions, and we parted. The younger man, whose name I still did not know, gave me a tight-lipped smile and began unloading stone from the barrow; Waring ascended to his lofty perch, and I walked back towards the market cross, with much on my mind.

Gideon Waring! This ascetic-looking man was the seducer, the sire of an illegitimate child – the man who had so flaunted his relationship with Eliza Hardacre, that Marianne had been able to observe them *in flagrante*? No – I could not believe it. That role would be more suited to his companion, the vigorous young fellow I had first encountered at Fourwinds, close to the cottage where Waring had lived and worked. My eyes blurred with confusion as I paused by a pipe-seller's window, and refused the attentions of a flower girl who offered me a sprig of lucky heather. Could there be two Gideon Warings, one of whom denied his name?

Impatient with myself, I felt that I was on a fool's errand. Clumsy and slow-footed, I was being led a merry dance, each step taking me in new and contradictory directions, till I hardly knew which way I was facing. As I wandered past the market cross and into East Street, the chief thought in my mind was the phrase Gideon had used, so similar to that of Ned Simmons, the other stonemason: *Take care to look about you.*

Chapter Twenty-five

A Rising Wind

It was not often that I found myself at odds with anyone in the household, beyond the most trifling difference of opinion. The argument with Samuel left me feeling ruffled, upset and angry; angry with myself for parting with him on such bad terms, and for having failed to carry my point; angry with him for his unfeeling obstinacy. My only hope was that he would fail in his mission to find Gideon Waring. Samuel seemed confident (on what basis, I did not know) that the villain could be found in Chichester; but I hoped that some whim, opportunity, or further misdemeanour, would have taken Waring elsewhere. Such was my loathing of the man that I could scarcely bear to think of him living in the same county; indeed, I would have been gratified to hear that he had set sail for the Antipodes, or some distant island idyll; anywhere, provided he did not trouble any of us again.

Prominent in my list of worries, though, was that Samuel *would* find Waring: and that the encounter might lead to him discovering prematurely that Juliana was the mother of the child supposedly Eliza Dearly's.

I would not have put it beyond Waring to mention the matter. One could not expect such a man to exercise discretion or restraint. If that should be the case, my plan – Mr Farrow's plan – for Juliana's future happiness would be ruined; for the subject could hardly be more sensitive, and must only be brought to Samuel's attention with the utmost tact and delicacy.

It must have been as plain to Mr Farrow as it was to me that something was badly amiss with Juliana. He must, of course, be at least partly aware of the reason; and I contemplated letting him know that I shared his knowledge, for then we could discuss what should be done to assuage her grief. She seemed bent on self-punishment, as though circumstances had not already conspired to punish her enough. Should she be sent on a vacation? Might a period of sea air help to restore her health, if not her spirits? I even considered making use of my grandmother's house in Eastbourne; though it would hardly cheer Juliana to stay in that gloomy mausoleum, redolent of recent illness and death.

However, I did speak to Marianne; for, since she was party to her sister's secret, she ought to know that I was, too. My approach was discreet, my manner confidential; but Marianne replied with an airy, 'Oh, so you have guessed at last? Yes, it is our secret, and Papa has made me promise never to tell, for Juley's sake – but I'm surprised it has taken you so long, Charlotte, clever as you are.'

It was disturbing, in fact, that Marianne seemed to think such a set of circumstances not much out of the ordinary. As to my raising the question of how her sister was to be consoled, she was shockingly matter-of-fact: 'Papa has everything in hand. She must marry Samuel. It's obvious. He will suit her perfectly, and she him.'

In truth, I had not given up this idea, although I reproached Marianne for her flippancy. As far as I knew, Samuel remained unaware of any scheming on Mr Farrow's part (or, indeed, on my own). But Juliana was quite right that he could only marry her in full awareness of her misfortune. To our advantage was Samuel's evident liking for children, shown in the pleasure he had taken in playing with little Thomas. Samuel was a generous, good-hearted young man, we were all agreed on that; but was he forgiving enough to accept the product of such an irregular liaison? Moreover, what should happen to young Thomas as he grew up? Mr Farrow had, no doubt, made some provision for him, and I supposed that his adoption by Eliza and Matthew Dearly had some financial basis, until the boy was old enough to be sent away to school. Presumably, he would remain unaware of his true parentage; but what of Juliana? The return of the Dearlys to our neighbourhood made for additional awkwardness, since she would hardly be able to leave the grounds without risking a chance encounter with her young son. She could not be expected simply to forget his existence.

Therefore, I was not surprised when Mr Farrow's jollity of manner, as he entered the morning room with news for us, smacked of desperation. 'Here's an invitation for the three of you, for this evening!' he announced; looking round the room, and seeing only Marianne and myself: 'Oh – where is Juliana?'

'She has taken Queen Bess for a ride on the Downs,' Marianne told him.

'Well, tell her this as soon as she returns. Mrs Greenlaw invites you all to dinner at The Glebe, to meet a special guest of hers. I am not included – it is to be an evening for ladies only, she says! I shall order the gig for you at six.'

When Juliana returned from her ride, just after four, I greeted her with this news. Since our painful conversation in her bedroom, to which she seemed determined not to allude, she had resumed her demeanour of passive, almost somnolent quietness. She received the news of our engagement with resignation, if not much interest, and at six o'clock the three of us were ready in the vestibule.

Once before, in company with Mr Farrow and his daughters, I had dined with the Greenlaws. The Glebe, in Staverton, was a stolid Georgian manse set in gloomy shrubbery, and since the Greenlaws were both fond of antiques, we seemed to have retreated a hundred years or more into the past. Elegance rather than comfort determined the furnishings; in the drawing room there were a great many little tables, Queen Anne chairs, a grand piano, and a chaise longue. Squarely in occupation of the latter was a lady introduced as Mrs Sophocleous. She was a strikingly bizarre figure: although some fifty years of age, she wore her hair long and loose, and coal-black was most assuredly not its natural colour; her hooded eyes were darkened with kohl; her plump body was clad in a voluminous robe of deep purple, bordered with frieze-like black; numerous necklaces and charms were draped around her neck, and the pudgy hand she extended was adorned with a heavy ring on every finger. 'Delighted, I'm sure,' she greeted each of us, in a throaty voice that came from deep in her capacious chest. She clasped our hands; hers, I noticed, were cold. Marianne's she took longest to relinquish, gazing at her in fascination. 'My dear, such a beautiful face!' she pronounced. 'You must be careful.' Marianne, I saw, was spellbound.

'Mrs Sophocleous is going to entertain us after dinner,' Mrs Greenlaw informed us, bobbing about like a coot, 'and I assure you, it will be something very special! Mr Greenlaw and my brother, Mr Eaton, have gone up to London to spend the night at their club, so no one will disturb us – we shall be all ladies together. Oh, such fun! And now here is Annette. You have not met my friend Mademoiselle Duchêne, have you, Miss Agnew? Annette – allow me to introduce Miss Charlotte Agnew.'

'*Enchantée*,' said the new entrant. Her name was instantly recognizable; both Samuel and Marianne had spoken of her after the dinner party at Fourwinds. Samuel had described her as very handsome. With a twinge of resentment, I saw that he was right; she was certainly a lady who knew how to make the best of her attractions. I caught a waft of expensive perfume; her gown, well cut and presumably French, showed off her figure to advantage, making Juliana and even

Marianne look dowdy and provincial. Her presence made me uneasy, for Samuel had hinted that she aspired to become the second Mrs Farrow. Not for a moment did I believe that Mr Farrow could be actively seeking a marriage partner; but might he become prey, even a willing victim, to such a woman as this? No, it was unthinkable! The idea of another woman insinuating herself into our lives at Fourwinds was repugnant to me.

These thoughts occupied me throughout the ensuing dinner, in the north-facing dining room. Marianne chattered amicably; Mademoiselle Duchêne made a number of flattering remarks and enquiries about Fourwinds; Mrs Greenlaw, in her gushing way, steered the conversation; Juliana said very little, and Mrs Sophocleous even less.

'She's a medium, you know!' Mrs Greenlaw told me, in a loud and penetrating whisper; for we were seated side by side. 'She is quite a marvel. We are so lucky to be honoured with her presence this evening, for she is greatly in demand. Wait till after dinner, my dear – I promise you, you will be quite astonished!'

'What manner of medium?' I returned, in an undertone. Although Mrs Sophocleous could hardly avoid overhearing, she made no response, and continued to toy with the food on her plate. 'Does she summon spirits?' I enquired. 'Communicate with the dead?' Barely could I hide my scepticism; I had no time for this kind of flim-flam.

'Oh, she is very versatile!' replied our hostess. 'I have seen her go into a trance and speak in voices –

quite alarming! I first met her at my friend Lady Brocklehurst's in Godalming, you know, and there she summoned spirits with a Ouija board. You know, it is all the rage in some circles! Quite fascinating, you know, the Life Beyond, and all that we cannot be aware of. Sometimes she uses a crystal ball – sometimes she simply places her hands on a person's head, and is able to see into their future. You look doubtful, Miss Agnew, but let me assure you that before this evening is out, you will be quite convinced! You see how silent she is – she is preparing herself, mentally, for the strain ahead.'

This gave me cause for concern: not for myself, for nothing short of the materialization of my late grandmother would persuade me that the dead could rise from their graves, but for Juliana and Marianne, both of whom were susceptible in their different ways. To protect them, I decided to treat the session ahead of us as a parlour game.

While we drank our coffee, a corner of the drawing room was prepared according to Mrs Sophocleous's very precise instructions. All the blinds were drawn; a single candle was lit. Screens were produced, and swathed in purple velvet; a circular table was fetched, and covered with a black chenille cloth. Finally, a large and throne-like carver chair was placed in position, and Mrs Sophocleous settled herself into it with much wafting and draping of her ample robe. The rest of us were ushered into a semicircle, facing her.

'Well,' I said brightly, 'who is to be the first victim?'

Mrs Sophocleous fixed with me a hard stare, and

Mrs Greenlaw whispered, 'You must not speak, my dear, until she is ready; it disturbs her concentration. She must have absolute quiet. She will choose, in her own time.'

Reaching into a large tapestry bag on the floor beside her chair, Mrs Sophocleous brought out a black veil, which she arranged over her head so that it obscured all of her face except for her mouth and chin; then a glass ball, which she put in the centre of the table. Marianne watched with rapt attention, Juliana with no more than mild interest; Annette Duchêne, I guessed by the quick, amused darting of her eyes, shared my cynicism, but was prepared to humour Mrs Greenlaw.

Moments passed; Mrs Sophocleous closed her eyes and began to breathe deeply; I suppressed a most uncharacteristic urge to laugh, and had to disguise it by coughing. Then her eyes opened in a wide, unblinking stare. With a theatrical gesture, she extended a bangle-clad arm in Juliana's direction, and beckoned her with a forefinger. Nervously, Juliana stepped forward. 'Kneel,' commanded the medium; Juliana did so, and the plump be-ringed hands were placed one each side of her head. Again, the eyes were closed, the trance-like breathing continued for some moments; then a thin, reedy voice issued from somewhere inside the matronly form.

'Yes, I see,' said the voice; 'yes, it is coming to me. I am reading the deepest desires of your heart, my pretty one. Let me gaze into my ball . . .' She removed her hands, turned in her chair, and replaced them on each side of the glass sphere, as though transferring thoughts from Juliana's head into its depths. 'Yes – yes – the pictures are forming. You are leaving church, walking down the aisle on the arm of a handsome young man – I see guests, I see white flowers, their scent fills the air – and it will be soon, very soon!'

'Can you see the man? Who is he? Can you describe him?' Marianne burst out, on the verge of leaping up to question the ball herself.

'Hush!' reproved Mrs Greenlaw.

'That is all,' said the childlike voice, and Juliana, visibly shaken, returned to her place. Marianne shot me a triumphant look; I gave the slightest shake of my head. The woman was a charlatan. She had only this evening met Juliana; most young women of nineteen or so would naturally look forward to marriage; what could be remarkable in guessing that?

'Who next?' Mrs Greenlaw whispered. 'We shall not all be so lucky. She will not have the psychic energy to look into each of our minds.'

After Mrs Sophocleous had refreshed herself with more deep breathing and a few groans, she stared and beckoned at Annette Duchêne.

'*Alors!* My turn!' The lively mademoiselle settled herself with a flourish of skirts. 'Shall it be marriage for me, too, I wonder?'

Mrs Sophocleous frowned sternly as she pressed her hands to each side of Mademoiselle Duchêne's stylish coiffure; then she spoke, and the voice was different this time, that of a hoarse old woman: 'I have you, yes, I have you, though you think I cannot – you like to enjoy admiration wherever you go. Everyone you meet has a high opinion of you, and that high opinion is shared by yourself—' At this, Annette Duchêne let out a giggle; she tried to look round for a reaction (and it was lucky she could not see *mine*, for I fear that my expression must have revealed my satisfaction), but the be-ringed hands held her firm. 'You are ambitious, yes, I see that – you are looking to rise in the world. Let me look into my glass . . . Yes, yes. It will happen, but not as you think. And you must wait, be patient – patience is not in your nature, but you must be prepared to wait.'

'Oh! Must I?' The recipient of this news, dismissed, rose to her feet, not in the least abashed by what she had heard. '*Alors*, she has read me as clearly as the pages of a book; I can hide nothing. Whose turn next?'

'Mine!' breathed Marianne; but Mrs Sophocleous, after resting for a few minutes as before, turned her gaze and her summoning finger towards me.

Sitting firm, I shook my head. 'No. Not I.'

'Come, child, do not be afraid,' she urged, in cooing tones.

'I am not afraid of what you might say to me. I do not choose to participate.'

'Please do, Charlotte! *I* want to know what she sees for you, even if *you* do not!' cajoled Marianne; but I was steadfast, and sat firm in my chair.

Why did I not put myself forward? My protective instincts were strongly aroused; I should have foreseen that hearing whatever nonsense this ridiculous woman pretended to read from inside my head would have prevented her from choosing Marianne. My only excuse is that by this time I had decided she was a harmless impostor, and had nothing but banalities to reveal.

We all waited. Mrs Sophocleous's hooded eyes closed again; her chest rose and fell with deep breathing; for a moment I thought she had fallen asleep. Then the eyes opened and fixed on Marianne, who, in a flurry of excitement, rushed obedient as a spaniel to kneel by her feet.

'Oh, you are beautiful indeed.' This time the voice was startling: loud, breathy, and with an unaccountable Italian accent. 'Beware, my dear – such beauty carries danger with it. You will always attract eyes, and thoughts. There is one now who longs for you, who dreams of you, who yearns to clasp you in his arms. And there will be others less honourable in their intentions. But you have something besides – you know it, do you not? – you have the gift, the gift of second sight. It disturbs you, you try to fight it, but you must not. I shall look into the glass, I shall see what I can read there.' She caressed a lock of Marianne's hair, twirling it in her fingers; she turned and gazed, clasping the orb; she seemed to recoil, then bent closer, examining it again. 'Take care, my beauty,' she continued, the voice becoming high and agitated, the accent more pronounced; 'for I see that your curiosity will lead you into danger, and very soon – a wind is rising, you are one with it, you will go where it blows you – you are searching for something lost, something hidden, yes, and you will find it— But oh! Beware—'

Abruptly Marianne rose to her feet. 'No! No more!' She struggled away from the table, crashed into a chair, overturning it, and backed against a sideboard on the other side of the fireplace. At once Juliana was beside her: 'Hush! Hush, Marianne, it is only make-believe – you must not take it to heart . . .'

Annette Duchêne was righting the toppled chair, and Mrs Greenlaw soothing the medium, who sat with eyes rolling, mouth open and panting, a hand clutched to her chest. 'Quickly! Ring the bell,' Mrs Greenlaw told me. 'Summon Emily – bid her fetch smelling salts and camomile tea. It is harmful to break the thread – she is in shock.'

I did as she asked, though my concern was more for Marianne than for Mrs Sophocleous's palpitations, which were, I had no doubt, part of the performance. Marianne's distress was genuine: she continued to stare at the older woman as though unable to break some psychic grip. 'Marianne!' I told her sharply. 'Come and sit down. Come, we shall drink tea.'

'I cannot!' Her hands were over her mouth; she spoke between spread fingers. 'Oh, Charlotte, she knows! She knows more than she has said – she saw that I shall find the West Wind! But the danger – she is right, I know she is right, and I fear it! I cannot tell what is hidden in my own mind, and it terrifies me sometimes – she read that, so accurately—'

'Come, come!' Assisted by Juliana, I led her towards the chaise longue, where she slumped as though exhausted. 'You must take no heed, dearest,' I told her, 'for it is only nonsense. Something lost, something to be found? A million people would find their own truth in that. It is the merest chance—'

'But the Wind! She spoke of the Wind!' Marianne whispered.

'She meant it metaphorically, I am sure,' I told her. 'Don't upset yourself, dear. It is only a game.'

She looked at me, wide-eyed. 'But you chose not to play. You were wise, Charlotte – for now what shall I do?'

Mrs Sophocleous had recovered sufficiently to rise regally to her feet, and was being escorted from the room by her hostess. She stopped by the chaise longue, and gave me a disdainful look. 'I must warn you, madam, that your scepticism risks serious harm to the sensitive girl there in your charge. She needs guidance, she needs understanding, she needs a confidante in tune with her temperament. And *that*, I am afraid, she will not find in you. You believe I am a fraud, do you not – a mere entertainment, an after-dinner diversion? Yet you feared submitting to my power. And now you encourage this girl to deny what she feels, what she knows! It is dangerous; you are unaware how dangerous it is; but it is dangerous. If she suppresses these feelings, these urges, she will only harm herself.' She gave me a curt nod, and laid a hand on Marianne's head. 'I have spoken. Now I must take my leave of you – for it has exhausted me, as it has exhausted her. Goodnight.'

With this, she swept out, Mrs Greenlaw scuttling in her wake. Annette Duchêne looked at me and raised one eyebrow; I found an unexpected ally there. 'Well!' she exclaimed in an undertone. 'I should very much like to see her on the Paris stage. Come, Miss Farrow – she was very flattering to you, was she not? Quite taken by your pretty looks! If I were you, I should remember that part of her verdict, and forget the rest.'

Marianne took no heed, but looked wildly about. 'We must go. Take me home, Charlotte, please.'

'Yes, it is quite late enough,' I said, rising to my feet. 'I shall summon Reynolds.'

As we wished Mrs Greenlaw goodnight, I had to curb my tongue, though my thanks for the entertainment were sharp-edged. I had arrived at The Glebe with one distraught girl on my hands; departing, I had two.

Chapter Twenty-six

North Walls

In good time for the appointed hour, I made my way to 4 North Walls. It was set in a terrace fronting a narrow street, a stone's throw from the cathedral. My mood, as I approached, was very different from the fury of indignation that had brought me to Chichester. Now, bemused and curious, I hardly knew what I expected to find.

My knock on the door was answered not by Waring but by his companion, whose name, I soon learned, was Richard Hobday; he was Waring's working partner. There was no female presence in evidence; neither of wife nor servant. I had hoped to find Gideon Waring alone; but Hobday was unobtrusive, for the most part silent, and, I soon learned, completely in Waring's confidence.

Inside, the place was simply furnished: a single room with a kitchen area behind; a fireplace with two wooden chairs facing it; a deal table and bench; a rag rug. A meal of bread, cheese and sausage was set on the table, with a jug of ale, and knives and mats for three. Much to my surprise, in view of Waring's guardedness earlier, I was urged to share the meal: 'Please join us. It is only a simple supper – not what you are accustomed to at Fourwinds – but you are welcome. Please, sit.'

His manner seemed changed; I wondered why. Maybe he had decided that I was not, after all, a spy sent by Mr Farrow. By now, indeed, I was so confused that I could not have explained what my motive was – only that I wanted to hear what he had to say, and to find out, if I could, what business Richard Hobday had had at Fourwinds. And it occurred to me now that Waring's reason for inviting me to eat could only be to find out what he could from *me*. I must be on my guard. Yet, whatever secrets he was guarding, he was the creator of the Winds I so admired – could I revere the sculptor, and despise the man? I did not think it possible.

While we began to eat, Gideon Waring asked me whether I had found lodgings for the night, and I replied that I had, in Eastgate Square; then I mentioned something that had struck me earlier. 'Mr Waring, when we spoke by the cathedral, you referred to yourself as a craftsman. I should rather call you an artist. Do you not think of yourself as such?'

A glance passed between him and Hobday – this happened often, I subsequently noticed, this fleeting, wordless communication – before he replied:

'I make no distinction, Mr Godwin. A craftsman is an artist, an artist a craftsman. The world may make a distinction; I do not. I am a carver of letters and embellishments by trade, a sculptor by inclination. I am paid for one, often not for the other – that is the only difference. Maybe, when I was younger, I had aspirations of finding recognition as a sculptor. But working as I do, following in the long tradition of masonry, working in the same places, handling the very same stone that has been handled by generations of masons, stretching back to medieval times – I find that humbling. To call myself an artist would be to set myself apart, to draw attention to myself. I do not require that. The work is enough. I do not put my name to it, for it needs no name. I am prolonging the achievement of others, preserving the spirit of the place. Their names are not known – only those of the master masons, and they were men of near genius – why should I wish for mine to be? It is of no matter.'

'But your carvings – the Winds,' I objected. 'What I so admire is the individual stamp you put on them – your own style, clear and distinctive. You were not simply following there, where others have been before.'

'But of course I follow. What else? How otherwise do we learn? Every sculpture I have admired, every carved figure, whether of wood or stone or marble, guides my hand. How have you learned to paint, Mr Godwin? I should say, how are you continuing to learn? For of course one never stops. Surely, by distinguishing between what you admire and what you do not; by experimenting and combining, by selecting and eliminating; that is how you develop what you call your own style. But it is all borrowed.'

That I could see in myself; for I suspected that I

could only ever be a skilled imitator, never a maker. 'But your work!' I persisted. 'I find inspiration in it, even if you do not.'

'That is not what I said,' he replied, with a patience that concealed impatience. 'My inspiration is in continuity. I am carrying on for a little while; when I am gone, others will continue. It is my one claim to immortality. I have no children, but the letters I cut yesterday will endure for centuries.'

I have no children.

He had said it quite guilelessly; unless he was as skilled an actor as he was mason, there was no intention to deceive. Could he be unaware?

Might I ask?

Hobday got up to refill my tankard with ale, and his own. Gideon Waring was drinking little. He finished eating a morsel of cheese from his plate, then went to the tiny kitchen and returned with a bowl of cherries, which he placed in the exact centre of the table. He was punctilious, I saw, in everything he did.

'Now, Mr Godwin. What of you?' he asked. 'What makes you paint? What do you aim to do, when you paint?'

No one had ever asked me this before, in quite these words. Only a short while beforehand, I should have replied that I wanted to make my mark, to achieve something unique, to win awe and recognition. After a few moments' thought, I said: 'I want to paint what I see. I want to show that objects are objects, and that light is light. That seems enough.'

It seemed inadequate, and I expected him to

challenge me; but he nodded, considering, and reached for a pair of cherries.

'Yes. Yes,' he said. 'That is good.'

I thought: I should like to paint this table, set for our supper. The brown plates, a crust of bread, the tankards, the fall of light from a high window; the vermilion of the cherries, shiny as lacquer. The thingness of things, their essence, their textures, the way they occupy space: that is what I want to paint, and so far I have not succeeded; the techniques I have so painstakingly learned, obstruct my vision. I did not say this, but he saw me looking, and seemed to read my thought; he nodded and, for the first time, smiled. I felt that I had passed some kind of test.

Against all my preconceptions, I was forming a strong liking for this man. I liked his precise movements, and the careful consideration he gave to every remark. I knew that even without painting the table-setting, I should hold it in my mind for ever; and the memory of what we ate, and what we talked about. Quite unlike the more obviously charismatic character I had imagined, he was a modest man, quietly wise, content with little, thoughtful, contemplative; a man to inspire devotion. I looked at Richard Hobday, who seemed to occupy the role of disciple to master, and to regard Gideon with silent respect. I rather envied him: I could, I felt, have happily trundled wheelbarrows and hewn stone under Waring's direction, gradually learning to make my own mark, unassuming but timeless, on the vast edifice of the cathedral.

I thought of my father; thought of his disappointment in me; knew that to be the son he wanted would be to deny an essential part of my self. For the first time I began to feel a sense of freedom from the bonds my father had imposed on me; to feel that accidental encounters may have as much power to shape our preferences and guide our lives, as those traits sown in us by heredity.

'Pardon me,' I said abruptly to Hobday, who sat with one ankle resting on the other knee, eating cherries and arranging their stones in a ring on his plate; 'but I believe I saw you at Fourwinds, early one morning. Is that not so?'

'You did,' he replied, in his unhurried way; 'you were swimming in the lake.' He smiled at me pleasantly.

'Might I ask what your business was there? And why you hurried away when you saw me, instead of identifying yourself?'

He glanced at Gideon Waring from under his eyebrows, as if seeking permission to answer; Waring sat forward, clasped both hands on the table, and said, 'I think the time has come to be frank with you, Mr Godwin. Samuel, if I may? We have each other's confidence, do we not?'

Chapter Twenty-seven

Gideon Waring's Account, as told to Samuel Godwin

I have told you that I care very little for worldly fame. This has not always been my view. For a while, recognition was what I craved; I believed my work was nothing if it was not sought out, exhibited and admired. I was resentful towards rivals, and jealous of any praise given to anyone other than myself. That, Samuel, is a state to be avoided, for no small success can be enough, every achievement of others is felt as a personal slight, and what really matters, the integrity of the work, takes secondary importance. The world's regard is fickle and deluding. It flickers from one subject to another, barely pausing before flitting off in some new direction.

I was given the opportunity to work as apprentice to a fashionable sculptor, and my ambition was first to follow and then to surpass him. After several years of this, working on elaborate statuary for rich patrons, many of them with more money than appreciation, I took what many would regard as a backward step, and became instead a stonemason, cutting letters for gravestones, sometimes memorial tablets, heraldic work and the like. To handle stone is to handle the stuff of life and death, and of time and change, and the mysteries of the Earth itself; there is something humbling and moving and immensely satisfying in it. And thus I preferred to earn my living. It was while I was working on a memorial tablet, commissioned by a gentleman in Guildford whose son had been killed in India, that Mr Farrow approached me. He flattered me, and admired my work; he was a man of very decided tastes. He was interested enough to return to view the tablet when it was complete and fixed in position on the church wall. After the service, he spoke to me in private, and offered me considerable enticements to produce the relief panels you are acquainted with, the Four Winds. His house was nearing completion, and my carvings – with a few other small pieces – were to be its final touches. In conversation he discovered my personal circumstances: that I am a single man, I have few material needs, and that above all I need solitude and seclusion. He offered me Yew Tree Cottage, in his grounds, for as long as I required it, and an outbuilding for my workshop.

Very gladly, I took up the challenge. I have since had cause to regret most bitterly the day I sold myself to him; but at that time, I saw only the good. Everything seemed to suit me perfectly. I installed myself, and spent many hours walking around the grounds, feeling the spirit of place, inspecting the house from every angle, considering how my Winds should look. They would be united in style, yet each should have its own character – well, you have seen three of them, and have been kind enough to say that you think I have succeeded, for which I thank you. I sketched all four before commencing, and obtained Mr Farrow's approval. After discussion with him, I ordered my Portland stone from Dorset. It is the finest limestone to work with: pure and true. Only the best materials are good enough for Mr Ernest Farrow; he was prepared to pay.

I set to. I work slowly and meticulously, with frequent pauses; it is important simply to stand and look. I spent long hours alone in my workshop and cottage; when I was not working, I wandered in the grounds or sat reading by the lake. But I was not always alone. Mr Farrow, as you may have found, likes to talk – especially late in the evening, and especially over a drink. On two or three occasions I was invited to dinner, and when Mrs Farrow and her daughters had retired to the drawing room, he and I drank brandy, and talked. – Ah, you have done the same? Yes, of course – he misses male company, in his house of women. I admit, Samuel, that I liked him – as, maybe, you do. Yes? I should rather say that I liked what I saw, for there was much that I did not see – was not allowed to see. Very occasionally he would come across to my workshop and talk to me there. He liked to see in progress the work he was paying for, to see it taking shape under his direction.

Mr Farrow, I thought at first, had every possible blessing. He had a devoted wife, two lovely daughters, a house built to his own specifications, and the wealth to furnish and maintain it. He was in good health, he had friends, influence and position.

But there was one thing he did not have.

A son.

The lack of a son and heir was a bitter disappointment to him. Oh, he has spoken of it? I see, yes. Yes, quite so. Whereas most men would – to use the trite phrase – count their blessings, he could not put aside the grudge that the one thing he most wanted, he could not have – and it could not be bought with money. I should go so far as to say that it was an obsession with him.

Worse, he allowed Mrs Farrow to believe that she was at fault, for failing to produce the son he so desperately wanted. I did not know the lady well, for she kept to herself. It was some unguarded remarks of her husband, when we were alone one evening, that suggested this to me. And then I noticed it whenever I saw them together. The formalities were observed, but, beneath, there was little affection. Mrs Farrow's health was variable, and her husband, I am sorry to say, less than sympathetic.

The two young girls found it a novelty to have a stranger living in their grounds. With their governess, Miss Hardacre, it became their habit to walk across to my shed, and to watch me at work, when I allowed it. I did not, always. For Marianne, it was the simple pleasure of watching a figure taking shape in the stone, and of guessing at its finished appearance. She was very much intrigued by the emerging personalities, and sometimes liked to draw while I worked – for she has a notable talent, Samuel, as no doubt you have seen for yourself. Juliana often came with her, and at other times besides. More and more frequently, she came alone. I wondered at the propriety of this, and whether I should discourage it; but I did nothing, and she continued to seek my company. Often, all she wanted was to sit by me, saying little. At other times she wanted to talk. After a while I sensed that something was troubling her deeply, something she had not confided to her mother, sister, or governess. One day, when she seemed particularly perturbed – indeed, she looked physically ill – I ventured to ask what was amiss, and if I could help her in some way. At first she would not speak, merely shaking her head in wordless grief. I persevered, and at last she did – hesitant, shivering, barely able to find the words – and, having told me, she became incoherent with weeping.

What she conveyed to me, Samuel, was that her father had been regularly coming to her bedroom during the night. He had – in short, he had used her as a substitute wife.

– Pardon me. I have shocked you. I know. I could hardly take in what I had heard – so obliquely did she convey this information, more delicately than I did just now. Forgive me – you have turned quite pale. Let me fetch you some water . . . Thank you, Richard. There. Shall I continue? Are you ready?

Well, then. My first thought was that she was deluding herself, that she was mistaken, that he had simply gone to her room to wish her an affectionate goodnight. But Juliana, as you will know, is not in the least given to exaggeration or dramatization. There was a pleading simplicity in her manner when she told me, a need to be heard and understood – to be believed. Afterwards she sat quietly sobbing in the corner of my workshop. Everything in her demeanour convinced me that she had spoken the truth.

I was at a complete loss. What should I do? I am still not sure that what I did was at all adequate. I have questioned myself again and again as to whether I should have acted otherwise.

I soothed her, assured her that it was not her fault, and not a punishment, but that it was wrong, very deeply wrong of her father and that it must not be allowed to continue. She must tell her mother, I told her, without delay. I urged and urged her on this point, until I had her assurance that she would. Mrs Farrow might consider it best to remove herself and her daughters from the family home – she has parents, I believe, in Ireland. Surely, after hearing what Juliana had to tell her, this is what she would do – I fervently hoped so – yet you tell me that the two girls are still at home . . .

Yes. I shall finish.

When I had calmed Juliana, and extracted yet another promise that she would tell her mother without delay, I escorted her back to the house. Then – and this is where I may have acted with unfortunate haste – I sought out her father, and told him that I could not continue to work and live on his premises.

He wanted to know why. I told him.

Immediately he flew into a rage – and if you have never seen Mr Farrow lose his temper, believe me that it is alarming to behold. He accused me of making up the most obscene slander against him; he accused me of behaving scandalously with Juliana myself; he accused me – and here I received another shocking revelation – of getting her with child, and making up malicious fabrications to conceal my disgrace. He told me that our arrangement was at an immediate end; that I must leave the cottage immediately, and that if I was found anywhere on his grounds by the next morning, he would not answer for my safety. He gestured towards the rifle he kept in a case on his study wall, oiled and ready for use.

– I am sorry. Yes. You see the effect he still has on me. I am not easily roused to anger, Samuel, I am not in the least a violent man, but I truly believe I could have killed him. Maybe I should not have restrained myself, for what restraint had he shown?

Poor Juliana, poor innocent girl. My heart went out to her – if it was true that she was with child, her plight was even more desperate than I had supposed. As I left the house, I hesitated, wondering still whether I ought to approach Mrs Farrow myself; but I glanced through the morning-room window, and saw Juliana seated with her mother on a sofa. Their postures were eloquent – Mrs Farrow was stooped, her face buried in both hands; Juliana, leaning against her, was weeping inconsolably – it was a heart-rending tableau. I could not possibly intrude into their distress; besides, I was aware that any intervention on my part could be misrepresented by Farrow as evidence of guilt. Propelled by impotent fury, I went back to my cottage and wondered what to do next.

To be brief: by next morning I had packed up my belongings, and arranged to be conveyed here by a local carter. I left my three completed carvings behind in the workshop, but the fourth – the West Wind, which I had only half done – I took with me. The stone having been paid for by Mr Farrow, I intended to return it when my carving was finished. I imagined that he would discard or destroy the other three – hence my astonishment when I learned from Richard that they are in place on the house walls, as intended.

I knew I could find work in Chichester, and soon did – but I have an outhouse here for storing my own projects, and in my leisure hours I completed the West Wind. Then I hired another carter to deliver it to Fourwinds. I don't know what Farrow has done with it – but I fulfilled my part of the bargain. I made him his Four Winds.

Soon after I arrived here, I met Richard, working here in the cathedral. We have become dear companions to each other – I think you understand. Hearing my story, he was curious about my Wind carvings, and travelled to Fourwinds with the sole intention of seeing them – expecting that, if they still existed at all, they would have been left in my workshop. Not finding them there, he approached the house, and saw my North, East and South in their intended positions – and the west wall, still blank. He returned to the cottage and workshop to look again for the West Wind – I had given him my key, which I had not returned – but he found no sign of it.

As for Juliana, I am deeply grieved to hear that

she and Marianne are still living with their father. I have reproached myself many a time for leaving so hastily, before ensuring that they were safe from him – I should have stayed, I should have done more. But I felt sure that their mother would take them away – make whatever arrangements could be contrived to remove them from—

– What? Dead? Mrs Farrow? When did this happen? But that is – pardon me, a moment – I – I— Good God! But this is— Are you quite sure?

Chapter Twenty-eight

Thomas

By Friday, missing Samuel more than I had anticipated, I awaited his return with a mixture of eagerness and foreboding. I longed to hear that he had been unable to find Gideon Waring, and hoped he had been so discouraged as to give up his search; also, I was most anxious to restore harmony between Samuel and myself. Several times I found myself planning what I should say to make amends for my brusqueness.

He had made no arrangement to be met at the station, but on Friday afternoon, needing to make some small purchases in Staverton, I asked Reynolds to harness the pony and drive me into town. Marianne came with me, but Juliana declined to accompany us, saying that she intended to exercise Queen Bess for an hour or two, for she had lately resumed her habit of riding out in the afternoons. Pleased at this sign of improving spirits, I did not press her. The excursion was carefully timed; on completing my errands, I suggested to Reynolds, as if on impulse, that we should call at the railway station to see if Samuel was on the afternoon train. Of course, Marianne believed

Samuel to have been in Brighton; in spite of my threat to tell Mr Farrow that he had lied, and was going to Chichester, I had kept this knowledge to myself.

The train duly arrived, disgorged two elderly passengers, then, with a hiss of steam, moved off. Marianne watched in dismay as it rounded the bend.

'Where is he?' she cried in distress. 'Where is Samuel? Oh, Charlotte, he is lost to us! He will never come back – I know he will not – we should never have let him go. Why must everybody leave us?'

'How you exaggerate!' I told her. 'There will be a simple reason. His friends have persuaded him to stay on for the evening, and catch the late train home. Yes, that will explain it.'

However, as we crossed the dusty forecourt, I felt a tug of disappointment on my own account; I wanted Samuel safely back with us. Reynolds, hearing the news, was displeased, complaining that he would have to return later. 'Might as well keep Hector between the shafts day and night, the amount of to-ing and fro-ing that's been called for lately,' he grumbled, as we took our seats. He picked up the whip, clucked his tongue, and we moved off, soon leaving the town behind us. The vista opened before us: the ridge of downs to our left, the pastures dotted with sheep, and the dusty chalk of the tracks, for the ground was parched after weeks without rain.

It was then that I had the idea of making another call that had been very much on my mind.

'Reynolds,' I called out, before the impulse left me, 'I should like to call at Rampions on the way home. Could you take us there, please?'

Marianne clutched at my arm. 'Rampions? Oh, Charlotte, must we? I – I want to go home.'

'I wish to speak to Eliza Dearly,' I told her. 'I shall not take more than a few minutes – then we will go home directly. Why should that upset you?' – for dismay was written all over her face.

'No – no, I am not in the least upset,' she said, recovering quickly. 'It is just that – you know – are you sure it is wise? Papa does not like us to see Eliza.'

'Then you may blame me,' I replied. 'You need not speak to her; you need not even get down from the chaise.' As Reynolds guided Hector into the lane that led to Rampions, the pony shook his mane with impatience, having thought his head was pointing for home. I told Reynolds to take us to the gardener's cottage, which was reached through a side entrance beyond the very grand gates which led to the mansion.

Orchard Cottage, which was, indeed, somewhat larger than one would expect a cottage to be, was set in an area walled off from the extensive gardens, walks and orchards surrounding the mansion. We pulled into a yard enclosed by various outbuildings: tool sheds, stables and the like. A few chickens pecked about, but there was no one to be seen.

Marianne tried once more to deter me. 'Please, Charlotte, can't we go home? I – I am not feeling well – it must be the heat.'

This was so transparent an excuse, and I was by now so determined, that I told her to wait in the chaise, and climbed down to go in search of Eliza.

Through a doorway in a high brick wall I saw a

formal kitchen garden, with symmetrical narrow paths, pear trees trained over hooped arches, and three green-houses in one corner. Two young gardeners were bent over their tasks, one weeding a vegetable bed, the other picking pea pods and laying them in a trug. Neither of these was old enough to be Matthew Dearly. On looking back towards the cottage, I saw that its front door stood open. I approached, down a flagged path bordered with pinks and marigolds, and rapped on the door. Inside, a narrow passageway, its floor covered with a rag rug, led to two more doors: one leading to a kitchen; the other, presumably, to a parlour.

Low voices were heard murmuring from that room. After a moment Eliza Dearly, in a flowered dress and apron, appeared from within, leaving the door ajar.

'Yes?' She did not seem surprised to see me; but then she could easily have glanced out of the window and seen Reynolds, Marianne and the chaise. Neither did she sound at all friendly. Of course, I had been markedly aloof with her when she visited Fourwinds.

'Good afternoon, Mrs Dearly,' I said. 'Please excuse this interruption. There is something I should like to discuss with you.'

'Oh?' She rubbed her hands together, then rested one of them on the swell of her belly. I saw what I had not noticed on our previous encounter: that she was with child. 'Has *he* sent you?' she asked me in a markedly imperious manner. 'Mr Farrow, I mean?'

'He has not. I am here on my own account.'

'Very well, then. We will talk in the garden,' said Mrs Dearly, giving a quick glance behind her. The child, Thomas, was toddling along the passageway; reaching her, he clutched at her skirts. With an exclamation of surprise or annoyance, she scooped him up, and marched purposefully out of the door. 'This way,' she commanded me. As I followed, I looked at the child, wondering if I could trace Juliana's features in his. How very clear his eyes were, how smooth and unblemished his skin, how round his cheeks! He returned my gaze, his mouth almost twitching into a smile, then hid his face against Eliza's shoulder. Truly, he was a most enchanting little boy.

'And how is little Thomas?' I asked.

'He is very well, thank you,' Eliza answered, leading the way to a small wooden bench at one side of the garden, shaded by apple trees. 'As you see, he will soon have a little brother or sister.' She set the child on the ground, where, holding her hand, he took a few steps, making little remarks to himself.

'Mrs Dearly,' I said, firmly, 'the child you are expecting will *not* be brother or sister to Thomas, will it? I am correct, I think, in believing that you are not, in fact, Thomas's mother – nor your husband his father.'

She made an attempt at prevarication. 'Oh? What can you mean by that?' However, she was an inadequate dissembler, and I was determined.

'Come, Mrs Dearly, let us not waste time,' I urged her. 'I am right, am I not?'

She looked at me squarely. 'So – you have worked it out for yourself? I cannot think that Juliana chose to tell you.' She jutted her chin. 'Tell me – does this raise me in your esteem, now that I am cleared of becoming a mother so indecently soon after my marriage? Or have I sunk lower, for entering into such an arrangement?'

'I should apologize for misjudging you,' I said, without warmth, for I could feel no liking for her; 'though I can hardly be blamed for suspecting what all appearances seemed to suggest. However, that is not what I wish to discuss. I have come to ask, Mrs Dearly, what arrangements have been made for Thomas's upbringing. More precisely, is he to grow up in the belief that he is in fact your son? Is he ever to be told the truth? And is Juliana expected to ignore his existence?'

Eliza gave me a haughty, sidelong look. 'I might ask what business it is of yours. Why do you not ask Mr Farrow? He has all the answers – you need not have troubled yourself to come here.'

'I am merely asking,' I told her, 'out of concern for Juliana. She was extremely distressed after your visit, Mrs Dearly. You know her, and I pride myself that I understand her as well as you once did. She must, for the sake of her health, find some way of putting this behind her – and that is well nigh impossible, now that you live so close. Obviously, the boy must be provided for, now and in the future; and I assume that his father takes neither responsibility nor interest.'

'His father?' Eliza looked at me steadily. 'My husband and I have a financial arrangement with Mr Farrow. The details need not concern you.'

'Precisely,' I agreed. 'He is, in effect, a member of the Farrow family, even if not acknowledged as such; his needs will be met. Yet the present arrangement, as you call it, is unsatisfactory for Juliana. She cannot venture into town without fear of meeting you and the child—'

'Fear!' Eliza repeated. 'Fear, you call it! You think you know Juliana, Miss Agnew, but let me tell you that you know only as much as she chooses to let you know. *I* am still her confidante; *I* am the person she trusts, and turns to.'

'Trusts *you!*' I could not prevent myself; the words burst from me. 'Why, it was under your supervision that she was led into this predicament! You must, surely, have known what was going on between her and Mr Waring?'

'Miss Agnew,' Eliza said, with a visible effort at keeping her self-control, 'you are free with your accusations, but plainly you do not know as much as you think you know. If you care what is best for Juliana, you will take her away from her father.'

'Away from her father?' I repeated, incredulous. 'Away from the one source of stability and comfort in her life? I cannot understand you, Mrs Dearly.'

'I thought not.' For a moment her chin jutted and she looked almost defiant; then her manner changed, and she spoke in a quieter, confiding voice. 'If he finds out – Marianne, too, before— I can do nothing, but I am afraid for them, both of them, I—'

Here she caught herself short, almost biting her lip; I looked at her, uncomprehending. At that moment, from the stable yard which the garden overlooked, I heard the scrape of hooves on cobbles. As I looked round, a white, bridled head lifted over one of the half-doors, ears pricked sharply. It was, unmistakably, Queen Bess. She gave a soft snickering sound, looking in the

direction of her companion, Hector, who was hidden
from my sight by the corner of the cottage.

'Oh!' I exclaimed. 'She is here – Juliana is here
with you now!'

How stupid I had been – how easily taken in! I
understood now whose voice I had heard through the
open door; understood Juliana's sudden insistence on
riding every afternoon. I felt myself flushing with
annoyance at being so wrong-footed.

'She is – and comes as often as she can,' Eliza said.
'I wish you would stop her, for Mr Farrow would be
angry if he knew. She takes up all my time – talking,
weeping, playing with the boy, going over and over
again that awful business of her mother's death – I
cannot think there is any more to say, but you see,
Miss Agnew, it is to me that she comes.'

So much for your sympathy, I thought, my heart
wrenching for poor Juliana.

'You were living at Fourwinds, were you not,' I said
coldly, 'when Mrs Farrow had her fatal accident? That,
no doubt, is why Juliana comes to you with her
anguish. You were present – I was not.'

'You call it an accident,' Eliza said quietly, 'but it
was no such thing. Mrs Farrow took her own life – in
desperation. I am certain of that, beyond all doubt.'

I took a moment to assimilate this; then retorted:
'How can you be so sure?'

'Wait a moment.' She rose to her feet and stood
for a moment smoothing her apron, as though undecided; then she walked quickly indoors, leaving me with
the boy. He gazed after her, stretched out his hand and

said something unintelligible before returning to a game he was making with twigs on the ground, arranging them in patterns. I sat on the bench, looking at his sturdy back and compact limbs, his dark silky hair, for of course, I now took the keenest interest in this child. How easily contented he was with a little patch of earth, a few sticks and stones; yet how alarmingly his horizons would extend, as he grew up and encountered the world beyond these gates, and learned, as surely he must, of the irregularity of his parentage! Yet he could be considered lucky, in comparison with many another child conceived unwanted and out of wedlock. He would not want for home comforts and care.

It was Juliana I was most concerned for. Turning, I looked towards the parlour window behind me; I glimpsed a quick movement as she darted out of sight. She had been looking out at me, as I sat here with her child. Her attachment to him had been drawing her here, day after day. Tender-hearted as she was, how would she face separation, now or in the future?

When Eliza Dearly returned, it was with secrecy in her manner.

'Step into the vegetable garden,' she whispered, 'for Juliana must not know of this – must not see.' She swept the child into her arms, making him wail for the enforced abandonment of his twig game, and set off towards the door I had glanced through earlier.

Very much perplexed, I followed her into the large cultivated expanse of the walled garden. The two youths were still at their tasks; glancing at them, Eliza led the way in a different direction, along a narrow brick path, past apple trees espaliered against the wall, ripening marrows and currant bushes heavy with fruit, and into the open door of one of the greenhouses. The air was warm with the smell of watered peat and tomato foliage. We were alone; still, she glanced in all directions before taking something from her apron pocket.

'You must not tell Juliana,' she urged me. 'Give me your word.'

'I do,' I replied, rashness and curiosity overcoming doubt.

She handed me an envelope. 'Very well, then – read this. No one knows of its existence, other than I.'

The envelope was small, and of good quality vellum paper; it was addressed simply to *Eliza*, in a lady's slanting hand. I took out the two folded sheets of paper it contained.

My dearest Eliza, I read, in a script which began neatly but became larger and less controlled as the writing progressed.

Forgive me, for I must confide in someone. There may be no sense at all in what follows, for I doubt my sanity. I have tried to speak, and cannot speak sense. Only by sitting here quite alone can I summon words of any meaning.

Yesterday, my husband told you that I am grievously ill. I overheard him. But if I am ill, he has made me so. He caught me making ready to leave Fourwinds in secret – to run away, taking my girls with me. But I cannot take them. I cannot have them near me. And now he has made other plans.

As for my reason, I hardly know how to convey it. I will try.

Two days ago, Juliana told me something so dreadful that I hardly know how to commit it to paper. She told me that my husband — not once but many times over the last year — has visited her at night in her bedroom. He has forced his attentions on her — he has behaved to her as a man to his wife.

To me he does not. He does not love me, I have known that. He has not entered my bedroom since my last miscarriage. I lost his baby son, and for that he can never forgive me. It is not my fault and I have grieved ever since, but he never touches me now. Never a kiss, never an embrace, never a kind word.

I thought poor Juley must be deluded. I tried to coerce, even threaten her into saying she was lying, or dreaming. She wept and wept but she said it was no word of a lie.

Most horrible of all, she is with child. I could not believe anything so monstrous, but she says it is true.

It is the stuff of nightmare. I doubt my own sense. For surely it is I who am dreaming or imagining. My husband rejects me and now I am jealous of my daughter and make up terrible accusations against her. Is anything more shameful than that?

And Marianne? Do I suspect her of the same? Do I suspect him with her?

I do not know. My head is a buzzing wasp's nest of fears and suspicions. I cannot think clearly.

I cannot bear to look at Juley, nor Marianne. I cannot bear to look at myself in the mirror, for I see only barrenness, and madness and fear.

I must go away from them. He says so.

I could not comfort poor Juley. I could only think and think myself into spirals of despair. Next day I went to Ernest. I was shaking and weeping so much that I hardly know what I said, but he understood me at once and was angry. I was afraid, and trembled like a child. He seized me and flung me into a corner. Or did I dream that? No, for I have the purpling bruise on my arm, unless that is painted by my mind. I am perverted, he says — I am crazed, insane and evil to imagine such things. He says that Juley has confided in him and that Gideon Waring is her seducer. He has forced the man to confess and has dismissed him.

Then he was calm and kind. He sat me down and stayed by me while I wept. He tells me that I am ill, and he is very sorry. I cannot stay here. I must be away from the girls, or I will infect them. I must go to a special sanatorium for illnesses of the mind. I will be made better there, he says. Two doctors are coming to see me, not our usual Dr Fletcher, but two others. They will see if I am as mad as my husband says I am. And I must be. I am very sorry, Eliza, for all you must have endured from me.

But now I am afraid. I shall be locked up with madmen and madwomen. I shall never be free. I shall never be myself again. And it is myself I fear most, for the foulness my mind invents.

How happy I was once, but how I depended on his good will. How powerless we women are, Eliza, once we lose the good will of men. It goes, and we are gone. Well, I am going.

Who would believe what I have written here? Do you? Do I? No one will ever doubt my husband. Good father. Good husband. He is respectable, blameless. Poor man, to be encumbered with such a wife as I, a madwoman. Everyone will say so.

My heart breaks to leave my girls, but leave them I must, this way or the other. They must not run mad like their mother. They will do better with him.

Arrangements are made — I am to leave Fourwinds

tomorrow. But I have a plan of my own. I must be away from him. I must be away from my darling girls. But there is only one way I can escape from myself.

Goodbye, Eliza, and thank you. You have been good to me. Look after my girls, and help them to forget their wretched mother.

My sincerest thanks and good wishes.

Constance

My eyes had devoured the letter with all speed, although the writing became difficult to decipher. Reaching the end, I began again from the beginning, conscious of Eliza watching me. At length, barely trusting myself to speak, I refolded the paper and inserted it into its envelope.

'Is this the rambling of a madwoman?' I asked, hearing the tremor in my voice. 'As she claims?'

Eliza shook her head and occupied herself with the child, who was trying to pluck unripe tomatoes that clustered, greenly tempting. 'I cannot tell.'

'Poor woman! But how did you receive this letter? Did she give it to you?'

'She pushed it under the door of my room, on the night of her fatal fall. By the time I saw it, she was dead.'

'But you showed no one the letter? You have kept it secret all this while? Surely, that was most irresponsible of you!'

'It is easy for you to say that, Miss Agnew,' said Eliza, raising her chin. 'You were not there. What was I to do, then – confront Mr Farrow? Let everyone know of his wife's torment? Was it true, or was it not? How could I tell? I kept silent, and bided my time – for my first duty was to Juliana and Marianne. Surely you must understand that! Surely, in my position, you would have been concerned for them, above all else?'

'Mrs Dearly' – I made an effort at self-control – 'is there any truth in this, any grain of truth? Tell me, please – who do you believe to be Thomas's father? Is it Gideon Waring, or—?'

'He is the son of Mr Ernest Farrow.' She spoke the words calmly, holding my gaze. 'I did not know it then, but I know it now.'

'Good God! Poor, desperate woman! To doubt her own sanity – to take her life!'

Eliza nodded slowly. I looked down at the letter in my hand. 'And the boy! Then he is—' I curbed myself. 'What is to become of him?'

'He is to be hidden from view – I mean, under the guise of being my child – until he is old enough to be sent away to school. Then, arrangements will be made for him to be brought up as a young gentleman. Eventually, I am sure, he will be acknowledged as Mr Farrow's son.'

'But this is insupportable!' Thrusting the letter back at her, I stood transfixed, staring at my surroundings, the dirt-streaked panes of glass, the thriving tomato plants, the ripening fruit, a watering can and a stack of flowerpots: all suddenly bright and unreal as though painted on a canvas. 'His father's son? His heir? What is to become of Juliana?' I looked again at the child: at his dark hair which, now that I knew, was so like his father's; at his delicate features, so like his mother's. But his mother was also his sister, and his father was also his grandfather, and I— My mind reeled, and I clutched at the potting bench for support. 'Why did you show me that letter?' I demanded.

'Because, Miss Agnew, you have shown nothing but the deepest suspicion of my motives.' She pulled the boy to her, so that he stood with his back against her knees; she fondled his hair, while he tugged at her restraining arm. 'Now, perhaps, you see that concern for Juliana has been foremost in my thoughts. And for Tommy.'

I considered this. 'You could have left Mr Farrow's employment as soon as you discovered the truth. You could have exposed him. Instead, you have entered into a financial arrangement which I have no doubt benefits yourself and your husband as much as it benefits this unfortunate boy. Pardon me if I conclude that you have compromised your integrity.'

Later, reflecting on the startling information I had just been given, I had time to reconsider and to judge her less harshly; but at that moment, the veil that barely concealed our mutual hostility was flung back.

'Well, you have been more than frank,' she said, with her cold smile. 'Let us see, then, how *you* will act, now that you know the truth. For surely you cannot continue to accept your wages, your bed and board, from such a man as Ernest Farrow. Will you leave Fourwinds? You speak to me of compromise – what, Miss Agnew, of your own position?'

Chapter Twenty-nine

Dark Water

The weather had changed; the period of unbroken sunshine had come to an abrupt end. A wind was stirring from the west, seeming to presage bad weather; the sky was heavy with cloud; the full crowns of the roadside trees writhed this way and that, their battered foliage producing a sound like that of a storm-tossed sea. As I walked uphill from the railway station, the gusts in my face seemed intent on forcing me back, so that I almost had to fight my way.

I was retracing the steps of my first journey, when I had set out so gladly from Staverton, all unknowing of what awaited me at Fourwinds. Then, I had been alert to every sensation; this time I marched, breaking into a run at intervals, barely noticing where I was in my fury. How to proceed when I confronted Mr Farrow I had not decided; but confront him I must, for I could not hide what I knew, could not pretend that it was otherwise.

'Take care,' Gideon had said, as his parting words; 'I am concerned for your safety, Samuel. He is a dangerous man when roused to anger. Be very careful if you make an enemy of him.'

I had promised to heed this advice, and to let him know what ensued. Most urgently I wanted to see Charlotte, for what had now emerged made our argument seem petty and foolish. I must tell her what I had discovered, for so decisively had she cast Gideon Waring as villain, that the truth would be even more startling to her comprehension than to mine.

What should be done, how the situation might be resolved, I had no notion. All I knew, as anger and urgency propelled me through the dusk, was that something was surely coming to an end, and that it was something I had come to cherish: my situation at Fourwinds, my intense involvement with its inhabitants, with the place itself, and its mysteries. But, in truth, Fourwinds was already changed to me. Beneath its immaculate surfaces, corruption lurked unchecked. I had been lured and seduced by its charms, but must now destroy what I had come to love.

The gates were open, their hinges creaking and sighing in the wind. There stood the house, four-square to the darkening sky; the North Wind would be frowning at me, though I could not see him. Beckoned by soft lights from the vestibule, I experienced a collision of emotions that struck me almost physically in the chest, bringing me to a standstill. This was not my home, and never would be, once I had done what I must do; yet as I stood looking, I had to resist the most powerful attraction – almost that, I imagined, of a man returning to his beloved, to a love not yet consummated, and all the more compelling because desire lay rather in expectation than in fulfilment.

Hardening my resolve, I told myself that this was Mr Farrow's house, built to his design, to his tastes, bought with his money, and that Juliana was his victim, Thomas scarcely less so, and that my own presence here was a part of his scheme. I marched on up the driveway, mounted the steps and tugged at the bell pull.

Alice opened the door, surprised to see me there, so late and so wind-blown. Letting me in, she shut the door quickly against the gale. 'Mr Godwin! Good evening – we had thought you must be staying on in Brighton after all. Do come in – what a night this is!'

So preoccupied was I, as to have forgotten that Brighton was believed to have been my destination. I muttered something about mistaking the time of a train, and fobbed off her enquiries about food and drink. 'Is Mr Farrow at home?' I demanded.

'Yes, sir. He is in his study.'

The door to the drawing room opened; Charlotte came to greet me. I stepped towards her, and clasped her hand.

'Charlotte! I—'

'I am glad you are back, Samuel – I have longed to see you—' Her expression was of unutterable relief; the effect on me was to produce a strong desire to weep, and to rage, and to be soothed by her. Indeed, I found it impossible to meet her gaze, for fear that she would read the conflicting emotions that battled to control me.

'But you are upset – what has happened?' she asked, her eyes searching my face.

'Nothing! Nothing at all – I must – I must speak to Mr Farrow – excuse me—'

'But wait until— You are tired, and it is late, and I—'

With an incoherent sound of protest, I broke away, and mounted the stairs two at a time to the half-landing. I rapped loudly on the door and, without waiting for permission, burst into Mr Farrow's study.

He was at his desk; what he found there to occupy him at this hour of the night, I had no idea. He looked up from his papers, surprised at the manner of my entry, but unsuspicious.

'Samuel?' he greeted me. 'You are back with us – and in a great hurry! Is something wrong? What can I do for you?'

'I don't know,' I blustered. 'But maybe you had better start by telling the truth.'

He stared at me in great puzzlement. 'I don't understand. What is amiss?'

'Amiss? Amiss? You pretend not to understand? When you know full well that *every*thing is amiss!' I marched over and leaned with both hands on the desk, thrusting my face towards his. Offended, he pushed back his chair.

'Calm yourself, Samuel – sit down, and let us talk rationally. What has upset you so? Maybe I can be of help—'

'It is not myself I have come to talk about. I have

no favours to ask of you – merely that you admit what you have done!'

'Whatever has come over you, to make you speak so wildly? Have you been drinking?' He sniffed; but, finding no lingering fumes of alcohol, gestured me to back off. 'Sit down, if you are staying. Though you have burst in without ceremony, we can at least be civilized.'

'Civilized! You talk to me about being civilized! You – how – you—'

'If there is something comprehensible you wish to say, by all means say it. If not, I suggest you retire to bed.'

He was the one who had been drinking. His voice was unslurred, but a cut-glass tumbler stood on his desk, a third full; a whisky bottle stood beside it.

'Yes! You have— I – I *know*!' I spluttered. 'Surely you—'

My inarticulacy seemed to give him relief. 'You are tired, Samuel. I will overlook your rudeness, for it is quite out of character – we will talk tomorrow. Mrs Reynolds will provide you with a meal before you retire. Now, goodnight.' He gave me a nod and a stiff smile, then pretended to return his attention to one of the ledgers before him; but I saw that there was a tremor in his hand.

'No! We will talk *now*!' I leaned towards him, thumping my clenched hand on the desk. Even in my anger I saw the flicker of doubt in his eye as he reached out to steady the glass and bottle.

'Very well – since you will not be denied.'

'I will not! You will hear me. I have found out, Mr Farrow, that things here are not as they seem – I have found out that Juliana has been most foully abused, and by yourself—'

I saw him flinch at my words; knew that they had struck home.

'And,' I continued, 'that Thomas Dearly is the product of this – this godless union—'

'How dare you!' He rose to his feet, his face pinched tight with anger. 'You presume to thrust your way into my study, at this late hour, and to accuse me of – of something so repellent that I cannot bring myself to give it words! Take care what you say, Samuel, or you will regret it. You have found out certain things – yes, you must have been asking questions, and prying, and drawing your dramatic conclusions. But let me assure you they are quite wrong! And I must warn you – do not repeat what you have just said, *do not* – or the consequences will be serious indeed.'

'Do you deny it?' I cried. 'Do you deny that Juliana gave birth to a son?' I clenched my hands; I had to hear him confess.

He sat, picked up a pen and put it down again; the muscles around his mouth tightened. 'That part, regrettably, is true. Juliana, poor girl, must have told you, though I have urged her to forget the boy and to put the past behind her. You are aware, of course, that I dismissed the sculptor, Gideon Waring, from my employment? The child is his. Surely you must have guessed.'

'That is a lie! Yes, I suspected, just as you

277

intended. But I have met the man – I have spoken with him – I know that you have used him as – as your scapegoat—'

He looked startled. 'Oh – you've met him, have you? Charlotte told me the fellow had come sneaking back. Well, of course he denies his perversion! Is that not to be expected?'

'No!' I shouted. '*You* are the denier! I am as certain as I can be that he has never fathered a child, and is never likely to—'

'What can you mean?' Farrow demanded.

'I mean, Mr Farrow, that I have seen Gideon Waring, and have formed the highest opinion of him, both as an artist and as a man. I have also seen that another man is his close companion – he is the last person to act as you accuse him, forcing his attentions on an innocent girl—'

I stopped there, wishing I had sooner bitten my tongue out than make this revelation. In my effort to supply proof, I had given Mr Farrow a piece of potent ammunition; he seized upon it at once.

'Ah, so that's it!' His eyes gleamed with triumph. 'He's one of *that* sort, is he? I wonder I did not guess. And you – another of the same, I don't doubt – no wonder he wheedled his way round you, flattered you, and I shall not ask what else has passed between you, for it would disgust me to know of it – *that*, Samuel, is the man I dismissed from my employment. And who would question my right to do so? A fellow that carries on in that perverted way – what will he not do? Faugh!' He almost spat with contempt.

I was wavering: not because I believed what Mr Farrow was saying, for his argument contradicted itself at every turn, but because his defences were so formidable. Who – other than I – would doubt him? Armoured, as he was, with money, status, respectability, and above all, the confidence that his word would be accepted?

'What you have just said is nonsense,' I forged on, 'regarding both myself and Mr Waring. Perversion – you dare to accuse *him* of perversion? I repeat – *you* are the father of Juliana's child, I am certain of it, and if you have any courage at all, you will admit it, instead of attempting to use a blameless, honourable man as your scapegoat. I have never exchanged a word with Juliana on the subject, but I know it is true. You have used your own daughter, used her to breed the son you so desperately wanted, in the most callous and heartless way possible. How you intend to account for the unfortunate boy, I cannot imagine.'

'Sit down, Samuel. *Sit down.*' He rose to his feet again; he leaned towards me, and for a second his physical presence was so powerful that, in spite of myself, I obeyed. 'That's better,' he went on. 'No need for hysterics. Now, let us talk some sense. My daughter has an illegitimate son – that much we agree. Through no fault of her own, she is compromised. She is befitted by temperament and inclination for marriage. How, though, can she marry? Either the existence of her son must be kept secret from any prospective husband – a deception to which she would never agree – or a considerable financial incentive must be offered.

That, and other inducements besides. This, Samuel, is why I have brought you to Fourwinds.'

'Yes! Do you think I have no notion of that? Well, you must eliminate me from your scheming. I will never agree to it, never!'

I began to rise from my seat, but he gestured for me to sit, and continued to speak in calm tones.

'Think about it, Samuel! Don't be so hasty. You know that I have money and connections. I have commissioned paintings from you. I have recommended you to others. There is already considerable interest in your work from influential people such as Mr Vernon-Dale. One might go so far as to say I am building your name.'

'Good God!' I pushed myself up from my chair; I turned away from him and faced the bookshelves.

'Yes, you see,' he went on, reaching for his whisky glass, 'I can transform you, Samuel – I *am* transforming you – from an unknown and, let us be frank, unexceptional student painter to an artist whose work is sought, who will soon be able to command whatever fee he names. Why not agree? Do you not see that it will benefit you in every possible respect? You would have a loving and attentive wife, a comfortable home, you need not want for anything, you would have a ready market for your work . . .'

So reasonable, so assured, so soothing was his voice that I allowed myself to consider the riches he spread before me. What was the alternative? To give up everything I had found here, to leave Mr Farrow's employment under a shadow, to bid farewell to

Marianne, Juliana and Charlotte, never to see Fourwinds again. Juliana! Juliana for my wife – I thought
again of my imagined tableau by the piano, my wife
ready to greet me with a smile and a warm embrace.
Many a man would think himself lucky. What if I agreed?
Who would be the loser? Not I, for sure; even though
Juliana was not the bride I should have chosen for
myself, and I should have to subdue all vestige of the
fascination Marianne held for me, or suffer many a pang
of thwarted desire. Juliana's future would be safe;
Marianne would, I felt sure, be glad to have me for a
brother-in-law; Charlotte would be happy for her charge;
even the sad ghost of Mrs Farrow, if she could be
consulted, might think this the best possible resolution.

I heard myself groan aloud. In that moment, the
cautious, spineless part of me almost yielded, agreed
that I had been hasty in leaping to conclusions; almost
sat me down in the chair to match Mr Farrow's matter-
of-factness, and begin discussing marriage plans. Was
it possible? Was it possible that he was speaking the
truth? But only if Gideon had lied. Gideon was a highly
intelligent man, of that I was in no doubt; and *one* of
them was lying.

Not Gideon. No, I was certain that Gideon had
not lied.

Against the coward in me, indignation rose up in
full force, and proved the stronger. I wheeled to face
my tempter. 'There is one thing you have omitted to
mention – that you would be my father-in-law. That,
I cannot think of without revulsion. You cannot *buy*
me – do you really think I am so easily compromised?

Marry Juliana, to cover your guilt? Is she to know that a husband is being bought for her?'

'Juliana has a loving, biddable nature,' her father said, with a complacency that made me want to grab him by both shoulders and shake some feeling into him. 'The arrangement will suit her perfectly.'

'*Will* suit her!' I retorted. 'How can you take my compliance for granted?'

'Sit, Samuel, have a cigar and some whisky. Let us discuss the matter more reasonably. You will see that my offer is too good to refuse.'

I made an impatient gesture. 'I will not sit! I do refuse! Open your ears, man! What of your son, Mr Farrow? This is where I can't follow your reasoning. You plan to settle Juliana comfortably and to obliterate the past – but here is young Thomas, living only a few miles away. How is Juliana to tolerate that? You have always wanted a son – you told me that yourself – and here *is* your son – but how shall you ever acknowledge him?'

'I have told you whose son the boy is. If you choose not to believe me, there is no more I can do to convince you. But do you imagine I have not thought of Juliana? Do you not understand that her happiness is my prime concern – always has been? If you marry, I shall buy you a London house, with a studio, garden, whatever you wish. You will be well set up, Samuel. You will not regret it.'

His complacency stirred me again. 'This is intolerable! Am I your puppet?' I flung at him. 'You have behaved monstrously, and you continue to deny it!

You believe your wealth can shield you, but it cannot!' Again I bounded towards him, leaned across the desk; I reached out, grabbing the lapels of his smoking jacket. He pushed back his chair, almost hauling me with him: stood and faced me, trembling with anger, while I released him with a gesture of disgust.

'Do not touch me. I warn you, do not!' he cried hoarsely. 'It will be the worse for you, if you lay hands on me!'

Our eyes met and locked; I stared at him with something approaching hatred. Never before had I felt such loathing for another human being, and yet it was fuelled by my former regard, and the knowledge that he had used and deceived me. His eyes flickered towards the gun case on the wall; I saw it, saw that of the two of us, I was closer. Extending my arm, I forestalled him as he lunged across the desk, and we stood grappling with each other in a silent contest of strength and will. I do not know whether I intended merely to prevent him from obtaining the weapon, or whether I should have threatened him with it, even used it – all I know is that my instincts clamoured to hit and hurt and shame him, to wipe the smug expression for ever from his face.

I never found out, for at that moment we were disturbed by a loud rapping at the door.

We broke apart, and I sprang back; Mr Farrow straightened himself, and smoothed the lapels of his jacket; the door opened, and Charlotte stood there, staring alarmed at the scene before her.

'Pardon me for interrupting' – she was rather short

of breath – 'but I have to tell you that Juliana has disappeared.'

'Disappeared?' Mr Farrow echoed. 'Are you quite incapable of supervising her? What do I pay you for?'

'Yes, it is my fault,' Charlotte said, meeting his eye, 'but we must search for her without delay.'

In a moment we were hurrying down the stairs, Charlotte and I abreast, our employer behind us.

'Where can she have gone?'

'I have sent Reynolds to enquire at the Dearlys' cottage,' Charlotte told me, 'but Marianne is convinced she went to the lake.'

'The lake! She is out there, in this weather?'

The front door had been left open, flung back by the strong wind, battered anew with each gust. Seeing this, Charlotte let out a cry of frustration. 'I told her to wait for me – Marianne – I should have known she would not!'

Almost as anxious at the thought of Marianne out alone in the storm, as at Juliana's slipping away, I broke into a run – out to the lawn, down the slope of garden and onto the rough grass of the approach to the lake. There was only a sliver of moon tonight, fitfully obscured by scudding clouds; I could see only dimly the tousled trees ahead of me, and the glimmer of water; I stumbled, plunged on towards the shore. 'Marianne!' I shouted, and again and again, 'Juliana! Marianne!'

No one answered. I reached the shore and stood looking out at the dark, inscrutable surface of the lake, pounded by the wind almost into waves, reflecting nothing. In the thudding of my heart I felt a renewal of the fear that had seized me in the water; a certainty that something was pulling me back here, waiting in the depths. The wind was so strong that my yelling could scarcely be heard. Straining my ears into the gusts, I heard at first only my own panting breath, until another sound reached me – a sobbing cry from the direction of the boathouse, and a disturbance in the water. Moving quickly in that direction, I heard a plashing sound, and the swimmer's voice, high-pitched and frantic: 'Juley! Juley—'

'Marianne!' I shouted again, with all the strength of my lungs, and with renewed energy dashed on around the water's edge; I tripped over a tree-root and sprawled headlong; I picked myself up again. Another figure had appeared at the shore – Juliana! Poised by the willows, she steadied herself against a leaning branch. I had only time to register that Marianne must have waded in, under the mistaken impression that her sister needed rescuing; then Juliana – ignoring my yell of alarm – launched herself forward. I heard the splash and gurgle as she plunged into the water, and her gasp of shock at the coldness. And now there were voices behind me – 'There! There she is!' – and the light from a lantern that swayed violently, casting eerie shadows – but I was occupied in divesting myself of jacket and boots, then scanning the water. I should lose them – once in and swimming, I should have only their cries to guide me. 'I'm coming!' I shouted, and waded in, waist-deep; then, fighting my reluctance, I plunged forward, the cold shock of wetness gripping my chest with fear that choked my breath, and weighting my clothes so that they seemed to enmesh my limbs like a trawlerman's nets. Keeping my head up, I swam towards Marianne; I heard her gasping cries; I saw the quick bobbing movement of her swimming; then she ducked under the surface and was gone. Behind me, at the shore, I heard the splash of another body plunging in; I saw the glimmer of the oil lamp; Charlotte, her skirt ballooning like a sail, was rushing up the little pier. There she clambered into the rowing boat, and as it rocked and swayed, held out her lantern over the water. 'There – there!' she cried. I saw where she pointed, swam closer, took a deep breath, and upended myself.

Beneath the surface I struggled against instinct to keep my eyes open, to peer into the murky gloom. Discerning only shadows, I threshed about with my arms, felt the fibrous stems of weeds, disentangled myself; lungs bursting, I flailed again, one hand making contact with the fabric of a garment; simultaneously, one foot struck the yielding softness of the lake-bed. I held fast to the cloth; I grabbed hold with my other hand; I kicked for the surface with all my might. Whichever girl I had, I hauled her roughly with me, got her head above water; whether she was breathing or not, I could not tell, but at that moment another body intruded, hampering my efforts in an attempt to assist, and a voice – Mr Farrow's – croaked: 'Juliana! Juley—'

'Don't touch her!' I shouted. Freeing one hand, I thrust him away hard; then looked round for Charlotte.

Hearing the plash of oars, I saw that she had rowed out from the pier and was now battling with the oars, trying to turn the little boat into the wind, ready to come to my assistance. I bundled Juliana towards her, our courses met, her hand reached out; as soon as she had Juliana in a firm grasp I turned again; for where was Marianne? Striking into darkness, I was struck by panic, for the choppy water showed me nothing – then I heard, a few yards away, her sobbing breaths, and saw the feeble strokes of her swimming. 'Marianne! I'm here!' I called; found her, and in a few moments held her in my arms, kicking back towards the rowing boat. Charlotte, unable to get Juliana over the side unaided, was attempting to control the list and sway; her face was lit by the lantern, as in a Renaissance painting; the incongruous thought struck me even *in extremis.* Between us, making the boat teeter precariously, we managed to haul both girls onto its boards, weighted as they were by volumes of sodden fabric; Charlotte plied the oars, and I swam in her wake towards the pier. As she moored there, I hauled myself out. Marianne, shocked and winded, attempted to rise; I helped her along the prow and onto dry land; then returned to Charlotte, who was bending over Juliana in the boat. I dreaded to hear what she might have to tell me; but she turned to me with relief.

'She is breathing,' she said; and I felt that my own breath had been arrested until this moment. 'I feared at first that she was not – but she stirred, coughed up a good deal of water, and is reviving. Look to Marianne – fetch your jacket – we must summon help.'

'Mr Farrow!' I exclaimed, looking round for him. 'Surely he is not still in the water!' I grabbed the lantern and held it out, illuminating only the ruffled surface – no bobbing head, no hand waving for help.

'I must help him!' I cried, preparing to dive; but Charlotte held tight to my arm, restraining me.

'He must wait. We have the girls to attend to.'

She spoke with perfect calmness, as if nothing out of the ordinary were happening. I looked at her, unable to read her expression; then twisted myself free, snatched up the lantern and held it high as I moved along the lake shore. I called Mr Farrow's name, over and over again; I stood on the end of the pier and cast the light as far as it would reach; failing to see him, I took to the rowing boat, and cast about in the water. At last, finding no trace of him, I went back to Charlotte, resigned and on the point of exhaustion. She had urged the two girls into the leeward side of a stout tree, for what protection it offered. Marianne was now on her feet, shivering almost violently, while Juliana still crouched on the ground, huddled into my jacket.

'Please, come indoors,' Charlotte urged me. 'You have wasted enough time on him. We must take the girls inside without delay.'

Chapter Thirty

Charlotte Speaks

I knew you would not bring him alive from the water, for I have killed him. I have killed my father.

Yes. Yes.

You are shocked. Of course. And you have had many shocks this evening. Come, wrap yourself in this blanket. Drink some of this brandy. It will bring the colour back to your cheeks.

You saved Juliana's life, Samuel. I suspect that she went down to the lake with the intention of taking her own life. And without your intervention, she could have taken Marianne with her. Marianne *knew* – I should have questioned her, listened to her—

I? No, I did nothing. All I did was—

I pushed him away, Samuel. When you swam back for Marianne, he attempted to board the boat. He looked exhausted. I could not stop myself – I was occupied with Juliana – I could not bear the thought of him touching her, placing his hands on her, even in that desperate situation. Samuel, I have found out – I have learned of—

289

I pushed him back in! I struck him away with an oar. I did not mean to kill him, it was not my intention – I thought he would swim to the shore, or haul himself out at the pier—

But perhaps it is best. Why should he live? Juliana cannot live while he is in the world. Now he is out of it.

Yes, we must have the lake dredged tomorrow. He will wait till then.

No, thank you – my mind is too active for sleep. I should prefer to stay here awhile – will you stay with me and talk, if you are not quite exhausted?

Gideon? You found Gideon Waring? Ah, and he – he knew of—? Poor man, how I have maligned him! – Yes, of course – that accounts for— I wish you had told me, on your return – Yes, yes – we have both received this same revelation, this same shock – How much I have failed to understand!

My father? Yes, Mr Farrow – he is – he *was* – my father – yes.

No, no, he never knew.

I had better explain. If you are not too tired? You are sure?

Samuel, we have urgent matters to discuss, and the most distressing things to confront – but first I must tell you what I have told no one else; what I have kept secret for so long that I have almost stopped acknowledging it as the truth – have scarcely even allowed myself to think of him as my father, nor the girls as my sisters—

Are you ready? A little warmer – not at all feverish?
Very well, then:

My mother, Violet, worked as a maidservant at the
Farrows' house in Belgravia. That is the house which
Mr Farrow later sold, in order to buy the land here. She
was then eighteen; Ernest, the elder of the Farrows' two
sons, was nineteen. They were lovers. I will not say that
he seduced her, though that must have been the case
– my mother, on the one occasion I met her, was
adamant that he loved her, and that she loved him. She
spoke of him only in terms of the highest praise. He
was away at Cambridge for most of that time; their liaison
was a brief one, over a Christmas when he was at home.

She knew that it could lead nowhere. She accepted
his advances in full knowledge of that.

When she found herself with child, he had already
returned to Cambridge. She must be a strong-minded
woman in many ways, my mother. She did not write
to him, did not make any attempt to communicate
the news that he was to be a father. She left the
Farrows' employment before her condition was discovered. She went home to my grandmother, who made
arrangements for her to stay with a family in Devon
until I was born, so that her ruination, as my grandmother saw it, could be concealed. It was never
acknowledged that Violet had a daughter.

So – yes – poor little Thomas and I have this in
common.

My grandmother made arrangements for my upbringing. Yes, that is correct: Mrs Newbold, the lady who has recently died. My mother sought employment elsewhere; she moved to Yorkshire, becoming a maid-servant on a prosperous farm there. A few years later she married the son of that family, and took his name. He, in disgrace for some reason, was sent to Kenya, which is I believe the destination of many a wayward son, to seek his fortune by farming there.

No – I never saw my mother throughout the whole of my childhood. Our one meeting took place two years ago. I said that my grandmother brought me up, but it would be truer to say that she provided for me – she sent me to a drab boarding school, well out of her way. Widowed soon after my birth, she quickly remarried; a son was born of this marriage, and I was even more superfluous. Although I had relations in name, I have always felt myself to be quite alone in the world. That is what I have accepted; that is how I announce myself—

I know, Samuel, and I am very sorry. I should not have deceived you, for you have always been honest with me; but I hope you will understand. It is my way of preserving some pride.

Yes, my mother contacted me. I was working then as a pupil-teacher. She was on a brief visit from Kenya, where she still lives. We met briefly in Hyde Park, and have not communicated since. How odd it was to meet this woman, a complete stranger, without whom I should not exist! I am still not sure why she suggested that meeting, unless it was to assuage her guilty conscience, or to have some current memory of me, for she has no other children. That day, I asked who my father was; she told me his name, and that I was the product of their passionate love. She was not ashamed of it, disastrous though the consequences had been for her. She told me that Ernest came from a wealthy family; although she warned me that he knew nothing of my existence, she thought that he might give me financial support, if I approached him and asked for it. I resolved to do no such thing, but was gripped by a powerful urge to seek him out, to see for myself what kind of man he was.

– Yes, I did so immediately. My mother had told me the location of the Farrows' Belgravia home, and next day I went there. I found that the Farrows were no longer in residence. The new occupant, Lady Merriby, told me that Ernest Farrow had been the previous owner of the house – which, as I saw for myself, was a very substantial one – but that he had sold up after the death of his parents, to build himself a new house in Sussex. Lady Merriby had his forwarding address, which she gave me.

At once resigning from my post, I came to Staverton. I had not enough money to support myself, so took employment at the Cross Keys—

Oh? Did he? Yes, it *is* true – working in the kitchen and waiting at table. It was hard work, more strenuous than I was accustomed to, over long hours and for low pay, but I had at least bed and board. More importantly, I was in a position to gather news of Mr Farrow, and of his new house, Fourwinds, which had excited much local interest. I learned of the recent tragic loss of his wife, and that he had two daughters. My half-sisters! No sooner had I learned of their existence than I longed to meet them. I had no intention of disclosing my identity, and in fact no further plan than to satisfy my curiosity. However, within the course of a few days I overheard several very intriguing conversations, beginning with news of a scandal. I learned that the governess, Miss Eliza Hardacre, had been keeping company with a male employee of Mr Farrow's; both she and he had fallen out of favour, and were dismissed.

Here was an opportunity, the best I should ever have! On my first free afternoon, I presented myself at Fourwinds, where I asked to see Mr Farrow. He was still, of course, in mourning for his late wife, and I – I – *then*, I felt for him most piteously, and for my sisters. Giving away nothing of my background, I said that I had heard of the vacancy for a governess, and offered my services. He was a little suspicious at first, but I was able to reassure him as to my suitability, and gave him character references from my school. I did not see either of my half-sisters on that occasion, and had to return to the Cross Keys in a fidget of agitation. The house itself, this beautiful house, so lovingly built, so perfectly crafted, had cast a spell on me, Samuel, as I believe it did with you, when you first saw it. I yearned to see it again, to examine every room, every aspect, almost as strongly as I longed to meet its inhabitants – my secret family, as I ventured to think of them. I had to wait almost a week before I received a letter offering me the post. Mr Farrow explained that the role I was to fill was partly that of governess, partly companion, in view of the sad loss of the girls' mother.

Yes. Charlotte Agnew is my real name. I had no choice but to use it, because of the need to procure a character reference. If the name Agnew had meant anything to Mr Farrow, I should have attempted to pass it off as coincidence; it is not an uncommon name. He made no comment, and I continued in my deception. Presumably, since her status in his parents' home was a lowly one, he knew my mother only as Violet.

My first impression? I could not help gazing at him in fascination – which I attempted to conceal. He struck me as a handsome man – I tried in vain to see any resemblance to my own unremarkable face. His manner was charming, reassuring. He seemed so – so *solid* – there in the stylish house he had built to his requirements, surrounded by all the accoutrements of wealth and stability. Yet he must be my father, for Violet had been adamant that he was her only lover before she was married; he was the great passion of her youth. I could not feel bitter towards him for the life of comfort he led; for, if he had known of my mother's predicament, who is to say that he would not have done all he could to help her?

And now I was to work for him, live in his house, come into daily contact with my sisters!

At first, of course, only Marianne was at home; Juliana, I understood, was convalescing with a relative. While I got to know one half-sister, I eagerly awaited the return of the other; and in June she came home. I, of course, was ready to believe whatever I was told. Now, it is abundantly clear that both girls had been scared into silence by their father, for never a hint was given of the real circumstances. As for me, I played my role to such perfection that I am quite certain no one in the house has ever guessed at my motives. In fact, I should have found them hard to explain, even to myself. You must remember, Samuel, that I have never known a family of my own; have never had sister or brother, though I longed for them. And here were two charming young women who not only accepted me, but needed me; the loss of their mother was still raw and shocking. As you cannot help but notice, Juliana has come to depend on me – more than is healthy for her, I fear. I am almost mother to my own sister. Relationships, as you see, are somewhat confused in this household.

But the dependency is twofold. Juliana depends on me; I depend on her, and on Marianne, and on my role here. I have become the person everyone believes me to be, and I can be no one else. I cannot bear the thought of separation from my sisters. Especially now that – now that – everything has changed, Samuel, even before tonight – I – I hardly know—

Yes, so much to— I cannot believe—

Thank you. Thank you, Samuel. I cannot tell you how much your friendship means to me.

Yes, it used to be my amusement to imagine myself living here as his rightful daughter; to think of how things might have been if my mother had been his social equal, and if he had been older when they fell in love. Still, by coming here and making myself useful, I have earned his respect, and shaped my life around his. At last I have found a place where I am needed and wanted. I have taken pleasure in observing his habits, in getting to know his tastes and his preferences, in finding him reserved and melancholy as befitted a man who had so recently lost his wife; a man who spent hours by himself, who kept a quiet watch over his daughters and their well-being; a man of dignity and feeling. Almost, you might think, I fell in love with him myself: fell in love with my father, and could not have wanted a better.

But now all is changed – I have found out—

– Yes, yes – I hardly know how to – the poor girls—

– Yes, my discoveries have irrevocably changed my view of him – I cannot bear to see him, to think of— And now? Now I do not know what is to become of us, any of us – for I have killed him, for Juliana, for all of us.

I have killed our father.

Chapter Thirty-one

The West Wind

I could not sleep. I made only a token gesture of lying on my bed; but was soon astir, unable to slow the racing of my brain, and the whirlwind of impressions that fought for dominance.

Standing at my open bedroom door, I listened for sounds of restlessness elsewhere in the house, but heard only the wind, whose temper gradually abated to fitful gusts. Charlotte had looked in on Marianne and Juliana before retiring to bed; she confirmed that both – restored by hot baths and warm drinks – were sleeping quietly. No creak of floorboard from Charlotte's room betrayed wakefulness there, either. Stepping quietly out to the gallery, I stood by the railings, looking down at the closed door of Mr Farrow's bedroom. There was a terrible absence, a void – for a moment I fancied that, without Mr Farrow at its centre, the house, fragile as a blown egg, would crack its shell and fly apart, sending us all spinning out into darkness, to the four winds.

Gripping the railing, I thought of his poor wife, Constance, releasing her hold on life, letting herself fall. From what Charlotte had told me, and from what I had already discovered, I knew that Ernest Farrow had driven his wife to her death as surely as he had abused his daughter. I should feel no sympathy for him; I should be glad he had drowned. And yet I could not shake off a sense of loss that only added to my bewilderment.

Activity was the only means of ignoring the turmoil in my head. As soon as day began to break, I dressed – indeed, there had been little point in undressing – and let myself out of the house. I was determined that, in order to avoid additional distress for the girls, I must find Mr Farrow's body myself. Or, maybe, I wanted to assure myself that he was dead – for I could not believe it, could not let myself assume that his tough and resilient spirit would have given in so easily. If, though, he had drowned in the lake, I must convince Charlotte that the responsibility was not hers; or at least not hers alone. Had I not thrust him away myself, with more than necessary force?

Low cloud loured; the sky was grey and wind-tossed; the willows swayed, lashing the water. Reluctantly I made myself approach the jetty, and walk out. The rowing boat was moored there, where Charlotte had left it; I looked along the banks in both directions, but saw nothing. Incongruously, from somewhere in the trees beyond the boathouse, a nightingale was pouring out its full-throated song: a song of choking plaintiveness and yearning. In ordinary circumstances I would have stopped to listen, tried to see the unremarkable little bird that produced such mesmerizing music. But now I tried to close my ears, and to think about what I must do.

The pit of my stomach chilled with the dread that had seized me before, for I knew that I should have to enter the lake again, dive under the cold waters and search for a body in the murk. Maybe I need not? Maybe it would be better to wait until full daylight, and enlist the help of Reynolds and the stableboy? But this excuse failed to convince even myself.

Hesitating, about to take off my clothes, I glanced back towards the house, and was disconcerted to see a figure approaching. Marianne! Clearly she was not sleepwalking this time, but hurrying across the grass; she had seen me. She was in her nightgown, clutching as she ran at the peacock shawl thrown over her shoulders. I hastened towards her, afraid of some new disaster; but, to my surprise, her face was radiant with gladness.

'You will find him now, Samuel, won't you?' she called, still several yards away. 'I knew! I knew you would, if I waited – and now I see! He is there – let me show you! I can take you to the exact spot.'

Not understanding, I looked at her in concern. 'Why did you not say so last night?'

'Last night?' she said, puzzled. For a moment I wondered if she had lost all recall of the traumatic events; but she went on: 'It was too dark to see. But that is why you have come, surely?'

'Of course!'

Giving me a strange look, she walked purposefully to the pier, where I had stood a few moments earlier.

She waited for me to catch up; then pointed out into the lake. 'There. There you will find him. I must have known it, mustn't I? All this time! Yet I had quite forgotten, until last night. How odd, the knowledge we conceal from ourselves!' She laughed, looking quite untroubled. 'I slept so well, Samuel – at last! – and awoke so refreshed! I did not think I had dreamed, and yet in my dream I saw him here. And, hark, Samuel! A nightingale – oh, how beautifully she sings! There, now all will be well. It must bring good luck, must it not, to hear a nightingale?'

I could not follow her at all; but this was no time to question her.

'I will do it,' I told her; 'but first I want you to go back indoors. I would rather you were not here – it will distress you.'

'No! No! I must be here, to guide you. Do hurry – it is cold.'

Unable to strip off my clothes in front of Marianne, I discarded only my jacket, necktie and boots. It was bravado that made me dive from the jetty, instead of wading in as I had done previously, for I was unsure how deep the water was here, or how weedy. After last night, though, and my desperate struggles in the darkness, the shock of immersion was mild. I swam out a few feet and looked round at Marianne.

'There! There!' she cried, pointing. It was hard to discern exactly where she meant, but I followed her instructions as closely as I could, and when she called out, 'Dive, Samuel – now, there!' I did so. I expected to find nothing, for how could she be so certain? But something loomed below me, something horribly human in shape; I pushed against the pressure of water and reached out both arms, grabbing what was undeniably a human arm, stiff to my touch beneath its cladding of cloth. I turned it towards me, saw the face, and immediately released my grip, making for the surface; there I gasped for air, ignoring Marianne's cries, and prepared for a second dive. I had seen enough to convince myself that this was indeed Mr Farrow, but I must look again at the horrible sight – at the bloated face, the mouth open, the hands reaching out hopelessly to grasp only water – to see what it was that held the corpse fast. Surely, otherwise, it would have floated free?

I remembered my own panic when I felt myself gripped and entangled by weed. My grisly task must now be to free the corpse and lug it to the shore; but I could not attempt this with Marianne watching. I swam a few yards towards her, and called: 'He – it – is there, your father's body, just as you said. I am sorry. It seems he became entrapped underwater.'

Her reaction was quite astonishing. 'My father? My father's body?' Both hands flew to her mouth. 'What? Father – is he dead, then? Oh – what can have happened? Did we forget him?'

She seemed unable to support herself; she crouched, seemed likely to topple. Afraid that she might fall into the lake, I swam fast towards her and scrambled out. Never, never would I understand this girl; never would I fathom what went on in her mind.

Soaking as I was, I took her arm. 'Come, Marianne,'

I said gently, urging her to her feet, 'I thought you understood. You must come back to the house now. Charlotte will take care of you.'

I gathered up her shawl, wrapped it around her and supported her with my arm, leading her off the jetty. Stopping, she turned to gaze at me. 'My father is dead?' she repeated. 'Dead, and in the lake?' She gave a childish giggle. 'Did you say that?'

'Yes. I am very sorry.'

'Sorry?' She looked at me and laughed. 'Why should you be sorry?'

'Marianne! I don't think you can have grasped—'

'Yes! I understand. He is dead – drowned!' She turned her face up to the sky and shook back her hair; her expression was wild, elated. 'Now I can breathe. Now we are free! I do understand, Samuel – I understand perfectly. But do *you*?'

Gazing at her in wonderment, I shook my head slowly; for maybe I knew more than she realized. 'I am not sure, Marianne. What is your question?'

'Then I must ask you again. Tell you.' Almost skipping, she pulled me round to face her, holding both my hands in hers. 'Sam! We are free! We can be happy. You won't go away, will you? Now, when we can live as we wish?' Her eyes, not quite green, not quite blue, held mine in a blend of exultation and pleading; her nails bit into the palm of my hand; she gave a strange, mirthless giggle.

I stood very still, feeling myself on the brink of a declaration.

Of course I shall never leave you, Marianne. How could

I, when I love you more than I have ever loved anyone in my life?

These words remained unspoken. Never had I desired more strongly to take her in my arms, to kiss and caress her, to pour forth my love and longing; and her posture seemed to invite it. However, I stood silent and undecided. In her face I read desperation, I read triumph; I feared madness, and in that instant I was afraid of her.

Only with an effort could I avert my eyes from hers. As I looked away, I saw a grey-clad figure advancing towards us from the lawn – Charlotte. Quickly I released Marianne's grip on my hands.

She followed my glance. 'Oh, now here's Charlotte.' She took two paces back and drew her shawl around her. 'She will see to everything. She always does.'

I was vastly relieved, for I had no idea how to deal with Marianne. Charlotte, who must have been amazed to see me soaked and dripping yet again, and Marianne in deshabille, hurried over the rough grass. 'What has happened?' she asked urgently, no doubt fearing that Marianne had walked in her sleep.

'Take care of her – she is very deeply shocked. Keep her indoors,' I told Charlotte in an undertone. 'I shall be back very soon.'

Charlotte gave me a quick, meaningful glance, but said nothing. She took charge of Marianne, who shivered, and giggled in that peculiar, unsettling way. Hurriedly I returned to the lake, anxious that I should not find the body again. Indeed, once in and swimming, it took me several minutes of casting around; I tried to remember exactly where Marianne had stood, and where she had pointed, and came again at last to the dreadful sight. I filled my lungs with air, upended myself and struck down, seeing now that both the corpse's feet were thickly entangled in weed, and that under its dark mass some bulky object lay on the lake-bed, wrapped in tarpaulin and tied with rope. Groping, tugging at the slippery weed, I saw what must have happened – one of Mr Farrow's feet had become caught beneath the rope. He would of course have kicked for freedom, but succeeded only in enmeshing himself in the weed. He could not have struggled for long, exhausted from his efforts, before the water choked him.

I had to surface. The relief of clean air filling my lungs, of the chill grey morning, the cluck of some water bird! Yet I must go again into the depths, must probe again, must free the poor corpse and bring it to light.

This time, till my chest was almost bursting, I scrabbled at the tarpaulin, succeeding in loosening it a little from its bonds.

My exploring hand touched stone, and in that instant I knew what I had found.

The West Wind.

The West Wind.

The stone figure of the West Wind.

This was what Marianne had meant. How could she know? And having known, how could she have forgotten?

Here it lay – had lain all this while – where Mr

Farrow himself must have committed it to the water!

I tugged and tore at the restraining weed, released the corpse's foot from the rope, and he was free. Grasping the body under both arms, as if pulling an imperilled swimmer to safety, I dragged him to the surface, and then to the shore. He was almost too heavy for me to manage alone; I had to leave him close to the edge, lodged in rushes. A gruesome sight indeed; but I must hurry, and make sure that no one strayed down here to see it unawares. I looked once at the bloated, terrible face, and wished I had not.

I hastened back to the house. There was much to do.

Chapter Thirty-two

Gargoyle

It was the strangest day I had ever known. There was much to do, and many visitors to the house, and all manner of questions to be asked and answered; yet I passed through the hours with numbed senses, as though not quite party to my own thoughts and actions.

After Samuel returned with the news that he had found both Mr Farrow's body and the missing West Wind, we set about summoning a police officer, a coroner and the family solicitor. Although I did my best to spare Juliana and Marianne from being too closely involved in the proceedings, it was inevitable that they had to answer questions from the police officer. The death had to be registered; the body was retrieved, examined, and later consigned to the mortuary in Staverton. There would be an inquest, of course; I could not think about that yet, for I dreaded to contemplate what honesty might compel me to reveal. The body could not be released for burial until the coroner had made his pronouncement.

Meanwhile, Juliana was my most urgent concern; for I feared that she had planned to take her own life, and that she, not her father, might have been pulled from the lake as a lifeless corpse. There could be no avoiding the truth; seeking her alone in her room, I told her all that I knew and suspected. Suffice it to say that many tears were shed, and an observer might have thought that our grief for the dead man was quite unlimited. I had not yet told her, of course, that although she had lost a father, she had gained a sister: that must wait.

'I loved him, Charlotte,' Juliana confided, 'even though I hated him as well. Does that sound possible? And now all I feel is bafflement – it is too big, too sudden to understand. How can a person be with us one day, then so abruptly vanished? I cannot grasp it – cannot get the simple fact into my brain, that he is dead. Where is he now, Charlotte? Where has he gone?'

I could provide no answer. Juliana was the church-goer, the believer; I went with her merely as a matter of form. I did not know where our father had gone. For his sake, I must surely hope there was no after-life; that his spirit as well as his life had been suffocated and extinguished, there on the lake-bed. If a vengeful God dealt out justice to departed souls, what torments would repay such wickedness? I shuddered, unable to contemplate it. My father was gone; his life had ended; and with it, I hoped, the worst of Juliana's sufferings.

We were interrupted by Alice, who told us that a messenger had brought a note for Miss Farrow, and that an immediate reply was requested. Juliana dried her tears, and made herself presentable, and we went downstairs.

The messenger was a young man on horseback, bringing a note from the family solicitor, Mr Jessop. Reading the letter, Juliana looked puzzled; she passed it to me.

Dear Miss Farrow, I read,

> *Following my brief visit this morning, let me convey once more my sincere condolences to you and your family. I mentioned then that I had seen your father only recently, with reference to the terms of his Will. In this connection, I should like to request a meeting with you and your sister, before the funeral takes place. The formal reading of the Will conventionally takes place after the funeral, but there are matters I should prefer to discuss privately beforehand with you and your sister, which I should not like you to hear for the first time in the presence of Mr Farrow's extended family. Would it be convenient for me to call on you this afternoon, at four o'clock? I should be grateful if you would send your reply immediately, by return.*
>
> *Yours most sincerely,*
> *Harold Jessop*

Juliana turned to me an anxious, tear-stained face. 'What can it mean?'

'I do not know,' I told her; though I guessed that the solicitor must be referring to Mr Farrow's provision for his illegitimate son. 'It is almost two now; you will not have long to wait.'

Juliana nodded. 'Kindly tell Mr Jessop that we will see him at four o'clock, as he requests,' she called to the messenger, who wheeled his horse round and spurred it into a fast trot. 'Charlotte!' She clutched at my sleeve. 'You must be present when he comes – you will, won't you, for my sake? I dread to hear what he will reveal!'

I attempted to reassure her; we found Marianne, who had been resting in the morning room since her upset by the lake, and told her of the forthcoming meeting. We had much to do meanwhile, for there were a great many letters to be written, but the time passed slowly and anxiously.

At last we heard hooves outside, which announced the arrival of the fly which carried Mr Jessop. Juliana composed herself enough to receive him politely. We had all seen him on previous visits to the house, for he had dealt with Mr Farrow's affairs for many years; he was a small, somewhat owlish man in half-moon spectacles, dressed very formally and correctly.

Juliana, followed by Marianne and myself, conducted him into the dining room, and offered refreshment. 'My sister and I should like Miss Agnew to be present at our discussion,' she told him.

Mr Jessop looked at her over the top of his spectacles. 'Miss Farrow, I must, er, forewarn you that some of the matters I have to disclose are of a very confidential nature. I should prefer to speak privately to you and Miss Marianne.'

Juliana, however, was firm. 'Miss Agnew is completely in our confidence, Mr Jessop. Whatever you have to say to us, we will immediately relay to her; so she may as well hear it from your own lips.'

'Very well – if you insist.' Mr Jessop had no choice but to give way. First, he produced a large folder of papers, and spent a few moments laying them out on the table. Through the conversation that followed, he never once glanced in my direction, addressing all his remarks to Juliana and Marianne.

'As you are no doubt aware,' he began, after a few preliminary remarks, 'your father was a wealthy man, who invested wisely and prudently. You will be more than adequately provided for.'

'That is all we require,' said Juliana, fumbling with her handkerchief, and glancing sidelong at Marianne, who gazed steadily at Mr Jessop and did not return the look.

'However,' the solicitor continued, 'I have to tell you that your father has made two substantial changes to his Will since the, erm, sad death of your mother.'

'I am not surprised by this,' Juliana commented. 'I imagine it is what a widower would be expected to do.'

He looked at her over the top of his spectacles. 'I am sorry, Miss Farrow, but I ought to warn you that you *will* find it surprising. I think it likely that your father's relatives may wish to contest the Will; it is even possible that you yourselves may wish to contest it, although, since I myself carried out the revisions and can guarantee that your father was in complete possession of his faculties, such an application is unlikely to succeed. This is why I was so anxious to see you today, in order to give you a few days to assimilate the, ah, information I am about to give you, so that it does not come as a shock to you when your relatives are assembled for the, erm, funeral.'

Juliana gave a nod of acquiescence; Marianne merely looked baffled.

'I wish to begin, Miss Farrow, Miss Marianne, by telling you how the Will stood before the recent changes,' Mr Jessop proceeded. 'During the lifetime of your, ah, late mother, the Will divided the major part of your father's fortune among the three of you. There were, besides, a few small bequests to members of the family, none of which need concern us. What *does* concern us, however, is the provision your father made for this house, Fourwinds.' He cast his eyes around the room, and upwards, seeming to encompass the whole dwelling in the sweep of his gaze.

'Please go on.' Juliana was pale, her hands clasped in her lap.

'If your mother had outlived your father, she would have been entitled to live here for as long as she wished. At the time the Will was drawn up, there was of course a possibility that your mother might give birth to a son, who would, ah, naturally be your father's heir. However, as we know, of course, the marriage produced no son.'

A quick, furtive glance was exchanged between Marianne and Juliana; Mr Jessop, occupied with his papers, did not see it.

'So the house is left to Juliana?' Marianne prompted, leaning over the table.

'I am afraid not.' Mr Jessop gave a small cough and adjusted his spectacles, while we all sat in suspenseful silence. 'Possession of the house, with all its land and effects, would go first to your father's younger brother, er, Mr Robert Farrow, and in turn to *his* son, James.'

'Sons! Sons!' Marianne half turned from the table, as if about to rise to her feet and storm out. 'Why must sons receive everything, and daughters nothing? So we are to be turned out of our house? Are we to beg on the streets?'

'Hush, Marianne,' I urged her. 'Mr Jessop is not finished.'

The solicitor looked grave. 'Indeed I have not. Please, Miss Marianne, do not anticipate what I have to tell you. You must remember that the Will I have been speaking of is the one drawn up before your mother's death. Your father made two subsequent changes, which affect things materially. Of course you are not to be turned out of your home. Your father has not neglected you – of course he has not.'

'Please tell us the rest,' Juliana said, in a low voice.

'The first revision,' continued Mr Jessop, 'removed all mention of your mother from the Will, and divided your father's fortune between the two of you; provision for the house remained exactly as I have outlined. However, your father amended his Will for a second time, in June last year.'

Juliana looked intently at her clasped hands; I saw what an effort it cost to sit passively and demurely while these uncertainties hovered before her.

'I have to tell you, Miss Farrow, Miss Marianne, that in this, the most recent version of the Will, your father's entire estate – money, investments, assets, this house, its land and all effects – is left to the, ah, child known at present as Thomas Dearly. I do not know if this name means anything to you. Ah, I see that it does.'

Juliana's eyelids fluttered, but she said nothing.

'Thomas Dearly!' Marianne burst out. 'And what of us? Do we count for nothing in our father's regard? So we *are* to be homeless, after all?'

'Most certainly not, Miss Marianne. Let me reassure you on that score.' The solicitor aligned his papers. 'The child known as Thomas Dearly is presently less than two years old. He is your father's, ah, illegitimate son; I am sorry if this, erm, information comes as a shock to you. I understand that the boy is currently in the charge of your father's erstwhile employee, Mrs Matthew Dearly, formerly Eliza Hardacre. Detailed arrangements have been made for his welfare, supervision and education until he comes of age, at which time he is to take the name of Farrow and to be acknowledged as your father's son and heir. I should add that a handsome provision is also made for Mrs Dearly, in recognition of, er, the services she has provided.'

'Thomas is to inherit everything – Juliana and myself, nothing?' Marianne exclaimed.

'Not quite nothing,' Mr Jessop answered. 'You are to continue to live here at Fourwinds, where all your needs will be met; you will each receive an annual allowance. Officially, until you each come of age, you will be under the guardianship of your uncle, Mr Robert Farrow.'

'Uncle Robert?' said Marianne. 'But he will not want to be troubled by us – we scarcely see him from one year's end to the next! And if he is to be denied the house, when he must have expected to inherit it, it will be a most unwelcome burden!'

'We will listen first to all Mr Jessop has to say,' said Juliana. 'There will be plenty of time later to think of the implications.'

'Indeed. I was about to, er, add that Miss Juliana Farrow is to receive a settlement of ten thousand pounds on the occasion of her marriage. May I – ah – I hope it is not presumptuous of me to assume that such a happy event is imminent? After a suitable period of mourning, naturally?'

'No,' Juliana answered, her voice barely audible; she looked down at her clenched hands. 'Please make no such assumption.'

'What of me?' Marianne asked. 'Am I to be given ten thousand pounds?'

'There is no mention of any such settlement. I inferred from these terms that Mr Farrow, ah, expected your sister to marry in the near future, and made this stipulation accordingly. I apologize if I am mistaken in that.'

Marianne turned to her sister. 'There, Juley! You can marry Samuel, and make him a rich man in the process!'

'I imagine that is what Papa had in mind,' Juliana said, in a voice which betrayed no emotion.

'Samuel?' queried Mr Jessop.

'Samuel Godwin, a young artist,' I told him. 'He

is – was – a protégé of Mr Farrow's, who considered him very promising.'

'Ah, so he has presented himself as a suitor?' said the solicitor. 'Yes, I see.'

'Juley, you ought to be pleased!' Marianne said, a touch peevishly. 'This is a piece of good luck, is it not?'

'Luck?' said Juliana, in a fierce undertone. 'You must forgive me if I do not see anything in my present situation that can be viewed as *good luck.*'

Marianne drew back, offended. 'I meant only to help. You are to marry Samuel – it is what Papa decided. Samuel will be ready enough to fall in with the plan, I am sure, for he is incapable of deciding anything for himself.'

The solicitor looked from one to the other, then back at his papers. 'This is all so very sudden – you will need time to, erm, assimilate this information at your leisure. You are shocked, of course; you need time to adjust to your sad loss. Miss Farrow evidently does not wish to contemplate marriage, while she finds herself so, ah, tragically, so unexpectedly in mourning.'

'Indeed not,' Juliana said resolutely, with a glance at me.

Marianne stood; with her eyes blazing and hair loose and wild around her face, she made an imposing figure. 'You are quite wrong, Mr Jessop, to suppose us sorrowfully afflicted by our father's death. I cannot speak for Juliana, but I can speak for myself. I am glad he is dead. I hated my father.'

'Hush, dear! You don't mean it!' Juliana clutched at her arm in an effort to pull her back to her seat;

Marianne, with a gesture of impatience, resisted. Pushing her chair away from the table, she went to the fireplace, from which new position she faced us defiantly. The solicitor glanced at me for the first time since we had entered the room, obviously considering it my job to cope with feminine hysterics. I rose and went to Marianne; almost violently she shook me off.

'I *do* mean what I say,' she burst forth again. 'You know I do! When you've had time to get over this shock, Juley, you will share my relief. I hated him! He used and controlled us, and he is trying to control us now – to make us fulfil his wishes. Thomas, Thomas is all that matters to him, or ever did! Thomas is the son he always wanted – Thomas counts for everything, and we for nothing – we have no home to call our own, we must live here with Thomas's permission . . .'

I had to quieten her, for Juliana's sake. Anxious as to what she might reveal, I went to Marianne and put an arm round her shoulders. Fortunately for us all, her voice faltered; she broke into a storm of weeping, and became incoherent.

'Juliana, please ring the bell and order tea and cake for Mr Jessop,' I said. 'I shall take Marianne into the morning room.' With an arm round her shoulders, I guided her through the door.

I had to know. Words must be found to ask the question, though I dreaded to hear it answered.

We sat together in the cushioned recess. Alice had just brought in a vase of flowers; the room was fresh and feminine, with its willow-leaf curtains, its curved stone fireplace, its white plaster frieze with a design of leaves and berries. I had always imagined that Constance Farrow, sitting here with her sewing, looking out at the lawn, must have thought herself the most fortunate of women. Now I could guess at the anguish she must have suffered, the self-reproach, the sense of failure that must have possessed her. I had misjudged her, as surely as I had misjudged *him* – the man I thought I knew so well, the father I had thought I loved.

'I am not sorry!' Marianne blazed at me. 'I will not apologize for what I said, for I meant it!'

'Marianne – forgive me, but I must know. Did your father – did he ever force his attentions on you?'

I feared her answer, but when it came, it was not what I had expected.

'No, never!' She faced me, with her head high. 'I feared it – thought it inevitable – and then I felt that he must love me less than Juley, that I am not good enough for him, not his special girl the way she is, and I hate him for leaving me out!' Her eyes brimmed over with fresh tears. 'Sometimes I even think I hate *her*, for dominating his attention as she does! I must be mad, Charlotte, must I not, to think such a thing? Not right in my wits?'

Of course, I told her, over and over again, as I had tried to impress on Juliana earlier in the day, that none of what had happened was her fault, and that her father, not she, must take all blame; but meanwhile my thoughts were churning. He had infected them all; the seeds he had sown so wickedly were springing up as live green shoots; he was dead, but what of his leavings?

All this while, Samuel, assisted by Reynolds and the stable-boy, had been busy down at the lake. When Mr Jessop had at last departed, and both Marianne and Juliana, exhausted by the traumas of the day and the night, had gone to their rooms to rest, I went in search of him.

I found him sitting alone beneath a willow tree. Near him, on the bank, was an object the size of a human body, shrouded in green. My heart thudded in my chest; for an instant I thought that a second corpse had been found in the lake. Then I realized that of course this was the West Wind statue; Marianne, before the solicitor arrived, had been exultant, telling me that it had been found. I thought of the obsession that had gripped her for so many months: that the inhabitants of the house would never rest at peace until the final sculpture was in place on the west wall. It was surely too late for that, but maybe its finding would give the poor girl some comfort.

'Samuel?' I called, from some paces off. 'Surely you cannot have managed that alone?'

He looked at me, his face mud-streaked, tired and haggard. With a painful wrench, I knew how dear he had become to me, now that we must surely part company.

He gave a rueful laugh. 'I did not. It took the combined efforts of Reynolds, Jack and myself, together with Hector pulling with all his might, to haul it to shore. They have gone back to the stables, and I don't know what to do. Look at this.'

I stared at the figure on the grass, barely identifiable as a human form to match our other three Winds; it was coated with green, slimy weed, studded with black snails, infested with small wriggling things, here and there matted into clots of oozing blackness. Only the face was discernible; Samuel must have attempted to clear it, though the features still had a green cast. Staring, I ventured closer, then drew back with a start of revulsion. The face was hideous – grotesque, slimed, leering like a gargoyle, but still a face that I recognized, a face I knew as well as my own: it was the face of Ernest Farrow.

'How . . . ?' I faltered, believing for a bemused second that my father's body, as though cursed for his sins, had turned to stone underwater, and that the corpse in Staverton mortuary was that of some other man.

'This is Gideon Waring's revenge,' said Samuel.

'I do not understand,' I told him, slow-witted with this fresh shock.

'Waring completed his commission – he is an honest man – he carried out the work he had been paid for,' Samuel explained. 'This is the sculpture he delivered to Mr Farrow, in completion of his contract. And this is where Mr Farrow hid it.'

'You knew?'

He shook his head. 'Marianne did; I do not know how.'

'But what is to be done with this – this despicable thing?' I looked again at the contorted face, shuddered, and looked away. 'We cannot put this on the west wall!'

'I shall have it towed back into the lake,' Samuel replied. 'And this time it can stay there for ever. Gideon Waring must produce another. He will do it, I know. He will complete the commission according to his original plan.'

'How can you be so sure of him?' I asked.

Samuel did not answer, and at first I thought he had not heard me; then he said quietly, 'I believe I am as sure of Gideon Waring as of anyone in my life.'

Chapter Thirty-three

Mr Rupert Vernon-Dale to Samuel Godwin

Rampions,
Staverton

8th July, 1898

S. Godwin, Esq.,
c/o E. Farrow, Esq.,
Fourwinds,
Staverton,
Sussex

Dear Mr Godwin,

It was a great pleasure to meet you at dinner at Fourwinds last Saturday.

As you will by now be aware, I take a great interest in fine art, and pride myself that I have an astute eye for new talent. I have been most impressed by what I have heard of you from your employer, my good friend Mr Farrow, who holds you in the highest regard.

Samuel Godwin

First let me assure you that I have discussed this matter with him before venturing to approach you in this way. I fully understand that you have paintings to complete for him before finding yourself free to embark on other commissions. However, I am most eager to secure your services for a similar project I have in mind. You will have heard that I have recently carried out substantial improvements to my house and gardens, and it is my proud hope that Rampions will soon be regarded as one of the foremost country houses in England. In recognition of this, I intend to commission a series of paintings, which will be prominently displayed in my picture gallery and which will reflect the changes as the garden matures.

I can assure you, Mr Godwin, that I have connections in the London art world which would be very much to your benefit, and would almost certainly result in further commissions and exhibiting opportunities. If you are interested in taking up my offer, please let me know as soon as possible. We shall then arrange a meeting at which we can discuss terms and remuneration.

In anticipation of further conversation, and with my heartiest good wishes,

Yours very sincerely,
Rupert Vernon-Dale

Chapter Thirty-four

Ashes, Earth and Dust

I read the letter quickly, then crumpled it up and stuffed it into my pocket, intending to discard it later. Mr Vernon-Dale, of course, had been unaware of Mr Farrow's death when he sat down to write it.

We seemed to spend the next few days in a strange limbo-like state, awaiting first the inquest and then the funeral. I had much to do, beforehand, to persuade Charlotte that nothing would be gained from her admission that she had repelled Mr Farrow with an oar, nor by my confessing to pushing him away. Unable for Juliana's sake to reveal our motives, we agreed to say, truthfully, that there had been a skirmish at the lake after Marianne, in search of her sister, had fallen in, and that everyone's efforts – compounded by panic, confusion and darkness – had been to pull Marianne, Juliana and later Mr Farrow himself from the water. The Coroner confirmed that Mr Farrow had met his death by drowning, with possible heart failure occasioned by the shock of sudden immersion in cold water, and the verdict was of Accidental Death.

The funeral could now proceed, and it was a relief

to busy ourselves with making arrangements for the grim occasion. Juliana and Charlotte spent hours addressing black-edged cards to Mr Farrow's relatives and acquaintances. At meals, and when we found ourselves at leisure together, we spoke of little but the practicalities we were attending to. It was as if all feeling had withered inside us, and must wait until after the burial to be revivified. Of course, I experienced many a painful reminder of the days following my father's death; try as I might to suppress them, I found myself heavy and subdued, little befitted to relieve the sufferings of my companions.

The burial service, at Staverton church, was attended by a great many people. Apart from the Vernon-Dales, the Greenlaws, Annette Duchêne, and various other acquaintances of Mr Farrow's, there were a number of relatives, none of whom, of course, I recognized. The family, naturally, took precedence, and Marianne and Juliana were escorted by their Uncle Robert – who brought with him his wife, his son of some ten years and a younger daughter – to the front pew, alongside various great-aunts, great-uncles and the like. Charlotte, who could have given the girls more comfort than anyone else present, found herself separated from them, and took a seat next to me in a pew several rows back. We could only gaze at them in sympathy – so young and frail Marianne looked, so unfamiliar, dressed all in black; Juliana so grave and dignified – and offer them our silent sympathy.

My own father's funeral was so recent that it

seemed no time at all had elapsed since I sat between my mother and sister in the Sydenham church. On that occasion, while Mama and Isobel sobbed, I found it a torment to sit in silence and to contemplate the coffin which held my father's worldly remains, while my mind replayed every impatient remark I had ever made to him, every piece of his advice I had discarded, every unkind thought I had harboured. Too late, too late, for one more word, one touch of his hand; he had slipped out of my reach.

Even now, as I gazed at the coffin, loaded with white lilies which filled the air with their scent, I found my eyes welling with unmanly tears. I felt that time had played a peculiar trick, that my father had died for a second time, and that if I gazed around the church I should find the pews occupied by my own family, and my father's friends and business partners. As I pronounced the *Amen*, I was bidding farewell to my own father; yet in a way I was mourning the loss of Mr Farrow too. I was mourning the man I had thought him to be; the man who had shown me more esteem and respect than my own father had ever done. I had convinced myself that Mr Farrow was the father I might have chosen for myself. Now, my disillusionment was bitter.

Kneeling for the prayers, I reflected that I might have listened more carefully to my father, to his insistence that my painting was a waste of time. He had been both right and wrong. Right: because although I should never have acknowledged it to him, nor, till now, to myself, I had not the talent to be more than mediocre; I was more enamoured of the idea of being an artist, than of art itself. Wrong: because the world does not know the difference. If first Mr Farrow, then Mr Vernon-Dale, chose to pluck an unexceptional painter from obscurity, and to broadcast the opinion that his work was of value, then it was generally believed to be so. Why should I not, like the Emperor in his new clothes, take advantage of such gullibility?

Mr Vernon-Dale's letter was in the pocket of the old jacket I had been wearing when the post was delivered. I had not thrown it away, thinking I might show it to Charlotte later. Now, I found myself reconsidering my hasty dismissal of the offer it contained. Circumstances had deprived me of job and home; why should I not seize this new chance? I should need money; I should need a home; I did not want to return lamely to my mother, admitting failure in my first attempt at independence; above all, I did not want to leave the three young women who had become, each in her own way, so dear to me. Yet, if I accepted Mr Vernon-Dale's offer, I should know myself to be an opportunist.

We stood for the hymn; my hand brushed against Charlotte's, and – tentatively – she clasped my fingers, giving me a sidelong glance. She, who missed nothing, had observed my tears, and must have thought they were for Mr Farrow; maybe they were. I returned the smallest of smiles, and for a moment we stood hand in hand. Of course, I must discuss my predicament with Charlotte. She would understand and advise; she would know what was best. As for her own situation –

she had not yet made her revelation to Marianne and Juliana, who already had enough to assimilate.

We filed out of the church and gathered around the newly dug grave. Jackdaws cawed from the tower while the coffin was lowered in, earth scattered over it, and heads bowed for the final prayers; Marianne sobbed, Juliana stood pale and resolute. The new grave would soon be given its covering of turf, and its head-stone put into position, where it would endure for measureless centuries into the future, crusted over, like the others beneath the ancient yew, with moss and lichen. Mr Farrow's final resting place would draw no attention to the manner of man he had been: passers-by, troubling to stop and decipher the mossy letters, would conclude that here was a loving family man, felled in his prime. To this we must all come, no matter how feverishly our hearts beat out the rhythm of our lives. Who could know what other stories, what lusts and desires, loves and aspirations and disappointments, crumbled with the bones beneath the grave-mounds?

At last this part of the ordeal was over; but there was more to come. The family party was driven, in several carriages, to Fourwinds; sherry and sandwiches, cakes and tea were served; more condolences offered. Throughout all this, Juliana performed the duties of hostess, conducting herself with quiet restraint. She had, however, another trial to endure – the reading of the Will. Now, I had the chance to observe the girls' Uncle Robert (Charlotte's half-uncle too, though he was not aware of it), at closer quarters. Five years or so younger than Ernest, he was very similar to him in feature, although with none of his brother's physical impressiveness. The likeness, however, was strong enough to disturb me; it was as if a less substantial Ernest Farrow, a shadow of himself, had returned to mingle with his funeral guests. The arrival of these strangers – to me – was newly unsettling, for what changes might they wish to impose?

Charlotte and I, while the family assembled with Mr Jessop in the dining room for the formal reading of the Will, walked together down to the stable yard, where the carriages stood ready to convey our guests back to the railway station. The horses had not been unharnessed, but had been given nosebags to sustain them for their return journeys, while the grooms and drivers took refreshment in the servants' quarters. The homely sounds of snortings, the occasional pawing of a hoof, the creak of harness and the jingle of bits, were soothing in their way. Charlotte and I wandered between the horses, admiring them – they were all black, of course, groomed to perfection, their summer coats so fine and glossy that the sunlight struck blues and purples from the sheen. I thought of the colours I should need on my palette, and how difficult it would be to reproduce what nature supplied so bountifully.

Mr Farrow's hunter, Guardsman, was upset by the intrusion into his domain. Turned out in his paddock, he paced this way and that along the fence, stamping up a cloud of dust from the bare ground; he pushed his chest into the rails as he turned, and shook his mane with annoyance, glaring defiance at the newcomers. Such vibrant energy, so pointlessly expended! – for by evening the yard would be empty again, and everything as accustomed.

'What will happen to him, poor fellow?' I asked. 'There will be no use for him here.'

'He will have to be sold, I suppose,' said Charlotte. 'It is generous of you, Samuel, to give your sympathy to a horse. This handsome animal is well trained and well bred; expert care has been lavished on him all his life. He will find a suitable new owner, I am sure. It is tempting,' she added, 'to think that more care goes into the breeding of valuable horses than of human beings. What of you and I?'

I had no reply to this. 'Poor Juliana!' I said instead. 'What torment she must be facing now, while Mr Jessop reveals the irregularities of her father's life. Thank God the family will never know – I assume they will not – the whole truth.'

'No. It will be Mrs Dearly whose reputation suffers – a risk she must have been prepared to take. As for Mr Farrow – many a man in his position has a mistress, an illegitimate son. Few can behave as barbarously as he has done – but that secret must stay for ever hidden, for Juliana's sake. Oh, it is so unfair! He has died, and died horribly, but he has ruined *her* life!'

We paused by the paddock fence; Guardsman stopped for long enough to push his nose into my chest and let me stroke his cheek before resuming his restless patrol. Much as I wanted to refute what Charlotte had said, I could think of no answer.

'Do you know anything of the girls' Uncle Robert, who is to be their guardian?' I asked her.

'From what Juliana tells me, he is busy with his own affairs in London, and his young children. He has never taken much interest in the girls, and is unlikely to do so now, as long as they are provided for.'

'So, you will stay here, with Marianne and Juliana?'

'Stay at Fourwinds?' she replied. 'No, that is quite impossible! Do you not see?'

'But, then . . .' I faltered. 'You cannot leave, surely – leave your sisters? When do you plan to tell them? You cannot intend to leave them in ignorance of what you have told me? Surely, Charlotte, you will not!'

She threw me an anguished glance. 'I am unable to decide what is best, though I go over and over it in my mind. Is it fair, to give the poor girls another shock, and such a startling one?'

'But you must! It would be the one thing to give them stability, security – to know that you will be with them – I am surprised you can think of leaving!'

'I have built my life here on a misconception,' she said flatly. 'I have deceived them, I have deceived you, and worse still I have deceived myself.'

'But—'

At that point, however, one of the carriage horses raised its head and whinneyed, and we saw, coming down the track from the house, Reynolds, with two of the visiting grooms.

'I must go back,' Charlotte said. Turning, she walked off fast, head down.

In perplexity, I gazed after her; considered following, then turned instead towards the lake.

There, in the still of late afternoon, the trees' lush canopy held coolness and shade. There, sitting by the water's edge, I reached a decision.

When I came back to the house, the guests had gone. Without seeing anyone on my way, I went to my room and changed out of my funeral garb, then wandered out to the lawn, smelling the warm grass, listening to the scream of swifts overhead. This summer had seemed everlasting. Not having known Fourwinds in any other season, I could only imagine it with the drawing-room doors thrown open, the curtains stirring in a breath of air, the garden seats arranged for shade beneath the cedar.

Piano music reached me faintly, so perfectly fitting the evening's mood that I did not at first register that Juliana was in the drawing room, playing Chopin, her favourite. I remained where I was for a few minutes, listening, debating with myself. Then, deciding that I must act now or procrastinate for ever, I walked slowly indoors.

She looked up at me, with a faint smile, and continued playing. Taking my position by her right shoulder, I stood ready to turn the page. I looked at the tender nape of her neck, with the hair swept up; at the lustrous black of her dress which became her so well, bringing out the delicate shades of hair and skin; I saw how beautifully and surely her hands moved over the keys, so that the music seemed to ripple from her fingertips and hover in the air like scent.

When she finished the piece, she rested her hands in her lap, and looked up at me. 'What would you like next? Will you choose?'

'Thank you, no. I wish to say something. Something important.'

With a feeling of unreality, I took both her hands in mine; startled, she almost snatched hers back, then submitted. Kneeling beside her, I looked into her face. I felt that I was acting a part in a play; and this self-consciousness seemed to prompt my words.

'Juliana,' I began hoarsely. 'Forgive my unseemly haste, for I know it is much too soon; you have had a great shock. But I must ask you, even though everything is in turmoil, and your feelings with it – perhaps *because* everything is so unsettled – I must put it to you that – would you do me the very great honour of – would you consent to be my wife? I have little to offer you – I mean in terms of wealth, security or status. Only the promise of my devotion, my everlasting regard. If you agree, you will make me the – the happiest of men.'

I had imagined this scene before, of course; and I felt sure of Juliana's response. She would drop her eyes, protest astonishment, make modest objections, and then she would blushingly, tearfully accept, and we would break the news, to everyone's delight and pretended surprise. Nothing could have prepared me for what she *did* say.

'Don't be silly, Samuel.' She pulled her hands away from mine and patted my shoulder, making me feel like a favourite dog.

'I beg your pardon?'

'I don't mean to seem rude,' she said, half-turning away. 'It's very kind of you, but I know that your offer comes from a sense of duty, even self-sacrifice. It's what Papa wanted, you know. Maybe you were aware of it?'

'Yes – yes, I was. But . . .' Aware of the ridiculousness of my position, I got to my feet and stood behind her chair as before, where at least she could not see my face. But she would not have that; she swivelled round to look up at me.

'And so you plan to carry out his wishes, even though he is dead?'

'No! It is only *because* he is dead – because he is no longer here to exert pressure,' I told her, in truth rather unsure, 'and I can act as if of my own accord.'

'Have you spoken to Charlotte about this?'

'No! I have spoken to no one. I suppose,' I added, for I had only just thought of it, 'I should have approached your Uncle Robert first, to ask his permission.'

'I am very glad you did not, for he will be as reluctant a guardian as you would be husband, and would no doubt have thanked you for taking me off his hands. Samuel, I thank you for your good will. Your offer comes from the kindest of motives, and I am grateful – please do not think otherwise. But my answer is No. And I do not say it in any spirit of bashfulness, to induce you to try again. Nor do I mean to suggest any personal rejection.' She hesitated. 'You believe that this is my chance to become a respectable married woman – for you are the one man who knows of my circumstances and yet is prepared to make this offer, even though it runs counter to your best interests.'

I began a half-hearted protest – for I was not as clear as she was that I had nothing to gain through this proposal – but she held up a hand to stop me.

'You see, Samuel, I do not believe that a woman's only chance of fulfilment is to be found in marriage. Yes, I might have embraced marriage, if things had been otherwise. But they are not, and I shall not. I have other blessings. I have Marianne; I have Charlotte; I am comfortably provided for. I have your friendship, Samuel, and I value it. But how do you think I should feel, if duty to me prevented you from marrying the person you love? Now, if you will excuse me, I shall go and change out of this gloomy black. Thank you for your kind and generous offer, but we will not speak of it again, and I shall not tell Marianne or Charlotte. Will you shake hands?'

We did so; and it was I who was left stammering, and blushing, and giving inadequate thanks, and Juliana who had shown gallantry. Pretending that *I* had been gallant, she released me from the obligation I had made myself.

When we reassembled downstairs, just before dinner, I was not sure how I should meet Juliana's eye, and was thankful for a diversion created by – surprise of surprises – Charlotte. To the amazement of all three of us, she was dressed in a blouse of bright scarlet. So accustomed was I to seeing her in drab grey, that it was as if a bird of paradise had alighted in our midst; I stared, we all stared. So self-conscious was she, that she might as well have been a walking pillar of flame.

'Charlotte?' I said, stepping towards her – indicating, with a sweep of my hand, the unfamiliar garment.

'Oh, this?' she said, plucking at her sleeve. 'It was an impulse purchase, and I thought – I thought now might be a good time to wear it, after the sombreness of the day. But it was a mistake – on the very evening of the funeral! Perhaps I had better go up and change into something more suitable.'

'No, it is very becoming!' declared Marianne, standing back to survey the complete picture. 'You make so little of yourself, Charlotte, but look at you now!'

Indeed, the vivid colour brought out the warmth of her hair – which was dressed with its usual severity – and of her lively brown eyes. I looked at her with affectionate amusement, and then at the other two. What a companionable group we made, I was thinking – and, with a pang of regret, that there would be few more such evenings, that my days here were numbered. My painting commission was over before it was properly begun, and Mr Robert Farrow would now be in a position to decide whether or not my employment as tutor should continue. I would be very surprised indeed if he thought it worthwhile to pay me to spend most of my time in idleness, with only the daily interruption of a drawing lesson. As soon as he reached that conclusion, Mr Jessop would pay me what I was owed, and I should have no reason to remain here.

I knew that my ill-judged proposal to Juliana had stemmed as much from my attachment to Fourwinds as from my misplaced sense of duty. If she had accepted, I should now – I knew it – have felt uneasily confined and compromised; but as she had not, I felt spurned, even bereft. It was not Juliana I had lost, but all three of my companions; for, on this peculiar evening, I felt that I loved them all equally, and should miss them most sorely. I should soon be gone from here, with only my memories, and my sketches and incomplete paintings which no one would want, to remind me of Fourwinds.

'Well,' said Marianne, after the coffee was served, 'none of us has spoken of what must be foremost in all our minds. What next?'

She looked at me, then at Charlotte, but it was Juliana who answered. 'What is the matter with us?'

'The matter?' Marianne repeated. 'What do you mean? Don't we have enough to perturb us?'

'I mean, what is the matter with us?' Juliana repeated. 'We are waiting to carry out our duties. We are waiting for Uncle Robert, and Mr Jessop, to tell us how we are to live our lives, and how to manage our money, and how to keep this house in perfect order for Thomas – for the next generation of Farrows. We are to be custodians – caretakers. That is what our father has decreed: that is what, as dutiful daughters, we are required to do.'

'Have you something else in mind, Juliana?' Charlotte enquired.

'I have.' Juliana faced us resolutely. 'Thomas is my

337

father's son – his heir – but he is also *my* son. Surely I am entitled to express some opinion about his upbringing? I want Thomas with me. I want to see him grow up. Yes, it will bring shame upon me, but I care nothing for that. It is not my shame, but my father's – *we* know that, even if no one else does.'

Marianne turned on Charlotte. 'Juley is right! But we must live elsewhere – we must leave Fourwinds and make a life of our own. Of course Juliana must have Tommy, but she cannot bring him here – cannot continue sleeping in the very room where—'

'Yes. I understand,' Charlotte said. She looked from Marianne to Juliana, then at me. 'There is something I have not yet told you – any of you.' We all gazed at her expectantly. 'I have inherited a house,' she told us, looking at each of us again, with a kind of defiance. 'A house in Eastbourne. It would not suit us to live there—'

'*Charlotte!*' exclaimed Marianne.

Charlotte held up a hand to silence her. 'But I could sell it, for a considerable sum, I am informed. We could use the proceeds to buy ourselves a house elsewhere – a house in a country village, maybe, where no one will know us. Then Fourwinds could be let, until such time as Thomas is old enough to make a decision about its future – for it must still be his, according to the terms of the Will.'

'I knew you had not told me everything!' I reproached her.

'Oh, Charlotte!' said Juliana. 'Why have you not told us this before?'

Marianne, though, was too caught up in this new idea to wait for explanations: she sat forward, clapping her hands. 'A house of our own! How delightful! We could live there all alone, the three of us – *four* of us, with Thomas. No one will disturb us – we can keep chickens, and maybe a cow, and beehives, and you can have Queen Bess, Juley – what could be nicer? We will be completely happy. And do let's live near the sea, Charlotte – I should love to live by the sea—'

I turned to the window. I should be best occupied packing my bags without delay, and making my arrangements.

'Oh yes,' said Charlotte to Marianne, with a laugh in her voice – something I had seldom heard till now – 'and I suppose you will soon be thinking of cheese-making and maypole dancing, to complete this bucolic picture?'

'But,' Juliana said, 'there is someone we must not forget.'

We all looked at her.

'Who?' said Marianne.

'Samuel, of course!' replied her sister, turning to me, with a slight flush crimsoning her cheeks. 'You may prefer to make other plans, Samuel – but maybe you would consider throwing in your lot with ours?'

Marianne's hand flew to her mouth. 'I am sorry! How could I not think of you, after all you have done for us? Do say yes, Samuel. How delightful! And you two – does this mean . . . ?'

I stared at Juliana in confusion, wondering whether she had reconsidered my offer; but she gave me the smallest of smiles, and replied to her sister, 'No, I wish to make one thing clear. There is to be no question of marriage between Samuel and me – for I was aware of Papa's connivings, as I think we all were. Everyone must understand that. We must be free to choose our own ways in life.'

Charlotte regarded me thoughtfully, and I wondered if she guessed what had taken place.

'Oh well, if you refuse outright, Samuel will be free to marry someone else,' Marianne said. 'Do say yes, Samuel – do say you will come with us! You could not leave us now, could you?'

'No,' I said, laughing. 'I don't believe I could.'

'What fun!' Marianne gave a little clap of her hands. 'How unconventional we shall be – three young ladies, one young man and one little boy, and none of us married! What will the world think of us?'

'We need not concern ourselves with that,' said Juliana. 'We shall be together, and away from here, and that is all I care about.'

'Samuel is an artist. That will explain it,' Marianne said gaily. 'Artists are allowed to break with convention.'

'Charlotte? We are racing ahead, too fast – what do you think of all this?' I gave her a searching look; she caught my expression, and read the question it conveyed.

'Well, there is a great deal to discuss and decide,' she said, with deliberate slowness. 'And of course we will need to discuss this with Uncle Robert, who may have objections. But I think Juliana is quite right. We must find our own direction. We have been controlled for too long by our father.'

I looked at her; saw that she had conquered the indecision that had overcome her earlier; saw that her scarlet blouse was a fanfare heralding change.

'*Our* father?' said Marianne, into the baffled pause that followed.

Withdrawing, leaving them to the exclamations, the reproaches and the wondering that followed Charlotte's revelation, I stepped out into the dusk.

I looked up at the sky, at the first emerging stars. As my eyes adjusted, I saw more and more of them – tiny and faint, they appeared, yet astronomers tell us that each one is a separate sun like our own. How unimportant we humans are, how minuscule, when set against the vast, incomprehensible scale of the cosmos! And yet how strong the pulse of our little lives, how vitally experienced, how sharp the pangs of joy and of anguish! How constantly we revolve around one another, held in our orbits like planets round a sun; how dizzily we would spin off into space if these holds were loosened.

By the cedar, I turned back to face the house. There it stood, in its solidity and grace; welcoming, in spite of all that had taken place there; so rooted, so perfectly proportioned, that it seemed a part of the landscape. In years to come, nothing would remain of the fears, the secrets, the torment of the lives lived here; visitors would see only the grace of design, the skill of craftsmanship, the beauty of materials, how perfectly right and harmonious the house was in every detail.

Why could Mr Farrow not have been content with this: his vision, his creation, his gift to the future?

Epilogue

Leavings

1920

The evening is over. Waiters collect glasses, bottles and ashtrays; the gallery owner and I retreat to his office for a final drink together.

'Well, I think we can call it a success!' He sinks back into a padded chair. 'Three good sales, and that American friend of mine is keen to give you a big commission. And I could sell *The Wild Girl* ten times over, if you'd only agree. You could name your price.'

I avoid his glance. 'No,' I tell him. 'She's not for sale. You know that. I shan't change my mind, so there's no point in discussing it.'

'Very well.' He holds out his hands in a gesture of

surrender. 'I was expecting to see your wife this evening. Was she unable to come?'

'She will, another day. She's bringing the twins up, some time next week. It'll be less crowded then, less overwhelming for the girls.'

'Fine. I shall be pleased to see them. All well, I hope?' He refills my glass, then pauses. 'And your son . . . ?'

I nod. 'Much the same.'

'Sad. Sad,' he says, shaking his head. 'Only, what? Twenty-five or so?'

'Twenty-three,' I say, automatically. 'He's with Marianne this week. I'll bring him home when all this is over.'

'Good, good.' But the conversation has faltered into awkwardness; he attempts briskness, changing the subject. 'Well! We must get together again soon. You'll be busy, but let me know when you're free. Come to dinner – I'll invite Walter Hickman, too, if we can fit it in before he goes back to Texas . . .'

Weariness tugs at me. This has become the world I inhabit, but I feel sickened by it; by all of it. By the fawning clients, their acquisitiveness, their flocking like vultures to what they assume to be valuable, their lack of real appreciation, the critics who can inflate a reputation overnight and burst it just as quickly. In my war sketches and paintings, especially the line drawings, I found honesty; I found simplicity and truth. What, now, shall I do with that? How can I go back to carrying out commissions for wealthy patrons?

And I know that I have painted my last painting.

Given my last exhibition. There is no more left in me; or, at least, what *is* left in me is not this.

I will soon be back at Fourwinds, where it all began.

This time, I travel down from London by car. I have not been here for many months. Staverton, like every town in England, shows the neglect of four years of war, and the loss of many of its menfolk. I notice several shops that have closed down, or changed hands; a brand-new war memorial stands in the market square. Beyond the town, hedges are untrimmed, ditches clogged, gates sag unrepaired. The trees are already well into their autumn flush; rooks and wood-pigeons peck over the harvested land. Who has done the harvesting? Old men and boys, it must have been – for so many of the young men are now dead in France or Belgium, and listed on the new memorial. I have seen for myself. I have seen the plain wooden crosses stacked up in readiness before a battle. I have seen the stragglers return, and I have seen how many failed to return.

Tom – Tommy! I murmur his name aloud. That simple affectionate shortening has come to stand for the ordinary soldier, the volunteer, the average young man sent willingly or unwillingly to his fate. And therefore I must suppose it fitting that our own Tommy, like so many, is lost to us, as surely as if he lay in an unknown grave in the Picardy chalklands.

At the copse of trees by the rise in the lane, I turn left for Fourwinds. Tyres crunch chalk stones; as I drive slowly, mindful of bumps and ruts, I cannot help but recall, as I always do, the first time I came here, all those years ago: as a young and impressionable man, walking towards the house and the people who would figure so largely in my life. So long ago, it seems now – before the war. People speak of *before the war* as if it belonged in a different world; and so it did.

The car swings through the high iron gates, and the house comes into view. As always, it works its spell on me. The ache of joy and loss, deep in my chest, almost stops me from breathing.

I park the car alongside two others; slowly I get out, and stand looking at the porch, the Gothic arch, the steps up, a rambling rose which bears scarlet hips. And above, the North Wind, calm and imperturbable, in its endless surveillance of the winds that blow over the house and fall and rise again. Fourwinds stands squarely in its landscape, mellowed now, and a home once more: home to Marianne and, officially, to Thomas, who owns it.

Here she is: Marianne, running down the porch steps. 'Sam! You're early!'

'Not very. Am I?'

'Then I'm late!' We embrace warmly; it is more than two months since we have met. I am allowed this.

'How is Charlotte? And the twins?' asks Marianne. 'And how are *you*?'

'All very well, thank you. And you? There is no need to ask – you are glowing.' I hold her at arm's length. Her beauty hurts me as much as it ever did; I am dazzled by her, as I have been since our first meeting. She is almost forty, but still full of girlish energy. Her hair, which to my regret she has cropped short in the modern fashion, is wound round with an Indian scarf; she wears a long, loose, printed garment with a paint-spattered apron over it; on her feet, work-manlike boots.

She laughs. 'I was working. I'll show you, in a bit. Tommy's things are packed and ready – he's down by the stables. Shall we go and find him? Or have coffee first?'

'Oh, Tom first. I've missed him.'

From the morning room I hear voices, male and female, in conversation; a gramophone plays jazz piano.

'Just a few artist friends,' Marianne says, glancing over her shoulder. 'You'll meet them at lunch.'

We take the dusty track that leads down to the stables. There are pigeons on the tiled roof; the trees are turning, green-gold in the soft light; the paddock where Guardsman and Queen Bess used to graze is now occupied by a retired riding horse, the stout cob that pulls the chaise, and a donkey. There, by the railings, Tom sits in the grass, hunched and absorbed, his back to us. The pose, the intent interest in something on the ground, are childlike, but I am looking at a grown man. The maidservant who accompanies him is seated on a stool beneath a tree, her sewing on her lap. She is a good girl called Enid, who looks after Tom whenever he is here, and knows his ways.

'He spends hours down here with the horses and the donkey,' Marianne tells me. 'He takes great delight in feeding them and grooming them, talking to them in his funny way.'

'Hello, Tommy!' I call out loudly, so as not to startle him with an unexpected approach.

Slowly, laboriously, he pushed himself to his feet. He comes towards me with arms held out, a beaming smile on his face; he makes incoherent sounds of pleasure as I clasp him to me.

'How are you, Tom? Enjoying this lovely day?' I say, though he cannot answer. I greet Enid, too, and ask how she is; but at once Tom is impatient, grasping my hand and pulling me towards the place where he was sitting, by the rails. He has a wooden pastry-board there, and some pieces of clay; he has been making models. In case I don't understand, he points in great excitement to the animals before us, the ponies and the donkey, then to the shaped clay on the board, and I see that he has fashioned all three. I admire them, although I cannot tell, in truth, which end of each figure is head, and which is tail.

'Gideon showed him how to do that,' Marianne explains. 'It was a clever idea. It gives him such pleasure.'

'Gideon has been here?'

She smiles. 'Last week. He called in on his way back from your exhibition. He was very complimentary – he especially liked the pen drawings.'

I nod, for Gideon has told me this himself. I think of him in the Mayfair gallery – how he stood, how he looked and looked with complete attentiveness, how calmness pooled around him. Turning back to Tom,

348

I try to understand the sounds he makes; I listen keenly. The doctors have said that speech may return, or it may not. He spent many months in specialist hospitals, until I became quite uneasy at the range of treatments that were being tried on him. We, his family, agreed that we should prefer to have him with us: mainly with Charlotte and myself in Alfriston, where Juliana visits frequently; sometimes here at Fourwinds, his rightful home. We do our best to keep him comfortable and amused. He seems content, even happy, apart from on the isolated occasions when he cries and whimpers and cannot be consoled. His condition has come to be known as shell-shock, and we can only be thankful that it has not afflicted him with the perpetual agitation or even terror that I have seen in others. Tom's shell-shock seems to have had the effect of obliterating all memory of trauma. In the face that looks eagerly into mine, I see a child's lack of self-awareness or guile, and beneath that – slipped out of focus – the features of the handsome, alert young man he used to be.

He rescued two men injured in a trench raid, bringing them back to relative safety when a shell barrage opened up. He showed no regard for his personal safety, the citation said. He showed immense coolness under fire. I think of this often.

Marianne steps close to him, taking his arm. 'Will you come indoors with us, Tommy?' she asks, speaking slowly and clearly, as we all do when addressing Tom. He watches her mouth, following closely, with deliberate nods of his head; he shapes his lips in imitation

of hers. She repeats the question; he seems to understand, but makes a sound of protest and pulls away.
He wants to carry on with his modelling.

'I'll stay with him here, Miss Farrow, and bring
him up in time for lunch,' says the girl.

We tell Tom that we will see him in half an hour,
and walk back up towards the house.

'Did you see Juley in London?' Marianne asks.

'I did; she came to the exhibition, and she'll stay
with us next week, to be with Tom.'

'She's as busy as ever, I suppose. It's no use my
inviting her to stay here, for she'll never come.'

We both understand too well why Juliana has never
once returned to Fourwinds.

'No. But you must come to Alfriston,' I tell her,
'and we can all be together.'

'That might not be till Christmas – I have so much
to do here. But I'll see Juley before then. Now, come
and see my work!'

Her studio is on the second floor, the room that
used to be mine. The door stands open, and the room
is full of light. There is no furniture in it other than
one chest of drawers; the fireplace is fronted by a huge
vase of leaves and berries. The room smells of oil paint
and turpentine. Canvases, stretched over their frames,
are stacked against the walls. Only one is on view, on
her easel: unfinished, I think, though it is hard to
know.

'What do you think?'

I stand and gaze at it. I don't pretend to understand the way Marianne works, with her broad gashes

of colour and her vivid palette, so like a child's painting. My tutor at the Slade would have said that she has no technique; and certainly she has forgotten or ignored all I ever taught her. But what she has is a kind of innocence; she sees to the heart of things. She has gone where I cannot follow; she is one of a new breed of artist, ignoring all the rules, caring nothing for tradition. This painting is of Tommy, slumped on a bench, smiling moon-faced. Behind him is a blur of leaves and blodged fruit that I suppose are apples. The naive style, capturing his look of puzzled sweetness, is perfectly right. It is almost too painful to look at, yet there is something wonderful in it.

'It's him,' I say, hearing the catch in my voice.

'Yes! Isn't it? I'm rather pleased.'

I decide to be pleased, too. This is the Tom we have now. I study the painting for some minutes, then move to the open window and look down to the lake, thinking of the West Wind with its face hidden for ever – or so I hope – in the mud and the silt. I wonder if a nightingale still sings there, as she did that summer? Never, since, have I heard a nightingale without recalling that chilly morning, and the two figures – one stone, one bloated flesh – that lay beneath the surface. Although Ernest Farrow's remains are in Staverton churchyard, I cannot help thinking that *here* is his grave, here is where his hopes and desires reached both their fulfilment and their end. Marianne never speaks of him, although her work includes a series of paintings of the lake in various lights and seasons, some of which make my flesh pimple and my skin creep at the remembered touch of those soft, hidden, slimy things.

A movement to the left of my view catches my eye; Tom, guided by Enid, is plodding towards the house, stumbling across rough grass towards the stable track. 'No,' says Enid, her voice carrying up to us, 'donkeys don't have lunch.'

What would Ernest think if he could see his ambition thus realized, and thus thwarted? Here is his son, his heir, at Fourwinds. Yet it would be a bitter blow to Ernest to know that his son's name is now Thomas Godwin, not Thomas Farrow; and that if Tom thinks of anyone as his father, it is me. And there will be no more Farrows to continue the name. Tommy will probably outlive his Uncle Robert; and Robert Farrow's son James lies in a grave near Vimy Ridge.

'Let's go down,' says Marianne. 'The garden is so lovely still.'

She is a mayfly, darting from one thing to another. There is something elated about her; I guess that one of the artists staying here is her new lover, and she will soon tell me, if so. I do not want to call it jealousy, this renewal of an ache that I almost relish; it would be ungracious of me to be less than content with my lot, and shamefully disloyal to Charlotte, who understands me better than I understand myself. And yet . . . I cannot stop myself from remembering my youthful passion for Marianne. That moment by the lake – the moment I have kept, and painted, and pondered, and brooded over – is constantly before me, as a tableau. I was too cautious, too circumspect.

If I had followed my feelings – if I had spoken—

The new generation of painters would care nothing for caution or circumspection. They would scorn me for my discretion, for my cowardice. For denying the passion in me.

I love Charlotte. Of course. But maybe I can only truly experience passion in this way: as a yearning for something out of reach, for ever unattainable, for ever desirable.

Marianne has had many lovers; how could she not? She attracts men, bestows herself upon them, tires, and moves on, always seeking, always restless. This is my consolation: that she loves none of them; she will neither possess, nor be possessed. The people she truly loves are not the men who come and go in her life, drawn like moths to her vitality, but her family – Charlotte and Juliana, Tommy and me.

We go down the stairs and through the drawing room. The doors to the lawn stand open; as we step out, I catch the resinous tang of cedar. That pungent scent recalls, sharp and clear in my mind, the hot summer's day more than twenty years ago, when I saw Thomas for the first time: when Eliza Dearly brought him to visit, and I played with him in the shade of this tree. Now the house and everything in it belongs to him, though he cannot know. Tom – Tom as he was – knew that he was adopted, that was all. Charlotte and I dreaded the task of telling him who his father was, when he came of age. Juliana was known to him as Aunt Juley, and that deception we had all decided to continue, for both his sake and hers.

Now he cannot know any of this, and maybe never will. Perhaps it is a blessing. As, perhaps, Tom's beatific smile is a blessing; as are the blanks in his memory that protect him from harm.

The garden has matured; it is more densely planted, more rampant than Mr Farrow would have liked. On the west side of the house, where Marianne leads me, there runs a long, wide border which was not there in Mr Farrow's day. A purple-leaved vine clothes the house wall, and the border is bright with Michaelmas daisies, with golden-rod, with the dried seed-heads of grasses and poppies, and others I do not recognize.

I stand looking up at the West Wind, fixed in its proper position: not the revenge piece, but the new carving made for us by Gideon.

I have seen him before, this Wind, but familiarity cannot diminish my sense of delight and of rightness. Here he is, the zephyr: the missing piece, the completion the house has awaited. Here he is, a young male figure, Pan-like, athletic, tumbled and twisted by gusts, arms outstretched, and his face – his face, mercifully, is nothing like that green-hued, snail-slimed, silt-stained visage drowned for ever in the lake, but full of joy, or mirth, relishing his own youth and vitality and the strength of the current that carries him. He is exuberantly himself; he is unmistakably the work of Gideon Waring. Someone has trimmed back the vine, so that he is not obscured; a few creeping tendrils obscure the edge of Portland stone and its fixing to the wall. I am caught, as always, by the grace and purity of line, and by the fine-grained beauty of the stone, perfect in its occasional imperfection. I have often watched Gideon, and have talked with him while he works. I know that while he plies hammer and chisel and carries on a conversation about the most everyday matters, his vision is always in his mind, clear and true.

Marianne comes to stand beside me. 'I told you,' she says, taking my arm, 'that the West Wind must be in his place. Once he was here, the house would be happy.'

'And I'm pleased you were right,' I tell her.

'I'm always right, Sam. Don't you know that, yet?'

I look at her and laugh; we stand for a few moments in silence.

I am thinking of the young man who stood here more than twenty years ago, his future open before him. How ambitious he was, how sure that he would make his mark, how complacent that his modest gift was only waiting for the world to appreciate it!

Well, he was a different person. The Samuel Godwin who stands here now is sadder, if not much wiser. I have, in a way, achieved my ambition, and found it brittle, crumbling to the touch. For truth, for something to sustain me through life, I must look elsewhere.

My gaze lifts again to the cleanness of stone, the purity of line, the ageless, timeless grace. And I know that this is what I yearn for. To handle the materials of life and death, as Gideon once said; to touch the mysteries of the Earth itself. I must make something simple, enduring and true.

I am thinking that, as soon as I can, I must see Gideon again, I must visit him in Chichester. I think of all I have learned from him, and of how much I have yet to learn.

The Times, October 22, 1941

Samuel James Godwin, 1878–1941

Samuel Godwin was one of several minor painters who came to public attention during the early years of this century under the patronage of Rupert Vernon-Dale.

Brought up in Sydenham, Godwin studied at the Slade School of Art, though he left before completing his course to take up commissioned work. Although his achievements never matched those of his more illustrious peers Augustus John, Wyndham Lewis and Paul Nash, Godwin's work became fashionable after the First World War. Vernon-Dale's sponsorship was a key factor in making Godwin's name; it was through Vernon-Dale's recommendation that Godwin was appointed as War Artist. Continuing to promote the work of Godwin and other artists after the war ended, Vernon-Dale had the London connections which led to Godwin's acclaimed one-man show at the Cork Street Gallery in 1920. Godwin never embraced the avant-garde; from 1920 he seemed to turn his back on the art world, and never exhibited again. The portrait entitled *The Wild Girl*, one of the works which helped to make his name, is believed to depict his sister-in-law, the artist Marianne Farrow. Of all his works, the most striking is surely *The Four Winds*, a series of oils which clearly shows the debt owed by Godwin to the sculptor Gideon Waring, with whom he formed a lifelong friendship.

In 1900 Godwin married Charlotte Agnew; they lived in Alfriston, near Eastbourne, at first with Mrs Godwin's sisters, Juliana and Marianne Farrow. Shortly after their marriage, the Godwins adopted a son, Thomas, who served in the Royal Sussex Regiment and was awarded a Military Cross before being invalided out of the army in 1918. Both Charlotte Godwin and Juliana Farrow were committed members of the Women's Social and Political Union until the outbreak of hostilities in 1914. Juliana Farrow served as a VAD nurse throughout the war years, afterwards continuing to campaign for women's welfare and for social reform. Marianne, her younger sister, became a successful painter in her own right. Although taught by Godwin in her youth, she developed a style very much her own.

From 1920 onwards, Godwin completed only a few insignificant watercolours, and turned his attention to stone-carving, becoming an expert at letter-cutting and a specialist in memorial plaques. His work can be seen in many a country church.

He is survived by his widow, Charlotte, by his son Thomas and by twin daughters, Connie and Grace (b. 1906).

100 Best
Games

100 Best
Games

BARRON'S

Original title of the book in Catalan: *Els Millors Jocs*
© Copyright Trevol Produccions Editorials S.C.P., 2000
Barcelona, Spain (World Rights)
Author: Eulàlia Pérez
Illustrator: Maria Rius

© Copyright 2000 of English language translation by Barron's
Educational Series, Inc., for the United States, Canada, and its territories
and possessions.

All inquiries should be addressed to:
Barron's Educational Series, Inc.
250 Wireless Boulevard
Hauppauge, New York 11788
http://www.barronseduc.com

Library of Congress Catalog Card No.: 99-69412
International Standard Book No.: 0-7641-1343-7

Printed in Spain
9 8 7 6 5 4 3 2 1

Introduction

Games and the act of playing them are a privileged source of learning and an answer to the need all children have for activity.

Through games, children develop their physical and intellectual abilities, as well as their communication capabilities.

Games supply pleasure and happiness, the opportunity for free expression, and the fulfillment of the child as an individual and as a member of a group. They clearly favor the integral development of the child.

In this book we suggest stimulating activities for children that are easy to carry out successfully and, at the same time, difficult enough to make them interesting and attractive.

"Man is truly human only when he plays".

F. Von Schiller

Justification

The games presented in this book are classified in two main groups: indoor and outdoor games. The games in these groups are, in turn, classified according to their main characteristics.

The basic aim of the games is for all the participants to have a good time. There should be active participation in the games, in that nobody is to be eliminated or excluded while the games are played. The cooperative group action of each game is more important than the player-opponent relationship.

The players can adapt the rules of the games as they wish, or they may even come up with a new game, thus avoiding monotony. These varations are decided on by the players on each occasion, based on their interests at that time.

Most suggested activities are designed to be carried out using easily found materials.

Each game description provides a targeted age range, the number of players, the organization or setup, and the development and rules.

Classification of the Games

 Introduction Games
Allow meeting new friends in a pleasant and amusing way.

 Games to Separate and Choose
Used to decide who counts, who starts the game, or who is in which group.

 Indoor Games
Those that can be played comfortably at home, in the classroom, in recreation centers...

 **Expression Games**
Representations and body imitations of characters, situations, things...

 **Games for Twosomes**
Used when participants are too few.

 Games with Recycled Materials
Learn how to create new materials for games from materials that can be recycled.

Outdoor Games

When open spaces—in the city or in the country—are available.

Games Played with a Ball

When a ball is available or one can be made.

Running Games

Designed to enjoy nature while playing.

Travel Games

Different activities that can be played in cars, trains, buses, or planes.

Games for Infants and Toddlers

Designed for the youngest members of the family.

Introduction Games

*Allow meeting new friends
in a pleasant and amusing way.*

Games to Separate and Choose

I'm Going to the Moon

Age:
6 years and older.

Participants:
a minimum of
6 players.

Organization:

All players sit in a circle on the floor.

Development and rules:

A player starts by saying: "I'm going to the Moon and my name is...," saying his name. The next player will then say: "I'm going to the Moon with... (saying the name of the previous player) and my name is... (saying her name)." The same process is repeated with all the players in the circle.

Names

Age:
7 years and older.

Participants:
a minimum of
6 players.

Organization:
All players sit in a circle on the floor.

Development and rules:
One of the players starts by saying his name (for example: "Mark!"). The player sitting next to him has to repeat the name of the first player while pointing to him and then add his/her own name (for example: "Mark, Christine!"). The next player has to say the previous two names and his own, and this continues until all the players have introduced themselves and memorized the names of the other players.

Variations: Pass a large ball to the player whose turn is next.

Organization:

All the players stand in a circle.

Development and rules:

One of the players walks to the center of the circle, says his name and something about himself while making a kind of salute (for example: "I'm Mike, I'm nice," and raises both arms), and then returns to his place. All the other players walk to the center of the circle, repeat what the first player said, and make the same kind of salute. The process is repeated with each member of the circle. The salute has to be a free gesture made up by each participant.

What Am I Like?

Age:
4 years and older.

Participants:
a minimum of
6 players.

Sun or Moon

Age:
5 years and older.

Participants:
a minimum of
10 players.

Organization:

One of the players will cover her eyes and the rest of players will make a line in front of her.

Development and rules:

The player at the head of the line will touch the hand of the player who is covering her eyes and will ask: "What am I?" and will be told "You are sun" or "You are moon." This is repeated with all the children in the line, so there will be two teams, one of suns and one of moons.

To have the same number of players on each team, when there are only a few players left in line, the player who chooses will be told how many more suns and moons she needs, for example: "You need one more sun and three more moons."

Who Is "It?"

Organization:

All players meet in a given place of the playground, one next to the other. They decide where they have to run, for example, to the fountain, to the wall in front,....

Development and rules:

All players run together to the place previously agreed to, and the last one to arrive is It.

Variations: Hop, skip, or jump to the selected place.

Age:
5 years
and older.

Participants:
more than
2 players.

Choosing Straws

Age:
5 years and older.

Participants:
minimum 2,
maximum 5 players.

Organization:

Get as many straws (or slips of paper, or toothpicks...) as there are players. All must be the same length but one, which will be shorter.

Development and rules:

One of the players holds all the straws in his hand in such a way that all seem to be equally long and presents them to the other players. Each player takes a straw, and the player who holds them keeps the last one. The player who draws the shorter straw is It.

Variations: Choose straws to divide into teams. The first one to get the short straw is on one team, the second is on the next team, and so on.

Rock, Paper, Scissors

Age:
5 years and older.

Participants:
2 players.

Organization:

Both players stand face to face.

Development and rules:

The players start by putting one arm behind them with their hand in a fist. Both players say at the same time: "Rock, paper, scissors, shoot," and bring their hands to the front, making one of the three figures. Rock is a fist, paper is an open hand, and scissors is formed with the index and middle fingers straight out while the other three fingers are still in a fist.

Paper wins over rock because paper can wrap around a rock; scissors wins over paper because scissors can cut paper; and rock wins over scissors because a rock can dent scissors. If both players make the same figure, there is a tie. Usually, two out of three wins.

Gold or Silver

Age:
5 years and older.

Participants:
2 players at a time.

Organization:

Both players stand face to face approximately 10 feet apart.

Development and rules:

Both players move forward one step at a time. The first player to take a step says "gold" and places one foot just in front of his other one. The second player does the same but says "silver." They keep doing this, always saying "gold" or "silver" each time they move a foot, until they are just about to touch. The player who has to take the last step, even when the space left is not big enough for his foot, is on one team; the other player is on the second team. This process is repeated until the whole group is organized in two teams.

 # Indoor Games

*Those that can be played comfortably at home,
in the classroom, in recreation centers...*

 Expression Games

Games for Twosomes

The Cow

Age:
7 years and older.

Participants:
a minimum of
5 players.

Organization:

Players sit in a circle and number themselves.

Development and rules:

The player who starts the game says: "The cow with no spots number 4 (if she is number 4) greets the cow with no spots number 10." The player who is number 10 immediately answers: "The cow with no spots number 10 greets the cow with no spots number 4."

When a player makes a mistake with the words or numbers, she gets a colored sticker that represents a spot and becomes the cow with one spot number__. The players who want to greet that cow will then have to say the number of spots the cow has.

Organization:

Make teams of 4 or 5 players each. The members of each team stand side by side holding hands and interlocking their legs in as little space as possible, as if they were a folded accordion. A box (or similar container) is placed at one end of the chain, and a line is marked on the ground three steps away from the other end.

Five small balls or balloons (or something similar) are placed on the other side of the line.

Development and rules:

Each team has to stretch enough so that the first player in the chain can take a ball from the other side of the line. The team then quickly folds back so that the player with the ball can drop it into the box. The first group to transport all five balls from one end to the other is the winner.

The Accordion

Age:
7 years and older.

Participants:
a minimum of
10 players.

21

Make-it/ Take-it

Age:
9 years and older.

Participants:
a minimum of
10 players.

Organization:

The players sit in a circle on the floor. Two equal objects are required (2 bean bags, 2 small balls,...).

Development and rules:

The player who starts the game has both objects. He passes one to the right and says: *"Here, have a make-it."*

The player who receives the object answers: *"Oh, a make-it! Thanks!"*

The player who started the game now passes the other object to the left, changing "make-it" to "take-it."

The second player on each side then passes the object to the next player, also saying: *"Here, have a make-it / take-it,"* and the players answer: *"Oh, a make-it / a take-it! Thanks!"*

The game continues in the same manner, with a fast oral exchange and trying not to make mistakes, until both objects arrive back to the player who started the game.

If a player makes a mistake, she has to give the object back to the initial player, who starts the game again.

I'm Going on a Trip

Organization:

The players sit in a circle on the floor.

Development and rules:

The idea is to pack a suitcase with the imagination and with as many objects as desired.

The first player says, for example: "I'm going on a trip and I'm taking pajamas." The next player has to mention the previous object and add another, for example: "I'm going on a trip and I'm taking pajamas and slippers." Each player will have to memorize the objects that have already been "packed."

The player who makes a mistake starts again.

Variations: Make a shopping list for the supermarket, take food for a picnic.... Pack the objects in alphabetical order, including one for each letter of the alphabet.

Age:
6 years and older.

Participants:
a minimum of
10 players.

Hidden Message

Age:
6 years and older.

Participants:
a minimum of
10 players.

Organization:

The children hold hands and form a circle, but one stands in the middle of the circle.

Development and rules:

The player who starts the game says: "I'm passing on a message to..." (and names one of the players). The message is a very light squeeze of the hand of the player who is to the right or to the left. The children pass on the message trying not to show the squeeze of the hand. When the message reaches its destination, the player says: "Message received." If the player in the center of the circle catches another player passing on the message, they exchange places.

The Color

Organization:

Before starting the game, a color and a leader are chosen.

Development and rules:

The leader will give a number of directions for the other players to follow, for example: "We will crawl under the table. We will take a ___ book...." When the chosen color or an object of that color is mentioned, the players must not follow the direction given by the leader but must quickly sit down instead. The last player to make a mistake becomes the new leader.

Drop the Beanbag

Age:
5 years and older.

Participants:
a minimum
of 10 players.

Organization:

The children sit in a circle on the floor. A beanbag, or another object of a similar size, is required.

Development and rules:

One of the players (It) holds the object and walks around the outside of the circle.

The other players ask: "What time will the sun rise tomorrow?" It gives a number from 1 to 12. The children sitting on the floor cover their eyes and start counting aloud up to the number mentioned, while It drops the object behind one of the other players.

When they stop counting, the players look to see if the object is behind them. The player who has the object behind her stands up and tries to tag the player who dropped the object (It), who, in turn, tries to sit down in the empty place to avoid getting tagged. If she is tagged, she continues to be It. If not, the other player is It.

Contrary Children

Organization:

One of the players will be the leader and will stand where all the other players can see him.

Development and rules:

The leader will give directions and the other children will do just the opposite; that is, if the leader tells them to be quiet, they will talk, if he tells them to sit down, they will stand up, and so on.

The last player to make a mistake becomes the new leader.

Age:
6 years and older.

Participants:
a minimum of
5 players.

I Spy

Age:
4 years and older.

Participants:
a minimum of
10 players.

Organization:
The children sit in a circle on the floor.

Development and rules:
One player begins by choosing an object in sight of everyone and saying: "I spy with my little eye something that is _____" and fills in the blank with a particular color, such as blue. The other players then take turns trying to guess the object. The player who guesses correctly gets to choose the next object.

The Detective

Age:
8 years and older.

Participants:
a minimum
of 4 players.

Organization:

One player is chosen to be the detective. This person takes a good look at the clothes the other players are wearing and then leaves the room or is blindfolded.

Development and rules:

Some of the players interchange something they are wearing. The detective then comes back or removes the blindfold. The detective has to discover who is wearing something different and also what it is. After this, another player will be the new detective. *Hint:* Wear different hats, shoes, belts, jackets, and so on.

29

Word Lightning

Age:
4 years and older.

Participants:
a minimum
of 3 players.

Organization:

One of the players will choose a letter to start the game.

Development and rules:

Taking turns, each player will have one minute to say as many words as possible beginning with the chosen letter. Players can take turns suggesting other letters and acting as timekeeper.

Variations: Use words that end in a given letter, or words that name objects to be found on a mountain, and so on.

Buzz!

Age:
7 years and older.

Participants:
a minimum of
10 players.

Organization:

All the players sit in a circle on the floor.

Development and rules:

A player begins counting and each player continues in turn. When a previously agreed-on number is reached, the player says "buzz." Older children can also include multiples of that number. For example, if the number is 3, the counting would go: "1, 2, buzz, 4, 5, buzz, 7, 8, buzz, 10, 11, buzz, buzz, 14, buzz..." and so on. Younger children would just say "buzz" on 3, 13, 23, and so on. The game ends when a player reaches 100 without making a mistake.

33

Where Am I?

Age:
5 years and older.

Participants:
8 players or more.

Organization:

All players stand in a circle, except one, who stands blindfolded in the middle.

Development and rules:

One of the players in the circle starts clapping her hands, and the player in the middle tries to guess who it is, walking toward the noise. If he guesses right, they trade places.

Organization:

Players stand in line, one behind the other. The player at the head of the line is the leader.

Development and rules:

The leader will move around the room making whatever kind of movement she wishes. The other players have to imitate her. Following the order of the line, keep changing the child playing leader until all the participants have had a turn.

Variations: If there is music played, the game is the same except that the leader has to create movements to the rhythm of the music.

Follow the Leader

Age:
4 years and older.

Participants:
a minimum of
5 players.

35

Charades 1

Age:
8 years and older.

Participants:
5 players
or more.

Organization:

Players sit on the ground forming a semicircle. One player stands in the middle.

Development and rules:

The player standing in the middle uses mime to represent a well-known character (Charlie Chaplin, Superman...). The player who guesses who the character is then represents another character and the game starts again. Animals, film titles, and so on, are also good subjects.

Charades
2

Age:
5 years and older.
Participants:
3 players or more.

Organization

One of the players uses his body to represent things without talking. The other players watch.

Development and rules:

The participants choose a general category to be represented (objects, animals, famous characters, careers, and so forth). The player chosen tries to act out a specific subject within that category in front of the rest of the players, who should guess what the representation is about. The first player to guess it becomes the new one to act out a different subject.

The Dog and the Cat

Age:
5 years and older.

Participants:
at least 3 players.

Organization:

Blindfold two children. One will be the dog and the other one will be the cat. The rest of players will sit on the ground in a large circle. The "dog" and the "cat" are in the middle of the circle and adopt a position that is typical of the animal they represent.

Development and rules:

The cat and the dog move around the circle, meowing and barking, while they try to catch each other. The players in the circle can help them by giving directional hints. When the dog catches the cat or vice versa, two other players from the circle take their places. This is repeated until all the children in the circle have imitated both animals.

Variations: Choose other animals, such as horse, sheep, rooster, hen....

The Message

Organization:

Form different lines of players, all sitting on the ground, one behind the other.

Development and rules:

The last player in each line "writes" a message on the back of the player in front (for example: a line and two dots). The message has to be passed on from player to player until it reaches the head of the line, where the message is checked to see if it coincides with the original one. Now the last player in the line sits at the head and the game starts again.

Age:
6 years and older.

Participants:
a minimum of 5 players.

The Director

Age:
8 years and older.

Participants:
a minimum of
10 players.

Organization:

One of the players walks away from the group. The rest of the players choose a director, and then they all form a circle.

Development and rules:

The first player comes back and stands in the middle of the circle. The chosen director, without being seen by the player in the middle, starts a series of movements the other players have to imitate. The player in the middle watches carefully, trying to find out who the director is. If her guess is right, the "old" director will be the new "guesser."

Noah's Ark

Age:
4 years and older.

Participants:
a minimum of
10 players.

Organization:

The players form pairs and choose the sound of one animal. One of the players in each pair gets a blindfold.

Development and rules:

The members of the pairs who are not blindfolded scatter around the room and start making the chosen sound. The blindfolded member of the pair tries to find the other member by following the sound. When all pairs have been reunited, the game starts again, changing pairs and sounds.

Find Your Partner

Age:
7 years and older.

Participants:
a minimum of
6 players.

Organization:

Players form pairs and become familiar with their partner's hands by touching them.

Development and rules:

Pairs separate and scatter around the room. All players cover their eyes with a blindfold and turn around three times before trying to find the other member of the pair by touching the hands of the players they bump into.

When the right partner is found, the blindfold comes off and the players watch while their friends finish the game. Different pairs can be formed and the game starts again.

Poor Cute Kitty!

Organization:

The players sit in a circle on the floor.

Age:
5 years and older.

Participants:
a minimum of
8 players.

Development and rules:

One of the players, walking on his knees, gets close to another player, imitating a cat and saying "Meow, meow" to try to make the other player laugh. The latter, very serious and not laughing at all, pats his friend, saying "Poor cute kitty!" The procedure is repeated three times. If, during this time, the other player does not laugh, the "cat" goes to another player. But, if the "cat" succeeds in making the other player laugh, then the latter becomes the new "cat."

43

Shapes

Age:
6 years and older.

Participants:
at least 2 players.

Organization:

Players form pairs. One of the players in each pair is blindfolded.

Development and rules:

The player whose eyes are not blindfolded adopts a certain body posture. The blindfolded partner touches the body position of the other partner to figure out his position. When she thinks she can recognize it, she warns her partner that she is taking the blindfold off, and her partner drops his position. The blindfolded player takes off her blindfold and tries to reproduce the position. Partners then exchange roles. It may help to set a time limit, such as 2 minutes, to discover the position and reproduce it.

44

Organization:

The children sit on the floor, one behind the other, forming a circle. One of the children is chosen to write the telegram.

Development and rules:

The writer will "write" a short message on any given part of the player sitting in front of him, who will do the same with the player in front of her. Each player will do the same until the message reaches the writer. The next person becomes the writer and the game starts again.

Telegram

Age:
8 years and older.

Participants:
a minimum of
6 players.

The Bag

Age:
4 years and older.

Participants:
a minimum of
6 players.

Organization:

Several very different objects are placed in a brown paper bag. It is best if objects are chosen and placed in the bag by someone not taking part in the game and without the players looking on.

Development and rules:

The children, sitting in a circle, put one of their hands in the bag, touch an object, say what they think it is, and then take it out of the bag to see if they have guessed correctly.

46

The Minute

Age:
8 years and older.

Participants:
a minimum of
2 players.

Organization:

A watch with a second hand or a stopwatch is controlled by one of the players.

Development and rules:

The player who checks the watch will signal when to begin, and the other players will have to guess, as precisely as possible, when a minute has passed. The player with the watch will try to confuse the other players by grimacing or making strange faces or telling them to hurry up or slow down. When a player thinks a minute has passed, she says: "Time!" The player closest to the right time is the next one to control the watch.

47

Hopscotch

Age:
7 years and older.

Participants:
a minimum of
2 players.

Organization:

Outline a figure on the ground like the one shown in the illustration on the right.

Development and rules:

The first player tosses a small, flat stone (or something similar) from the line at the bottom of the figure, trying to throw it into the first box. If the stone falls on lines or out of the figure, then the next player tries. If the stone falls into the desired box, the player hops through the figure but skips the box where the stone is. The player hops into boxes 4-5 and 7-8 with both feet at the same time, and hops back to regain the stone.

If the player succeeds in hopping all the way and back without stepping on lines, then he tosses the stone again but into the next box. The winner is the first player to toss the stone into all the boxes and hop back and forth.

48

Games with Recycled Materials

*Learn how to create
new materials for games from materials
that can be recycled.*

Concentration

Age:
6 years and older.

Participants:
a minimum of
2 players.

Organization:

The game requires several empty containers (such as paper cups or cans) of equal or different sizes, as well as several pairs of objects, such as 2 buttons, 2 bottle corks, 2 stamps, 2 pebbles,.... Prepare a minimum of 15 pairs of objects and have a container for each object.

Development and rules:

Each object is covered by a container. The containers are then mixed up. In turn, each player uncovers two objects. If he finds a pair, he keeps it, if not, he covers both objects again and it is the next player's turn.

The player who finds the most pairs wins.

Variation: Keep the empty containers in the game. The game then becomes more difficult.

Organization:

Prepare six empty plastic bottles. Number six small pieces of cardboard from 1 to 6, and glue each piece to a bottle. Draw a line on the ground. Stand the bottles in a triangle formation about 4 feet (3.5 m) from the line. Construct balls with paper and adhesive tape. There should be one ball for each player.

Development and rules:

Players take turns throwing a ball to try to knock down as many bottles as possible. Each player totals the points on the fallen bottles. The player with the highest number of points after each player has had a turn is the winner.

Bottle Bowling

Age:
6 years and older.

Participants:
a minimum of
2 players.

Bucket Brigade

Age:
6 years and older.

Participants:
a minimum of
8 players.

Organization:

Form teams of 4 players each, who will stand in line with an empty can or plastic cup in their hands. There should be a bucket full of water at one end of the line and an empty bucket at the other end.

Development and rules:

The first player in the line fills his can with water and empties it into the can of the second player, who in turns does the same with the third player, and so on. The last player in the line pours the water into the empty bucket. The first team to successfully transfer the water wins.

Organization:

Use newspaper and adhesive tape to make a very large paper ball. Players lie in a circle on the floor and raise their legs.

Development and rules:

The players pass the ball to each other just using their feet.

The Paper Ball

Age:
6 years and older.

Participants:
a minimum of
8 players.

55

The Basket

Age:
4 years and older.

Participants:
a minimum of
6 players.

Organization:

A box or bucket or similar container is needed, plus some small balls (as many as there are players minus one). One of the players is chosen to start the game.

Development and rules:

All small balls go into the box and all the players turn their back to the box, except the one to start the game. This player suddenly empties the box and each of the other players tries to pick up one small ball. The player who cannot get one will be in charge of the box next.

Outdoor Games

When open spaces—in the city or in the country—are available.

 Games Played with a Ball

 Running Games

Octopus

Age:
4 years and older.

Participants:
a minimum of
10 players.

Organization:

A large play area becomes the "ocean" and clear boundaries are marked on either side to be the "shores." One of the players stands in the middle of the ocean. She is the Octopus. The rest of the players (the Fish) stand side by side on one shore.

Development and rules:

When the Octopus yells "Swim!" the Fish run to the opposite shore, dodging the Octopus. Those players who are tagged stay in the middle, joining hands with the Octopus, thus becoming her tentacles. The last Fish to be tagged becomes the new Octopus.

Organization:

Form two lines in the middle of the playground, so that all players are back to back. One of the lines will be "heads" and the other one "tails." At the head of the lines there will be another player who will toss a coin in the air.

Development and rules:

If the tossed coin indicates "heads," the players in the "heads" line have to run to the end of their side of the playground, while the other players try to tag them. If the coin indicates "tails," the process is reversed. Any player who is tagged becomes a member of the other team.

Heads or Tails

Age:
7 years and older.

Participants:
a minimum of 10 players.

Cats and Mice

Age:
6 years and older.

Participants:
a minimum of
10 players.

Organization:

Form two teams with the same number of players on each. One team will be the cats and the other will be the mice. Define the playground boundaries.

Development and rules:

The cats will have to catch the mice. When a mouse is caught, he has to keep still in the place where he was tagged, legs apart. To be free again, another mouse has to crawl under his legs. When all mice have been caught, roles are reversed and the game starts again.

In this game it is important that cats and mice can be clearly told apart. Use colored handkerchiefs, make-up, or paper ears, or some other method of defining the teams.

Organization:

Decide first on an object that will be the sardine, or make one. The game can also be played with a small ball or a rubber chicken.

Development and rules:

One of the players will be the cat and another will hold the "sardine." The cat runs after the sardine, which can be tossed to another player while saying his name and adding the word *sardine.* For example: "Jack sardine!" Then the cat has to run after the player who now has the sardine. The player who is tagged or drops the sardine becomes the new cat.

The Cat and the Sardine

Age:
6 years and older.

Participants:
a minimum of
8 players.

Blindman's Bluff

Age:
5 years and older.

Participants:
8 players or more.

Organization:

Form a circle and blindfold one player, who will step into the middle.

Development and rules:

The players in the circle hold hands and walk around the player in the middle (the blindman).

When the blindman claps three times, the players must stand still. The blindman then points to one player in the circle, who walks to the blindman and stops. The blindman tries to identify this player by touching his face, hair, and clothes.

If his guess is right, then the blindman goes into the circle and the player whose name has been guessed becomes the new blindman.

Organization:

All players except one, who will remain standing, sit on the ground, one in front of the other, legs apart and holding on to the waist of the player in front.

Development and rules:

The player who is standing will try to pull the onions by pulling the arms of the player at the head of the line. When the onion is pulled, the new player joins the player who is standing and then both try to pull the next onion.

Pulling Onions

Age:
6 years and older.

Participants:
a minimum of
6 players.

Prisoners Rule

Age:
8 years and older.

Participants:
a minimum of
6 players.

Organization:

A player is chosen to be It. She stretches one of her arms and all the other players have to touch her hand.

Development and rules:

It closes her eyes and starts to count from 15 down to 0. The rest of players have to hide. When It finishes counting, she names all the players she can see, who then become prisoners and have to help her spot more players. When no one else is in sight, It shouts "come out" to the players who are still hiding and starts the process again, but this time counting down from 14. The game continues like this until all the players have been made prisoners.

Organization:

A player (It) is chosen to chase the others and try to tag as many as possible.

Development and rules:

A player being chased can stand on an elevated place and then he cannot be tagged. But if all the players are safe on an elevated place, It can say, "Jack and Jill get off the hill!" and then they must change safe zones. The first player who is tagged becomes the chaser.

Age:
6 years and older.

Participants:
a minimum of
6 players.

65

The Train

Age:
7 years and older.

Participants:
a minimum of
6 players.

Organization:

The players form lines of 5 or 6 players each. Each line is a train. Each player holds the shoulders of the player in front of him. All close their eyes or are blindfolded, except the last player in the line, who will be the train engineer.

Development and rules:

The train engineer drives the train with a system of signals that pass from player to player until they reach the first in line.

- *a tap on the head, the train goes straight*
- *a tap on the left shoulder, the train turns left*
- *a tap on the right shoulder, the train turns right*
- *a tap in the middle of the back, the train stops*

Organization:

All the players but two form a circle. They hold hands with their arms in the air.

Development and rules:

The remaining two players have to tag each other while they run under the arms of the other players. The player who chases (It) has to follow the path of the running player. When the runner is tagged, she becomes It. The player who was It decides which of the players in the circle will now be chased, and takes his place in the circle.

Under the Bridge

Age:
4 years and older.

Participants:
a minimum of
10 players.

Hunters and Pigeons

Age:
8 years and older.

Participants:
A minimum of
20 players.

Organization:

Form two teams and mark the playground as shown in the illustration. One team will be the pigeons and the other team the hunters. The hunters take up both sides of the corridor and the pigeons are at one end of it.

Development and rules:

One by one, the pigeons toss a ball in the air and run to the other end of the corridor. The hunters try to catch the ball and throw it to touch the running pigeon (below the neck only!). If the pigeon is touched with the ball, he has to freeze on the spot. He becomes free again if another pigeon succeeds in going and coming back without being touched with the ball. The hunters cannot keep the ball in their hands; they have to toss it from one to the other continuously. They also cannot walk holding the ball in their hands. When all the pigeons have gone and come back along the corridor, count the number that have been touched and reverse roles.

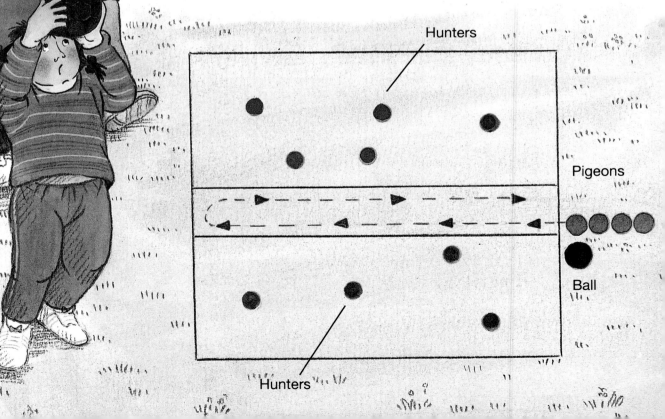

Hunters

Pigeons

Ball

Hunters

Organization:

The players all form pairs in which one will be the plane and the other the pilot. The "plane" will wear a blindfold. Before the game starts, the players in each pair secretly agree on the codes they will use for instructions to go right, left, ahead, back, or to stop. For example, they can use colors, such as: "blue" to go ahead, "green" to go back, and so on.

Development and rules:

First, all players agree on the place where planes have to arrive. Then all pairs stand at the starting line, with the plane in front of the pilot. All planes are driven by the instructions given by their respective pilots, who cannot move from the starting line. The winner is the first plane to arrive at the finish line.

The Plane Without a Pilot

Age:
8 years and older.

Participants:
a minimum of
6 players.

Object Tag

Age:
6 years and older.

Participants:
a minimum
of 6 players.

Organization:

A player (It) is chosen to try to tag as many of the other players as possible. The latter will, of course, try to avoid being tagged.

Development and rules:

It begins by saying: "I went to the store and I bought a..." (and mentions an object in sight). The other players quickly run to touch that object. It tries to tag as many players as possible before they touch the "safe" object. The last untagged player becomes the new It.

The Frog and Grasshoppers

Age:
5 years and older.

Participants:
a minimum of
6 players.

Organization:

Draw a big circle on the ground. The grasshoppers hop (with both feet kept together) inside the circle. A player is chosen to be the frog.

Development and rules:

The frog can only jump in a squatting position and tries to catch the grasshoppers. Each grasshopper who is tagged becomes a frog. The last grasshopper to be caught will become the new frog when the game starts again.

Freeze Tag

Age:
4 years and older.

Participants:
a minimum of
6 players.

Organization:

The players scatter freely around the playground while It counts to 10.

Development and rules:

When It tags the other players, they must "freeze" in the position and spot they were in. They can become unfrozen if tagged by another player. It wins if she can freeze all the players.

Organization:

Form two teams. It is important to differentiate both teams clearly: by the color of the T-shirts, using handkerchiefs or ribbons,....

Development and rules:

One of the teams passes the ball among its players while the players on the opposite team try to catch or intercept it. The team that catches the ball starts tossing it again.

When a player has the ball in his hands, he can only make a maximum of three passes.

Variations: The first team to pass the ball 10 times without dropping it or being intercepted wins. Use a large ball for younger children.

Keep Away

Age:
6 years and older.
Participants:
6 players or more.

Croquet Ball

Age:
6 years and older.

Participants:
a minimum of
10 players.

Organization:

The players stand forming a circle, legs apart and hands on their knees.

Development and rules:

A player steps to the center of the circle and uses her feet to make the ball pass under the legs of the other players, who can stop the ball using their feet or knees, but not their hands. When the ball goes under the legs of one of the players, that player takes the position in the center of the circle.

The game is over when each player has been the one in the center of the circle.

The Fox

Age:
between 8 and
12 years old.

Participants:
a minimum of
10 players.

Organization:

The playground is divided by a line drawn on the ground. All the players but one scatter around the playground and keep still, remaining on one side of the line or the other.

Development and rules:

The free player is the fox, who has to run among the other players. The fox can cross the line. The other players toss the ball from one to the other, trying to hit the fox with the ball (below the neck). The player who hits the fox with the ball becomes the new fox.

Open Ball

Age:
8 years and older.

Participants:
a minimum of
15 players.

Organization:

Form two teams of 5 players each, who will stand in line one behind the other. The player at the head of the line will hold a ball.

Draw a line on the ground 35 to 50 feet (10–15 m) away from the head of the line.

Development and rules:

One of the players shouts "Open ball!" and the two

players at the head of their respective lines run to the line drawn on the ground. From there they throw the ball to the next players. These two then run to the line and throw the ball from there to the next players. The procedure is repeated until all players are at the line. The ball can never touch the ground. A player who drops the ball has to go back to the end of the line.

The team whose players are all at the line first wins.

Ball Tag

Age:
8 years and older.

Participants:
a minimum of
10 players.

Organization:

Define a playing area, approximately 50 by 50 feet (15 by 15 m), in which the players will move freely.

Development and rules:

One of the players (It) tries to tag the other players by hitting them with a ball (below the neck). The player who is hit must sit down. In order to be free again, the tagged player must catch the ball and throw it to hit one of the standing players. Or, a standing player can help a sitting player by catching the ball and throwing it to him.

The round ends when all players have been tagged and are sitting down.

78

Organization:

The players form a circle. One player stands in the center holding a ball.

Development and rules:

The player in the center of the circle says the name of an animal and tosses the ball to one of the other players, who has five seconds to say if the animal belongs to land, sea, or air. If she is wrong or drops the ball, she will have to imitate the named animal. If her answer is correct, then she takes a position in the center of the circle. The five seconds are counted aloud by the rest of players.

Animal Ball Toss

Age:
7 years and older.

Participants:
a minimum of
6 players.

Up, Up

Age:
6 years and older.

Participants:
a minimum
of 2 players.

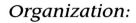

Organization:

A ball is required. Younger players should use a large ball.

Development and rules:

Players take turns tossing the ball in the air and keeping it up by using fingers or a flat hand. The ball should never stop moving.

Count the number of times each player hits the ball into the air. The winner is the player who can keep the ball going the greatest number of times. If a player drops the ball, the next player takes a turn.

Organization:

All players but one form a circle. Younger players may hold hands. The remaining player is in the center of the circle.

Development and rules:

One of the players in the circle starts by kicking the ball to another player in the circle. The player in the center tries to get the ball without using his hands. If he succeeds, he trades places with the last person to have kicked the ball. That person gets a penalty point. When the players decide to end the game, the person with the fewest penalty points wins.

Soccer Keep Away

Age:
6 years and older.

Participants:
a minimum of 10 players.

Spud

Age:
6 years and older.

Participants:
a minimum of
10 players.

Organization:

One player (It) holds a ball and the rest gather around her.

Development and rules:

The player with the ball tosses it in the air and calls the name of another player. The player whose name has been called has to catch the ball as quickly as possible. In the meantime, the other players run away. When the player catches the ball, he shouts "Spud!" and all players have to freeze. The player with the ball takes three steps and throws the ball at one of the players. If that player gets hit, she gets an *S*. If not, the thrower gets an *S*. The person who gets a letter begins the next round. The first person to get four letters—*S, P, U, D*—loses and becomes the next It.

Drop the Ball

Age:
6 years and older.

Participants:
a minimum of
5 players.

Organization:

All the players but one (It) stand in a circle. It holds a small ball.

Development and rules:

It walks around the outside of the circle and at a given moment drops the ball behind one of the players and starts running. The player behind whom the ball has been dropped takes the ball and starts running in the opposite direction. The last one to arrive at the empty place in the circle is It, and starts the game again.

The Five Islands

Age:
between 8 and
12 years old.

Participants:
10 to 20 on
each team.

Organization:

Draw five circles on the ground, as the illustration shows, or use hula hoops. Form two teams. The players of one team (the island team) will be inside the circles and the players of the other team (the sea team) will be scattered around the playground.

Development and rules:

The members of the island team have to pass the ball among them, avoiding interceptions from the members of the sea team. If the sea team gets the ball, then they take positions in the islands, and the other players become the new sea team.

Bounce

Age:
4 years and older.

Participants:
a minimum of
9 players.

Organization:

The players stand in a circle, legs apart.

Development and rules:

The game consists of passing the ball from one player to the other, using only one hand and always making it bounce once inside the circle. The ball cannot be caught with both hands. Players count aloud the number of bounces to see how many they can get. If the ball goes out of the circle or bounces more than once, the game starts again and a new count begins.

The Tower

Age:
7 years and older.

Participants:
a minimum of
15 players.

Organization:

All players but one (It) form a circle, leaving about half a yard between one another. One player holds a ball. It stands in the center of the circle alongside an object (such as a bucket, a marble, a box, and so on).

Development and rules:

The players in the circle try to hit the object with the ball. They can pass the ball from one to the other but they cannot move from their place. The player in the center has to stop the ball from hitting the object. When one of the players succeeds in hitting the object, he becomes the new It.

Grab Tag

Age:
5 years and older.

Participants:
a minimum of
10 players.

Organization:

One of the children is chosen to be It. The other players run free all around the playground to avoid being tagged by It.

Development and rules:

It chases and tries to tag the other players. When she succeeds, the tagged player becomes the new It. The condition is that the tagged player has to run with his hand "grabbing" the spot where he was tagged. The game continues until each player has been It.

Organization:

Two lines are marked in the middle of the playground, about five or six feet apart. This is the wall. Three players are chosen to be the taggers and stand on the wall. They can only move between the two lines. The rest of the players will stand on one side of the wall.

Development and rules:

The idea is to run across the wall and back as many times as possible without being tagged by the players who are on the wall. The player who is tagged joins the taggers on the wall. The game is over when all the players have been tagged.

Variations: The player who is tagged has to stand on the wall with legs apart. If a player passes under her legs, she is set free. In this case, the game is over when all the players have been tagged and they are standing on the wall, legs apart.

The Wall

Age:
6 years and older.

Participants:
a minimum of
10 players.

Grab the Tail

Age:
6 years and older.

Participants:
a minimum of
10 players.

Organization:

Each player has a handkerchief (or a piece of cloth or ribbon) hanging from the back of his pants so that it looks like a tail.

Development and rules:

All the players run freely around the playground trying to take the tails from the other players and trying not to have their own taken away. Each time a player succeeds in taking away one of the tails, he will add it to his own at the back of his pants.

The game is over when most players have lost their tails.

Organization:

One of the players (It) has to chase the other players, who are scattered all around a large playground.

Development and rules:

It chases one of the players until she catches her. Then the player who has been caught becomes the new It. A player being chased can be saved if another player gets in between him and the chaser (It), who now will have to start running after the player who has gotten in the way and "cut the thread."

Cutting the Thread

Age:
6 years and older.

Participants:
a minimum of 10 players.

Couples Tag

Age:
8 years and older.

Participants:
a minimum of
10 players.

Organization:

Pairs of players stand next to each other, scattered all around the playground.

Development and rules:

One of the pairs will start the game. One player will chase the other member of his pair all over the playground. To avoid being tagged, the player who is being chased can stand either to the right or the left of another pair. Then the member of the new pair on the opposite side has to start running, since she becomes the new player being chased.

If she is tagged before she can stand at the side of another pair, she becomes the chaser and the other player the chased one.

Planted

Organization:

A player is chosen to be the chaser (It), and the rest of the players run around the playground trying not to be tagged.

Development and rules:

When a player is about to be caught, she can become "planted": she freezes on the spot, legs apart and arms out, and then she cannot be tagged. To become free again, another player has to pass under her legs. While a player is passing under the legs of another, he cannot be tagged either. If It tags a player before she becomes planted, then the tagged player becomes the new It.

Age:
6 years and older.

Participants:
a minimum
of 8 players.

93

The Worm

Age:
5 years and older.

Participants:
a minimum of
10 players.

Organization:

Form groups of 3 or 4 players holding hands. Distribute them around the playground.

Development and rules:

The player at the head of each group tries to cross through the other groups. When the first player in a group succeeds in touching a member from another group, the latter has to raise his arms to let the group cross under.

Variations: When a group crosses under another one, both groups become one. The game is over when all the players form just one group.

Changing Places

Age:
6 years and older.

Participants:
a minimum of
5 players.

Organization:

Inside the playground, mark as many places as there are children playing minus one. These places can be indicated by hula hoops, drawing circles with a piece of chalk, and so on.

Development and rules:

Each player stands inside one of the indicated places and the extra player goes to the middle of the playground. Once there, he shouts "Change!" and all the players, including the one in the middle, have to change places. The player who does not find a place will then go to the middle of the playground and repeat the watchword. No player can take the same place twice in a row.

95

Steal the Handkerchief

Age:
6 years and older.

Participants:
a minimum of
10 players.

Organization:

Form two teams. The members of each team number themselves. Each team stands at opposite ends of the playground, behind a line drawn on the ground. One player stands in the middle of the playground with one arm extended, holding a handkerchief.

Development and rules:

The player in the middle calls out a number and the players on each team with that number run toward the player holding the handkerchief and try to take it. The player who first takes the handkerchief then runs back to her place and the other player tries to tag her before she gets there.

If a player succeeds in getting to her place with the handkerchief, the one chasing after her becomes trapped and has to stand next to the player in the middle, also extending an arm. Another member of his team then gets his number and adds it to his own. A player who has just taken the handkerchief can free her teammates by touching their hands while she is running back to her place.

The player in the middle calls out numbers until all the players on a team have become trapped.

The Spider and the Flies

Age:
8 years and older.

Participants:
a minimum of
10 players.

Organization:

Mark a path all around the playground, as shown in the illustration. One of the players will be the spider and will have to catch the other players (the flies). All of them have to run inside the path.

Development and rules:

The spider stands at one end of the corridor and the flies stand at the other end.

The spider starts chasing the flies in one direction. The flies may move forward or backward, but the spider may only move forward. When a fly gets caught, he freezes on the same spot where he was tagged, moving his arms so as to be an obstacle for the other players.

The game is over when the spider has caught all the flies.

Flies

Flies

Flies

Spider

Carry Tag

Age:
5 years and older.

Participants:
a minimum of
10 players.

Organization:

Define a playing area, approximately 50 by 50 feet (15 by 15 m). The players cannot go out of these limits. Have an object (such as a ball) to be carried.

Development and rules:

A player is chosen to be It. Another player will have an object in her hands. It has to chase the player who has the object, who in turn can pass it on to another player by touching him with the object. Then It has to start chasing the player who now has the object. When the player carrying the object gets caught, she then becomes the new It.

The player who drops the object or goes out of the limits immediately becomes It.

99

Line Tag

Age:
6 years and older.

Participants:
a minimum of
8 players.

Organization:

Two teams are formed with the same number of players on each one. Each team is at the opposite end of the playground, behind a line drawn on the ground.

Development and rules:

Draw lots to decide which team is the first to start the game. The chosen team sends the first player to the opposite line, where the members of the other team will be waiting with their arms extended in front. The player slaps the hand of an opponent and starts running back home.

The player whose hand has been slapped runs after the first player. If he can tag her before she gets behind her line, then he can take her back to his team as a prisoner. When a player catches another from the opposite team, he can exchange her for one of his own team who is also a prisoner.

The winner is the team that succeeds in catching all the members of the opposite team.

Color Tag

Age:
5 years and older.

Participants:
a minimum of
6 players.

Organization:

A player is chosen to be It. She calls out a color and starts running after the other players.

Development and rules:

In this game of tag, the players are safe (that is, they cannot be tagged) if they are touching the mentioned color. The player who is tagged before he can touch an object that is the color mentioned becomes the new It.

Travel Games

*Different activities that
can be played in cars,
trains, buses, or planes.*

Word Chains

Age:
6 years and older.

Participants:
a minimum of
3 players.

Organization:

Players take turns, usually clockwise from the starting player.

Development and rules:

The first player says a word. The next player has to say a new word that begins with the same letter as the last one in the previous word. The game continues until someone repeats a word.

Variations: Geography: Use names of countries, states, rivers, mountains, and so on. Anyplace in the world is fair game. Younger children can be told the last letter and given hints about places they know that start with that letter. Older children (and adults) are on their own.

Organization:

Players try to find objects in the landscape, beginning with each letter of the alphabet.

Development and rules:

Players can take turns finding objects or they can play competitively. The first player to complete the alphabet wins. Younger children who are just learning their letters may be given help.

Alphabet Objects

Age:
4 years and older.

Participants:
a minimum of 2 players.

The Parson's Cat

Age:
6 years and older.

Participants:
a minimum of
3 players.

Organization:
Players create sentences around a letter of the alphabet.

Development and rules:
Players begin with the letter *A* and fill in the blanks of a given sentence: "The parson's cat is a(n) _____ cat and his/her name is _____." Each person uses the same letter. For example, the first player might say: "The parson's cat is an angelic cat and her name is Alice." The second person uses different *A* words. When the round gets back to the first person, *B* is used. Players may not repeat alphabet words.

License Plates

Organization:
  A pencil and paper are helpful.

Development and rules:
  Each player tries to find a license plate for different states, provinces, or even countries. At the end of the trip (or when "time's up" is called), the player with the most states wins. To keep things honest, players can call out each state as they spot the license plate.

Participants:
a miminum of
2 players.

Name That Car

Age:
9 years and older.

Participants:
a minimum of
2 players.

Organization:
Set a time limit or a score to reach.

Development and rules:
Players try to be the first to identify passing cars by make and model. Each correct guess wins a point. When the time is up, the player with the most points is the winner. Or, the first person to reach a particular score wins.

Games for Infants and Toddlers

Designed for the youngest members of the family.

Horsey Rides

Age:
6 months and older.

Participants:
An adult and a baby.

Organization:

The baby sits on the lap of the adult, facing him.

Development and rules:

The adult holds the baby's hands and makes the baby bounce while singing a song or reciting a rhyme. For this rhyme, follow the guidelines below.

This is the way the gentlemen ride, bumpety, bumpety, bump. [Bounce knees slowly and stately.]

This is the way the farmer rides, galumpety, galumpety, galump. [Jostle knees one at a time, side to side.]

And this is the way the little ones ride, bumpety, bumpety, bump. [Quick, energetic bounce.]

Organization:

This game can be played while changing diapers or at any other time when the baby is lying down.

Development and rules:

The adult plays with the baby's toes and fingers while reciting a rhyme. For "This Little Piggy" begin with the big toe. Wiggle each toe with each line. When reciting the last line, "walk" your fingers quickly up baby's body to lightly tickle him under his chin.

This little piggy went to market,
This little piggy stayed home.
This little piggy had roast beef,
This little piggy had none.
And this little piggy cried "Wee, wee, wee,"
    all the way home!

Tickle Time

Age:
birth and older.
Participants:
an adult and a baby.

111

The Mosquito

Age:
3 years and older.

Participants:
a minimum of
6 players plus an
adult.

Organization:

Form a circle with all the children. An object is needed (such as a small, soft ball) to represent the mosquito.

Development and rules:

The adult walks around the circle holding the "mosquito" and saying: "The mosquito flies, flies, and lands on a..." (and places the mosquito somewhere on the body of one of the players—for example, his nose). The chosen player has to mention this part of his body ("nose!") and then the other players say aloud: "Itchy, itchy nose!" The game continues with another child and a different part of the body.

Thumbkin, Pointer

Organization:

The adult will take the baby's hand and open it.

Development and rules:

The adult will point to each of the baby's fingers in turn while reciting the rhyme. With the last words, the adult rolls the baby's hands around each other.

Age:
3 months and older.

Participants:
An adult and a baby.

> *Thumbkin, Pointer, Middleman big*
> *Silly Man, Wee Man,*
> *Rig-a-jig-jig.*

Hand on Hand 2

Age:
3 years and older.

Participants:
4 players or more.

Organization:
All players sit down in a circle.

Development and rules:
The first player places his right hand palm down in the center of the circle, the next player puts his right hand on top, and the rest of the players do the same in turn. When all the players have put in their right hand, they repeat the same process with their left hand.

Once the pile of hands is completed, the first player takes his hand out from the bottom and places it on top. In order, the rest of the players do the same but getting faster each time. When the pile of hands gets undone, the round is over.

Organization:

The adult places the baby on her lap and holds the baby's forearms.

Development and rules:

The adult guides the baby's hands while singing a song.

Pat-a-cake, pat-a-cake, Baker's man, [Clap four times.]
Bake me a cake as fast as you can. [Cup one hand; use a finger to stir.]
Pat it, [Gently pat with baby's palm.]
And prick it, [Use an imaginary fork.]
And mark it with a "B" [Trace a B on baby.]
And put it in the oven [Pretend to do so.]
For Baby and me! [Point to each of you. Hug baby.]

Pat-A-Cake

Age:
3-4 months and older.
Participants:
an adult and a child.

The Rainbow

Age:
3 years and older.

Participants:
a minimum of
6 players.

Organization:

The players form different lines, except one player, who will be the director. Each line will have the name of a color.

Development and rules:

When the director mentions a color, the players in the line with this color have to squat. When the director mentions a different color, they can stand up again, but if the same color is repeated, they have to remain squatting. Colors should be mentioned faster and faster, trying to force the players to make mistakes. When a line makes a mistake, the first player in this line becomes the new director and the old director takes the last place in this line.

Finger Play

Organization:
The child will open his hand and show it to the adult.

Development and rules:
The adult helps the child count his fingers to a rhyme.

Age:
1 year and older.

Participants:
an adult and a child.

One, two, three, four, five, [Count fingers.]
Once I caught a fish alive. [Wiggle hand like a fish.]
Six, seven, eight, nine, ten, [Count fingers on other hand.]
Then I let him go again. [Throw fish back.]
Why did I let that fishie go? [Shrug shoulders.]
Because he bit my finger so. [Shake finger.]
Which finger did he bite?
This little finger on the right! [Hold up finger on right hand.]

Row the Boat

Age:
2 years and older.

Participants:
2 players.

Organization:

In pairs, players sit on the floor facing each other, with their legs apart and their feet touching. They stretch their arms forward and hold hands.

Development and rules:

The idea is to move the body back and forth. When one child goes forward, the other goes backward, and vice versa. The players follow the rhythm of the song as they rock back and forth.

Row, row, row your boat
Gently down the stream.
Merrily, merrily, merrily,
  merrily
Life is but a dream.

See-saw, Margery Daw
Jack shall have a new master.
He shall have but a penny
  a day,
Because he can't work any
  faster.

Peek-A-Boo!

Age:
3 months and older.

Participants:
an adult and a baby.

Organization:

The baby is lying down or sitting on the adult's lap, face to face.

Development and rules:

The adult puts a cloth diaper, towel, or open hand in front of the baby's face. The cloth or hand should be lowered gently while saying: "Peek-a-boo! I see you!" with a big smile. The following rhyme can be recited:

> *Peek-a-boo, peek-a-boo,*
> *Who's that hiding there?*
> *Peek-a-boo, peek-a-boo,*
> *_____'s behind the chair!*

119

Complements to the Games

This section includes several ideas for creating additional material for some games. They are basic creative activities that allow the child to personalize as well as participate in the development or evolution of a given game. Materials used are easy to find, and objects are simple to make. Each participant may put his imagination to use and invent new objects with whatever material is available.

The educational side to creating objects for a game is in the manipulation of different materials, as well as in the intellectual processes the child uses when proceeding through the various steps.

A crown

In "Follow the Leader," the player who is the leader may enjoy wearing a crown she has made.

Material needed: oak tag, some dry macaroni, ribbons and bows, markers, and white glue.

Use a piece of ribbon to measure the child's head around and then mark this length on the oak tag.

Use a pencil to draw a crown on the oak tag and scissors to cut it out.

Color the crown with the markers, putting in as many details as desired, and glue some macaroni to it.

Make some cuts at both ends of the crown, as shown in the illustration, and it will be ready.

A sardine

To make a sardine for "The Cat and the Sardine," use a cardboard tube, like the one toilet paper comes on.

Material needed: a cardboard tube, an old newspaper or magazine, a couple of buttons, and some white glue.

First, cut one side of the tube as shown in the illustration. Then fill it in with newspaper to give it some weight. Finally, staple both ends so the paper will not come out.

Decorate the cardboard tube as desired, adding a tail, fins, and scales made from magazine paper and glued to the tube.

122   Two buttons can be glued on to make the eyes.

A mask

For games in which a blindfold is called for, make a mask. It will be a mask without eyes, because the player wearing it cannot see the other players.

Material needed: oak tag, a pencil, colored pencils or markers, and a long piece of elastic.

Draw an oval on the oak tag, making it as big as the player's face.
Cut out the mask, the mouth, and the nose.
Paint the mask. Each player may decorate it to taste.
Make two small holes on the sides, pass the elastic through, and tie it to the mask with a couple of knots.

Goggles

Make some goggles for the game "The Plane Without a Pilot," but ones that will not allow the pilot any vision.

Material needed: two small disposable cups, clean and dry, a length of elastic band, paint, and some small pieces of cloth.

Make two small holes in each cup, as shown in the illustration.

Measure the elastic band needed for the distance between the eyes as well as for the distance around the head.

Pass the elastic band through the holes and tie knots at the ends. Now try the goggles on to adjust the size.

For decoration, paint the goggles or glue some small pieces of cloth onto them.

INDEX

100 Best Games

Travel Games

Games for Infants and Toddlers

Alphabetical Index

100 Best Games